ALSO BY MARY DAHEIM

CLAM WAKE

A Bed-and-Breakfast Mystery

Mary Daheim

wm

WILLIAM MORROW

An Imprint of HarperCollins*Publishers*

This book is a work of fiction. The characters, incidents, and dialogue are drawn from the author's imagination and are not to be construed as real. Any resemblance to actual events or persons, living or dead, is entirely coincidental.

HarperCollins books may be purchased for educational, business, or sales promotional use. For information please e-mail the Special Markets Department at SPsales@harpercollins.com.

FIRST EDITION

Library of Congress Cataloging-in-Publication Data has been applied for.

ISBN 978-0-06-231772-8

14 15 16 17 18   OV/RRD   10 9 8 7 6 5 4 3 2 1

In loving memory of Judith Marie Marshall Collins.
You are still with me, dear Coz.

Author's Note

The story takes place in January 2006.

Clam Wake

Chapter 1

Judith McMonigle Flynn stared at the mail on the credenza, glared at the thick packet's return address, and squared her broad shoulders before marching out of the front hall to confront her husband in the kitchen.

"It's here, Joe," she announced. "Come and get it."

"What's here?" he asked, after swallowing a bite from a ham-and-cheese sandwich.

"The mail," Judith said, hands on hips. "Phyliss brought it in when she was sweeping the porch."

Joe's green eyes looked suspicious. "So? Did your cleaning woman figure somebody sent a bomb to Hillside Manor?"

"A bombshell as far as I'm concerned," Judith retorted. "It's from New Zealand."

"Wow!" Joe stood up and hurried past Judith on his way to retrieve the packet.

Phyliss Rackley came through the back hall from the basement. "Satan's familiar is hunting. There must be a mouse there. Or a rat."

"At least Sweetums will probably nail whatever rodent it is," Judith said glumly. "Do you have any *good* news?"

It was the wrong thing to ask her fanatically religious cleaning woman. "I sure do! Hallelujah! Christmas is over!"

"That's good news?"

"It certainly is," Phyliss asserted, setting a pile of clean kitchen towels on the counter. "We don't have to listen to those heathens gripe about the holiday and that Santa Claus is our savior."

"There is that," Judith allowed, opening the refrigerator. "Of course Santa is based on a Catholic saint. A bishop, in fact."

Phyliss's beady eyes were suspicious. "You're making that up."

"No," Judith said, removing some leftover salad from the fridge. "Surely you've heard the legend about him."

Phyliss slammed the drawer in which she'd put the towels. "Legends! More hocus-pocus. What's that one about Sleepy Hollow? Did your bishop take off his head and ride a horse?"

"Not even close," Judith retorted. She wasn't in the mood to argue.

As Phyliss left the kitchen, Joe returned. "This is really one hell of a trip. I'm going over to see Bill as soon as I finish lunch. I already called to tell him I got the packet."

"Good for you," Judith muttered, sitting down with her salad.

Joe hurriedly finished his sandwich, then leaned forward to put a hand on his wife's arm. "Hey—I honestly don't know why you're so irked about this New Zealand fishing trip Bill and I are taking. It cost us less than four hundred dollars apiece. We weren't serious about bidding on it at the church auction, just trying to hike up the price for Father Hoyle. Was that so wrong? How did we know the other guests were going to suddenly get tightfisted?"

Judith set her fork aside. "First of all, the parish council shouldn't have moved the auction to November instead of May. Yes, I know Father Hoyle's taking a month off to visit relatives when the auction's usually held. But scheduling the event so close to the holidays was a big mistake. What's more, the fishing trip has to be in January because it's summer in New Zealand. I suspect that even some of the wealthy parishioners couldn't take time off right now. But what really got me—and Coz Renie—

was that after the first hundred bucks, you and Bill were the only people bidding—against each other."

"That was because . . ." Joe sat back and sighed. "Okay, so maybe we shouldn't have been the bartenders before the bidding started."

Judith narrowed her dark eyes. "You were told to get the other parishioners juiced, not each other."

"You have to admit it's a hell of a deal," Joe asserted. "If we had to pay the full freight, it'd be almost three grand apiece."

"Which, I may point out—again—prohibits Renie and me from going with you and Bill. Admittedly, it's a slow time here at the B&B, but she has annual reports to design and can't get away even if we could afford it. You could've earned some big bucks investigating the crooks behind that recreational development project up north. The only thing that kept me barely above water this month is New Year's and the Martin Luther King three-day weekend. The reservations until St. Valentine's Day are few and far between."

Joe refused to look contrite. "Even if you two went, you'd be bored. Besides, you know how drunk Renie gets if she has to fly. Do you realize how unbearable your cousin would be by the time we got to Auckland?"

"She'd be unconscious," Judith said. "I wouldn't have to listen to her. We could stay in the city and explore. I've heard New Zealand is a lovely country." She finally managed a small smile. "Okay, I give up. I'm being a brat. January's always a downer."

"I know." Joe smiled back before standing up. "How come you're eating salad again?"

Judith shot him a dirty look. "I'm still trying to lose the seven pounds I gained over the holidays. I've got three to go."

"Hey," he said, reaching down to put a hand on her shoulder. "You're tall. I can never tell when you gain or lose weight."

"Your eyes are probably going." She poked at his slight paunch. "It wouldn't hurt you to shed some weight, too."

"I've gained less than ten pounds since we got married fifteen years ago." Joe glanced at his midsection. "I think my muscles have worked their way down to my stomach since I retired from the police department. Being a private investigator forces me to spend too much time sitting on surveillance. I'm off to show Bill the packet." He kissed his wife's forehead.

Judith smiled again. "Say hi to the Joneses for me. Renie's probably working on her graphic designs in the basement."

Joe started out of the kitchen, but paused. "We'll have to be at the airport Thursday morning by six for the flight to San Francisco. We can take the shuttle."

"And you will," she agreed. "I've got two Wednesday reservations."

"It's only Tuesday. You might get another one."

"Ha ha," Judith said. But she wasn't smiling.

It figures," Gertrude Grover muttered when Judith went out to collect her mother's lunch tray from the converted toolshed apartment. "Dopey and Dummy will be upside down in New Zealand. Although I don't think it'll make much difference with that pair. What brains they've got will probably fall into outer space. Say, why don't you ask your goofy cousin Serena and her daffy mother to come over some night so the four of us can play bridge? That might cheer you up."

"That's not a bad idea," Judith said. "Renie and I haven't played cards in ages. I hope we can remember all the bidding cues. We might be kind of rusty."

"It'll come back to you," her mother asserted. "Just like riding a Popsicle. You never forget how to do it."

"A Popsicle?" Judith echoed. "You mean a bi—"

"I know what I mean," Gertrude interrupted. "When you were a kid and it got hot in the summer, you'd put a Popsicle on your bicycle seat to cool it off."

"I only did that once and it was a mistake," Judith said. "The Popsicle melted and it looked like I wet my pants."

Her mother shrugged. "Seemed like a good idea at the time."

"It wasn't. Maybe Renie can come over Thursday night. I've only got one reservation so far. Luckily, the weekend's looking a little better."

Worry surfaced in Gertrude's faded blue eyes. "You going broke?"

"No, Mother, it's always like this in January." She stood next to Gertrude's chair and put a hand on the old lady's rounded shoulder. "Things will pick up in March. They always do."

"Hunh. There's talk of a recession. Maybe just like the thirties. Soup kitchens and homeless camps. Where's FDR when we need him?"

"The last I heard," Judith said, "he and Eleanor were still buried at Hyde Park."

Gertrude sighed. "Seems like only yesterday that I heard FDR had died. I was babysitting Serena while your aunt Deb and uncle Cliff were off on some appointment. I left you napping with Grandma and Grandpa Grover. Your dad was teaching at the high school. Serena and I were prank-calling Realtors when Deb and Cliff pulled into the driveway. We both went to the back door——"

Judith was aghast. "You let Renie prank-call people? She was six."

"Don't interrupt. She's always had a deep voice. Anyway, as soon as Deb and Cliff got out of the car—their old '37 Plymouth—we knew something terrible had happened. They'd heard the news about President Roosevelt on the radio. You were too young to understand."

"That's true. I don't remember anything about it."

"All the Grovers were in mourning. Even Auntie Vance, who's tougher than a logger's tin pants. She was working for the navy at the time. Then Aunt Ellen joined the Red Cross. Oh—speaking of Auntie Vance, she and Uncle Vince are coming down from

Whoopee Island Thursday. I hope they bring clams. I've got my mouth set for chowder."

"They might," Judith said, edging for the door. "She's definitely tough enough to brave the January cold to dig them at Obsession Shores. But she has a heart of gold and you know it."

Gertrude sneered. "She's got you fooled, Toots."

Judith smiled and headed back to the house. When it came to being tough, her mother could give most people a run for their money.

On Wednesday, a last-minute reservation came in. A reporter for a Midwest newspaper chain was doing a series on Pacific Northwest getaways and hadn't liked the looks of the motel reserved for him at the bottom of Heraldsgate Hill. He'd checked nearby hostelries, deciding that Hillside Manor was close to downtown and would be a nice change from the nondescript accommodations he'd been staying in as he worked his way north.

Judith had given Jack Larrabee her warmest welcome, hoping he might have a good word about the B&B in his articles. Jack, who was about forty, tall and lean with rather unruly fair hair, had kept a poker face. She figured him for a hard sell, though he would stay two nights.

For now that news was good enough. After the guests' social hour, Judith got caught up in Joe's trip preparations. Being a man, he couldn't find half of the items he needed. In fact, he couldn't even remember where he'd stored his suitcase. By nine o'clock Wednesday night, Judith finally found it in the basement behind the furnace.

"Why," she demanded, after dumping it in the hall by the back stairs, "did you put it there instead of with the rest of our luggage?"

"So I'd remember that was the one I want to take instead of something bigger. Or smaller," Joe explained.

Judith shook her head and went into the living room to relax. As soon as she collapsed on one of the matching sofas in front of the fireplace, the phone rang. With a sigh, she hurried across the room to the cherrywood table to take the call.

"What," Cousin Renie demanded, "has two legs, two arms, an ornery disposition, and no eyes?"

"Your husband," Judith replied. "Please don't tell me Bill's lost *his* suitcase."

"Oh, he's got that," Renie said. "But he can't find the big envelope with his plane ticket and reservations. He thinks I set the whole thing on fire. Is he nuts? I never got a chance to look at all the stuff Joe brought over here. I'll be glad to see Bill go. If I weren't afraid to fly, I'd pilot the plane myself."

"In twelve hours the husbands will be airborne," Judith reminded Renie. "We'll be left in peace. Oh—did you know Auntie Vance and Uncle Vince are coming into town tomorrow?"

"Yes, Mom told me. Six times. You know how she likes to call to make sure I haven't been kidnapped by Somali pirates. Gee— do you suppose that before they sail, their wives have to find all their weapons and list of demands and the how-to-negotiate guidebook?"

"Probably," Judith said, hearing a loud yelp in the background followed by a lot of cussing. "What's that?" she asked.

"Bill. What else? Hang on."

Judith could hear her cousin inquiring if Bill was dying. Since he answered, she figured he wasn't. The exchange between husband and wife was surprisingly calm. Too calm, since Judith couldn't hear what they were saying.

"Sheesh," Renie finally uttered. "Bill found his stuff. He was sitting on it. If he didn't use four pillows on his favorite chair when he watches TV, he might've . . . never mind. Crisis averted. I'm going downstairs to finish the gas company's annual report concept." She hung up.

It was after eleven by the time Joe finally got himself organized—with Judith's help, of course.

"I have to get up at five to get ready for the shuttle," Joe groused as they climbed the stairs to the family quarters on the third floor. "I'll try not to wake you."

"You bet you'll try," Judith said, taking her time. The day's hectic activity had made her artificial hip ache. "But wake me before you leave."

"You sure you want me to do that?" Joe asked as they reached the top of the stairs.

Judith smiled. "Of course. I really will miss you."

The gold flecks danced in Joe's green eyes. "Then maybe we should have a little farewell party now."

"Won't that mean you'll get even less sleep?"

Joe put his arm around Judith, leading her into the bedroom. "I can sleep on the plane."

Judith leaned against him. "I really hope you have a good time."

"I will." Joe brushed her lips with his fingers. "Starting now."

At six thirty the next morning, Judith barely recalled Joe's mumbled words of farewell. Struggling out of bed, she blinked several times before looking out the window. It was still dark, but she could hear the patter of rain on the shrubbery next to the house. She was in the kitchen by seven, ready to face the day— without Joe. Judith already missed his help preparing the guests' breakfast. Even when Joe was on a PI assignment, he rarely stayed out all night. That was a promise he'd made after retiring as a detective for the police department.

Phyliss arrived at nine. The elderly couple from Topeka had almost finished breakfast. Their son was picking them up at nine thirty. The British Columbia sisters hadn't yet come downstairs, but Jack Larrabee showed up just as the golden agers rose from the table.

"Is it true it never stops raining?" he asked.

"Yes," Judith replied. "January is usually wet. We often have a lot of wind, too. Sometimes it snows."

"It wasn't raining in Portland," Jack said.

"That's further south. But the Oregonians have a reason for calling themselves Webfoots. Have you never been to this part of the country?"

Jack shook his head. "The farthest north I've been until now is San Francisco. Talk about wind—and fog. Don't you people get depressed?"

"Yes. I think we-—along with San Francisco—have the high-est suicide rate in the country. Unless, of course, cities in Alaska have got us beat. Those endless days—and endless nights, you know."

Jack shuddered. "I gather you're not a good PR type for travel-ers."

"No. So many visit when we have our four or five days of sun-shine. Then they want to move here. We're getting too crowded. Traffic is horrendous. There are a lot of terrible accidents, with a high rate of fatalities. Newcomers don't know how to drive in the rain."

Jack seemed mildly surprised. "You make this city sound like hell."

Judith shrugged. "I'm only being candid. You may find some people with other opinions. But they probably got here only a month or so ago. I do recall a sunny day in early December. After the fog lifted, of course." *Good grief,* Judith thought, *am I turning into Renie? I'm being utterly perverse. I need a vacation.*

"Yes," Jack murmured. "I'll do that. Where should I go to find these more upbeat people?"

"Try the zoo. Locals like watching the animals in the rain." Hearing the spinster sisters in the hall, she scurried back into the kitchen.

"What animals?" Phyliss asked, pausing in her task of cleaning the backsplash by the sink. "With all this rain, they're lining up two by two."

Judith ignored the comment, lest the cleaning woman start in on Noah, which would inevitably lead to Judith asking where he'd found penguins and kangaroos in the Holy Land. Phyliss's answer would be that those kind of creatures didn't exist back then.

By eleven, the sisters from BC had checked out. Shortly before noon, Auntie Vance and Uncle Vince arrived.

"Okay, twerp, we got clams," Judith's buxom aunt declared, setting a large bucket on the hallway floor. "How many do you and my addled sister-in-law want?"

"Um . . ." Judith gazed at the pile of littleneck, Manila, and butter clams. "Nice. Can I take a couple of gallons? In the shell, I mean."

Auntie Vance looked irked. "How else? I dig, you clean." She turned to Uncle Vince, who was leaning against the wall with his eyes closed. "Hey, Weber, wake up! Didn't you get enough sleep while you were driving from the ferry dock?"

"Wha'? Oh, right, Little Girl," Vince said, using his affectionate, if not accurate, pet name for Vanessa. "Hi, Judith." He pecked her on the cheek and immediately headed for a kitchen chair.

Judith smiled faintly, accustomed to the nickname that he'd always called his Amazonian wife. She was also used to her uncle's habit of nodding off any place, any time, and under any conditions. He'd been a dairy deliveryman for his entire career and had never recovered from getting up at three A.M. Thus he had never been able to break the pattern of going to sleep in broad daylight. The Webers had dated for years, marrying late in life, and had never had children. Instead, they lavished good deeds on the entire Grover clan, though Auntie Vance would only scoff at efforts to repay them for their kindnesses.

"Get some jars," Vance ordered. "You sure you want two gallons?"

"Yes," Judith said, before going in the pantry. "Even with Joe gone, Mother and I can eat that many clams before the weekend's over."

"No, you can't," Vance asserted. "You won't be here for the weekend. Vince and I leave tomorrow to visit Ellen and Win in Beatrice, Nebraska. You're going to house-sit for us. It's all arranged. Now, how many clams do you really want?"

Chapter 2

Judith's mouth fell open. "What?"

"You heard me," Vance said. "I already told Gert and talked to the Rankers. They'll fill in for you here while you're on Whoopee Island. You'll probably want to take Renie with you, so we'll stop off to give her the news on our way back home."

Judith started to protest. "But—"

"No buts, butt-head." Vance laughed. "God, I haven't seen you look so surprised since you and Renie made yourselves into a horse for my birthday party forty years ago. You fell down and Renie lost her rear end. She looked kind of surprised, too. Talk about a couple of horse's—"

"Stop!" Judith held up her hands. "I need to sit. Please, Auntie Vance. Wouldn't you like some coffee?"

"I'm fine. Stick Vince's head in the pot and maybe he'll wake up. Or drown." She charged ahead into the kitchen.

Despite her harsh words, Vance poured coffee for Judith and Vince before joining them at the table. "Okay, here's why we're going to Beatrice. Aunt Ellen's having shoulder surgery today. You know how she works three jobs and is involved in at least two dozen volunteer organizations. Uncle Win can't keep up with all that while she's in the hospital, so we volunteered to help. We won't be gone more than a week. My sister can't stay put any longer than that, and once she's mobile, we'll take off before Ellen and I kill each other."

Judith nodded faintly. Uncle Vince just nodded off.

"As for you and Renie coming up to our place," Vance went on, "there's an emergency meeting tomorrow night of everybody who lives at Obsession Shores. In the past few months there's been a lot of wrangling with some of the local morons, including a couple of new owners who bought land that won't percolate. You know that means they can't put in a septic tank. The dumb-asses should never have bought in, but that's what dumb-asses do—dumb-assed stuff. Anyway, they're trying to run a sewer line through the development, and if you think the rest of us want to pay for something like that, then you're a dumb-ass, too."

"Of course you wouldn't want that," Judith agreed. "But if there are only two couples, aren't they outnumbered about thirty to one?"

Vance shook her curly graying blond head. "You're right about the number of owners, but the original population has aged since we moved up there after Vince retired. Close to a third of them head south for the winter. And there are another dozen or more who only live at Obsession Shores in the summer. I doubt many—even any—of them will bother coming to the island for the meeting."

"So," Judith said, "what are Renie and I supposed to do? Blow up the place wherever this civil war is going to be fought?"

"That's right," Vance asserted. "I've named you and Renie as our proxies. That's legal, so you'll represent us. Of course you'll vote no."

"Of course." Judith made a face. "Did I just say that?"

Vance slapped her hand on the table. "Yes. Now be damned sure you take an early ferry. It may be winter, but there's still quite a bit of weekend traffic over to the island. Off-season for crab pots, by the way."

"Darn," Judith said softly. "Are you sure all of this is okay with Arlene and Carl?"

"You bet your ass it is, twerp. I gave them a pile of clams, too. Lucky we were able to catch the Rankerses before they head for Palm Springs at the end of the month. Carl and Arlene are glad to get out of the house. Their downstairs is being painted starting on Monday."

"Monday?" Judith echoed. "Won't Renie and I be back by then?"

"Well . . ." Vance paused to nudge Vince, whose face was getting dangerously close to his coffee mug. "Knowing you, somebody on the island might get killed over this fracas and you'll want to stick around to figure out whodunit."

"That's not funny!" Judith cried. "I've retired from doing that."

"Oh, hell," Vance said, standing up and hauling Vince to his feet, "half of the people who live there are retired. You'll fit right in. You sure you want two gallons of clams?"

Judith had also gotten to her feet. "Oh . . . maybe just one. I suppose Renie and I could dig our own. It'd help pass the time. Of course she may not come with me. She's working on some annual reports. Are you going to see her now?"

"Right." Vance dragged Vince down the back hall. "She'll come. She can always work on them at our place. She just draws a bunch of stuff anyway. How hard is that, unless she busts all her crayons?"

"It's a lot more complicated than—"

"By the way," Vance broke in, "I made my beef noodle bake, so your dinner's ready to heat. I baked ginger snaps and made Grandma Grover's coffee cake. Oh—I made a boysenberry pie, too. You won't starve."

"Thanks," Judith said, feeling overwhelmed. "You didn't need to—"

But Vince interrupted, his pleasant face wearing the familiar worried look that was only noticeable when he was fully conscious. "Don't take my boat out. It gets real choppy out there in January."

Vance glared at her husband. "You think dead calm is choppy. That wreck of a boat hasn't been out in six years."

"It just needs a bit of work," Vince murmured. "Good to see you, Judith. Have fun on The Rock. Stay warm and dry."

"Thanks," Judith replied. "We'll try our best to do . . . both."

Vance laughed. "Did I ever tell you we were married for three years before I realized Vince could talk? Let's go," she said, giving her husband another nudge. "You need to take a nap behind the wheel."

Judith watched the Webers walk away, arm in arm. Or maybe Vance was holding up Vince. It was hard to tell with her aunt and uncle.

Renie called half an hour later. "Okay, so I caved. What is it about Auntie Vance that makes everybody do her bidding? Except maybe Aunt Ellen when she visits from Beatrice? They're two of a kind. Sort of. Aunt Ellen always seems like she's on speed."

"I know. Auntie Vance is an irresistible force. Both Grover sisters are . . . awesome. The brothers were never introverts. My father was the quietest of the bunch, but he certainly was immovable when he expressed his opinions."

"My dad was, too," Renie said, "but in a droll, succinct sort of way. When he wasn't cussing and throwing things, of course."

"You're sure you can work on your projects at the island?"

"Yes. My contribution is all smoke and mirrors. If I tell them my design concept conveys their message to shareholders or customers or wombats, they believe me. By now, I've got street cred. Those bozos in the corner offices don't know a concept from a contraceptive. Well . . . they might know that, but you get what I'm saying."

"After spending fifteen minutes with Auntie Vance, I'm not sure I get what *I'm* saying," Judith admitted. "Okay. I'll check the ferry schedule. I have one here for guests. I'll pick you up at ten tomorrow."

"Ten?" Renie shrieked. "I won't be awake at ten. Make it eleven."

"Fine. If we have to wait in line for three ferries, it's your fault."

"I'm willing to take that risk," Renie said. "Oh, no! Mom's calling me. Maybe Auntie Vance and Uncle Vince stopped off to give her some clams, too, and Mom knows we're leaving town. You know what that means—I'll get a dozen calls a day from her asking if I've been swept away by a tsunami or devoured by giant geoducks. Bye." Renie hung up.

Judith had no sooner put down the phone when Gertrude wheeled herself through the back door. "What's wrong with you?" she demanded, putting on the brakes just short of running over her daughter's left foot. "Have you made chowder yet? My lunch was kind of skimpy."

"I haven't had time to clean the clams," Judith said. "I was just about to do it. We'll have chowder for dinner."

"Make enough for my lunch tomorrow, too," Gertrude ordered, ignoring Sweetums, who was weaving in and out under the motorized wheelchair. "Or did Arlene and Carl get clams, too?"

"They did," Judith replied as Phyliss reappeared via the dining room. "Maybe she'll bring theirs over here."

Phyliss wrinkled her nose. "Clams are ungodly. Did you ever hear of our Lord multiplying the loaves and the clams? He wouldn't bother."

Gertrude took umbrage. "You ever hear about the nectar of God? That was clam nectar. Guess you never read the Bible."

Phyliss stiffened, clutching her cleaning rag as if she were trying to shred it. Or planning to wrap it around Gertrude's neck. "You think I never read the Bible? Are you crazy? I read it every day. I never heard of any such thing. Or is that in your weird Catholic Bible?"

Gertrude was undeterred. "That's right. It's what the apostles drank when they played bingo. Kept 'em really juiced."

Phyliss dropped the rag and put her hands over her ears. "Blasphemy! I won't listen to another word!" She rushed back through the dining room, oblivious to Sweetums, who was right behind her.

Gertrude laughed. "I know how to shut up that crazy old bat. *You* try to reason with her. Trust me, kiddo, it can't be done."

"You shouldn't tease Phyliss," Judith said. "Someday she might really get mad and quit. I don't know what I'd do without her."

Gertrude was still chuckling. "I know what *I* can do with her—and that's get her goat. Hey, at my age I need to have a little fun now and then. And yes, I do know it's 'nectar of the gods.' One of those Greek myth things, if what's left of my memory still works."

"Your memory works just fine when you want it to," Judith said, picking up the rag that Phyliss had dropped. "I suppose you're looking forward to having Carl and Arlene here."

"You bet. They treat me right."

Judith looked down at her mother. "And I don't?"

"That depends," Gertrude replied. "Are we playing bridge tonight?"

"I have to ask Renie and Aunt Deb if they can come."

"As annoying as Deb can be, she's not as lippy as Vance. As for my dingbat niece, she's a decent cardplayer, but don't tell her I said that. Fact is, compared to Serena, you're kind of mealy-mouthed. You may look like me, but she speaks her mind more like I do. Don't tell her that either. She might get swellheaded."

"I won't," Judith promised.

"Okay." Gertrude revved up her wheelchair. "In that case, I'll go back to my so-called cardboard box of an apartment and start marking the cards. See you in the funny papers." She rolled off, just as Sweetums meandered out of the dining room before streaking through the kitchen and down the hall.

Two of a kind, her mother and the cat. Both were old and ornery, but still lovable.

There was no bridge game that Thursday night. Judith ended up with an unexpected party of four at the last minute. Two couples from Santa Barbara had arrived at a B&B across the ship canal only to discover there was a power outage in the neighborhood and no word on how long it would last.

Meanwhile, Renie had flat-out rejected the cardplaying get-together because she wanted to finish another annual report project before leaving town. Aunt Deb couldn't make it because some old friends had dropped in unexpectedly from the eastern part of the state and stayed on for dinner. Gertrude was disappointed, but Judith consoled her by promising to bring back some of her favorite chocolates from the candy store on Whoopee Island.

By the time Judith had taken care of her guests' needs, made dinner, consulted with the Rankerses, played three games of cribbage with Gertrude, checked her larder, packed a suitcase, discovered Sweetums hiding under the kitchen sink, and listened to her mother's lecture about not picking up sailors on the island, it was going on midnight. She dragged herself up to bed, but couldn't settle down. She wondered if Joe and Bill had arrived in Auckland. Trying to figure out the time changes finally put her to sleep.

Morning came too soon. Routine was the only thing that got Judith through serving breakfast. She put herself on autopilot, wearing a smile she hoped didn't look like it belonged to a robot and praying that her natural empathy for people would come through. Apparently, it did. The guests all seemed cheerful—except Jack Larrabee, of course.

Arlene arrived just after ten thirty. "You told me you wanted to leave before eleven," she said, slipping out of her all-weather jacket. "Have the departing guests checked out?"

"All but a reporter named Larrabee who should be coming down shortly," Judith replied. "He's moving on up north today."

"How far north?" Arlene inquired, looking suspicious.

"Uh . . . I'm not sure, but eventually he'll go to a couple of cities in British Columbia. He's writing a newspaper series for people who want to visit our part of the world."

Arlene's blue eyes danced. "Wonderful! I love to see the tourists come to town. I always tell them this is the best city to visit while they're on vacation. Did you tell him about the recent measles epidemic?"

"Darn. I left that out. You'll get your chance with him. Don't forget the bicyclists who think they own the streets, yet ignore traffic laws."

Arlene nodded. "The two-wheeled assassins. Yes, I could hardly omit them. What about the tolls on the floating bridge? When the bridges don't sink, of course."

"I forgot that, too. You're going to have quite a list."

Arlene's pretty face lit up. "Oh, I can think of so many things! Most of our streets have lumps, potholes, and cracks. Those huge cranes that occasionally collapse at all the construction sites, the dangerous old viaduct, the changes with no warning when a one-way street suddenly becomes a two-way . . . Goodness, I could go on forever."

Judith gripped Arlene's shoulder. "If anybody can do it, you can. *I'm* going now."

"Just hope the ferry doesn't run into a smaller boat or go aground . . . again," Arlene called after her. "Have a wonderful trip!"

Judith felt more alert after driving her Subaru over the top of the hill and halfway down the north side to Renie's house. She honked twice in front of the Joneses' Dutch colonial. And waited. She honked again. Another minute passed before she decided to see if knocking would rouse her cousin. But as Judith started to turn off the ignition, Renie staggered onto the porch, managed to let the storm door slam her halfway back inside, cussed a blue streak, dropped her keys, and scrambled around to pick them up by the milk box. When she finally fell into the passenger seat, she was panting.

"Stupid mornings," she muttered. "I hate them. They come too damned early."

Judith waited to speak until they were crossing the old stone bridge above the gully. "Have you heard from Bill yet?" she asked.

"Bill who?" Renie growled.

"Your husband."

"Are you kidding? He hates the phone. What's wrong with this seat belt? It's busted."

Judith braked at the six-way stop before making the loop to the main drag that led to the freeway. "You're putting it in backward."

"Oh." Renie finally clicked herself in. "What about Joe?"

"Nothing yet. Maybe they'll wait until they get to the fishing resort. What took you so long to come to the door?"

"I had to say good-bye to Oscar. He's miffed because he didn't get to go to New Zealand. Frankly, he's not a good traveler. Bill decided not to take him anywhere after we went to Vegas and he had Oscar sit next to him at the blackjack table. The little twerp wouldn't let go of the silver dollar Bill gave him. It caused quite a scene when—"

"Stop. Please. I was just getting into a good mood for a change. I don't want to hear any more anecdotes about your stuffed ape."

Renie folded her arms across her chest and pouted briefly. "You might at least ask about Clarence."

"Okay," Judith agreed. "He's a real live animal. Who's caring for your bunny?"

"A De Rosario grandkid from around the corner. Clarence is fairly self-sufficient. He puts himself to bed at night, you know."

"Very clever of him," Judith allowed for the sake of peace while she maneuvered into a steady stream of northbound traffic.

The cousins both were silent until they reached the freeway. Judith had thought it best to allow time for Renie to regain complete consciousness. Otherwise, they might get into an argument that would set the trip off on a wrong note.

It was Renie who finally spoke while Judith maneuvered around heavy northbound traffic. "I'm not sure I understood the issue with the homeowners at Obsession Shores. Is it a vote on whether or not to put in a sewer system instead of septic tanks?"

"That sounds right to me," Judith agreed. "Of course there are probably some personality clashes involved."

"We've met a couple of the neighbors over the years," Renie said. "Dick and Jane Sedgewick come to mind. Did Auntie Vance mention them?"

"No. Maybe they're part of the snow-bird group that goes to California or Arizona this time of year. Oh—the Friedmans. Sarah and Mel, right? They live close to the beach."

"Yes, cute gabled cottage." Renie didn't speak again until they'd passed the city limits. "I'm trying to remember the name of that couple Auntie Vance didn't like. They live across the road and always shoo the deer over to her garden to nibble on the rose-bushes."

Judith nodded. "The Leonettis. I don't know if I ever heard their first names. Auntie Vance always called them something unprintable."

"She calls a lot of people names like that," Renie said, "including most of us in the family. At least we know she loves us. In the Leonettis' case, venom is in her voice."

"The Bennetts," Judith blurted. "That name just came back to me. They started out as summer people, but moved to the island when he retired. I don't remember much about them except that they lived directly below Auntie Vance and Uncle Vince."

Renie grew thoughtful. "He owned his own company. For

some reason, I remember that. What was it . . . ?" She finally shook her head. "Some kind of manufacturing, but I don't recall what they made."

"Trouble?" Judith said.

"I hope not. Once we cast our votes tonight, I assume we *could* head home tomorrow."

Judith glanced at Renie. "Do you really want to do that? I'd like to stay through the weekend. It's been three years since Joe and I took Mike and his family to the island. The grandkids loved it. Besides, I figure Auntie Vance will want a full report of reactions to the voting results and the meeting itself."

"Probably," Renie agreed. "If we do that, we should wait to go back Monday morning. Ferry traffic Sunday night can be ugly. It's a short crossing, but they don't have superferrys on the route."

Judith signaled for the turn off the freeway that would lead them to the dock. "We might as well stay in the car," she said.

"Not me. I'm going up to get popcorn. I'm hungry."

"Fine."

They lapsed into silence until they were in the lane that led to the terminal. They noticed a security officer with a sniffer dog going from car to car, a precaution that had begun after the tragic events of 9/11. Man and dog passed by them with only a glance. And presumably a sniff.

A ferry was heading into the dock. Judith surveyed the half-dozen lanes of vehicles waiting to go aboard. "We're lucky. We'll make this one."

"It's not yet noon," Renie remarked, checking her watch. "The rush will be on a little later. You sure you got the right senior fare for us?"

"How could I get the wrong one?"

"Just asking. If I'm getting old, I want my perks."

"It isn't as if there are two different rates for seniors. You expect 'old' and 'really old'?"

"As a matter of fact," Renie said, "I suspect that'll happen the way people are living so long. You do realize that there are now two generations of so-called seniors. Everybody fusses about the baby boomers gobbling up all the Social Security. They should work longer."

"What about young people looking for jobs?" Judith asked in a reasonable voice.

"Most of them don't know what they want to major in, assuming they're going to college. Why not a one- or two-year public-service requirement for both sexes? Why doesn't anybody except me have good ideas?"

"May I remind you that both our husbands took advantage of retirement at sixty-two?" Judith pointed out.

"True—and it galled me. But they're still earning, with Joe doing PI work and Bill seeing a few of his nutty patients. The only glitch is he nods off more often while they're unloading their problems on him."

The ferry had docked. The disembarking foot passengers came off first, followed by a long double line of vehicles that included a school bus, a moving van, and a cement mixer.

Ten minutes later the cousins were aboard and on their way across the Sound. Renie immediately got out to search for popcorn on the second deck. Luckily, Judith had been able to pull into an outside lane where she could get a porthole view of the water. She felt the engines kick into high gear after they cleared the docking area. The only other vessel she could see was some kind of freighter heading south toward the city. Seagulls swooped and squawked as they circled the water for food. Or, she thought, waiting for Renie to appear on deck with her popcorn. Her cousin tended to be a messy eater.

Judith's attention was diverted by a man getting out of his SUV a couple of cars ahead of her. He looked familiar, but she couldn't place him. He, too, headed toward the stairway that led to the upper deck.

Renie returned by the time the ferry had slowed as it

approached the dock in the little town of Cliffton. "Wanthum?" she asked, thrusting the almost-empty paper bag at Judith.

"No thanks," she replied, long ago having learned to understand her cousin when she talked with her mouth full. "Those six kernels might spoil my appetite for lunch."

"Lun," Renie said, emptying the bag. "Wheh?"

"At the Webers," Judith said. "Didn't Auntie Vance tell you she had a ton of food waiting for us?"

Renie swallowed. "Yes, but I thought it might be fun to eat at the Chowder House up on the hill above the dock. It *is* twelve thirty."

"We can go there for dinner if you really want to eat out."

"No, we can't. The meeting's at seven. We'd be rushed."

"Tomorrow night, maybe," Judith offered.

"Okay. We could go into Langton instead. They have more restaurants. It's always fun to shop in their little stores and boutiques. I always like to go to the Sun Store, where they . . . hey, I know that guy," Renie said, nodding at the man Judith had seen get out of his SUV. "That's . . . I forget."

Judith nodded. "I thought I recognized him, but I don't remember his name."

"Neither do I. It's Eddie or Edgar or something like that."

"The only thing I remember about him is that he looked a little like my father," Judith said. "Same height, same weight, glasses."

Renie smiled. "Uncle Donald was better-looking."

"True," Judith agreed as the ferry bumped some of the pilings leading into the dock. "I suppose we should call on some of the people we actually know, like the Sedgewicks and the Friedmans. They should be able to tell us more about who's for and who's against this sewer line."

"I can't figure out why anyone would be for it, especially if there are so many retirees living at Obsession Shores," Renie said as the cars began to disembark. "Unless they're all rich, that's a pricey idea."

"Well . . ." Judith turned the ignition key. "We had a septic tank at one of our seedy rentals in the Thurlow district. They can cause problems. We had our share even though Dan and I lived there less than a year before we got evicted."

"How many times were you kicked out during your ill-fated union with Dan? I forget, if only because he was such a jackass that he never let any of us visit while you spent nineteen years in exile from the rest of the family. The only house I saw was when Bill and I came out the night Dan died and listened to the rats partying inside the walls."

Judith didn't answer right away, waiting her turn to get off of the ferry. Her marriage to Dan McMonigle wasn't her favorite topic of conversation. She'd met him while she was already engaged to Joe. As a rookie cop, his first encounter with OD'ed teenagers had led to his own overdosing on Scotch in a nearby bar. The woman known to Judith as Herself—Vivian—had promptly hijacked Joe to Vegas. When Joe sobered up, he discovered he was married to the wrong woman. In what seemed like a gallant effort at the time, Dan offered to marry Judith despite the fact that she was carrying Joe's baby. It didn't take her long to realize that his chivalry had been motivated by his quest for a meal ticket. Dan had a severe allergy to work.

"We were evicted only three times," Judith said as they followed the other vehicles up the hill and away from the dock. "Of course we actually lost the first house that we'd bought while Dan was still running The Meat & Mingle Café. You may recall he forgot he had to make regular mortgage payments. Not to mention that he got into trouble with the IRS after the café went under."

"It all comes back to me now," Renie murmured. "I have trouble remembering because I've spent so much time trying to forget what you went through all those years. I could only talk to you on the phone late at night after Dan went to sleep—or passed out."

"Just as well," Judith said. "Joe's marriage to Herself was equally miserable. She drank as much as Dan did. Still does, as far as I can tell, but at least now she guzzles in her Florida condo on the Gulf."

"That's a safe distance." Renie leaned forward in her seat. "Do you remember where we turn to get to Obsession Shores?"

Judith nodded. "I make a left and then another left. It's toward the south end of the island, but on the side with the western exposure."

"Sounds right," Renie agreed, rubbernecking along the winding road. "Wow. There's been a lot of building around here since I was on the island. Of course some people commute to the mainland."

"We're on Worthless Bay Road," Judith said. "I've never figured out why the native tribes called the bay worthless."

"Maybe they were looking for gold," Renie suggested. "Or couldn't get a permit for a floating casino."

Judith darted an ironic glance at her cousin. "Good thing they didn't. You'd spend all your time gambling while we're up here."

"I only go to a casino when Anne's in town and I can bond with my daughter. Or when Bill has a yen to play baccarat. Or when—"

"Stop," Judith broke in. "I vividly recall your manic gambling mode when we all went to the Stillasnowamish Casino by the family cabins."

"Oh, that." Renie looked out the window. "I see the bay."

Judith smiled. "I feel better already. It must be the saltwater air."

"Oh? Interesting, given that you haven't rolled down the window or gotten out of the car since we left home. Or does the absence of rain improve your disposition?"

"You know the rain doesn't bother me. I'm a native, like you. Besides, the sky looks very gray and gloomy. I expect it'll rain before the day is out."

"No doubt." Renie leaned forward. "Slow down. There's the sign for Obsession Shores."

"Got it." Judith braked and hit her right-turn signal. "What the . . ." She frowned as she saw a sheet of paper that had been attached to the sign. "Am I crazy or is that a skull and crossbones?"

Renie gaped at the crudely drawn artwork. "It sure is. Gee, coz, you may be back in business."

Chapter 3

No!" Judith shrieked. "Did you forget I retired from sleuthing last fall? The only reason I got involved back then was because Joe wanted to solve it for Woody Price's sake. It was his partner's first unsolved homicide."

"I know." Renie scowled. "Why are you stopping?"

Judith smirked. "To read the small print under the skull and crossbones. 'Say Nay to the Naysayers.' It's politics about the sewer vote."

Renie leaned over to read the sign for herself. "That's a gruesome way to win voters."

Judith released the brake, heading down the gentle hill above the beach. "This isn't some ritzy enclave," she said. "These people are mostly blue-collar types like Uncle Vince, with a few upscale folks who like the setting and the proximity to the ferry." She nodded to her right, where an older gray three-story house sat on the edge of the forest. "There's a height restriction to prevent blocking the view. Whoever owns that place wanted a bigger house and had to build away from the beach."

"The home on this side is much newer," Renie said. "Don't look or you'll hit the mailboxes. It's octagonal with lots of glass and stonework. Nice, really, if you like that sort of thing."

"I'll take your artist's word for it until I can see for myself."

Judith took a left into the paved driveway that led to the Webers' garage. "I suppose Uncle Vince's little boat is down on the beach."

"It's been beached as long as I can remember," Renie said, collecting her purse from the car floor. "If there's even the slightest hint of a big wave or a whitecap, he insists it's too choppy out there."

Judith undid her seat belt and opened the car door. "In all the years they've been up here, I think I've only been out in that boat once."

Renie waited to comment until she'd grabbed her overnight bag and had gotten out of the Subaru. "That sounds about right. I got seasick, which probably heightened Uncle Vince's fear of going far enough out that he was no longer scraping bottom."

"Auntie Vance insists the boat's not seaworthy," Judith said as they started up the stairs leading to the house's main floor. She paused to sniff the air. "It does feel different, doesn't it?"

Renie nodded. "There's a saltwater tang to it. Fresh and yet sort of pungent. You got the key?"

Judith stared at Renie. "No. I thought Auntie Vance gave it to you. She was at your place after she left Hillside Manor."

"She never mentioned a key to me."

"Damn!" Judith scrutinized the twenty-foot-long deck where Renie was already making a search. "Any luck?" she asked.

Renie shook her head as she peered into various seashells, under the doormat, and between pieces of driftwood. "You're stuck relying on the lockpicking skills you honed while married to Dan."

"I'm rusty," Judith admitted, digging in her purse for an item that would trip the lock. "I haven't done this in ages, unlike when I had to open Dan's safe every week to see if there was money for food."

"I've got my trusty nail scissors," Renie volunteered.

"I can't seem to find anything that will do the job. Give me the . . ."

Renie turned the knob. The door opened. "Voilà!" she exclaimed.

Judith stared. "How'd you know it was open?"

"I didn't. But it never hurts to try."

The cousins entered the big paneled room that served as kitchen, dining room, and living room. The house plan was simple: the master bedroom off the living room section, a half bath, and a hallway with a guest room at one end and the laundry room at the other. The main bath was in the middle. There was also a partial basement that was entered from the garage, but had no access from the main floor. The furnishings were comfortable and solid. Auntie Vance wasn't one for flash and dash. Uncle Vince could go to sleep anywhere.

Judith espied a note on the kitchen counter. *Hi, Idiots,* their aunt had scrawled. *We took off this morning at five and figured nobody would bother robbing us because we don't have anything worth taking, so we left the door unlocked. If we gave you two boobs a key, you'd probably lose it. Have fun and stay out of trouble. XXX OOO, Auntie Vance.*

"Typical," Judith said, laughing. "I don't think I've ever heard of a break-in around here."

"It's a small community," Renie noted, setting her overnight case, tote bag, and purse on the floor. "Maybe fifty houses, and some aren't occupied all year. I never heard of a neighborhood watch, but they probably don't need one. Obsession Shores is off the beaten track."

Judith gazed through the big window that faced Worthless Bay, the Sound, and the mountains over on the Peninsula. "From what I can tell, the tide's either almost in or starting to go back out."

"Check the bulletin board," Renie said, opening the fridge. "There should be a tide table there some place. Oh, wow! Auntie Vance made us her clam chowder. A green salad to go with it. Let's eat."

Judith found the table in plain sight while Renie put a kettle on the stove to heat the chowder. "Low tide is at ten to two."

"We can walk the beach later on," Renie suggested, finding a box of crackers in the cupboard by the stove. "The tide won't come all the way in again until this evening. Of course, you'll want to start meeting and greeting the suspects. I mean, *neighbors*."

"Don't say things like that," Judith said sharply. "Are you looking for trouble?"

Renie shrugged. "We do have a way of finding it. Sometimes."

"For once, let's not," Judith said in her normal voice. "The last thing I want is a dead body to spoil my improving mood."

Renie was putting bowls and silverware on the table in the dining area. "You're rarely in a funk. What set you off besides the normal postholiday blues? Joe? Your mother? Do you feel okay otherwise, aside from your artificial hip sometimes bothering you?"

Judith sat down, but waited for Renie to take her own place at the big pine table. "Well . . . physically, I feel okay. The last few days getting Joe ready for the trip have been hectic. I admit I was kind of jealous of him going off without me. Did it bother you to have Bill take such a big vacation while you stayed home?"

Renie shook her head. "Heck no. It's good for him to get away from me once in a while. Sometimes I drive him nuts and vice versa. You and Joe haven't been married for almost forty years. We have. I miss Bill, and I'll be glad when he gets back. An occasional break does us both good." She glanced at the stove. "Let me get the chowder."

"I understand that," Judith said. "I resented the money Joe spent at the auction, but given the actual cost of the trip, it was insignificant. Now that he's gone and I'm not in my usual B&B whirl, I'm happy for him. Except for a long weekend up in Vancouver, we haven't had a real vacation since we all went to Scotland almost two years ago."

"So," Renie said, her brown eyes probing as she sat down after pouring the chowder, "what is it that set you off?"

"Ohhh . . ." Judith ran a hand through her shoulder-length dark hair with its pale gold highlights. "This sounds stupid, but I think I'm still mad at myself for flubbing that cold case and fingering the wrong killer. I've never made a mistake like that in all my years of accidentally getting mixed up in murder."

Renie looked as if she were trying not to laugh. "No kidding. Gosh, coz, you only missed by choosing one prime suspect over the other. Your usual logic and keen people skills made the solution fit perfectly. Both of those two people had motive, opportunity, and not quite airtight alibis."

"I still got it wrong," Judith asserted. "I should've stayed retired. I've gone out a loser."

Renie held her head. "That's about the dopiest thing I've heard from you. Unless I count saying yes to Dan when he proposed."

"It galls me to screw up a murder investigation."

"Please. You're ruining my taste buds for Auntie Vance's chowder."

"Nothing could do that. Skip it. If I remember, Dick and Jane Sedgewick live in the second house down on the right as you enter Obsession Shores. I mean, if we walk up there, they'd be on the left."

"That sounds right," Renie said, brushing cracker crumbs off her nubby green, gold, and bronze sweater. "Or left, I mean."

Judith got up to go to the counter that divided part of the kitchen from the rest of the larger room. "Auntie Vance keeps all her important stuff here with the phone books and catalogs and . . . ah! Here's a list of homeowners in the development. And," she went on with a hint of triumph, "I found a copy of the measure we're voting on."

"Spare me," Renie said. "All I need is no."

Judith sat down again. "Don't you want to be informed?"

"No. No, no, no." Renie viciously speared a lettuce leaf with her fork. "You think I haven't had to work on designs for conning people into voting whatever way I was dragooned by earning big bucks from whichever civic or public utility outfit hired me?"

"Fine. *I'd* like to know the details." Judith downed more chowder while reading through the proposal. "It sounds clear to me. This measure is to establish a private nonprofit sewer system to serve the—"

Renie held up a hand. "Serves them right if it's passed. I get it."

Judith put the single sheet of paper aside. "Has it occurred to you that this could be a *good* thing?"

"No. You want Auntie Vance to kill us for treason? If she and Uncle Vince are against it, I'm with them."

"I'm considering the opposition," Judith said reasonably. "Some of these other people might really prefer sewer lines. Not to mention the properties that don't percolate, so that a septic tank isn't an option. Over the years the forest has reclaimed the land they couldn't sell. You may recall that when the Webers were talking about building up here, my parents considered buying in, too. But the site they were looking at didn't perc. Then my father died and Mother lost heart in the idea."

"Your mother had a heart back then? I always wondered where it went. And no, I don't remember that. I was in high school at the time."

"No, you weren't. You'd graduated from college."

"So I was too caught up making serious money by creating graphic designs for brain-dead corner-office types."

"That sounds right. Are you finished with your latest foray into piggery?"

"Hey, I didn't spill much." Renie stood up. "Let's go be neighborly."

"At least you didn't dress in your usual nonprofessional bumlike wardrobe," Judith noted as they cleared the table.

"I figured we were going public," Renie said, opening the dishwasher. "A lot of these people must be really old. I don't want to scare them."

"Sometimes your bummy outfits scare *me*."

Renie made no comment. The cousins put on their jackets and headed outside. After closing the door, Judith grimaced. "I don't like not locking up. But we have no key. Does that bother you?"

"Kind of," Renie admitted. "But if that's how the locals live, I guess it shouldn't worry us. We're used to living in a big city, surrounded by the everyday threat of criminal activity. It keeps us alert."

The cousins took their time walking alongside the road. Overhead, the clouds were getting lower and darker. Accustomed to the gray of winter, neither Judith nor Renie paid much attention. The old joke was that the standard forecast was "overcast with a high of fifty-five, a low of forty-three, and a ninety percent chance of rain." It was more of a truism than a joke during much of the year.

As they turned to follow the stone walkway to the front door, Judith glanced back to take in the view. "Maybe a storm is coming this way," she noted. Moving figures crossing the main road halfway to the beach caught her eye. "Some clam diggers are out. A couple of people are pushing somebody in a wheelchair. Do you recognize them?"

Renie made a face. "From here? I'm farsighted, but they look like blobs to me."

Judith shrugged and kept going. Dick and Jane Sedgewick were out on their deck, arguing about something. "Hey," Dick called, waving at the cousins, "button it up, Jane. We've got company. It looks like the Webers' nieces. I'll be damned."

"You probably will be," Jane said with a cutting glance at her husband. "Hi, girls! Come on up. It's almost cocktail time."

"At one thirty?" Renie called back as they approached the staircase. "Isn't that kind of early?"

"Not at Obsession Shores," Dick shot back with a grin. He was a big, hearty man with a full head of steel-gray hair. "We figure anytime is cocktail time during the winter."

Jane took what Judith hoped was a playful punch at her husband's midsection. "Don't listen to my bitter half. He wishes we could drink a lot more, but his ulcer and my high blood pressure have short-circuited our former party days. Come on in. We're trying to decide if this piece of so-called driftwood he picked up this morning is a coiled cobra or a worn-out tire. Dick doesn't see so well anymore, but I figure the Firestone imprint gives it away."

"Damn!" Dick exclaimed. "I should wear my trifocals when I go for a morning stroll, but they get blurred when it's foggy."

"*You're* foggy, Lover Boy," Jane said, taking Dick's arm as they ushered their guests inside. "Vance told us you were going to stand in for them at the meeting tonight. I just hope you can stand the meeting. It's going to get ugly."

Judith smiled. *Ugly* was not a word that would describe Jane Sedgewick. Age had not diminished her tall, voluptuous figure or her auburn-haired beauty. The silver streaks among her natural curls only emphasized the sparkle in her hazel eyes.

"Come into the nook," Dick said, leading the way past the kitchen with its gleaming black appliances. "We call it our 'love nest,' but," he added, "sometimes with my wife, it's more like a 'crow's nest.' Either way works with me." He slapped Jane's rear.

"Just don't say *Old* Crow," she murmured. "I make a mean hot toddy. Real rum for this occasion. How about it, girls?"

"Sure," Judith said. "Can I help?"

Jane looked askance, but her hazel eyes danced. "You think I'm doddering?"

"I probably dodder more than you do," Judith replied. "Hip replacement, you know."

"Oh, yeah, I remember Vance telling me about that. Dick got a new knee last year. Go ahead, you can help carry the mugs," she continued as they backtracked into the kitchen. "Renie will entertain Dick. She's a sport, as I remember."

"She is that," Judith agreed. "Speaking of sports, she and I should probably know who to watch out for as the enemy tonight."

"Oh, they'll be hard to miss," Jane said, turning on the teakettle. "Of course, we don't know how everybody will vote. Some of these people are virtual strangers. That is, they're mostly a younger crowd, second generation of the original owners, or newcomers. They tend to keep to themselves."

Judith nodded. "Typical, I imagine. Are there many children living here these days? In the early years after Auntie Vance and Uncle Vince moved up here, there weren't any young families."

"It's like everywhere else in this part of the country—lots of newcomers moving in from all over the place." She paused to get a bottle of rum from a well-stocked liquor cabinet. "As time went on, more people with children inherited or bought in. The school bus stops here now. There are about two dozen kids who ride it. That's quite a change in the last six, seven years. Until then, the only children we saw were usually just visiting."

The teakettle whistled. Jane made the drinks while telling Judith to grab a notepad from the kitchen drawer near the phone. "You'll want to write down the names," she said. "I don't know everybody, but I can at least identify some of the players, both pro and con sewers."

"Got it," Judith said, finding a ruled notepad on top of some kitchen appliance manuals. "By the way, who's the old guy we saw being pushed by a couple on the way up here?"

"Quentin Quimby," Jane replied. "He's in his midnineties, but he can still walk. He'd rather ride, though, so his son and daughter-in-law have to push him around." She paused and laughed. "Wrong term. Nobody pushes that old guy around. He's ornery, but he may be on our side against the sewer line. Unless he changes his mind, of course. His wife died a few years ago. Frankly, we thought she'd finally run away."

"Gosh," Judith said, "maybe my mother would like to date

him. They'd make a good pair. They could have an ornery competition."

Jane smiled. "As I recall, your mother is a character. I like her."

"So do I," Judith agreed as Jane handed her two steaming mugs. "But she sometimes frustrates me."

"Understood." Jane's expression was bemused. "Sort of like being married a long time."

Going back into the nook, Judith and Jane joined Renie and Dick, who were talking about his former career in construction for a regional company specializing in skyscrapers.

"Never did like heights," Dick was saying. "They had to make me a foreman because I wouldn't get off the ground."

After handing out the steaming mugs, Jane called for attention. "Let's get back down to earth, Dick," she said, sitting in a wicker-back chair. "As in what should go *in* the ground around here. Friedmans against." She glanced at the cousins. "You know them, right?"

Judith nodded. "Are they around this afternoon?"

"No," Jane said. "They went into town to see Mel's doctor. He has to have elbow surgery."

Dick held up a finger. "The Logans, Kent and Suzie. Dark green house one up from the beach and four over from this road on your left. He's an attorney, still practicing part-time. She's a pianist, still practicing the damned thing. She'll never get it right. I can't think how she made any kind of living off that when it sounds like she's wearing boxing gloves."

"The Johnsons, Charles and May," Jane put in. "Older than God, but still sharp. You remember them? They're four doors past your aunt and uncle with about twenty hummingbird feeders around their house."

Judith frowned. "Um . . . not offhand, but I might know them when I see them." She looked at Renie. "How about you, coz?"

"I'm blank," Renie replied.

"No problem," Dick said. "In fact, maybe the best way is for you two to sit with us tonight and we'll clue you in as we go along."

"Probably," Judith agreed after tasting her toddy. "This is delicious," she added, smiling at Jane.

Her hostess shrugged. "I still had some mix left over from the holidays. We might as well use it up. It doesn't keep forever."

Renie held out her mug. "I already finished mine. How about a refill? I wouldn't want what you have left to go to waste."

"It won't go to *your* waist," Judith asserted, then turned to her hosts. "She eats like a hog and never gains an ounce. It drives me nuts."

The Sedgewicks both laughed while Renie curled her lip at Judith. "Go get it," Jane said. "There's just enough left for a refill."

"I'll do that," Renie said, and exited the nook.

Judith glanced at a note she'd made on the tablet. "I'd like to know about one pro-sewer couple—the Crowleys. Auntie Vance mentioned them in particular. What's their story?"

Dick made a face. "They're younger, late thirties, got two kids—a boy and a girl—who go to the grade school. They live next door to Mel and Sarah Friedman. Big on the environment, which I guess is why they want sewers. I don't know how that makes a difference, but it does to them."

Judith nodded once. "The Bennetts? Pro or con?"

"Not sure. Kind of an odd couple. Been here a long time, but I don't know their take on this deal."

Renie returned to the nook. "Hey, coz," she said, "ask about the guy we recognized from the ferry."

Judith paused before offering a description. "Older man, average size, glasses, and his name was something like Eddie or Edgar."

Jane was quick to answer. "Ernie Glover. He and Edna used to be summer people before he retired from the state working as an auditor. He's on our side, so his wife probably is, too."

Judith made another note. "Is there one person who seems to be leading the charge for the sewer line?"

Jane and Dick exchanged inquiring glances. He held up a hand, indicating his wife should answer the question.

"It's hard to tell," Jane admitted. "The most vocal—or maybe the loudest—is Zach Bendarek. Kind of goofy, but likable."

"Ex–football player," Dick said. "Probably didn't remember to put on his helmet before he got off the bench and into the game. Went on from the University to play in the pros for a few years before his knees went south. Wife's a little squirt of a thing." He glanced at Renie. "Even littler than you, but cute."

"I'm not cute?" Renie shot back. "Watch it."

Dick chuckled. "Hell, you always had a mouth on you, right? Not as bad as Vance, though. She's a damned hoot."

"She certainly is," Judith asserted, looking out the window. "As long as the Friedmans aren't home, Renie and I should get our beach walk in now. It looks like it's going to pour fairly soon."

"It's that time of year," Jane said. "But then it can rain up here almost any time of the year except July and August."

The Sedgewicks saw the cousins out the door. "If you run low on food," Jane called out as they went down the steps, "come to dinner while you're here. But knowing Vance, you're well stocked."

"We definitely are," Judith shouted back. "See you at the meeting."

"Nice people," Renie commented as they walked down the road to the beach. "They're holding up quite well."

"They enjoy sparring with each other." Judith glanced at Renie. "Kind of reminds me of you and Bill."

"We don't spar, we viciously attack. Verbally, I mean."

"No, you don't. You two just have bigger vocabularies." Judith glanced at both sides of the road. "It's quiet around here. Everybody seems to be hunkering down. Maybe they know a big storm is coming."

"You're used to being up here in the summer when the weather's good," Renie said. "Careful with the steps to the beach."

"Right. You go first so that if I fall I'll land on—"

"Yeah, yeah," Renie shot back. "I'm the human buffer."

Judith held on to the railing and made short work of the ten steps. "The wind's come up," she noted. "Shall we see if we can find Uncle Vince's boat?"

"Why not? He always tied it up over there by that big log. In fact, I can see it from here. Barely. Maybe nothing's left but the prow. No loss. Watch your step. There's always a lot of junk that washes up on the beach. Or what slobs leave after they've frolicked here. Unfortunately, it's not a private beach. Anybody can access it without coming through the development if they're willing to walk a bit."

"There's nobody out here now that I can see," Judith said. "At least the sand isn't very wet this close to dry land. Have you noticed all the new construction on the north side of the bay by Scratchit Head?"

"Yes, growth everywhere you look." Renie kicked at a discarded beer can. "If I hadn't been raised by My Mother the Germaphobe, I'd pick that up and take it back to the garbage. Look over there," she said, pointing to a bundle of clothes. "Somebody must have left their laundry by that big piece of driftwood."

Judith peered at what looked like a pile of rags. "Now, why would . . ." She paused as they got within twenty feet of the large bundle. "Oh, coz . . . I have an awful feeling."

"About what?" Renie stared at Judith, then quickly walked closer. "Good Lord!" she exclaimed. "It's a person!"

Judith picked up her pace. "Is it a man?"

Renie nodded. "He must've passed out." She rummaged in her purse to take out her cell.

Judith moved closer to the man, who was facedown in the wet sand. A horrible yet all-too-familiar feeling overcame her. She tried to figure out if he was breathing. "Can you take his pulse?" she asked Renie. "I shouldn't try to bend down that far."

But Renie had moved a few feet behind her, apparently calling 911. After disconnecting, she moved to Judith's side. "I can, I guess," she said in a tremulous voice, "but I don't think he's got a pulse. If he's facedown, he can't be breathing. Damn! Coz, I think you just found another freaking corpse!"

Chapter 4

That doesn't mean the guy's been murdered," Judith said with fervor. "He's got a full head of gray hair. He may've had a heart attack. He's certainly not young."

"But he certainly is dead," Renie said, sounding more like herself. "The emergency folks will be here in under ten minutes. They come from the fire station by the second turnoff from the ferry dock."

Judith felt the first raindrops fall on her face. She put her car coat's hood up more securely around her head and grimaced. "Remember how Uncle Vince always called us the Gruesomes when we were kids because we liked murder-mystery stories so much?"

Renie rolled her eyes. "It was prophetic. I'd forgotten all about that nickname."

"We're stuck here. Maybe we should go sit in Uncle Vince's boat."

"I'd rather sit on that log," Renie said. "If it rains really hard, the overhang from the ground above might keep us from getting soaked."

"Good idea," Judith agreed. "The seagulls are diving and swooping all over the place. That's always the sign of a storm. I hate to walk off and leave him lying here alone." She chewed her lower lip as she studied his inert body: navy all-weather jacket, tan pants, sturdy brown walking shoes, blue rainproof cap lying near his head. "I wonder how long he's been here?"

"That's up to the experts," Renie said. "Keeping a vigil won't matter to him, but it matters to me if I get pneumonia from standing over a stiff. Let's go. Or, as Bill would say, boppin'!"

Yet both cousins moved with dragging feet to the big log. "We should've worn boots," Renie muttered. "It's cold, too. We need mittens."

"I've never seen you wear mittens," Judith said, wiping moisture off of her face.

"That's because I don't have any." Renie made a face. "I'm too old to wear mittens. Mom finally let me stop wearing them when I was twenty-two. Have you forgotten I had horrible sinus infections as a kid?"

"No, but you outgrew them when you were twelve. Why didn't Aunt Deb let you stop wearing mittens then?"

"Mom wanted to be sure," Renie retorted. "Besides, I stopped growing then. That's why I'm so much shorter than you are. You know how she's always worried about me."

"Do you think she'd worry more if she knew we were sitting twenty yards away from a corpse?"

Renie shook her head. "That kind of thing doesn't bother her. She's used to it by now. So's Aunt Gert."

Judith didn't comment. The rain was falling harder. The overhang protected them except when the wind blew the hard, cold drops into their faces. "Do I hear a siren?" she asked, raising her head.

"No. It's a seagull." Renie checked her watch. "I called at two ten. It's now two twenty. They should be . . ." She paused. "Now I hear sirens. We'd better make sure they can see us."

A minute passed as the sirens—at least two of them, Judith realized—grew louder before they stopped. The cousins stood up, hurrying toward the staircase. Before they covered the last ten yards, the EMTs came racing down the steps and onto the beach. They were carrying their kits and a gurney. The cousins waved their hands.

The three medics looked very young. Judith wondered if they were volunteers. The taller of the trio asked if they could show them the victim's location. Judith indicated the driftwood and what appeared to be a pile of rags, but, alas, was not. The medics trotted off just as four firefighters came down the stairs.

"Guess they don't need our help," Renie said, grimacing into what had become a downpour. "The overhang doesn't help with the wind blowing from the northwest. What's the point of getting soaked?"

Judith frowned as she brushed water off of her face. "We can't just walk away."

"I can," Renie declared. "But," she added after a pause, "I won't, because you may need help getting back up the stairs."

"Go without me," Judith said. "To quote your mother, 'Don't worry about me.'" She made clucking noises with her tongue.

"Oh, for . . ." Renie dug into the damp sand, setting her elbows on her knees and propping her chin on her hands. "Fine."

Judith was craning her neck to look back at the steps. "Where are the cops? Don't they always come with the medics and firefighters?"

"Only when they get called to *your* house," Renie said in a grumpy voice. "Or somewhere else in your cul-de-sac."

One of the firefighters approached the cousins. "Are you the ones who called in?" he asked, stopping a yard or so away from the log.

"Yes," Judith replied. "The poor man is dead, right?"

The firefighter, who looked closer to forty than thirty and had keen blue eyes, nodded. "I'm afraid so. Heart attack, maybe, though we don't like to guess. Do you know him?"

Judith shook her head, noting that his nametag read BREWSTER. "We don't live here. We're staying at our aunt and uncle's place."

Brewster nodded once. "Okay. We're not needed, so if you want, you can ride with us back to your relatives' place. After we get there, I can take your names and contact numbers just in case."

"Just in case *what?*" Renie asked.

"Well . . ." Brewster looked faintly embarrassed. "It probably sounds silly, but we have to always allow for the possibility of a person's death being . . . suspicious."

Renie burst into laughter. "That's too funny! I never heard of such a thing!" She nudged Judith with her elbow. "How about you, coz?"

Judith barely stopped herself from kicking Renie. "You can't blame the authorities for being cautious," she said primly. "Yes, thank you. We'll take your offer of a ride up to the Webers' house."

Brewster signaled to his fellow firefighters. "Let's go," he said, leading the way to the staircase.

At the top of the steps, Judith was faintly dismayed to see the type of fire engine that she remembered from her youth. "This is . . ah . . . ?"

Brewster looked grim. "We have problems passing bond issues on the island. Very fiscally conservative kind of folks. But this old baby still runs. The hoses and pumps work fine. That's what matters. It's got real seats, too. Squeeze in next to each other before I get behind the wheel."

"I'll go first," Renie volunteered. "Coz needs a boost, Brewster. She doesn't have all her original parts. Neither do I, but what the hey." She awkwardly scrambled into the engine's cab.

"You," Judith said under her breath after the firefighter had eased her into a sitting position, "don't have much trouble with your partial shoulder replacement. Why even mention it?"

"Why not?" Renie shot back. "It's like a . . . badge of survival, maybe? More perks of getting old. Sympathy's nice. I think."

"Just try to keep your mouth shut," Judith whispered as Brewster opened the door on the driver's side.

"Okay," he said, after making sure his fellow firefighters were in position. "Where to?"

Judith gave him directions. "It's easy. The Weber house is off this road on the right, almost to the top of the hill."

"Got it." The gears seemed to grind as Brewster started the engine. "This relic was new not long after World War Two. I kind of like it."

"Gee," Renie said, "I was only thirty-five back then."

Judith elbowed her cousin, but Brewster laughed obligingly. "Quality lasts," he said. "You two seem remarkably undisturbed by finding that poor dead guy."

"We're used"—Renie began, but switched her own gears after another, sharper jab from Judith—" . . . car dealers. This antique engine fascinates us."

"Oh?" He glanced at the cousins. "You have your own dealership?"

"No," Judith replied before Renie could get them any deeper into fantasyland. "She means that we have an interest in older-model vehicles. My husband has a classic red MG."

"That's awesome," Brewster said. "How close are we?"

"The next street," Judith said, noting that a few homeowners had braved the heavy rain to come as far as their porches and decks. Obviously, they were curious about what had brought emergency personnel to Obsession Shores. No doubt, Judith thought, more were staring from their windows. With any luck, maybe nobody would notice their arrival via fire engine.

The old truck slowed to a stop. "Hang on," Brewster said. "I'll help you get out."

To Judith's relief, nobody in the immediate vicinity seemed to be witnessing their return. Thanking Brewster profusely, she moved quickly through the wind and rain to seek sanctuary inside.

"Wow," Renie said, closing the door behind her, "you can almost run when you want to."

Judith was taking off her car coat. "I wanted to avoid the thrill-seekers. Besides, I'm cold and wet. Aren't you?"

Renie nodded. "I'm just surprised that you didn't ask more questions, like if the emergency crews knew the deceased. You seem to have left your customary curiosity back on the mainland."

"We'll find out soon enough," Judith said. "We don't know most of these people. A name probably wouldn't ring any bells."

"True," Renie allowed, joining Judith, who had sat down on the sofa. "Unlike your usual encounters with death, it didn't happen in your home or your immediate neighborhood."

Judith gave her cousin a reproachful look. "As you recall, the last case was sixteen years old and occurred in the Thurlow district after I moved from there. The more recent homicide investigation I got involved in happened on the other side of the mountains, a hundred and twenty miles from Hillside Manor."

"I sit corrected," Renie said. "If the dead guy is an Obsession Shores resident, I wonder if they'll call off the meeting tonight." She glanced at the phone on the kitchen counter. "I don't think Auntie Vance and Uncle Vince have an answering machine. They live the simple life up here on The Rock, as the locals refer to the island."

"You're right," Judith agreed. "Not long ago, Auntie Vance was bitching about people who have phone add-ons. I told her I had to do that because I was running a business. She told me to go stick my head in the soup pot. She also told me where I could put my computer."

"I've heard that from her, too," Renie remarked, then tensed before getting up to look out the window. "Speaking of hearing things, did somebody just let out a yell?"

"Maybe it was another seagull," Judith said.

"I don't think so." Renie went outside to the deck, but returned after only a few seconds. "The medic van is parked in front of the second house in from the road below us. I wonder if that's where the dead man lived." She grimaced as she brushed some raindrops off of her face. "What's their opening line? 'Are you the Widow Whoozits?'"

"Oh, dear." Judith stood up to join Renie by the window. "They're probably informing his wife what happened. I wonder how long he'd been gone before he collapsed."

"Not too long," Renie said. "He didn't look wet or rumpled. It was as if he'd just fallen down. Maybe he was still warm."

"Now who's being a ghoul?" Judith inquired with a smirk.

The phone rang before Renie could respond. Judith went to the counter and grabbed the receiver.

"What's going on by the Glovers' place?" Jane Sedgewick asked. "We heard sirens a while ago and now there's an aid car parked by the house. Have you seen any excitement around here?"

"That's Ernie Glover's house?" Judith said in surprise.

"Yes. I wonder if something's happened to Edna or Ernie."

Judith swallowed hard. "Ernie's dead. Renie and I found him on the beach. Apparent heart attack, we were told. Renie called 911. We just got back from there a few minutes ago."

"Oh, no!" Jane exclaimed. "Poor Ernie! Poor Edna! Maybe Dick and I should go over there. Talk to you later." She hung up.

"Ernie?" Renie said. "The guy you saw on the ferry?"

"Right." A helpless feeling overcame Judith. "Jane and Dick are going to offer Edna help. Maybe we should . . . No, we're strangers. We'd be intruding. The neighbors can provide aid and comfort."

Renie's brown eyes danced. "But none of them will ask the right questions because they don't have your rampant and often grisly curiosity."

"I'm not that curious about a guy having a heart attack," Judith declared. "It isn't as if he was riddled with bullet holes or had a knife sticking out of his back."

"Hey," Renie responded, holding up her hands, "I can't help it if you're disappointed because somebody died of natural causes."

"Don't say that," Judith snapped. "I quit sleuthing."

Renie glanced outside, where the wind drove the rain against the big window. "So what do we do for fun? I'm not playing cribbage. I've done my duty with Aunt Gert and gotten my rear kicked in the process."

Judith regarded her cousin with a wry expression. "I thought you had work to do."

"You're right. Thanks for the reminder." Renie grabbed her laptop from the counter and settled in at the dining room table.

Judith's watch informed her it was just after three. If she were home, guests would arrive in two hours. She'd be scurrying around, making sure their rooms were ready, overseeing Phyliss's housecleaning progress, studying hors d'oeuvres recipes, figuring out the dinner menu, looking in on Gertrude, taking new reservations . . .

She flopped back down on the sofa. Maybe she'd take a nap. Judith rarely had time to relax. But a much-needed nap was necessary in November after she and Renie had confronted a killer. Almost getting killed tended to tire her out. Nor was she as young as she used to be. While still sitting up, Judith was drifting off into sleep when someone pounded on the door.

"Dammit!" Renie cried, jumping off the chair. "Just when I was about to be brilliant . . ." She yanked open the door. "Hi. Who are you?"

Judith struggled to her feet, hearing a male voice identify himself as Brose Bennett. By the time she joined Renie, he was introducing his wife, Fou-fou, and asking where the Webers might be.

"Halfway to Beatrice," Renie replied. "If you want them, call Aunt Ellen. Wait—don't call her. She may be in the hospital. Or not. I forget."

"Bee Atris?" the small, blond Fou-fou squeaked. "Who's that?"

"It's not a who, it's—" Renie began as Judith offered her hand.

"Hi," she said. "I'm Judith Flynn and this is Serena Jones. We're the Webers' nieces. We're house-sitting while they visit our aunt Ellen and uncle Win in *Beatrice, Nebraska*. Do you want to come in?"

Since the wind was practically blowing the couple through the door, they didn't have much choice. The cousins stepped aside. Judith suggested they sit on the sofa and offered them something to drink.

The Bennetts sat down. "Didn't mean to barge in," Brose apologized. "If Vance and Vince told us they were taking off, we forgot." He looked at Fou-fou for confirmation. She shrugged, her bright blue eyes darting around the room.

"We didn't know they were going until a couple of days ago," Judith explained, sinking into a recliner that felt like a bottomless pit. "Aunt Ellen is having shoulder surgery. Maybe you met her the last time they visited from Beatrice."

"They have a lot of company," Fou-fou said in her tiny voice. "Ambrose and I can't keep track. You must come from a big family."

"We sure do," Renie asserted, dragging a kitchen chair over to sit next to Judith. "Dozens of us, all over the place. Do you want something to drink or what?"

"Oh . . ." Brose stared up at the ceiling. "Guess we wouldn't mind an inch or two of Scotch." He poked Fou-fou in the arm. "You'd be surprised at my little gal. She can hold her liquor."

Renie got up to head for the kitchen area. "I hope so. I'd hate to have to hold it for her."

"Hey!" Brose said, laughing lustily. "That's a good one."

Fou-fou wrinkled her button nose. "I don't think it's funny."

Her husband turned serious, his long face beaglelike. In fact, Judith realized, he had unusually long ears as well. "The wife here isn't much for jokes," he said in a somber tone. "We stopped by to see if the meeting tonight was canceled. I guess poor ol' Ernie Glover bought the farm this afternoon. Helluva thing."

"We haven't heard anything about the meeting," Judith said. "We're here because the Webers gave us their proxy votes."

"You don't say," Brose murmured.

Fou-fou glared at her husband. "She did, too, say it. I heard her."

"Right, right," Brose said under his breath. His jowls sagged, making him look even more houndlike. "I wonder how Ern would've voted."

Judith shrugged, reluctant to lead into any reference to the cousins' discovery of his body. "We never met him."

Renie carried a tray with four glasses to the Bennetts. "The drinks are all Scotch except mine. Take your pick."

Fou-fou craned her neck to look up at Renie. "I like Scotch with fruit juice. It keeps away wrinkles."

"No kidding," Renie said, turning her head this way and that. "How far away? If they're outside, they probably blew south by now."

Fou-fou looked mystified; Brose frowned.

Judith forced a laugh. "My cousin's teasing. She's a real joker."

"Then she should tell us a joke," Fou-fou piped in a cross tone.

Brose patted his wife's arm. "Just take the damned drink, sweetie pie. These ladies are real nice."

Fou-fou rolled her eyes, but picked up the glass nearest to her small hand. "Fine," she grumbled, settling back into the sofa cushions.

"I don't suppose," Brose said, after taking a sip of Scotch and smacking his lips, "you'd tell us how the Webers are voting."

"That's right," Renie retorted, after handing Judith her glass and sitting down. "For all we know, the meeting's off."

Brose slowly shook his head with its fringe of graying brown hair. "Don't think Ern'd want us to do that. He was the kind of guy who thought the show must go up." He made a face. "Or is it *on*? The curtain goes up, but the show . . . Never mind." He paused again, shaking his head. "Poor ol' Ern. He retired about the same time I did, two, three years ago."

Judith reached back into her memory, trying to recall any

information about Ambrose Bennett. "You were in manufacturing, right?"

Brose nodded, his long chin almost touching his narrow chest. "You bet. I manufactured the best danged weenie and burger buns in the West. Bet you've scarfed 'em down over the years."

"Ben's Buns?" Judith said in surprise. "Oh, yes, of course."

Brose nodded sagely. "You betcha. Kept the operation small, only marketed on the West Coast. I sold out to some big wheels from California, but they keep up the quality. I hope," he added in a less certain tone, before polishing off his drink in two big gulps. He poked his wife again. "Come on, sweat pea, we better get ourselves in gear. It's gonna be serious drink time in a few. Better hoist one for ol' Ern."

Fou-fou had already drained her glass. "Why? I didn't think you liked him," she said, letting her husband haul her up from the sofa.

"Awww . . . Ern was a good guy. I just liked kiddin' around with him." He turned to the cousins, who had gotten up. "Nice to meet you. Thanks for the hit. Nice way to start the evenin'."

After the door was closed behind them, Judith and Renie stared at each other. "That doofus ran a business?" Renie gasped in disbelief. "Thank goodness I never buy Ben's Buns."

"I do," Judith said. "They're . . . good. I mean, a bun is a bun. But I wonder if Brose is putting on an act."

"It's a good one. Who else but a dumb cluck would marry Fou-fou?"

Judith collected the empty glasses. "She *is* a bit strange. I'm wondering about these Obsession Shores people. Do the retirees just sit around during the winter and wait for the cocktail hour?"

Renie grimaced. "There isn't much else to do in January. I'd hate to be stuck here. If you like sports and culture, it's a round trip via ferry and a long drive into town."

"That costs—" Another knock interrupted Judith. "Now

what?" she muttered, opening the door to a stocky six-footer in a sheriff's uniform.

"Excuse me," he said. "Are you Mrs. Flynn or Mrs. Jones?"

"Flynn," Judith replied. "She's Jones. Come in. What's going on?"

The officer entered, removing his hat and introducing himself as Lieutenant Erik Jacobson. "I believe you two found the body of Ernest Glover earlier this afternoon. Is that correct?"

Judith nodded. "Do we need to fill out a form?"

"I have some questions for you." He cleared his throat. "Mr. Glover didn't die of natural causes. He was stabbed to death. I'm afraid we're talking about a homicide."

Chapter 5

Renie staggered, grabbing Judith's arm. "Oh, no! I feel faint!"

Judith managed not to glare at her cousin. "Maybe you should sit down, *dear,*" she said, trying to free her arm without wrenching it from Renie's grasp.

Renie let go, leaning against the counter. "I'll be all right," she said in a feeble imitation of her usual voice. "It's just such a shock."

"Maybe," Judith suggested to Jacobson, "we should all sit down."

The lieutenant nodded, following Judith and an unusually docile Renie into the living room area. The cousins sat on the sofa; Jacobson lowered himself into the recliner before taking out a notebook from the inside of his jacket and clicking a ballpoint pen. Apparently the island's law enforcement agency relied on old-fashioned handwriting and real paper. After jotting down their names, addresses, phone numbers, and relationship to the Webers, he asked why they had gone to the beach that afternoon.

Judith responded. "We're natives. Rain doesn't bother us. We wanted to walk a bit before it got too stormy."

Jacobson nodded. "Several people had done that in the early afternoon, including the victim. The locals know when a storm is brewing." He paused. "Mr. Glover hadn't been dead for more than half an hour."

"You mean," Judith said, "there were footprints around the scene?"

He nodded again. "The high tide usually comes close to where you found Mr. Glover's body. There'd been a break in the weather before noon, so some prints were still faintly visible."

Judith leaned forward slightly. "I don't understand. The rain didn't wash them away? Or do you mean the prints were away from the body? Could you take casts of them?"

If the questions surprised Jacobson, he didn't show it. His ruddy face with its sharp green eyes remained impassive. Judith guessed him to be in his early forties. There was no gray in the auburn buzz cut, though the lines around his wide mouth and broad forehead indicated he laughed and worried in equal measure.

"At least four other people saw Mr. Glover on the beach," he said, ignoring her second question. "What time did you go down there?"

"A little after two," Judith replied. "We found the body only a few minutes after getting to the beach."

"Two-oh-nine," Renie said sitting up straight and no longer sounding feeble. "I called 911 at two ten. They showed up ten minutes later. But you know that already." She folded her arms and leaned back on the sofa. "I think I've recovered from the shock."

"So it seems," Jacobson murmured. "Yes, I've noted the time that you called. You were described by the 911 responder as 'calm.'"

"I suffer from delayed reaction," Renie said with a straight face.

Judith wondered if it wasn't better if Renie *didn't* talk. "My cousin performs well in a crisis," she asserted.

Jacobson didn't comment. Instead he asked if they'd seen anyone else on the beach. They hadn't, Judith said. "But," she continued, "we saw no blood. Where was he stabbed?"

"In the chest," Jacobson replied. "Three times. He bled out into the sand. You wouldn't have seen it. The EMTs didn't notice until they were pulling him out onto the gurney."

Judith grimaced. "Did you find the weapon?"

He remained impassive. "Not yet."

"I wonder," Judith said, "if he died right away. He must've, if we saw no signs of a struggle, right?"

The officer frowned slightly. "You're unusually observant, Mrs. Flynn. I take it you didn't know Mr. Glover?"

Judith shook her head. "I'd actually seen him on the noon ferry. He looked vaguely familiar and I recalled he might've been pointed out to me on a previous visit. I never met him, though."

"And you, Mrs. Jones?" he asked.

"No. Same thing—a passing remark by our aunt and uncle."

Jacobson studied his notes, frowning slightly before speaking again. "Did you see anyone or anything unusual after you left here?"

"We didn't leave from here," Judith replied. "We'd been at Dick and Jane Sedgewicks' house. They're close friends of the Webers. We've known them fairly well over the years, too."

He gave another nod. "I'll talk to them as well. We're questioning everyone in the development."

"How many deputies are here?" Judith asked.

"I have two working with me today." He made as if to close the notebook, but stopped, glancing first at Judith and then at Renie. "Did you touch the body?"

"No," Judith said. "I thought we should take his pulse, but Renie pointed out that being facedown, Mr. Glover couldn't breathe and therefore he must be dead."

Jacobson seemed puzzled. "An odd reaction, don't you think?"

"Why?" Renie demanded sharply.

The officer fixed her with a hard stare. "Most people don't assume someone lying on the ground is dead," he stated with a hint of incredulity. "They react by thinking the person is unconscious."

Renie lifted her short chin. "Try logic. It's my cousin's strong suit, by the way. I have some, too. It runs in the family. If someone is obviously unable to breathe unless he's got a tube in the ground that goes all the way to Beijing, then he's probably a goner."

Jacobson and Renie stared—or glared—at each other for what seemed to Judith like a long time. Finally, he closed the notebook and stood up. "Thanks for your cooperation. We'll be in touch." He started for the door. "You're not going anywhere, are you? That is, outside of Obsession Shores."

Judith struggled a bit getting up to her feet. "We might go to the grocery store up at the junction or into Langton."

"Don't. We'll let you know when you can leave Obsession Shores."

Jacobson opened the door and strode off.

At least he didn't slam the damned thing behind him," Judith said, closing the door. "Are we actual *suspects*?"

"Sounds like it," Renie said, putting her feet up on the sofa. "It wouldn't be the first time."

"Coz!" Judith cried. "It's one thing to find another corpse, but now I have to prove we're innocent. That means—"

"You have to start sleuthing," Renie finished for her. "Go ahead. You'd do it anyway. I wonder if Auntie Vance has enough Pepsi? If she doesn't, that could be a problem."

"For *you*," Judith snapped, pacing the living area. "I can drink water. I usually do. It's better for me than pop."

Renie ignored the comment and propped herself up with a couple of throw pillows. "How many real suspects are there? I'd guess well under a hundred, if you don't count kids. Probably not too many visitors this time of year. You can do it."

Judith sank back into the recliner. "I do not intend to interrogate a hundred people. I couldn't. Besides, some of them might not have known Ernie very well. This is like any other neighborhood. People bond through common interests, not addresses."

"See? You've already eliminated half of the suspects. Keep

going. Don't forget, some of these houses are vacant because their owners went south for the winter."

Judith turned stony-faced. "Okay. I'll start with you. What did you notice on the way to and along the beach before we found Ernie?"

Renie gazed up at the open beamed ceiling. "Not much. I tend to keep my eyes on the ground, especially when I'm on unfamiliar turf. In case you've never noticed, I'm kind of a klutz."

"That's because when you get in gear, you rush around too much," Judith said, still annoyed. "Are you sure you didn't notice anything?"

"Yes." Renie turned to look at her cousin. "And you?"

Judith made a face. "I didn't either. The locals probably stayed inside because they know when a storm's coming. Heck, *we* should've known better than to go out." She paused, her anger dissipated. "Why didn't I roll down the window and say hello to Ernie when I saw him on the ferry? I'm usually outgoing and friendly."

Renie had gotten up to rummage in the cupboards, apparently seeking snacks. "Because you didn't know he'd be your next victim?"

"So he is," Judith muttered. "I wish I could remember if I've met Mrs. Glover. Edna, that is."

Renie had found some saltwater taffy. She popped a piece into her mouth. "Widonyaser?"

"I won't ask her if we've met," Judith shot back. "The poor woman's husband just died. I'd feel cheeky barging in on her." She paused again while Renie sat back down. "But we *should* offer condolences on behalf of Auntie Vance and Uncle Vince."

Renie had swallowed the taffy. "Now?"

Judith shook her head. "Tomorrow. Even I'm not that pushy."

Her cousin merely shrugged. Judith started going over the notes she'd made at the Sedgewicks'. The names were no longer those of mere neighbors. Now they were the names of suspects.

The storm had passed over shortly after Jacobson left. Judith and Renie sat down to dinner at exactly six, lapping up Auntie Vance's legendary beef noodle bake. As usual, there was enough left to last for two or even three meals. The boysenberry pie was predictably delicious. They finished cleaning up from dinner by six thirty, with ample time to get to the seven o'clock meeting. Jane had called shortly after five to assure Judith and Renie there was no cancellation. She also gave directions to the clubhouse in case they'd forgotten where it was located. Which, in fact, they had. Neither cousin had ever been inside the gray frame building that stood at the south end of the development.

"Nondescript," Renie murmured when they pulled in next to a big black SUV. "Don't they have an architect living around here?"

"The clubhouse was the original sales office. They enlarged it later."

"They sure didn't improve it," Renie said, before exiting the car.

Judith waited to respond until after they were both on the paved path that led to the entrance. But before she could say anything, she saw Mel and Sarah Friedman coming their way.

"Hi," Judith called out. "How was the doctor's appointment?"

Both Friedmans laughed as they joined the cousins. "Are there no secrets at Obsession Shores?" Sarah asked, after the quartet exchanged hugs. "It was fine, the surgery's set for early February. I asked Dr. Miles to prescribe tranquilizers for *me* because Mel will be a terrible patient."

"Enough with the griping," Mel remarked in his deep, dry voice. "We heard you two found poor Ernie Glover on the beach this afternoon."

Judith blinked against the bright lights in the small clubhouse lobby. One wall featured a collection of glass balls nestled in beach netting. The rest of the decor consisted of homely watercolors that Judith figured had been done by local amateurs. It appeared that there was one large meeting room with a tiny kitchen and a restroom.

Judith was discreet. "It's so sad. Have you talked to his wife?"

"Yes," Sarah replied, lowering her voice as they entered the main room, which was beginning to fill up. "We stopped by before we came here. A terrible shock. Poor Edna."

Judith noticed the Sedgewicks coming in behind Quentin Quimby's son and daughter-in-law, who were pushing the old man in his wheelchair. Jane waved to the cousins and the Friedmans.

Sarah waved back, indicating the next-to-last row of chairs. "At least we've got Jane and Dick on our side," Mel said under his breath.

"Who's at the end of the row?" Renie asked as they kept moving.

"Kent and Suzie Logan," Sarah said softly. She led the way, exchanging greetings with the Logans. Mel sat beside his wife, while the cousins followed. Several sets of eyes stared at the newcomers. Renie had just sat down when an elderly couple finished filling up the row.

"Johnsons," Mel whispered to Judith and Renie. "Both deaf."

"So why are you whispering?" Renie said in her normal voice. A half-dozen heads swiveled to look at her. She gave them a toothy, if phony, smile. "Hi," she all but shouted. "Isn't this democracy thing *fun*?" They all turned around again. "Guess not," she declared loudly.

"Coz . . ." Judith said in a low, warning voice.

"Fine." Renie crossed her arms and scowled. The Johnsons didn't seem to notice.

Judith gave a start as a tall, sixtyish, fair-haired man banged a gavel at a rostrum up front. "I'm calling this meeting to order," he barked. "You got one minute to plant your butts in the seats before we have a moment of silence for the dearly departed etcetera."

"Hank Hilderschmidt," Mel said out of the side of his mouth. "Honorary jerk. His wife is Hilda."

"Okay," Hank said, scratching at one of his long sideburns.

"Let's do it. Heads down. Ernest Glover, rest in peace." He raised his left arm, eyes on his watch.

"Jeez," Renie murmured, but bowed her head.

A shrill voice shattered the sudden silence. "What the hell is going on now? Is this some damned church? Where are we? What's Hank doing up there? Where's Hilda?"

Judith's eyes slid to her right, where she could see part of Quentin Quimby and his wheelchair at the end of the row near the wall. Frantic whispering ensued, probably from his son, who apparently was seated in the last row. At least a couple of stifled laughs could be heard, one of them from the silver-haired man in front of her.

"Time's up," Hank announced, banging his gavel again. "Meeting's called to order. All those in favor of skipping a big blah-blah discussion raise their hands."

A dozen or more hands went up from Judith's estimate of at least forty people. Renie was among them. Hank banged his gavel. "Motion carried. Let's vote. The little woman will pass out—"

"She'd better," yelled a male voice up front. "Stick it, Hank. The damned motion failed. Shut the hell up and let some of us talk."

"Frank Leonetti," Mel whispered to Judith. "Pro on the issue."

Judith nodded. Renie was staring straight ahead, a sure sign that her brain was somewhere other than in the clubhouse.

"Hey," Hank responded, "we've talked this sucker to death. Let's get it over with. Yea or nay. It's not real hard to choose."

Kent Logan stood up. "Hold on, Mr. Chairman," he said in a resonating voice that Judith figured had served him well as a courtroom lawyer. "I suggest we *not* vote for the measure this evening." Several people started speaking at once, but Hank banged his gavel—and Kent kept talking. "The so-called study for the sewer system wasn't specific in details. Putting together a couple of estimates from out-of-area contractors isn't an efficient way to determine cost or effectiveness."

Kent sat down. A few people clapped. Hank frowned. Frank Leonetti spoke up again: "Yeah, especially when one of the estimates was from somebody's brother-in-law in the big city."

Hank glowered. "Hey, leave Tank out of this. He does great work."

Judith barely heard the last few words. A hubbub had begun and was growing more hostile by the second. Quentin Quimby stood up, yelling obscenities. A female voice wailed, "I feel faint!" Hank started banging his gavel in a futile effort to restore order. He finally tossed it aside, grabbed his parka, and stalked out through the rear door.

"I guess," Dick practically shouted after tapping Judith on the shoulder, "the meeting's over. Let's go."

A dozen people had made the same decision, rushing to the main door. The last Judith saw of Quimby, his son and daughter-in-law were propping him up against the wall. He was still cussing, apparently at his overturned wheelchair. The cousins, along with the Sedgewicks and Friedmans, escaped the clubhouse without getting trampled.

"Gee," Renie said as fog settled in over the island, "that was so much fun I think I'll go back to the house and shave my head with a cheese grater. I'd hate to see the evening end on a low note."

Judith was edging her way to the car, trying not to bump into any of the other fleeing residents. "Are the meetings always so heated?" she asked of nobody in particular.

"Not quite," Dick replied. "Hey, how about a lift back up to our place? I could use a drink. Mel? Sarah?"

"Thanks, but we'll walk," Sarah called back, a vague figure as the Friedmans kept going into the foggy night. "We need to collapse."

The Sedgewicks got into the backseat. "So," Jane asked after Judith started the car, "how do you like the way we live on The Rock?"

"It's . . . rocky," Judith replied. "I'm afraid to reverse. I can't see very much behind me."

"Wait," Dick advised. "The building must be almost empty by now. Some of the others may've gone out the rear exit."

"The problem is," Jane said, "so many of the people at the meeting are retired or semiretired. They don't have anything to do except quarrel with each other. And drink," she added more softly.

Renie turned to look at the Sedgewicks. "I'm never going to retire. I like what I do and I'll keep working even if I end up using chalk to make patterns on the sidewalk in front of our house." She glanced at Judith. "And don't add that's what Aunt Gert says I'm already doing."

Judith smiled, but kept quiet, slowly easing the car onto the road.

"You're lucky," Dick said. "I didn't hate my job, but I got sick of listening to bitching, especially from our subcontractors. Tank Hilderschmidt was one of them. A real pain in the butt."

"How," Renie asked, still looking at the Sedgewicks, "did Hank get to chair the meeting? He really is a jerk."

"He volunteered," Jane replied. "Nobody else would do it. He's not stupid, just rough around the edges. He and his twin, Tank, came up the hard way. Hank worked for the ferry system. He started buying up old mom-and-pop grocery stores. As city real estate prices soared, so did his bank account—and his ego. We couldn't see if his wife was up front, but she may not have been there. She's kind of a loner."

"I'd be a loner if I was married to Hank," Renie said, turning around. "Careful, coz. You're close to the road's edge on my side."

"Got it." Judith turned the wheel to her left. "I'm curious. When Obsession Shores started almost forty years ago, it wasn't very expensive to buy in. Have prices risen up here like they have in town?"

"Not as much," Dick replied. "We bought before Vance and Vince did, back in '71. Cost us fifteen grand, including the money to build the house. Now we could get half a mil without much trouble."

Judith nodded. "That sounds right. Heraldsgate Hill has some of the most city's most expensive real estate. It's all about location."

"South slope," Renie said. "Coz lives on the hill's rich side. Bill and I live on the north side above the ship canal, otherwise known as the Poor People's Place. We don't care—we call it our own little slum."

"Nobody up here is megarich," Jane said. "It's more blue than white collar among our age group. Then there's Quentin Quimby. Nobody knows how much money that old coot has."

Judith stopped at the Sedgewick house. "How did he earn it?"

Dick guffawed. "You don't know?" Seeing the cousins shake their heads, he continued. "Over a hundred years ago, what's now Obsession Shores was the Quimby family's small farm. In the late sixties, after the senior Quimby died, Quentin's wife, Blanche, got fed up with trying to eke out a living from a few cows and chickens. She insisted they start selling off the property. But not in the usual way. It was more like the English do it. In effect, you buy in for a stated amount of years. Face it—now that his wife's dead, old Quimby owns Obsession Shores."

Chapter 6

The cousins declined the Sedgewicks' invitation for drinks. Even though it wasn't yet eight o'clock, Judith was tired. She was also anxious to put the car in the garage for the night. The drive back to the house was short, but the fog had settled in, preventing visibility of anything much beyond the Subaru's hood.

"What a waste of time!" she exclaimed after they entered the house. "I realize I'm old enough to retire, but like you, I don't want to sit around all day staring at Joe. We're lucky our mates work part-time."

"You bet," Renie responded, flopping on the sofa after grabbing a Pepsi from the fridge. "Otherwise, we might kill each other."

"Don't say that," Judith said grimly. "For all we know, Edna whacked Ernie."

"Good plan," Renie murmured. "Get him out of the house—which maybe he didn't do very often this time of year. No mess to clean up afterward. Maybe you've already solved this one."

"That would be too easy," Judith said, forgoing the too-low-to-the-floor recliner for an overstuffed chair on the other side of a small table.

"Bill loves coming up here," Renie said. "At home, he takes long walks around the hill, but what he likes best is a beach. One time when we were up here, he was gone for over two hours. It was bliss. Too much of a good thing, as my dad always said, is *un*good. Unless it's honeycomb covered in dark chocolate. Don't they have a candy store in Langton?"

"I think so, but we're not supposed to go anywhere until the sheriff's department says so."

"That's too dumb. Who'd know?"

"Coz . . ." Judith gave Renie a hard stare.

Renie ignored the look. "We can go tomorrow. Hey, maybe for once the real detectives will find the killer. There's no dark chocolate in this house. I looked. That's how I found the taffy. Auntie Vance watches her weight, but she still tastes everything she cooks as she goes along."

Judith sighed. "Now I'm hungry for more of that pie," she said, getting up and going to the kitchen. "You want some?"

"Not yet," Renie replied. "I'll get a megasnack later."

"Which often turns into another meal," Judith pointed out, reaching for a plate above the counter. Her hand fell away. "Coz! Did you write something on Auntie Vance's magnet notepad on the cupboard?"

"No. Why would I?"

"Come look. I don't want to touch it."

"What the . . . ?" Renie got up and hurried to join Judith.

The hand-printed note in black ink said BUTT OUT OR ELSE!!!

"Damn!" Renie said under her breath. "So much for leaving the door unlocked. That's creepy."

Judith rubbed at her strong chin. "Yes, it is. We're locking up tonight. We've got to show this to Jacobson. I wonder if we should notify the sheriff's office now?"

"Why not?" Renie was already at the door, making sure it was now locked. "It might help eliminate us as suspects. If we really are, I mean."

"You're right. Hand me the phone book from the shelf by the door. I don't want to make a 911 call. That's overkill. So to speak."

There were several listings for the county sheriff's department. The headquarters was located in the largest town on the island, some thirty miles to the north. There were two other stations, the nearest being in Langton. Judith dialed the number, but a recording informed her the office was closed and to call the main number or try again between 8 A.M. and 5:30 P.M.

"I forget what life is like away from the big city," she grumbled, dialing the headquarters listing. "People in small towns and rural areas do live at a slower . . . Yes," she said, changing gears as a reedy-voiced woman answered. "Is Lieutenant Jacobson available?" He wasn't. Judith asked if he could be reached. She was informed he was off duty. Could someone else help? Judith started to say yes—and thought better of it. "No. I'll get in touch with him tomorrow." She rang off and began perusing the island directory for Jacobsons.

Renie looked puzzled. "He should've left his card. Isn't that what Joe used to do when he was on the force?"

"I'm not sure they did that back then," Judith said. "There are four Jacobsons, two with the initial *E*. Same family, maybe. Erik, right?"

"Yes," Renie agreed as the phone rang.

Judith grabbed the receiver. "Hello?" she all but shouted.

"Jacobson here," he responded in his now-familiar calm, authoritative tone. "You called?"

"I did, Lieutenant," she said to alert Renie. "How did you find out?"

"I'm off duty, but still on the case. Whoever answered the phone noticed it came from Obsession Shores. What were you calling about?"

Suddenly feeling foolish, Judith took a deep breath. "I don't mean to be an alarmist, but after we returned from a meeting at the clubhouse, we found a rather menacing note that someone left here."

Jacobson asked what the note said. Judith read it to him,

adding that it was printed. "Where was this note found?" the officer inquired.

"On a kitchen cupboard door," she replied.

"Did you leave the door unlocked?"

"Yes." Judith winced. "My aunt didn't leave us a key."

A brief silence seemed to echo over the line. "Our longtime residents have some bad habits," Jacobson finally said. "They're living in a time warp. The island has changed with the population growth. I'll stop by in about ten minutes." He rang off.

Judith looked at Renie. "Auntie Vance and Uncle Vince apparently think we're still in the twentieth century. According to Jacobson, The Rock really isn't paradise."

Renie shrugged. "I never thought it was. Most people who move to retirement communities insist it's heaven on earth. They don't want their judgment questioned. Remember when Bill took that seminar before he retired? The first thing is don't move, not even out of your house, let alone out of the area. Second is don't move anywhere that doesn't have nearby medical facilities. Third is—"

"I know, I know," Judith interrupted with a wave of her hand. "Do not buy an RV if you're half blind or scared to get your driver's license renewed. What we have to do now is figure out how to secure the house. No access to the main floor from the basement, but that still leaves the front door and the back door in the laundry room."

Renie was unwrapping more taffy. "It's a good thing Bill never wanted to buy an RV. They don't have room service and honor bars."

"You're spoiled," Judith declared. "Hillside Manor doesn't have those amenities either."

"That's why I've never stayed at your B&B," Renie said before popping a piece of taffy into her mouth.

"You've stayed overnight with me there."

"Ewahfwee."

"Yes, I know it was free." Judith scowled at the door. "Maybe we can put the overstuffed chair in front of the door for added security."

Renie swallowed the taffy. "Hey, if they really want to get in, they can break a window." She paused, suddenly looking alert. "I think I hear a car. It's sure quiet around here at night."

"It's quiet during the day. Except for finding corpses and going to meetings," Judith added, dropping her voice.

"You think the walls have ears?" Renie asked. "What does that mean? Really. Think about it."

"No, I won't," Judith retorted, moving to the door. "I should have left it unlocked. Then Jacobson could just walk in."

"Darn," Renie said. "He might give us police protection."

"You want to spend the night with a sheriff's deputy?"

Renie shrugged. "Why not? You've been sleeping with a cop for years. Jacobson's not that bad-looking."

After the first rap sounded, Judith opened the door. "Come in," she said, stepping aside. "You must think we're foolish."

"No," Jacobson replied, nodding at Renie, who had shoved some more taffy in her mouth. "Your relatives are, though. We've had three break-ins this past month on the other side of the bay at Scratchit Head. Where's the note?"

Judith pointed to the cupboard. "I didn't touch it," she assured him. "We haven't spent much time in the kitchen area since we got back from the clubhouse. You might want to check the counters for—"

Jacobson paused in the act of putting on a pair of latex gloves and glared at Judith. "You think I don't know my job, Mrs. Flynn?"

Embarrassed, Judith leaned against the counter. "Sorry. I guess I . . . watch . . . too . . . much TV." The last words were mumbled. She grabbed Renie by the arm. "Let's sit down."

Assuming their previous places, both cousins tried to keep from watching Jacobson. That was not a problem for Renie, who was eating more taffy, but Judith had to force herself to keep her eyes from darting into the kitchen area. A glance at her watch showed it was 8:25. Somehow it seemed as if it should be much later.

"Okay," Jacobson said as he put the note in his evidence kit. "I'd better take your prints now. I assume neither of you is on file anywhere?"

Renie almost choked on her taffy. Judith gaped at the deputy. "Well . . . actually, we may be," she finally replied. "You see, we were once involved in a homicide case. Well, more than once, but somewhere along the way we had to have our prints taken."

Jacobson had come out from behind the counter. "Which jurisdiction was that, Mrs. Flynn?"

"Offhand, I'm . . . not sure." She winced. "Do you remember, coz?"

Renie swallowed the taffy. "The family event at the B&B?"

"Which one?" Judith asked.

"The . . . first one, with Otto Brodie and his ghastly gang?"

Judith thought for a moment. "Maybe. Or was it the one up at church with the Easter Bunny?"

Renie shook her head. "I think it was more recent. Maybe when Herself found the dead guy under the tree in her yard."

"I don't think so. It had to be before that. What about the body at the apartment house down at the bottom of the hill?"

"The corpse behind the wall or the one on the bed?"

"Hold it," Jacobson ordered in less than his normal calm tone. Apparently, he felt the need to sit down in the recliner. "Maybe it'd be easier for me to check you through the system."

"Really, we don't mind," Judith insisted. She gave a start. "Wait," she said, looking at Renie. "Your fingerprints don't take, right?"

Her cousin nodded. "I lack grooves." She wiggled her thumbs as if to prove the point. *Or,* Judith thought, *the lack of* . . . But she decided it was best not to think about how really weird Renie could often be.

"Forget it," Jacobson said, with a hint of exasperation. "I ran you two through the system. You're married to a retired homicide detective, Mrs. Flynn. I assume that's how you became acquainted with murder cases. We law enforcement types try not to take our work home with us, but it happens. Sometimes we need to vent in a safe place."

"Yes, of course," Judith agreed. "I understand."

"As for you, Mrs. Jones," he continued, "your husband is a psychologist. While he probably wouldn't breach patient confidentiality, he might occasionally share certain symptoms he's treating."

"True," Renie conceded. "He never names names. Bill's very professional. It's always Mr. Goofball or Mrs. Nut Job or Ms. I-Can't-Believe-She's-Allowed-in-a-Public-Venue."

"Ah . . . right." Jacobson opened his notebook and turned back to Judith. "What time did you leave here?"

"About ten to seven," Judith said, though she hadn't really noticed. "It's a short drive to the clubhouse, as you know."

Jacobson nodded absently. "What time did you get back?"

The cousins exchanged glances. "Seven-thirtyish?" Judith replied.

The deputy made a note. "Did you leave the lights on?"

"Yes," Judith said. "The porch light and the ones that are on now."

"That," Jacobson said, "was a short meeting. Did you leave early?"

"No," Judith replied. "The meeting ended abruptly because it got . . . sort of out of control."

He leaned forward, hands on his knees. "Can you explain why?"

Judith took a deep breath. "It was supposed to be a vote on whether a sewer system should replace the current septic tanks. Before they could do that, there were some people who felt they didn't have enough information to cast an intelligent vote."

"Or," Renie put in, "they didn't have enough intelligence, period. All hell broke loose."

Jacobson sat up straight again. "In what way?"

"Arguing and shouting," Judith replied. "I think one woman may've fainted. Then the chairperson—Hank Hilderschmidt—adjourned the meeting. Sort of, that is. He tossed his gavel and walked out. Everybody headed for the exits."

"I see." The deputy frowned. "Then it had nothing to do with Ernest Glover's death. I thought they might have canceled the meeting, given the circumstances."

Judith realized that Jacobson found the Obsession Shores residents' behavior odd. "Hank did ask for a moment of silence in Mr. Glover's memory."

"In a half-assed way," Renie said. "I'm using our aunt's terminology here. A less obscene version thereof, by the way."

Jacobson evinced mild interest in the comment. "Are you insinuating that Mr. Hilderschmidt didn't like Mr. Glover—or that the deceased wasn't well liked in general?"

Renie glanced at Judith. "You answer that one, coz," she said. "You're a better people person than I am."

Judith frowned. "It's hard to say. We were near the back. Renie and I don't know these people, except for the Sedgewicks and the Friedmans. A few others have been pointed out to us over the years, including Mr. Glover. But that's it."

The deputy again nodded before looking at the few notes he'd jotted down. "Can you be more precise about when you returned here?"

Judith turned to Renie. "Maybe a little before seven thirty? We were sort of in the middle of the pack going out the main door. Some of the others went out the rear exit where Hank Hilderschmidt had gone. Oh! I see what you mean. It's unlikely that anyone attending the meeting could also have come here to leave the note."

"No," Jacobson said. "It's quite possible. There was enough time for someone who was at the meeting to have gotten here before you did. In fact, whoever left that note might still have been inside the house when you arrived and went out the other door at the end of the house."

On that chilling note, Judith changed the subject. "Did you ever find the weapon?"

He shook his head. "It may have been thrown into the water or buried in the sand some distance away."

Judith decided to press her luck. "Have you been able to figure out what kind of weapon was used? That is, from the entry of the stab wounds."

"Something sharp," Jacobson replied, looking grim. "Pointed and tapering to a width of at least five inches."

Before Judith could say anything else, he stood up and announced he was taking his leave. But first he produced two padlocks with keys. "It's not safe for you to be unable to secure the house. Given our preliminary investigation, you're free to leave Obsession Shores tomorrow. I don't need to remind you there's a murderer on the loose. Of course," he went on, moving to the door, "I have the impression you're both aware of the danger this sort of situation can present."

Judith and Renie nodded. There really was nothing more to say. When it came to murder, "been there and done that" was too glib. The cousins realized they'd been very lucky over the years. But luck had a way of running in streaks. Eventually it always ran out.

Chapter 7

Well," Renie said after Jacobson was gone, "when do you start grilling suspects? It's too foggy to go door-to-door."

"I told you, I won't do anything until tomorrow." Judith started for the hall, suitcase in hand. "The first person I want to call on is the grief-stricken widow. I refuse to do that tonight. Her family is probably with her." She looked up and down the short hall. "Do you want to sleep in the master bedroom or the spare room?"

"Auntie Vance and Uncle Vince have a king-size bed," Renie said. "Why bother making two beds?"

"Because you chew gum in bed," Judith replied. "You almost drove me nuts when we had to share a room in Little Bavaria last October."

"So why didn't you bring earplugs?"

"Damn," Judith said under her breath. "I should've thought of that. Did you bring gum?"

"Of course. I can't get to sleep without it."

"Then you take the spare room."

Renie shrugged. "Hey, do the Sedgewicks play bridge or pinochle?"

"I don't know. I think the Webers play poker with them and the Friedmans. You want to call to see if they're bored?"

"Oh, they're bored," Renie responded. "Murder notwithstanding, I'm kind of bored, too. Really—what do people do up here in the evenings, especially this time of year?"

"They watch TV, like normal people. Even Joe and I do that. You watch TV with Bill."

"I watch what Bill watches," Renie said. "If I don't like it, I read or do a crossword or jigsaw puzzle. Besides, it's hard to focus on any TV program with Mom calling me three times every night. I also missed the part in the wedding vows about a man promising to have and to hold not only his wife, but the TV remote."

Judith smiled, but a knocking sound startled both cousins.

"I'll get it," Renie muttered before going to the door. "Are you armed and homicidal?" she shouted.

A muffled female voice seemed to say no. Renie cautiously opened the door as Judith came across the room to join her. The young woman with red curls peeking out from under her brown hood looked upset.

"Where's Vance?" she asked in an uncertain voice.

"Out of town," Renie replied. "You are . . . ?"

"Katie Blomquist, Ernie and Edna Glover's daughter."

Renie opened the door all the way. "Come in. Sorry about the query, but you must know we're all a bit on edge."

Judith offered her hand as Katie came inside. "We're the Webers' nieces. I'm Judith and this is Renie. We're house-sitting. I'm very sorry about your father. Do sit down."

"I can't stay," Katie said, red-rimmed green eyes darting this way and that. "I wanted to borrow a heating pad. Mom told us Vance and Vince had an extra one. Hers broke and she needs it for her arthritis. It's . . . well, it's going to be hard for her to sleep tonight as it is." Katie sniffed once as if to underscore the comment.

"I'll look for it," Renie volunteered, heading for the master bedroom.

"Do sit," Judith urged, pulling out a kitchen chair. "We didn't really know your dad. But what happened to him was a terrible thing."

Hesitating, Katie sat. "I can't take it in. Who would do such a thing?" She shook her head, causing the hood to slip down to her shoulder-length curls. "We heard two strange women . . ." She stopped. "Was it you and your sister?"

"We're cousins," Judith said with a kindly smile. "Our dads were Vance's older brothers."

"Oh." Katie sniffed again. "I didn't mean *you* seemed strange. I meant . . ." She fumbled in her pocket and pulled out a Kleenex to blow her nose. "You know what I mean. That must've been awful for you. It makes me shudder just to think about it."

"Do you live nearby?" Judith inquired. No comment about finding the corpse was necessary. In fact, it felt redundant.

Katie shook her head. "No, we live just north of the city. My husband, Greg, teaches at the local high school. That's where I met him. I mean, I taught there, too. Now that we have kids, I do some tutoring." Her freckled hands clenched into fists. "Why? Why would anyone stab Dad? He was the nicest man in the world. It must be some crazy person. Maybe an escapee from an institution or someone on drugs."

"That's possible," Judith allowed as Renie finally came into the room with the heating pad. "How is your mother holding up?"

Katie sighed. "She's a fairly strong person. If it had been a heart attack or something like that, it'd be bad enough. But murder?" She shook her head and couldn't seem to go on.

"Do you have siblings?" Judith asked to change the subject.

"Yes, a brother. Dave lives in Denver. He's flying in tomorrow." Katie rubbed at her forehead. "I'm sorry, I've been trying to be brave for Mom. Greg's a big help. He actually likes his in-laws. His own parents died young, before we met."

Renie had sat down next to Judith. "Are your kids here?"

"Yes. The boys are four and two, but they loved Grandpa. Greg and I figured they'd be a comfort to Mom. I don't think they understand what's happened."

"Probably not," Judith agreed. "Having young children around helps. It demonstrates the cycle of life. And death," she added more quietly. "Your father must've had a lot of friends in this community."

"He did," Katie declared. "Dad got to know so many people here, especially after he retired. We're not sure if we should have the funeral on the island or in the city. He had lots of friends there on the Bluff."

Judith knew the neighborhood well, since it was adjacent to Heraldsgate Hill. "That's a nice area," she remarked.

Katie nodded in a distracted manner. "They had a nice house there—nothing fancy like some of the mansions."

"Yes," Judith said, not daring to look at Renie. Several years had passed since the cousins had helped host a party at one of those mansions. A relative by marriage spoiled the festivities by getting shot to death. "That neighborhood really grew after World War Two," she continued. "Wonderful views of the Sound."

Katie struggled to get to her feet. "I must go. Thanks for the heating pad. I hope the pills the doctor prescribed will help Mom sleep."

"Who *is* the doctor around here?" Judith asked as she and Renie walked their visitor to the door. "Our aunt and uncle have remained patients of their longtime GP in the city."

"His name is Dr. Payne," Katie said, wincing. "With a *y*. He's retired, too. Thanks for the heating pad. Good night."

Renie sighed. "Let's lock up. I'm not in the mood for more company. Our guests tend to be on the grim side."

Judith retrieved her suitcase in the hall. "I'll make sure the back door's locked. If I'm not back in sixty seconds, call the sheriff."

Flipping the switch to turn on a couple of lights on the pine-paneled walls, Judith gazed around the spacious bedroom with its adjacent half bath. In all the years they'd visited the Webers, she'd never spent the night. As a kid, Mike, as well as the three Jones offspring, had stayed with Auntie Vance and Uncle Vince for a few days every summer. None of them had minded their great-aunt's rough tongue, even when she disciplined them. They instinctively knew how much she loved entertaining children. Vince was a sport, too, at least when he managed to stay awake.

To Judith's relief, she saw no sign of an intruder in the bedroom. That was a comfort. Until she realized that there had been nothing to suggest an intruder in the kitchen—except for the warning note.

"Coz," she said, coming out of the hall via the door that led into the living area, "did you see any footprints in the kitchen when we got back from the meeting?"

Renie, who had moved to the sofa, set aside the *Sunset* magazine she'd been reading. "No," she replied, staring at the wall-to-wall carpeting. "This is all that indoor-outdoor stuff. Auntie Vance got it because everybody spends so much time on the beach. It's designed to not show scuffs or prints."

Judith sat down in the overstuffed chair. "You're right. The whole house is covered in it. Auntie Vance got a deal through somebody Uncle Al knew. You know about Uncle Al and all his deals."

"A master of the art," Renie murmured, referring to their well-connected sportsman uncle. "Did you really expect Jacobson to check for hair and fibers?"

"No," Judith admitted. "I'm so used to people coming in the back door at home who track stuff into the back hall and kitchen. At least the carpet in the entry hall covers most of the floor for the guests." She grew silent for a moment. "I wonder how many people have an airtight alibi for the time of the murder."

Renie's expression was droll. "House-to-house canvassing tomorrow?"

"Of course not. But this is Friday. I'll bet a lot of people grocery-shop and run errands before the weekend. For one thing, they can get the specials, which I imagine most of the older folks watch for. Have you seen their weekly newspaper anywhere?"

"Oh, jeez," Renie groaned, "how do ads for pork chops and pickled pig's feet help figure out who murdered Ernie?"

"They don't," Judith asserted. "But the local paper would list a calendar of events. I'm trying to get a feel for this place."

"You're not writing a novel, you need to work on not getting us killed. Give it a rest until tomorrow." She made one of her usual futile efforts to snap her fingers. "I know! Let's watch TV!"

"Fine." Judith reached into the magazine rack next to the chair. "I'll see what's on. Oh—here's the *Whoopee Weekly Word*."

"Great," Renie remarked in a bored voice. "Read me the funnies."

"They don't have funnies," Judith said, scanning the front page. "Lots of planning news on other parts of the island. Storm-watch report . . . argument over beach rights . . . obit for ninety-six-year-old Ignatz—"

"Stop!" Renie yelled. "Just get to the calendar, for heaven's sake!"

Judith flipped through the pages. "Here it is. Nothing for Obsession Shores." She checked the publication date. "The paper comes out Wednesdays. The locals may not have had time to get the special meeting in before the deadline. It's not stop-the-presses kind of news."

Renie yawned. "It sure isn't. Can we watch TV now?"

"Go ahead, turn . . . wait. Here's an article about Brose Bennett finding what he claims is an English gold coin dated 1798. It was washed up on the beach earlier this month."

"Could be. Captain Vancouver plied these waters at the end of the eighteenth century. The coin wouldn't be hard to authenticate, though I doubt it's worth much."

Judith summed up the six-inch article. "He found it after a high tide last weekend. It's a guinea with George the Third on it.

Here," she said, tossing the newspaper to Renie. "There's a picture of the coin and one of Brose."

Renie skimmed the article. "Brose looks full of himself. Did you spot him and Fou-fou at the meeting?"

"I couldn't see who was up front," Judith said, finding a copy of *TV Guide* in the magazine rack. "Drat. Not much on tonight. *Bloopers, Trading Spouses, Killer Instinct—*"

"Stop!" Renie cried. "No college basketball on Friday nights either. This is when Bill and I get out a DVD to watch *Brideshead Revisited* for the umpteenth time."

"Oh?" Judith barely heard what her cousin had said. "I wonder if other rare coins have been found around here."

Renie sighed. "You're going all numismatic on me? Forget it. Not in January weather."

"No," Judith responded with a glare. "I'm talking about motive."

Renie shook her head. "We'd have heard about that hobby. Serious treasure seekers use a metal detector. I gather that's not mentioned in the article. In fact, Uncle Vince might stay awake for more than fifteen minutes at a time because he's interested in history. You know how he tells stories about being in the army during World War Two."

Judith smiled. "I always liked the one where the ship he was on for the D-Day invasion got lost in the fog. They ended up landing back in England and scaring the wits out of an entire English village."

"I always wondered if he was navigating," Renie said, laughing. "He might've dozed off."

"That was before he became a milkman," Judith remarked. "Turn on the TV. Maybe you can find an old movie we haven't seen lately."

Renie picked up the remote and stared at it. "How do you use these things? I don't think they've got cable up here. Don't they all have a dish? Or maybe one great big one?"

Before Judith could answer, yet another knock sounded outside. "Now what?" she murmured. "I thought retired people went to bed early."

"I'll get it," Renie said, tossing the remote in Judith's lap. She leaned against the door and called out, "Password, please!"

"Hell, Vance," a male voice shouted, "stop clowning around! It's cold out here."

"That's not it," Renie yelled back.

Judith stood up, reaching around the chair to peek through the blinds that covered the window. "I can't see who it is from here."

"Fine," Renie said, heading back to the sofa.

Whoever it was didn't give up easily. Their visitor pounded even harder on the door, now shouting both Vance and Vince's names. "This isn't funny! There's a killer out here!"

Judith turned to stare at Renie. "Do you think he means literally?"

Renie shed her shoes and put her feet up on the sofa. "If a killer's out there, he's not in here. Ignore the knock."

"Oh, for . . ." Judith started for the door. "It sounds like Hank Hilderschmidt. If he acts menacing, hit him with the remote. Hold on!" A muffled grumble responded. She finally got the door open. "Hi. The Webers are out of town. I'm Judith, their niece. Come in, Hank."

Hank gave a start. "You know me?"

"My cousin," she said, nodding at the sofa, "and I were at the meeting tonight. You probably didn't see us. We were at the back."

"Oh." Hank stamped his feet on the floor. "That's one thick fog out there. Third night in a row." He looked at Renie, who hadn't budged and was staring straight ahead. "Is she okay?"

"Uh . . . yes, she's fine. Did you want something? I mean, can I help you? I don't think we've met."

"Awww . . ." Hank paused, scratching at one of his long sideburns. "No, I guess not. I just wanted to talk to Vance and Vince about the cops coming around to question all of us after Ernie . . . you know. Bought the big one."

"Have a seat," Judith said, indicating a kitchen chair. She didn't dare suggest the living area. Renie seemed to be in one of her socially zoned-out moods. "You're good friends of the Webers?" she asked, sitting down at the end of the table.

"Good enough to ask if they have a drink," Hank said. "My wife didn't make it to the liquor store today."

"Oh. That's too bad." Judith was about to let the comment pass, but caught the pitiful look in Hank's dark eyes. "Would you like a short shot of Scotch?"

"Yeah, that'd hit the spot. Nasty night out there."

Judith got up to fetch the liquor. She decided she might as well join Hank. "I didn't realize the police had interrogated everyone."

"Oh, they sure did. You'd think I'd done in poor ol' Ernie. Hell, nobody around here would do a thing like that. Must've been a nut case walking the beach. It happens."

"What happens?" Judith asked, putting ice into the glasses with their inch of liquor.

"Nuts. Not so much this time of year, but in the summer. Yeah, right, it's a public beach, but still . . . they make trouble and leave a mess. That's not right. Wish we had a retired cop living here. He'd know how to handle 'em."

"Were you and Ernie good friends?" Judith inquired after she'd set down the drinks and resumed her place at the table.

"Oh—we got along fine, but Ern was still settling in after he retired. I keep working. Took my pension with the state ferry folks two years ago, after thirty years in the boiler room, but I do part-time stuff helping out at the dock on weekends and holidays. Just did a turn for the Martin Luther King three-day deal. Here's to ol' Ern." He lifted his glass.

Judith joined him in the toast. "Did you work today? Being a weekend, I mean."

Hank shook his head. "Nope. Not so busy this time of year.

Probably won't do much now until the weather gets better. Easter comes along in April. Might be nice by then."

Judith noticed that Hank had downed almost half of his drink in the first gulp. "Why did you get to chair the meeting?"

"Hard to get everybody to agree on much of anything around here," Hank replied. "Too damned many fractions."

Judith assumed he meant *factions*. "Is that because some younger people have moved here in recent years?"

Hank dug a finger into his left ear. "Well . . . in a way. Those folks got what you call more liberal ideas. That makes 'em kind of fractious."

Judith figured Hank was right the first time. "Such as?" she asked.

Hank almost polished off the Scotch in another big gulp. "You know, who can buy in. Not that there's a rule about color or stuff like that, but we've kept to our own kind. If you know what I mean." He winked.

"That's it!" Renie yipped, vaulting off the sofa and hurtling toward the kitchen table. "Say it, Hilderschmidt. What *is* your own kind other than stupid?"

"Hey!" Hank's long face darkened. "What's with you? We got lots of different people. Jews, Catholics, even a damned atheist."

"They're all white," Renie snapped. "Has anybody sued you dolts?"

Hank finished his drink and stood up. "How would I know? Ask that old goat Quimby. He's the one who really runs the show. I just live here." He stumbled a bit over his own feet before heading out the door.

Renie hurried to set the lock. "Why have we never gotten a whiff of what really goes on up here?" she demanded.

"Vance and Vince may ignore it. Or else they're embarrassed."

"I vote for Door Number Two," Renie said, having secured the house for the night. "Face it—they're like most people. They don't want to let on that this place isn't ideal."

Judith had gotten to her feet. "I've never asked what goes on here, besides clam digging and putting out crab pots and deer eating rosebushes. That's the trouble—we all take things for granted."

"True," Renie muttered, heading for the sofa and grabbing the remote. "Let's watch something mindless and forget about all this mess. I'm beat." *Click, click, click. . .*

The cousins settled in to watch *Mississippi Burning*. Somehow it diverted Judith from thinking about Ernie Glover's murder. The movie was set in the past. A killer lurked in the present.

Chapter 8

To Judith's surprise, she slept like a brick that night. Renie had spared her the gum chewing by going to bed in the spare room. It was almost nine by the time Judith had showered, dressed, and gone into the kitchen. Glancing outside, she noted overcast gray skies but no rain. Assuming Renie would sleep until at least ten, she made a breakfast of bacon, toast, and coffee. Renie could fend for herself.

Shortly after ten thirty, Jane Sedgewick called. "You survived the night," she said, sounding faintly relieved.

"Yes," Judith replied. She didn't want to mention the second visit from Jacobson—or the threatening note—but acknowledged Hank's visit.

"What," Jane inquired archly, "did that jackass want?"

"A drink," Judith said. "He thought the Webers were home."

"His wife probably drank all their booze. She wasn't at the meeting last night. Vance thinks Hilda's pass-out time is early evening, then she gets up at five in the morning to go on the prowl. Your aunt takes more of an interest in people than I do. It's her nature. I spent my career as an executive secretary dealing with personnel issues. I vowed not to get mixed up in other people's problems when I retired."

"Do you know what's the point of Hilda's prowling?" Judith asked.

Jane sighed. "No. She walks the beach for hours even if the weather's on the crummy side. When she goes home, she probably starts drinking. Their son used to visit every few months, but I haven't seen him in ages. Hilda's weird, very unfriendly. Maybe she collects shells or bottle caps. I keep my distance."

Judith refrained from further comment and changed the subject. "I intend to call on Mrs. Glover today. Do you think that'd be okay? Her daughter stopped in last night to borrow a heating pad."

"Why not go see her?" Jane said without hesitation. "Vance and Vince would do that, so they'd appreciate you filling in for them." She laughed, a throaty sound. "In fact, Vance is going to be madder than a wet cat when she finds out she's missed the biggest excitement around here in ages."

"Uh . . . I suppose she'd want a piece of the action," Judith admitted. "Auntie Vance has never been one to avoid risks."

"Curiosity seems to run in your family. Say, would you and Renie like to come for dinner tonight? I've got some T-bones in the freezer."

"That's kind of you to offer, but Auntie Vance left—"

"Vance left, period," Jane interrupted. "Sure, you've got enough beef noodle bake to feed half of Obsession Shores, but Dick and I are bored. Come around five thirty and have cocktails first. No arguments."

To make her point, Jane hung up.

"Who," a tousled Renie demanded from the hallway, "was that calling in the middle of the night?"

"Jane," Judith replied. "And did you have to wear those scary tiger stripes? It's a wonder you don't have nightmares about getting stalked in the jungle."

"This is my travel set," Renie snarled, plucking at the marabou-trimmed sleeves of her peignoir. "I dreamed I was on safari. The one we never went on because I got married instead. What was I thinking?" She shook her head and went into the bathroom.

Judith decided to unlock the door and step outside. The gloomy skies weren't as threatening as her cousin in the morning, especially in those orange and black tiger stripes.

The air smelled damp, but not particularly cold. Judith checked the thermometer next to the big front window. It registered forty-nine. No chance of snow, which was a relief. Maybe they could drive into Langton and browse the shops.

"Hey!" a booming voice called out from somewhere below.

Judith scanned the road just below the house. A very tall, very broad man was striding in her direction. "Where's Vance?" he shouted, his butterscotch-colored hair ruffled by the morning breeze.

"Nebraska," Judith called back. "Who are you?"

"Zach Bendarek," he replied, taking the stairs two at a time. "You the cleaning woman?"

Judith managed to stifle a sharp retort, awed if not intimidated by Zach, who was at least half a foot taller than her five-foot-nine. "I'm Judith Flynn, Mrs. Weber's niece. My cousin and I are house-sitting."

"I'll be damned." He held out a hand. "Sorry 'bout that. Been out of town for a few days. I scout."

Judith winced as he crushed her fingers in his huge paw. "Scout?"

"Right. High school athletes, even some junior high kids. Played the game twenty-odd years ago. Kind of an odd time for me, now that I think about it. Got the coffeepot on?"

"Yes, come in."

He went first, which was a relief to Judith. She was afraid he might mow her down if she led the way. But Zach stopped in his tracks just inside the door. Judith almost ran into him.

"What the hell is *that*?" he asked as Renie whipped out of the bathroom and back down the hall in a flurry of tiger stripes.

"The other niece," Judith murmured, trying not to rub her sore hand. "She's a late riser."

"She's a . . . sight. I played for the Bengals. Not often and not long, but what the hell." He pulled out a chair and flopped himself into it with a big sigh that almost masked the sound of creaking wood. "You like football?" He held up one of his paws. "Never mind. I didn't come to talk about that. I hear Ernie Glover got whacked. Helluva thing. You know anything about what happened? Just asking."

Judith was pouring coffee. "My cousin and I found his body."

"Wow! That must've fried your fritters. I heard he was shot six times by a jealous husband. Doesn't sound like Ernie, but you never know about people. Damned unpredictable. I take it black."

"What? Oh—the coffee. Sure." Judith set the mug on the table. "He was stabbed," she continued, carrying her own coffee refill and sitting down. "You must have quite a rumor mill up here."

Zach nodded absently. "Right. Kind of a hobby, along with drinking. Stabbed, huh?" He didn't wait for confirmation. "Glad he wasn't shot. Too much gun violence these days. Oh, it's fine on the football field, but otherwise . . . not so good. Not that anybody uses a gun when they play football." He scowled. "Can't think of a penalty for doing that, though. Illegal carrying, maybe? But you know what I mean."

Judith wasn't sure she did. Zach was probably midforties, making him one of the younger Obsession Shores residents. Thinking back to the aborted meeting, she'd calculated that the average age of the attendees was around sixty, maybe more, not counting children.

"Do you live here full-time?" she asked.

"Yeah, but I'm on the road quite a bit. I scout both football and basketball. Flew in from L.A. on the red-eye this morning. Becca'd locked me out." He guffawed. "Thought the killer might be after her. I had to break down the damned door."

Judith's expression was questioning. "Becca is . . . ?"

"My better half," Zach replied. "She got really mad. It's tough to get workmen here on the weekend. I'm kind of afraid to go back home. That's why I thought I'd walk over to see what was up with the murder. Vance always knows what's going on."

"Did you know Ernie very well?"

"Yeah, fairly well. That's why his playing around surprised me. You say it's not true? How do you know? You make a pass at him and got turned down? That's too bad. You're a nice-looking lady."

"I never met Ernie," Judith said rather stiltedly.

"You saw him yesterday. Oh, sure, he was dead and harmless, but still . . ." Zach shrugged his broad shoulders.

Renie appeared dressed and looking almost like a human being. "Hi, Moose," she said, brushing past him and going to the coffeemaker.

Zach looked stunned. "She knows me? That was my nickname as a player. Is that why she looked like a mess of Bengal stripes?"

"I'm not deaf," Renie shouted from the kitchen. "I saw you play in college and then—briefly—with the Bengals, Rams, and Redskins."

"Wow. I'm flattered." Zach looked almost as if he were blushing.

"That's my cousin Renie," Judith said. "She and her husband follow sports more closely than I do."

"I guess," Zach said, still looking faintly flabbergasted. "Thanks, Weenie. You made my day." He stood up. "Guess I'd better go home and see if I can do anything about that damned door. Thanks for the java."

Judith got to her feet to show Zach out. "I don't suppose you've heard anybody say why they think someone would kill Ernie? I mean, other than wild rumors."

Zach grimaced. "You mean about Ernie playing around? I don't know if they are that crazy. I've heard some stuff about him and . . ." He stopped and shook his head. "Hell, I'm not talking trash about a dead man. You know how it is in football—a guy goes down and the other players all back off. Afraid an injury is catching. See you around." Shaking his head, he stalked out of the house.

Judith closed the door and leaned against it. "I don't know what to make of him. Is he one of those concussion victims?"

"Probably," Renie said, sitting down at the table with a mug of coffee. "He was a defensive lineman. They get cracked now and then. Where's the newspaper?"

"Oh—I forgot to look. I didn't check for it on the porch."

Renie gave her cousin a disdainful stare. "This isn't the city. They put it in the paper box by the mailboxes. I'll get it later." She glanced out the window. "No fog, just clouds. I see some people on the beach."

"Uncle Vince has binoculars somewhere around here," Judith said absently. "Zach seems to have an alibi," she continued after a pause. "He was on an airplane coming from L.A."

Renie had moved away from the window. "Do you believe him?"

"At this point, I'm not sure I believe he's Zach Bendarek. Or Moose, for that matter."

"That was his nickname at the University," Renie said. "I don't think reserve linemen get nicknames in the pros."

"He scouts."

"So I overheard. If he covers two sports for colleges and universities, I assume he gets paid fairly well, though not like a pro scout would. In fact, I wonder if it's under the table via the sports-loving alums. I've never asked Bill about it. Or Uncle Al, for that matter."

"Are you going to eat? We have to go see Edna Glover."

Renie shrugged. "You can't go without me?"

"I'd just as soon have backup."

"Okay, I'll get some cereal. I'm not in the mood to have a big breakfast. I got up too early."

Twenty minutes later, the cousins were trudging down the

hill and turning left. The Glovers' stained cedar-shake house was where they'd seen the ambulance parked the previous day. As Judith climbed the five wooden steps, she noticed a wreath on the front door.

"Is that a mourning wreath?" she asked in a quiet voice.

"I don't usually do mornings," Renie responded. "I don't think you do either. It's a St. Valentine's wreath. I see red hearts, white cupids, and a small mailbox, presumably for love notes. Cute, in a pedestrian sort of way. Probably handmade. I'd have used a different approach if I'd designed this thing."

"Maybe now it's for condolence notes," Judith said somberly. She rang the bell, which chimed what sounded like the first few notes of the old song "Ebb Tide."

Katie, encumbered by a small boy hanging on to her left leg, opened the door. "Oh! Mrs. . . . I forget!"

Judith gently reminded her of her and Renie's first names. "If you've met our aunt and uncle," she said as they entered the house, "you know we don't come from a very formal family."

Katie disengaged the toddler. "I met your aunt once," she said, leading them into an overly furnished living room. The older boy was playing with a brightly colored contraption that had several flashing lights and emitted peculiar whooping noises. "That's Josh, the younger one's Brad," Katie shouted, indicating the cousins should sit on the sofa.

Judith and Renie both hesitated, noting the cushions were almost completely covered with throw pillows, many of which seemed to have been decorated by hand.

"Mom's getting dressed," Katie went on while the cousins tried to arrange themselves into somewhat precarious positions. "Even with the pills, she had trouble sleeping. But she finally settled down around three o'clock and she slept in until almost nine thirty. My parents have always been early risers. Dad usually took a beach walk every morning and afternoon." Her face crumpled slightly. "Coffee?"

"No, thanks," Judith said, still trying to get reasonably comfortable. "We've had plenty of coffee at home," she added, noting that Brad was trying to commandeer some part of the multifaceted toy from his brother. Josh pushed him away. Brad started to cry and rushed to his mother, who had sat down in a rocking chair.

"Boys," Katie said in a plaintive voice. "Please share. And take your Wobble-Dobblemobile into the bedroom."

"No!" Josh shouted.

"No!" Brad squealed.

"Hey," Renie said, getting off the sofa and dislodging a couple of pillows that tumbled to the floor. "That's good. You guys can agree on something. Let's haul this thing somewhere so I can see how it works. Where should we go? I'm lost."

To Judith's surprise—and Katie's obvious relief—Josh hefted the toy and led the way out of the room and into the kitchen.

"My cousin raised two boys—and a girl," Judith explained. "I only have one son."

"Dad bought them the Wobble-Dobble," Katie said. "They love it. Oh—here's Mom."

Edna Glover didn't fit the preconceived matronly image of Ernie's wife that Judith had in mind. She was a slim, fairly tall woman with fine features and a graying dark pageboy haircut. Her widow's weeds consisted of blue jeans, a white cable-knit sweater worn over what looked like a tailored shirt, and black suede boots with a dash of fringe. The fine facial lines indicated she could be sixty or so, but except for a slight limp, she could have passed for ten years younger.

"Hello," she said, putting out her hand. "I overheard some of what you two were saying. You're the Webers' niece?"

"Yes." Judith noticed that the joints in Edna's hands were slightly swollen, no doubt from arthritis. "We—my cousin Renie is with your grandsons—wanted to convey our sympathy in your loss. I know Auntie Vance and Uncle Vince will be very upset about Mr. Glover's death."

Edna sat down in a straight-backed chair by the small fireplace. "It's a horrible shock. There's nothing I can say that conveys my reaction. I'm utterly stupefied. It's as if there's no rational explanation."

"It's all this violence, Mom," Katie said. "We live in a dangerous world. And too many people have untreated mental disorders. You know this has to be a random act."

Edna's dark eyes sparked at her daughter. "Is that supposed to make me feel better? You can't dismiss death."

"I know, but . . ." Katie looked away.

"There are tragedies that seem inexplicable," Edna went on, "but that hardly lessens their impact." Her gaze shifted to Judith. "You're in my peer group. Do you agree?"

"Of course," Judith replied. "But are you implying a crazed stranger killed your husband?"

"Does it matter?" Edna rubbed her hands, massaging her knuckles. "I forgot. You and the other niece found Ernie. What was your first thought?"

Judith was taken aback. She could hardly tell the truth and say, *Oh, damn! Not another stiff!*

"We thought he'd had a heart attack," Judith said. "He was facedown, so we had no idea he'd been stabbed. We only found out later."

Edna's face was very earnest. "Then what did you think?"

Judith didn't dare give voice to what flashed through her mind: *Damn, this time I'd better not screw up on fingering the perp.* "I wondered who'd done it," she replied solemnly.

Edna frowned. "You did? That's odd."

Katie finally found her voice. "No, Mom. I think that's a natural reaction. Even if it's some head case or druggie, it still matters."

"Of course it matters," Edna said. "But only in legal and moral terms. The one thing we can be sure of is that it was a stranger. Everybody liked my husband, despite any common gossip you might hear to the contrary. People distort the smallest disagreements, especially over such things as a sewer-plan proposal. Ernie's integrity was absolute. It had to be, given his many years as a state auditor. He was well respected by his peers."

Judith didn't want to argue. "That must be a comfort," she murmured, getting up from the cluttered sofa. "By the way, do you do crafts? You have so many lovely pillows."

Edna also got to her feet. "I used to do many things I can't do now with my arthritis. Embroidery, crochet, knitting, decoupage." She shrugged. "It's very frustrating. Time literally lies heavy on my hands."

"I'm sorry," Judith said, beginning to feel redundant. "I must let my cousin know . . ." She stopped as Renie came into the living room. "Here she is now."

Katie rose from the rocker. "Where are the boys? They're so quiet."

"Valium," Renie said. "Works every time. They'll come to in a few hours. Bye." She headed for the door, seemingly oblivious to Katie's shriek and Edna's aghast expression.

"I guess I'd better go," Judith said, hurrying after her cousin while calling out farewells to the Glover women. She caught up with Renie on the road. "You're horrid! Did you really give them Valium?"

"Hardly. I had them play Log, like Bill did with our kids on long car trips. It worked, at least for some sixty miles of peace and—"

"Stop!" Judith poked Renie. "What did you really do to those boys?"

"I just told you. They did what our kids did when they played Log—they went to sleep. I couldn't stand the racket that awful Wobble thing made. Just to make sure, I took out the batteries." She winced. "Damn. They're still in my pocket. Oh, well."

Judith shook her head. "Did you listen in on our conversation?" she asked as they headed back up the hill.

"Yes, Edna's a piece of work. She still embroiders. One of those pillows was dated Christmas of this last year. She's higher than a kite, too, in my opinion. I haven't seen so many antidepressants since I got a little too rambunctious at our HMO's pharmacy and vaulted over the counter to get my allergy pills."

"Really?" Judith felt stupid for not suspecting Edna might be taking more than a sleeping pill or two. "They were in the kitchen?"

Renie nodded. "I wanted to check the bathroom, but I was afraid I'd get caught. I'll bet Edna's cranked up most of the time. I doubt they ever have company. There's no room for guests."

"I agree," Judith said. "Katie talked about how many friends her dad had made in the last year or so. She didn't mention her mother."

"True," Renie agreed, stopping by the Webers' mailbox next to the road. "I'll grab the paper, you get the mail."

"Mostly junk," Judith murmured, flipping through the small stack. "No delivery yet today. The flag's still up. Or do I mean down?"

"No idea," Renie said, starting up to the deck. "Too rural for me. I haven't seen a postal van yet, though. Do you want to drive into Langton and have lunch?"

"Lunch?" Judith checked her watch. "It's not yet eleven."

"We could shop and then eat," Renie said. "I'm getting hungry."

"Oh . . . why not? It's always kind of fun to browse the shops."

The cousins reached the front door. Judith paused to look out across the Sound. "It'd be nice if the clouds would lift enough so we could see the mountains over on the Peninsula."

"I think they're still there," Renie said. "You do have the padlock keys, right?"

"Yes." Judith dug them out of her pocket. "Having this thing outside must make us look like a couple of alarmists."

"Well? Unless a random nut really did get loose, there *is* a murderer somewhere in the vicinity. I realize that's not a new concept for us, but it doesn't hurt to be cautious."

"I know," Judith said as they went inside. "I just hate to advertise the fact." She set the mail down on the kitchen counter. "Circulars, real estate come-ons, travel brochures, a senior-citizen flyer, AARP insurance offers, the Public Utility District bill—I'd better save that one." She set the envelope aside. "More senior activities. That's it."

"Shall we head on out?" Renie asked.

Judith hesitated. "Let's wait until it's closer to noon. You'll want to eat as soon as we get there and I'm not hungry."

Renie made a face. "Okay. I'll read the newspaper. I'm glad the Webers still get a real paper from a real city."

"They like keeping up with the city's news," Judith said, gazing out the front window. "It's clearing off. I can see almost across the Sound. Several people are on the beach and two—no—three more are walking along the roads. I guess these folks go outside when the weather's decent. Maybe I'll take a little stroll to work off my breakfast."

Before Renie could respond, a phone rang. "Is that my cell or yours?" Judith asked.

"Not my ring," Renie replied, her eyes glued to the *Times'* front page. Judith went to the kitchen counter and reached into her purse to dig out her cell.

"It's three in the morning and I can't sleep," Joe announced. "The seventeen-hour time change has thrown Bill and me for a loop. Are you really hang gliding over Mount Woodchuck? That's what your gruesome mother told me. Where are you?"

"Whoopee Island," Judith said a little breathlessly. She was surprised at how thrilled she was to hear her husband's voice. "We're house-sitting for Auntie Vance and Uncle Vince. They're in Beatrice, helping Aunt Ellen and Uncle Win. She had shoulder surgery. Except for not sleeping, are you having fun?"

"We really are," Joe said. "It's light tackle season as you may recall, which means we can't start fishing until later in the afternoon. We've had some action off the jetty, but tomorrow—that's Monday here—we'll spend two nights at sea, probably around Lizard Island."

Judith grimaced. "That sounds a little creepy."

Joe chuckled. "Not even close. It's beautiful around here. We swim in the mornings and we'll try snorkeling today. The people are great, the food's terrific, the weather's balmy. It's all worth losing a little sleep. What are you two doing on The Rock?"

Judith's initial euphoria had waned. "Well . . . we've met a lot of people. We'll have lunch in Langton, maybe at the place above the variety store. Then we'll browse the shops that aren't closed during the winter."

Joe chuckled again. "That sounds . . . good. Too bad you can't find a dead body. As I recall from visiting up there, some of the residents looked as if they were already dead."

"They aren't *all* old," Judith asserted. "Renie and I spent time this morning with small children."

"What happened? Did their parents take a wrong turn?"

Judith started to say something waspish, but didn't want to quarrel from half a world away. "Never mind," she said. "I take it Bill's enjoying himself, too?"

"What's not to enjoy?" Joe retorted. "Bill's sorry Oscar isn't here, though I guess the little guy gets seasick. It's probably just as well he stayed home."

That comment almost sent Judith over the edge. If Joe had bought into the Oscar mythology, maybe he should stay on Lizard Island. "I'd better let you go," she said, *before I feel like locking you out of the house when you get back.* "You should get to sleep so you'll feel fresh when you and Bill go snorkeling tomorrow."

"That's today here," Joe reminded her. "But you're right. Tell Renie Bill says hi. Stay safe." He rang off.

Renie looked up from the newspaper. "They're having a wonderful time," she stated. "I can tell by the sour look on your face.

Spare me. I don't want to hear about it. It'd make me even madder than you are."

"I don't want to repeat it," Judith countered. "I'll walk it off. You want to come along?"

Renie shook her head. "I'm not that fond of walking in general. You get rid of your snit while *I* finish reading the news."

"Fine." Judith put on her jacket. "Lock up—but don't lock me out."

"Use a code word so I know it's you," Renie said, still hiding behind the *Times*. "Oscar will do."

Judith didn't say anything before going outside. A freighter was halfway across the Sound, heading north. She'd walked more than halfway to the beach steps when she saw a frail, fair-haired woman carrying a canvas bag coming up the hill toward her. "Hi," she called to the stranger. "How are you this morning?"

The woman stopped some twenty feet away, eyeing Judith suspiciously. "*Who* are you this morning?" She clasped the bag to her breast. Then she screamed and ran back down the hill.

Chapter 9

Judith stood still, her dark eyes following the woman's frantic path. She veered right onto the last road before the beach, disappearing by a drab-green one-story house. It was pointless to follow her, especially if she was seeking sanctuary at her home. All of the half-dozen modest dwellings just above the beach had been built early on in the development of Obsession Shores.

By the time Judith reached the steps leading to the beach, she could see all the way across the water to the mountains on the mainland. Farther south, a ferry glided from the Peninsula to the landing just north of the city. As seagulls cried and swooped above the great swath of wet, sandy beach, Heraldsgate Hill seemed very far away. Judith involuntarily shivered.

"Well, well!" a male voice called out, making her jump. "If it isn't the house-sitter. Looking for another dead body?"

Trying to regain her composure, Judith turned around to attempt a smile for Brose Bennett. "Hi," she said. "I'd rather not do that again." *At least not here.* "Were you at the meeting last night?"

Brose nodded. "Last to come, first to go. Bunch of bull crap. Fou-fou stayed home. She hates meetings. Don't blame her. You going down to the beach? The tide'll be all the way out in another hour. You never know what might wash up next." He chuckled.

"I think I'll stay up here," Judith said. "I understand you found a rare coin a few weeks ago. Have you had it checked out by a collector?"

Brose shook his head. "There's an old guy in Langton who knows something about old coins, but I'll take it into the city, where I can get a real expert. You know—somebody who's more up-to-date and in touch with big-time collectors."

"Did you use a metal detector?" Judith asked, noting that a couple of children were walking with an adult near the boathouse.

"Nope, but I'm getting me one," Brose said, brushing at the graying brown hair that was blowing in disarray. A breeze had suddenly come down from the north. "I ordered it from the Internet. It should be here today or Monday."

"So you just spotted the coin lying on the beach?" Judith asked.

"Not quite." Brose tugged at the collar of his all-weather jacket. "I was looking for clam holes. Saw a rock that looked kind of interesting—I like to collect 'em to put around the garden. When I picked it up, there was the coin, plain as day. Kind of worn around the edges, though."

"Do you think someone dropped it?" Judith asked, then quickly added, "Recently, I mean."

Brose's expression was droll. "You think somebody was wandering around and just sorta dropped a coin like that? I figure it was washed up from someplace else or maybe worked its way up through the sand over the years. Earthquakes, maybe. They move the ground, you know."

"So they do," Judith said dubiously—and changed the subject. "What's going to happen with the proposed sewer project?"

Brose shrugged. "Who knows? The only one who can really decide is ol' Quimby." His long face hardened. "Too bad he didn't get knocked off instead of poor Ern."

"Are you saying a vote wouldn't change anything?" Judith asked.

"Only if it went Quimby's way." Brose looked down at the

beach. "Hey—do you think some of those folks are looking for old coins? Maybe I started a fad."

Judith followed his gaze. Three people were bent down not far from the boathouse. "Maybe. But they could be clam digging."

"No buckets," he noted.

"You're right. Can you tell who it is?"

"Well . . ." Brose craned his neck and squinted his eyes. "Not till somebody stands up." He paused. "Ah! It's the Johnsons, Charles and May. Old-timers here. Surprised they can still bend." He pointed to the drab-green house behind Judith. "That's their place."

"They were sitting in our row last night," Judith remarked. "They moved fairly fast when the meeting was over."

"Probably scared they'd get trampled." Brose took another look at the beach, where the third person in the group had stood up. "That's Mel Friedman. You were sitting by him and his wife, right?"

"Yes," Judith said. "I'd met them on an earlier visit here. Maybe I'll go join him and the Johnsons."

Brose nodded. "See if they were looking for more old coins. See ya later." He started up the hill.

Just as Judith reached the steps, she saw Mel coming away from the Johnsons and heading toward her. She decided to wait. The wind was blowing harder, but at least it was dispelling the clouds.

"Hey," Mel called as he moved a bit faster. "You coming down?"

Judith shook her head. "It looks like you're coming up."

"I am," he said with a grin as he started up the steps. "I'm not in the mood for buried treasure."

Judith didn't speak until Mel joined her. "Is that really what you were looking for?"

"No," Mel replied, "but the Johnsons were. They swear that an English ship was wrecked around here a couple of hundred years ago. I've never heard of that, but it could be true. Both Sarah and I are from Southern California. We didn't move up this way until after we were married and I finished dental school at the University while she got her nursing degree."

"How long have you lived here, Mel?" Judith asked as they moved away from the steps.

"Full-time?" Mel's high forehead creased. "Almost three years. But we bought in over twenty years ago." He gestured to his right. "That gabled cottage is our house. Do you want to step in for a cup of coffee and say hi to Sarah?"

Judith wanted to say yes, but she figured Renie was getting anxious to leave for Langton. "Could I bring my cousin later today? I left her in charge of our aunt and uncle's house. She may be dismantling it."

Mel laughed. "Sure. Come down anytime, okay? We'll have cocktails instead of coffee later on."

Judith figured that if she and Renie had drinks with the Friedmans and then with the Sedgewicks, they might both be hammered by the time Jane served dinner. But she didn't want to refuse. "That sounds fine. See you then. Tell Sarah I'm looking forward to the visit."

"Will do. Say," Mel said, lowering his voice, "do you stay up late like your aunt does?"

"Fairly late," Judith responded. "Why?"

"I don't imagine Vance or Vince mentioned it," he said, his voice almost a whisper, "but the last couple of weeks Sarah and I've noticed a boat that goes out after midnight. That's about the time we go to bed and our bedroom looks out over the water. Vance and Vince have seen it a couple of times, too. I wondered if you noticed anything last night. We weren't sure because the fog didn't start to lift until about then."

"We turned in before that," Judith said. "What do you think it is?"

"We don't know. You hardly ever see a small boat from here so late during the winter. It usually disappears out of range by

Scratchit Head. It must come back, but we've never stayed awake long enough to notice."

"Maybe we'll stay up later tonight. Renie's a real night owl."

Mel made a face. "Now I feel kind of foolish for mentioning it. Vance was curious, too." He chuckled softly. "I guess this time of year we're pretty hard up for amusement on The Rock."

Judith smiled. "I call it human interest. It's normal to be curious."

She didn't add that sometimes being curious was also dangerous.

When Judith returned to the house shortly before noon, Renie was on the sofa, doing the newspaper's crossword puzzle.

"What's a six-letter word for a pain-in-the-butt relative?" she asked as Judith came through the door. "Don't tell me. It's *J-U-D-I-T-H*. I'm perishing from boredom."

"I'm not the entertainment committee," Judith declared. "I thought you brought work with you."

Renie sneered. "I told you I finished most of it before we left. I only have to do some tweaking."

Judith was brushing her windblown hair. "I picked up some bits of news, including a really weird woman."

Renie feigned shock. "You picked up a weird woman? You couldn't find a weird man?"

"No." Judith sat down by the front window. "I saw an older woman coming up the hill. When I said hello, she asked me who I was and then shrieked before running off down the last road before the beach."

"Sounds like par for the course on The Rock. Boredom and booze can make anybody goofy."

"You're exaggerating," Judith retorted. "We're here during the quiet season. You know from visiting the island in good weather that these folks have plenty to do. It's as if they hibernate in winter."

"If you saw a bear on the beach, I'm leaving. Especially if he was wearing a bathing suit."

"Get serious. What happens to us when it snows on the hill and we're marooned?"

"Okay, okay," Renie said, looking resigned. "We're stuck unless we want to ski or sled. Which I do not. The one time I went skiing a little kid skied between my legs. That did it. Where did Weird Woman go?"

"For all I know, she went home. I did find out the Johnsons live in that green house on the corner. They were on the beach with Mel Friedman looking for rare coins. Brose Bennett thinks he started a fad."

"Ah." Renie grinned. "I assume you interrogated him?"

"We chatted," Judith said. "Brose insists the vote on the sewer line is meaningless because Quentin Quimby will do whatever suits him. He also felt it was a shame that Quimby wasn't the victim instead of Ernie."

"I doubt Quimby would agree," Renie murmured. "So the old coot really runs this show. How did the Johnsons feel about that? They're kind of old, too."

"I didn't go to the beach," Judith replied. "Mel left the Johnsons to their treasure hunting. He told me that he and Sarah, along with Auntie Vance and Uncle Vince, have seen a boat that goes . . . Oh—here's the postal van. I might as well get the mail now." She got up, opened the door, and shouted down to whoever was parking by the mailbox. A short, spare man in crimson all-weather gear hopped out of the vehicle and looked up at her.

"Excuse me," she called out. "I'm coming down to get the mail."

"Don't bother," he said, staring up the stairs. "It's all junk. My hernia's killing me." He met her halfway and handed over a dozen pieces—of junk. Judith thanked him and went back inside.

"Do you want to go into Langton now?" she asked Renie.

"Yes. I'm hungry."

"Of course. I am, too. Let's do it."

The cousins made sure everything that needed turning off was actually off and headed out to the Subaru. As soon as they were on the county road, Judith remembered to finish telling her cousin about the mysterious boat that had been spotted going out after midnight.

"A phantom ship?" Renie said after her cousin concluded the recital. "That sounds intriguing. No theories?"

"Mel indicated they had no idea," Judith replied, taking the turn to the highway that would lead them into Langton. "Auntie Vance has a good imagination, so if she could think of any explanation she'd have said as much. If she hadn't been in such a hurry to get ready to leave, she might have told us about it."

"She was probably worrying about Aunt Ellen," Renie said. "I wonder if Uncle Vince and Uncle Win will get a chance to complete a sentence with our aunts around."

"Uncle Vince won't stay awake that long and Uncle Win may've forgotten how to talk." Judith slowed down as she saw a big truck ahead of them. "Will you stay up to see if that boat appears after midnight?"

Renie laughed. "We both will. You don't have to get up at six."

"You're right," Judith agreed. "This is almost like a vacation."

"Complete with corpse," Renie said. "Gosh, when have we had a real vacation without one of those?"

"When we went to Europe back in 1964," Judith replied, finally seeing sufficient straightaway to pass the plodding truck. "I wonder if we should tell Jacobson about that boat. He may know something about it."

"You think somebody has reported it?"

"One of the locals might've mentioned it when they were being questioned about Ernie's murder."

"Maybe," Renie allowed. "Where shall we eat?"

"How about the café above the the Sun Store?" Judith suggested. "We can browse the shop on the main floor afterward."

"Sounds good to me."

Five minutes later they were on Langton's main street. The town was perched high above the water, facing east to the mainland. The summer flowers were gone from the sidewalk planters and the trees were bare of leaves. No tourists strolled from shop to shop, ogling the local wares. Foot traffic was sparse. Judith thought the little town looked a bit bleak without the summer bustle in the three blocks that made up its commercial area.

But the upside was that there were plenty of parking places. Judith pulled into a spot only two doors down from the café.

The second-floor dining section was fairly busy. The cousins were shown to a table for two overlooking a pocket park off the street. The only thing in bloom was a cluster of winter crocus, pale as a cloud, but thriving among the moss that covered boulders claimed from the beach.

"Smoked salmon!" Renie exclaimed, practically licking the menu.

"Sounds good to me," Judith agreed. "A small salad to go with it?"

"Of course." Renie was beaming.

Judith wasn't. She was facing the entrance and saw Quentin Quimby being wheeled into the restaurant by his son and daughter-in-law. "His Majesty has arrived," she murmured. "Don't stare."

Renie did just that, though she kept her voice down. "They're being seated right in back of you."

Judith brightened. "Maybe we can overhear them."

"The window!" Quimby shouted. "Move me closer, dammit!"

Renie grimaced. "You really want to hear that?" she asked under her breath.

"Why not? I can't see them." Judith stopped speaking, intrigued by the old man's barked orders to his mumbling—and apparently bumbling—caregivers.

"He's a caution," Renie muttered. "Maybe they'll push him out the window. Then you could chalk up another corpse."

A ponytailed young man approached the cousins with one eye on the Quimbys, who had subsided into merciful silence. Renie put her menu aside. "Is it illegal to yell 'obnoxious' in a semi-crowded café?" she asked the server, assuming her best aging-ingénue expression.

"Not a chance," the server replied softly. "The old guy owns part of the island. I'm Jonathan and I'll be running your interference with Mr. Q." He leaned even closer. "Sometimes he asks the other patrons to move. It's nothing personal."

"It is if it's me," Renie said. "I'll have the lox with all the trimmings and a small Caesar salad with a pound of shrimp."

Jonathan seemed unfazed as he turned to Judith, who ordered the same thing, but added, "My cousin's exaggerating. She's kind of a pig. A small pig, I mean. The usual amount will do."

Jonathan grinned, revealing dazzling white teeth. "Okay. I'll see what I can do for you and Piglet." He headed back to the service counter.

Renie wrinkled her nose at Judith. "Does that mean you're Pooh?"

"I feel like Eeyore," Judith said. "Who keeps bumping my chair?"

"The King of The Rock," Renie replied. "He's still twitching. Do you remember the names of his son and daughter-in-law?"

"I don't think I ever heard them." Judith winced as the sound of banging startled her from behind. "What now?"

"I think," Renie said, leaning sideways to get a better look, "Mr. Q. wants to be served. Or else he's rearranging his utensils piece by piece."

"I'd like to rearrange *him*," Judith said. "Maybe we're the ones who should ask to be moved."

"But then you couldn't overhear him," Renie pointed out.

"They aren't actually talking," Judith responded. "Maybe his family members aren't allowed to speak in public. Ah! Here comes a young woman to take their orders. A very pretty young woman, I might add."

"She's a dish, all right," Renie murmured as the smiling strawberry blonde passed by. "Why do I think she's not just another server?"

"Maybe," Judith whispered, "she serves something other than food. What's she doing?"

"She's not taking off her clothes yet," Renie murmured just as Judith heard a hearty, if raspy, guffaw erupt behind her. "Q.'s mood is improving. Do you remember Auntie Vance talking about him? I don't."

Judith shook her head. "Not really. She occasionally mentioned—and I quote—an 'ornery old codger' and a 'horse's ass,' but I don't recall her giving him an actual name. Our aunt prefers not discussing people she doesn't like. She just ignores them and does as she pleases. With her big, bad, and often bawdy mouth, maybe even Q. wouldn't confront her."

"He's acting coy at the moment. Oh, ick—Pretty Woman's tickling his chin. And tugging his earlobe. Double gack."

"Spare me," Judith said. "Here comes lunch."

Jonathan set down their orders, glancing briefly at the other table. "Poor Ginger," he said in hushed tones. "She and her husband, Jens, lease the café. Mr. Quimby owns the building. Does everything look all right?" he asked in his normal voice.

"Just fine," Judith said with a smile. "Thanks."

"Talk about lord of the manor," Renie murmured. "Do you suppose Ginger and Jens live at Obsession Shores?"

Judith made a shushing gesture. Renie shrugged and ate a big forkful of salad. Several other patrons had finished their meals and were leaving. Judith could catch some of the conversation behind her.

" . . . even murder wouldn't scare you, dear Mr. Quimby," Ginger was saying. "You're such a brave man."

Unfortunately, Judith couldn't hear his reply, but Ginger giggled. "I *have* seen your war medals, *Major* Quimby. You were very brave to run that social hall so the troops could be entertained. Fighting men can get out of control, especially if they drink."

Once again, Q.'s mumbled rambling was impossible to decipher. Ginger, however, had become serious. "Oh, Mr. Quimby," she said, "you mustn't try catching the killer by yourself. Let the sheriff's staff do that. Of course you may be right about who killed Mr. Glover, but you mustn't endanger yourself. You know how much we all love and respect and admire you."

"She's gone a couple of verbs too far," Judith whispered.

Renie shoved some lox and trimmings into her mouth. "Ahdintherdat."

Judith scowled. "Skip it. You probably couldn't hear over your chewing." Taking a bite of romaine lettuce, she caught most of Ginger's farewell to the Quimbys.

" . . . to be very careful, you darling man," she was saying, though there was a strain in her voice. "I doubt a killer would go after anyone as revered as you are. Now I have to help out downstairs. Kisses!"

Judith saw Ginger practically run through the café. "Did she really kiss the old twit?" she asked Renie.

"Air kisses," Renie said between mouthfuls. "Even Ginger wouldn't stoop that low. Unless she was revealing her décolletage. Luckily for her, she's wearing a turtleneck jersey."

"Not so lucky for Quimby," Judith murmured. "I wonder if he really does have a suspect in mind."

"Do *you* want to play with his earlobes? Please!"

Judith shuddered. "No, but I wouldn't mind talking to his son or the daughter-in-law. I wonder if Quimby takes naps."

Renie again leaned to her right. "He may be taking one now. He's facedown in his place setting."

Judith was wide-eyed. "Are you kidding?"

"No," Renie replied. "His caregivers don't seem concerned.

They're just staring out the window. Maybe he often does that. Good Lord, I hope he didn't order soup. He'll drown."

Judith kept quiet, trying to concentrate on her food. But it wasn't easy. There had to be some way to speak to Quimby's relatives without taking on the overbearing old man in the process.

"We could have car trouble," Judith said softly.

Renie shrugged. "I suppose. Your Subaru is kind of old—like our Camry. Did you notice it making strange noises on the way here?"

Judith glared at Renie. "I mean as a ruse."

Renie held her head. "Sheesh. Why not just go ask the geezer who he thinks killed Ernie? He's sitting up now. Sort of."

"Maybe I will," Judith retorted. "As soon as we finish our lunch."

"Count me out," Renie said.

"Fine." Judith ate a little faster.

A couple of minutes later, Jonathan and a young Asian man rolled a cart up to the Quimbys' table. Judith and Renie both stared at the covered dishes on the cart.

"Gee," Renie said, "maybe we should've ordered what they did. I think it's all of the menu items."

Quimby let out a sharp cry. "I don't want no Chinaman serving me! Beat it, Fu Manchu!"

"But, sir," Jonathan said in a polite voice, "Jake's an American. His grandparents are Vietnamese."

"That's worse," Quimby shot back. "We're still fighting those damned people. That so-called war's never going to end. He's probably a spy. Tell him to go back where he came from."

"But Jake was born and raised on Whoopee Island," Jonathan said, still sounding polite. "His parents are from San Diego."

Jake nudged his fellow server. "He's all yours. I'm going on break." But before he moved away, he leaned down to speak to Quimby. "The Cong have surrounded the building. Good luck with that." Jake briskly moved away. Jonathan began to remove the covers from the plates of food. Quimby paid no attention, muttering so quietly to himself that Judith couldn't hear a coherent word.

"That's it," Renie declared, tossing her debit card at Judith. "I'm done. See you in the shop."

Judith sighed and resumed eating, though her appetite had faltered. When the Quimbys finished making their choices, she asked Jonathan for the bill. Accosting the cantankerous old goat seemed like a bad idea. The last she saw of Quimby, he was pontificating about Calvin Coolidge and why he was almost as good a president as Rutherford B. Hayes. Judith wondered if the old man was so ancient that he'd actually voted for both men. After paying for the meal, she headed downstairs.

She found Renie browsing through sweatshirts and chatting with Ginger. "Hey, coz, meet my new best friend, Ginger Kopf. With a *K*. This is Judith, the other niece. Ginger knows Auntie Vance."

Ginger laughed as she shook Judith's hand. "Everybody knows Vance," she declared. "She's amazing."

"As amazing as Quentin Quimby?" Judith asked.

"Oh God!" Ginger cried, looking disgusted. "You must've heard or seen some of what I have to go through with that old turkey. I'd feel sorry for Quincy and Nan, but if they offend him even unintentionally, he'll cut them out of his will. He's already done it four times, but they always fall all over themselves with apologies—and constant attention. Frankly, it wouldn't be worth it to me."

"But," Judith pointed out, "you have to make a fuss over him."

"Jens and I have to eat," Ginger said. "We've got two kids still in grade school. When we moved up here five years ago, we had no idea what we were getting into."

Judith sympathized. "I get it. Do you live at Obsession Shores?"

"No, thank goodness," Ginger responded. "We live here in town, just three blocks off the main street. Luckily, Quimby doesn't come here too often. I can imagine how hard it must be to cart him up the stairs in that wheelchair. I've heard he can walk, at least a short distance, but I don't see why he doesn't have an elevator put in the building. It'd make sense and be convenient for lots of the retirees who live in the area."

"Perverse," Renie declared. "He'd rather make everybody suffer. And he's a racist."

Ginger nodded. "He's everything awful. We never knew his wife, Blanche, but she must have been a saint."

"Maybe," Judith suggested, "he was nicer while she was still alive."

Ginger shrugged. "That's possible, I suppose. It's too bad he couldn't meet an old lady who's as nasty as he is."

Renie elbowed Judith. "Hey—how about your mother, coz?"

"Even she isn't that horrid and you know it," Judith said with a touch of indignation. "Mother's just set in her ways." She turned back to Ginger. "Did Quimby tell you he knew who killed Mr. Glover?"

Ginger sighed. "Yes. It's too stupid. In fact, I won't repeat it. Rumors fly around this part of the island like seagulls. I'm amazed someone hasn't tried to murder Quimby. Excuse me—I see a customer who looks as if she wants to buy something. Got to feed the family." She hustled off toward the housewares section.

"Gosh," Renie murmured, "you flunked an interrogation session."

"That's okay," Judith replied. "Quimby may think we killed Ernie."

Renie sneered. "Maybe somebody will kill *him*."

Judith didn't comment, but it wasn't her cousin's worst idea. In fact, she wondered why no one had ever tried to do in Quentin Quimby. Instead, Ernie Glover, a man who seemingly didn't have any enemies, had been the murder victim.

That gave her more than lunch to digest.

Chapter 10

The sun was out when the cousins returned to the main street. They passed a hobby shop, a cobbler's, and a drugstore before pausing at chipped gold letters spelling out EXONUMIA on a murky window.

"I wonder," Judith mused, "what that means?"

"It sounds like a disease," Renie replied, tugging at Judith's arm. "It may be contagious. Let's move on."

But Judith shook off her cousin's hand. "Look—the other window says 'Numismatics.' It must be the collectors' shop Brose Bennett mentioned to me when I went for my walk. I wonder if there've been any other rare coins found on the beaches around here. Let's ask."

Renie looked puzzled. "Why? Do you think Ernie found one that was worth a lot of money and that's the motive for murder?"

"No," Judith replied, opening the door, "but I'm curious, okay?"

Renie didn't argue. An elderly bald man was behind the counter, studying something through a high-tech magnifier. He looked up to offer a faint smile. "Yes?" he said, rubbing his hands together.

The shop was small and faintly musty. The rough wooden walls were decorated with license plates from what looked like every state in the union. The rear wall displayed most of the Canadian provinces, various vanity plates, and some oddly shaped foreign hardware that Judith didn't recognize. A small engraved sign on the counter by the ancient cash register read L. D. MOFFITT, PRO-PRIETOR.

"Hello, Mr. Moffitt," Judith said. "You *are* Mr. Moffitt?"

The proprietor nodded once. "However," he continued in a surprisingly deep voice for his small stature, "L.D. was my father. I'm D.L. Papa started this business here in Langton after he came home from the Great War. Hardly anyone lived here back then."

"That was"—Judith paused—"very brave of him. I must admit my ignorance. What exactly is exonumia? I understand the *numia* part being about coins, but not the *exo* at the beginning."

"Ah," Mr. Moffitt said, his dark eyes lighting up, "basically it means 'other than.' As in coins that have no monetary value. Like these on the bottom shelf." He tapped the front of the counter. "Those are—if you will—tokens that could be exchanged for goods in company-owned communities. Logging, fishing, mining towns, and such where regular currency wasn't used. Very convenient."

"Interesting," Judith remarked. "But you also have quite a few rare coins from all over the world. I was wondering if many older coins are found on the island."

Sadly, Mr. Moffitt shook his bald head. "Not in recent years," he said. "I don't think anyone has brought in a coin older than the 1950s in the past decade. Any rare coins I've acquired have come from collectors or their estates."

Apparently, Renie was tired of being quiet. "What about the man from Obsession Shores who found the 1798 British coin recently? We read about it in the local newspaper."

Mr. Moffitt chuckled. "Silly man. There were no English ships in these waters that late in the eighteenth century. He's been duped. I wish he'd stop by to show me the coin. I'd tell him it's worthless, but why spoil his fun, eh?"

"You're right," Renie said. "I should've known that. Captain Vancouver was the last Englishman to come through the local waters."

"Not precisely," Mr. Moffitt said gently. "Vancouver never sailed this far south, but sent some of his lieutenants to explore the area. That gentleman with the bogus coin doesn't know his history. I suspect someone is pulling a shenanigan. There is, I fear, money to be made by counterfeiting old coins. Very vexing. I've heard of people who have bought up expensive property just because they think there's buried treasure in the ground. Nonsense, of course."

"Has that happened on the island?" Judith asked.

"Not that I've ever heard of," he said. "I was born and raised here. I still live in the family farmhouse a half mile from here. It's not a farm anymore." The expression on his thin face grew poignant. "We were forced to sell off most of the acreage during the Great Depression when I was still a lad."

"At least you kept the house," Judith pointed out.

Mr. Moffitt lowered his eyes. "Yes, yes. We did that. Indeed."

Judith decided to move on to a more cheerful topic. "What's the rarest coin you've ever seen?"

The old man's face lit up. "One of our own—a 1907 Saint-Gaudens double eagle. Gold, and beautifully designed. It was a joy to behold."

"Did you sell it?" Renie asked.

Mr. Moffitt blushed. "I did. Fifteen years ago, for a pretty price. It was part of a collection that had never been properly appraised. People are often foolish about what they save, even collectors. They acquire such things for the sheer joy of the acquisition itself. I don't blame them, really. I understand."

"Did you sell it to someone around here?" Judith inquired.

"Now, now," he said, shaking a finger, "I can't disclose that kind of information. One has to be discreet about buyers and sellers. For their and my protection, you see."

Judith smiled. "Of course. Thank you for enlightening us. We appreciate your time and your dedication."

"My pleasure," he said with a little bow. "Enjoy yourselves and come again. A visit from comely ladies always delights me."

" 'Comely'?" Renie gasped after they exited the shop. "I've been called a lot of things, but that's a first for me. I wonder what it'd take to get Bill to call me comely? It sure beats homely. Too bad they don't rhyme. I could make up a little poem for Mr. Moffitt."

Judith laughed. "He's really an old dear. He obviously loves his work." She turned serious. "Who lives around here that would buy such an expensive coin?"

"The buyer might not be local," Renie said as they reached the corner. "I'll bet he does some Internet business. I could see what looked like a computer monitor in the little office at the back."

"You're probably right. I wonder if he has any family. He doesn't wear a wedding ring, but some men—especially older ones—don't."

"Bill doesn't. He wears the ruby ring that belonged to his father. Where are we going? You know I'm not that fond of walking. I'm not that keen on wearing shoes either."

"There's a women's apparel shop across the street," Judith replied. "Would that pique your interest?"

"It might," Renie said. "As long as they have more than sweatshirts that read 'I Made Whoopee on Whoopee Island' or 'The Rock Rocks!' They're a little short on imagination up here."

"Let's find out." They crossed the street after waiting for two cars to pass by. The shop's name was Adele's. Renie looked put off by the window display that featured uninspired winter separates on what looked like real sand. Judith hesitated before they reached the entrance. "I sense this isn't your sort of thing," she said.

"It's not," Renie declared, her eyes suddenly sparkling. "The candy store's two doors down. Let's go."

Judith refused to be tempted. "I'll wait outside."

Renie was already several paces ahead. "Fine. I'll be quick."

Taking her time, Judith strolled past a secondhand store and a jewelry shop. She reached the Sweet Suite, but refrained from looking in the display window. Instead, she kept her dark eyes riveted on the bank across the street. A familiar figure wearing a raincoat came out and got into a dark blue midsize sedan.

I know that guy, she thought to herself. *I must have seen him at Obsession Shores.* But as Renie exited the candy shop carrying a large white paper bag, Judith realized she was wrong. "Guess what?" she said to her cousin. "I just saw Jack Larrabee."

Renie looked puzzled. "Who?"

"Oh!" Judith clapped a hand to her head. "He was a B&B guest this past week. Jack's a journalist who's doing a series on this part of the world. He told me he was heading north."

"I guess he did," Renie said, reaching into the big bag and taking out a dark-chocolate-covered cluster of raisins. "Want one?"

"No thanks," Judith replied. "Let's move on to the Mermaid. I see the sign on the corner. It may be an apparel store."

"That might be more upscale," Renie agreed after devouring the cluster.

But the Mermaid was a bar, not an apparel store. "How about the gift shop we just passed?" Judith asked.

"Seen one gift shop, seen 'em all," Renie said. "Hey, if you want to chat up the locals, why not have a drink at the Mermaid? Loose tongues and all that."

Judith grimaced. "If we're having cocktails at the Friedmans' and then at the Sedgewicks', we shouldn't get an early start here."

"We can order a beer or a glass of wine," Renie said. "We didn't have a drink at lunch."

"You don't like beer. You aren't that fond of wine either."

"So I'll bitch a lot. So what? You're used to it."

"How do we know anybody of interest is in the bar?"

"As in 'persons of interest'?" Renie smirked. "You'll find somebody. You collect that sort of person. Remember what your old bat of a former mother-in-law used to say—you never met a stranger."

Judith sighed. "I wish Dan's mother had said it nicely."

The cousins entered the Mermaid, which was so dark that they paused until their eyes adjusted. Judith finally zeroed in on an amber lampshade by the bar. "I think I see a table. Or a vase."

Renie took a few steps. "It's a hat rack. But there's a table beyond it. I think."

The table turned out to be occupied by a man. Judith tried not to stare as she recognized Kent Logan. The other chair was unoccupied, but two glasses sat on the table.

"Hi," he said. "Aren't you related to the Webers? I saw you last night at the meeting."

"Yes," Judith replied. "I'm Judith and this is Renie. We're the nieces who are house-sitting for Vance and Vince."

"Oh, that's right," he said, his eyes darting off to his left. "There are some empty booths just past the statue of the mermaid by the bar. It's a bit dark in here, isn't it?"

"Yes, it is," Judith agreed. "Nice to see you again." She all but pushed Renie off in the direction Kent had indicated.

"Why," Renie said as they became accustomed to the gloom and found a booth on the other side of the wooden statue, "do I think he wanted us to go away?"

Judith didn't answer immediately. She was facing the rear of the establishment and saw a familiar figure coming in their direction. "Maybe that's why," she finally said as Fou-fou walked briskly past the cousins.

"The plot thickens," Renie noted. "Yes, she's heading for Kent's cozy table for two. Wouldn't it be more discreet for them to be seated away from the front?"

"Maybe they couldn't see that far," Judith said. "We couldn't."

A portly middle-aged man with a soiled white towel tied around his midsection clumped up to their booth. "What'll it be, ladies?" he asked in a wheezy voice.

"Your best sweet berry wine," Renie said. "No year of choice, but preferably from this century."

"Got it. And you?" he inquired of Judith.

She told him she'd have the same.

He chuckled. "You're going to share a glass? You want straws?"

"No," Judith replied with as much dignity as she could muster. "I'd like my own glass. My cousin is a messy drinker."

The man chuckled again and wended his way to the gloomy bar.

"I wish I'd ordered malmsey," Renie muttered. "I'd like to hear what snappy comeback he'd have had for that."

"I'd like to be able see more of the customers," Judith said, leaning sideways as far as she could without falling on the floor. "There are only a couple of men on the bar stools and I don't recognize either of them. I'm beginning to think this wasn't a good idea."

"You already saw Kent Logan and Fou-fou Bennett having what I assume is some kind of tryst," Renie said. "Now let's figure out how that could be a motive for murdering Ernie."

"Affairs can always be a motive," Judith responded, "but then blackmail might be involved. We don't really know Ernie, but somehow I doubt he was the type for that sort of thing. For all we know, Mr. Logan and Mrs. Bennett may merely have run into each other. They *are* neighbors. I suppose it'd be a good excuse for starting the cocktail hour in the early afternoon."

"Good Lord," Renie said with an incredulous expression, "you can sound like such a dip sometimes. You know your brain is working at two hundred miles an hour figuring out what those two see in each other and how long the affair has been going on."

"They *are* in public," Judith replied primly.

Their wine arrived. "Want some snacks?" the portly man asked.

"What are they?" Renie inquired.

"Crackerjack, right out of the box," he said. "You might get a prize. Somebody got a little plastic pickle last night."

Renie wrinkled her nose. "We'll pass."

"Suit yourself," he said wearily, and ambled away.

"Why," Renie murmured, "do I like it better when you find a body in the city, where we can hang out in classier bars and upscale bistros?"

"Why," Judith whispered back, "do I see Brose Bennett coming this way from the rear of the bar?"

"How can you tell where the rear is?" Renie responded.

Judith shook her head and greeted Brose as he approached the booth. "Are you having . . ."

Brose kept going. "What's with him?" she asked Renie. "He looks angry. Can you see where he's headed?"

"Are you kidding?" Renie shot back. "I'm lucky I can see at all in here. This wine tastes like melted jelly."

Judith sampled her portion. "You're right. It's kind of icky. I'm not sure I want to . . ." She stopped, hearing men's raised voices. "What's going on up front?"

"I'll go look. Stay put." Renie scooted out of the booth.

She was barely out of sight when Judith heard more shouting, a woman's screech, breaking glass, and a crashing noise that made her jump. Despite the warning, she hurried out of the booth. Renie was plastered against the wall in an attempt to keep clear of the mayhem. Brose and Kent had faced off in front of a screaming Fou-fou.

Before Judith could speak, Brose swung part of a broken chair at Kent, knocking the other man against the hat rack, which toppled to the floor. As the portly man chugged out from behind the bar, Brose grabbed his hysterical wife, kicked the hat rack aside, and exited the premises. A half-dozen customers were now clustered at the near end of the bar, but kept their distance from what was left of the combat zone.

Judith couldn't help herself. She moved to where Kent Logan was slumped against an undamaged chair. He shook himself, rubbed at his jaw, and looked up with a dazed expression. "Is Brose gone?" he asked.

"Yes," Judith replied. "He took Fou-fou with him."

Kent struggled to his feet. "Good riddance. They're both head cases." He picked up his Gore-Tex jacket and reached for his wallet. "Here, Dundee," he said to the portly man. "Take my credit card to cover the bill. Then total up the damage and I'll pay for my share later."

Dundee looked uncertain. "You didn't start that. I saw it."

Kent ran a hand through his disheveled hair. "At least let me pay for the drinks."

Dundee shook his head. "I'll put those on Mrs. Bennett's tab."

Kent shrugged as Dundee handed the credit card back to him. "That's the last time I offer free legal advice about a divorce," he said, and slammed out of the Mermaid.

Judith and Renie, along with the other patrons, headed back to their respective places. Dundee was last seen fetching a broom from behind the bar.

"So," Renie said, after they were reseated, "the Bennetts are pfft?"

"I guess," Judith replied. "We misread the tête-à-tête. Maybe we should pay for our so-called drinks and get out of here before the roof falls in. I didn't recognize any of the onlookers."

"Good idea," Renie agreed, tossing a ten-dollar bill on the table. "Let's go. I'll throw up if I have to drink any more of this slop."

"Brose must've come in via the back. Why not leave that way?"

The rear exit was plainly marked—once they got close enough to see the sign. "Ah—I can breathe again," Renie said, sniffing at the salt-tinged air. "This is quite a view."

The cousins were standing on a small expanse of grass, high above the beach. "I can see the mountains over on the mainland,"

Judith said. "There's Mount Woodchuck by the family cabins. We ought to go up there this spring. Wouldn't that be fun? My grandsons would love it."

"It's been a while," Renie noted. "If I had grandchildren, they'd probably like it, too. How come you aren't speculating about Fou-fou running off with Ernie? Didn't Zach Bendarek say Ernie played around? Somebody else hinted at that, too."

"Brose, maybe," Judith said, and stared at Renie. "I suppose it could happen. Boredom and booze can lead to a lot of bad things."

"I can believe anything on this island. I can even believe you talked us into going to the Mermaid."

"It was *your* idea," Judith declared.

"It was?" Renie grimaced. "Well, not all my ideas are good ones. What's next on your agenda?"

Judith checked her watch. "It's almost three. We should head back to Obsession Shores if we're going to have drinks with the Friedmans before we have drinks with the Sedgewicks before we have dinner."

Renie looked askance. "That's too many befores. Frankly, I'm looking forward to an after, as in when we can collapse by ourselves."

The cousins trudged around the building to reach the main drag. The Subaru was parked almost directly across the street.

"I wonder," Judith said after they got in the car, "if Jacobson's making any progress with the investigation."

"Why would he be? We're not."

"Unfortunately, that's true," Judith conceded as she waited for a battered pickup to go by before pulling out from the curb. "The truth is, there are so many possible suspects we haven't met."

"You could call your own meeting at the clubhouse and take turns interrogating them."

"That's Jacobson's job," Judith said. "I kind of wish he'd touch base with us, but I don't know why he would."

Renie laughed. "He doesn't know you're FATSO."

Judith glared at Renie as they paused at the arterial. "Don't use that garbled nickname! You know it's *FASTO* and I hate it either way."

"Hey—so you've got a fan club out there in cyberspace. I think it's kind of nice they came up with the code name for Female Amateur Sleuth Tracking Offenders. Do you ever look at the site?"

"No! It's too embarrassing."

"You're too touchy," Renie said as they reached the highway. "Hey, why are you driving so fast? The speed limit is forty on this stretch of road. Are you in that big of a rush to get your next drink?"

"Just hang on and shut up," Judith retorted, her eyes on the rearview mirror as a siren suddenly sounded behind them. "Guess I'd better pull over." She slowed way down and steered the Subaru to the first wide spot in the road. "We got busted. So far, so good."

Renie merely shook her head.

The county cruiser pulled in behind them. "How lucky can we get?" Judith murmured. "It's Jacobson."

"You're an idiot," Renie shot back.

The lieutenant appeared beside the driver's window, which Judith had already rolled down. "Would you please step out of the . . . Mrs. Flynn?" Jacobson said in surprise.

"Yes. I'm sorry. My foot slipped."

"You were doing seventy in a forty-mile zone," he said solemnly.

"I was? I didn't think my foot slipped *that* far."

Jacobson sighed. "Why did you speed up right after I pulled onto the road behind you? And why did I end up pulling a weekend shift?"

"I wondered about that," Judith said. "I was surprised that it was you. We need to talk."

"We do?" he asked, looking surprised. "Why?"

Judith chose her words carefully. "Quite by accident, my cousin and I have discovered some interesting information about various Obsession Shores residents. It's the sort of thing that an official police investigation might not learn without a lot of tiresome work."

He removed his hat and rubbed his buzz cut. "Are you serious?"

"Yes."

The deputy slowly put his hat back on. "Okay. But first I have to write you up. The fine for speeding on the island is five dollars for every mile over the posted limit."

"Does it count if it was intentional?" Judith asked.

Jacobson's shoulders slumped. "Oh, hell. I could let you off with a warning. I'll meet you back at the Webers' place. Let me go first."

"Of course." Judith smiled. "Thank you, Lieutenant."

"I can't believe you got away with it," Renie declared while they waited for the deputy to drive off in his cruiser. "You lead a charmed life."

"At least I saved a hundred and fifty bucks," Judith said. "I knew Jacobson seemed like a reasonable person."

"It'd serve you right if I told him you're FATSO. I mean, *FASTO,*" Renie said with an impish grin. "Why don't you bribe me with that hundred and fifty bucks so I don't reveal your lurid past?"

"Because you won't rat me out, that's why." Judith drove back onto the road. "The problem with telling him what we've found out so far is that it sounds like gossip. He won't like that."

"It *is* gossip," Renie said as two bicyclists appeared up ahead. "The young are exercising. The tide's still out. We should be digging clams."

Judith gave the bicyclists a wide berth. "We're digging for truth and justice. How come you're not insisting I run over that pair?"

"Because Jacobson would arrest you and then I'd be bored," Renie replied. "I only get upset when they don't observe the rules of the road."

Judith followed Jacobson onto the Obsession Shores turnoff from the main highway. The sun was still out. She caught peekaboo views of the sparkling bay off to her right. There had been only a handful of other vehicles on the road from Langton. It was a different world from Heraldsgate Hill where a half-mile drive up to Falstaff's Market could take ten minutes in traffic. Five minutes later, Judith pulled into the Webers' garage. Jacobson had parked on the verge above the mailbox.

"This better not be a waste of time," he said as they headed up the steps to the front door.

"Why?" Renie asked. "You got a big crime wave going on up here?"

"I've got a homicide investigation," he shot back. "Isn't that enough? I'd like to be able to knock off highway duty at four and kick back with my wife and kids."

Judith managed to open the padlock with a minimal amount of bother. The first thing she did when she got inside was to pull the blinds that looked out to the bright sunlight. "We natives aren't used to the glare," she explained.

"I'm a native," Jacobson said, sitting in the same recliner he'd used on his previous visit. "I grew up on the island."

"Would you like some coffee?" Judith asked.

Jacobson shook his head. "I'd rather have a beer right now, but I'll wait until I get home. Start dishing. It's three o'clock."

Renie sat down on the sofa, kicking off her shoes. Judith joined her cousin. "As virtual strangers," she began, "we don't know most of the locals, but we've met a few of them since we arrived."

"And?" the deputy prodded.

"You probably already heard Mr. Glover didn't have an enemy in the world," Judith said.

Jacobson looked impatient. "Right."

Judith decided to come up with some serious data. "Do you realize that the so-called meeting last night was a sham because

Quentin Quimby runs the development and only allows freehold agreements?"

The deputy looked puzzled. "What do you mean?"

"It's a form of lease," Judith explained. "After a certain period of time, the property reverts to Quimby—or his heirs."

"I never heard of anything like that," he said in a dubious tone.

"It's not common in this country, but it is in the UK," Judith asserted. "To my knowledge, it's legal."

Jacobson took out his notebook. "I'll check this out," he murmured, still sounding skeptical. "The courthouse should have the records. What else?"

"There may be some sort of scam going on regarding counterfeit rare coins," Judith said, no longer feeling on such firm ground. "Talk to Brose Bennett—who, I should add, may be divorcing his wife."

"That's all iffy," Jacobson declared. "What would that have to do with the victim?"

"I don't know," Judith admitted, "but Brose and Kent Logan came to blows at the Mermaid about fifteen minutes ago. We saw it happen. Fou-fou—Mrs. Bennett—had been consulting Mr. Logan about a divorce. There've been some rumors that Mr. Glover may've played around."

"I don't deal in rumors," Jacobson said. "Go on."

Judith shrugged. "We paid a condolence call on Mrs. Glover. She didn't seem like a typical grieving widow. Her attitude was very strange."

"Shock, maybe," Jacobson said. "She did strike me as capable of controlling her emotions. Some people are like that. Are we done here?"

"Not quite. Have you any idea about who left the note here?"

"No." He got to his feet. "We'd need DNA from everybody in the development to figure out who warned you off." The deputy took a couple of steps toward the door, but stopped. "What have you two been doing? Interviewing suspects on your own?"

"Of course not!" Judith exclaimed. "We just keep running into—"

"Stop." Renie got off the sofa and put a hand on her cousin's arm. "Judith is writing a mystery novel. She's doing research. You can't blame her for that, can you?"

Jacobson looked faintly nonplussed. "No. No, I can't. But be careful. There's a killer out there."

Judith and Renie already knew that. But they weren't going to tell the sheriff's deputy there usually was.

Chapter 11

You," Judith said to Renie after Jacobson had left, "just told a bigger whopper than I *ever* did. I only tell fibs for a good reason."

"That *was* a good reason," Renie countered. "You were having trouble extricating yourself. Should we call Auntie Vance now?"

"It's three thirty," Judith said. "Two hours time difference, right? She may be making dinner. Let's wait. We should be back here by seven thirty. Auntie Vance stays up late."

"Right," Renie murmured. "Oh, good grief! You forgot to ask Jacobson about the phantom ship!"

Judith clapped her hands to her cheeks. "You're right. I wonder if I should call him. He must have a cell. But he may be chasing a speeder. I don't want to aggravate him."

"Maybe we should talk to the Friedmans and the Sedgewicks about the boat," Renie said, flopping back onto the sofa. "Mel and Sarah have seen it. I don't know if Jane and Dick have, though."

Judith sat down in the overstuffed chair. "I hope Jacobson can find out about the freehold lease thing. It struck me as weird, but the more I think about it, the more I can see why the people who buy in here would do such a thing. Depending on how reasonable the price is and how long the lease is good for, people of retirement age wouldn't care if it was for, say, fifty or a hundred years. They'd still be able to leave the property to their heirs.

After that, who knows if the kids or whoever would want to live up here."

"I can see that," Renie said, "but what I don't get is why Quimby did it that way in the first place. Control, I assume. He thinks he can dictate from beyond the grave."

"Probably," Judith agreed. "I'd like to know more about his wife."

"Blanche? Why?" Renie asked.

"She's only been dead a few years. Blanche had the idea to sell off the old family farm. Did she allow her husband to handle the finances or was she the one who came up with the freehold lease idea instead?"

Renie looked bemused. "Interesting. How do we find out?"

"I don't know," Judith admitted. "I'm not sure that calling on the Quimbys would be a good idea."

"But you'll do it anyway."

"Maybe." Judith turned thoughtful for a moment. "I do wonder if Quimby changed after his wife died. Face it, he's a mystery man to us."

"You can't let *that* go on for very long," Renie said with a grin.

"He has to sleep," Judith murmured as much to herself as to Renie. "Maybe a late-night visit is in order."

"That sounds prudent," Renie said, seemingly serious. "I can't wait to run into the killer waving a saber at us."

Judith sighed. "Right, right. We could take along our own knives. Which reminds me—there's something wrong with Jacobson's theory that the killer tossed the knife into the bay. Think about it. The tide was still way out, so he or she had to walk a long way to get to the water. Even if no one else was on the beach, all these people have binoculars or telescopes." She nodded at a shelf under the kitchen counter near the door. "A second pair is in the master bedroom. Then there's the matter of blood on the knife. What would you do about that?"

"Stick it in the wet sand," Renie said, but quickly retracted the statement. "No. The sand by the body was above high tide and the rain hadn't started until after he was killed."

"Right," Judith agreed. "I think the knife is somewhere, maybe not far from where we found Ernie's body. Let's take a look. We have to go down near the beach steps to get to the Friedmans' house."

"We still haven't met the Crowleys or the Leonettis," Renie said. "When do we pay them a call or do you figure they're out of the loop?"

"Nobody's out of the loop," Judith replied, getting up. "We'll deal with them tomorrow. Let's go."

They were on the beach five minutes later. A breeze had come up off the water, but the sun was still out, edging ever downward toward the mountains on the Peninsula. The ubiquitous cry of the seagulls could be heard as they swooped for food over land and sea. Two small boats were off Scratchit Head, each apparently occupied by a lone fisherman.

"Maybe," Renie said as they walked to the log where broken crime-scene tape fluttered in the wind, "we should've brought a shovel."

Judith shook her head. "I don't think the killer buried it. That's a guess, though."

Renie frowned. "Don't you figure Jacobson and the other deputies scoured this area?"

"Of course, but they're men. You know they never can find things."

"True." Renie knelt down on the dry sand by the log. "The roots on this thing are really gnarled and twisted. You could shove a knife inside, but I suppose Jacobson thought of that."

"Probably," Judith said in a vague voice as she studied some of the smaller driftwood pieces that had piled up behind the log. Her gaze strayed to the boathouse. "I imagine they looked in there, too, though I doubt the killer would use the boathouse as a hiding place."

"Are you talking to me," Renie asked, "or to the seagulls?"

"I'm talking to myself," Judith replied. "I really believe that the knife has to be here someplace." She glanced to her right and saw two figures cautiously coming down the staircase. "Is that the Johnsons?"

Renie, who had stood up and was brushing sand off her slacks, didn't respond.

"It *is* the Johnsons," Judith said after the couple had descended the steps. "They're coming this way."

Renie shot Judith a wry glance. "Good. Now you're answering yourself. I'm off the hook."

"Stop," Judith said. "Charles and May, right?"

Renie made a thumbs-up gesture. "Yes! Tell yourself you got their first names right. That's ten points."

"Someday I'll . . ." Judith shut up. "Never mind. If I did strangle you, I'd have to turn myself in." She broke into a smile and waved to the Johnsons, who were slowly trudging toward them. He was carrying a contraption that Judith guessed was a metal detector. "Hi," she called out loudly, aware that they were deaf. "Nice day."

There was no response. "Try yodeling," Renie said. "We heard people do that in Little Bavaria."

The Johnsons stopped a few feet away. "Howdy," Charles said with a faint smile on his wrinkled face. "Don't we know you somehow?"

Judith smiled back. "We sat by you during the meeting at the clubhouse," she said in a loud voice.

Charles used the hand that wasn't holding the metal detector to cup his ear. "Eh? Eating at the Chub House? Never been there."

Judith shook her head and pointed in the clubhouse's direction. "The meeting. Sewers."

"Sue who?" Charles responded, looking puzzled.

May poked his arm. "The meeting," she said in an almost normal voice. Maybe, Judith thought, Charles could read her lips.

"Oh, sure." He smiled sheepishly. "I'm a bit hard-of-hearing."

"No kidding," Renie said under her breath.

Judith moved closer to the Johnsons. "I'm Judith and this is Renie." She glanced around, noting that her cousin hadn't budged. "We're the Webers' nieces."

"Got the sneezes, eh?" Charles said, shaking his head. "It's all the damp around here. Try steam."

"Thanks," Judith said, smiling before pointing to the device he'd just set on the ground. "Is that a metal detector?" she virtually yelled.

May nodded. "Yes. We bought this in Langton yesterday. We've already found some interesting things with it."

"Coins?" Judith asked.

Charles apparently caught that word. "Not yet. But we will. Got to be more than Brose Bennett found. Nobody loses just one coin."

May patted her husband and laughed. "Listen to him! Last fall he forgot to tell me he had a hole in his pants pocket and almost two dollars in change fell out in our front yard. So far we've found only the sort of things that people leave on beaches." Her expression grew serious. "Beer cans, soda cans, rusted bolts, kitchen utensils, silverware—not sterling, though. Nothing of value. This is our second foray of the day. Maybe we'll have better luck over here near the boathouse."

Charles scowled at his wife. "I kind of hate to search around this part. Poor Ernie was killed here. Might be bad luck. It sure was for him."

May looked indignant. "That wasn't bad luck, that was some crazy person's doing. This is a good place to try. People coming off their boats must drop all sorts of things. You always did when we had our boat."

"Maybe so." Charles tipped his baseball cap. "Nice to meet you folks. We'd better get going before that wind blows in some rain."

The Johnsons ambled off.

"You seem to have lost your voice," Judith said to Renie.

"I get tired of yelling at people. Why don't they get better hearing aids? At least May's not quite as deaf as Charles."

"They seem like very nice people. Admit it, they get out and do something. That's a plus at their age."

"True," Renie allowed. "Shouldn't we head for the Friedmans? It's going on four, time to start getting blitzed like the other people do here."

By the time they reached the steps, the wind had picked up, creating whitecaps out in the bay. Judith fastened her car coat and pulled up the hood. Even the seagulls were seeking cover, flying off from the beach onto the utility wires at the edge of the surrounding forest.

Mel greeted them at the door of their gabled cottage. "We saw you down on the beach," he said. "Did the wind blow you up the stairs?"

"It threatened to," Judith replied as they stepped into the small foyer. The smell of baked bread hung in the air. "There's a lovely odor around here," she noted, sniffing in appreciation.

"Sarah baked challah bread for dinner," Mel replied, leading them into a surprisingly modern-looking living room with its stark black-and-white furnishings. "Have a seat. She'll be right here." He went over to a sleek mahogany cupboard and removed a bottle of wine. "A Bartenura Asti. It's kosher. How does that sound?"

"Fine," Judith said while the cousins settled into matching black-and-white-striped chairs that were more comfortable than they looked.

Sarah entered the room. "Ah!" Mel exclaimed. "The baker has completed her task." He filled a fourth glass.

Sarah greeted their guests before settling onto a backless white divan by the leaded-glass front windows. "I'd offer a slice of fresh bread, but it has to cool before I can cut it. Have you heard any news about the murder? I saw a cop car by your aunt and uncle's house earlier."

Not wanting to alarm their hosts, Judith didn't mention the

threatening note, and shrugged. "I suppose the sheriff's deputies will continue their investigation," she said, accepting a glass of wine from Mel.

He sat down next to Sarah. "We've only talked to a deputy once late yesterday afternoon. There wasn't much we could tell him since we weren't around when Ernie was killed." He glanced at his wife. "Carson was the deputy's name, right?"

Sarah nodded and held up her glass. *"L'chaim,"* she said. "A toast to life." They all raised their glasses. "That seems apt," she went on, "given that we've lost one of our own."

Judith took a sip of wine before speaking. "Were you able to tell Carson anything helpful?"

Mel grimaced. "Not really. All we could offer was that Ernie seemed like a good guy. Oh, he had the occasional minor disagreement with somebody, but he was an affable sort."

"It's strange," Sarah said. "Nobody seems to know anything about what happened. Wouldn't you think there'd be *some* witnesses around here? Yes, the weather wasn't great, but people are always looking out at the water or down onto the beach. It doesn't make sense that not one person seems to have come forward."

Mel nodded. "The only locals I know of with cast-iron alibis are us and the Crowleys. They picked their kids up early from school and headed out of town for the weekend to a family birthday party in Oregon. They live next door and I waved them off before noon. I was just heading to get the car. We were probably on the same ferry, though I never saw them. Sarah and I stayed down below."

Judith frowned. "The Crowleys left town before last night's meeting? I thought they were very much pro-sewer."

Sarah nodded. "They probably arranged for proxy votes, just like Vance and Vince did with you."

Renie leaned forward in her chair. "Who would the Crowleys pick?"

"No idea," Mel said. "Maybe the Hilderschmidts."

A pounding on the front door startled the foursome. Mel glanced out the mullioned window and winced. "It's Betsy. Again. What now?" He got up and wearily walked to the foyer.

"Who's Betsy?" Judith asked.

"Quimby's daughter," Sarah whispered. "She's a head case, but who wouldn't be, living with that old jerk? Hi, Betsy," she said, standing up. "Have you met the Webers' nieces?"

Judith tried to conceal her surprise. Betsy was the strange woman she'd met earlier on the road to the beach.

Betsy's eyes flickered in Judith's direction. "No. What's wrong with the Webers?"

"Nothing," Mel replied. "They're visiting relatives in Nebraska."

The fair-haired woman put a fist to her thin lips. "No! That's not good. I'm going now." She turned around and left.

Mel shrugged. "Don't mind her. She's not quite all there."

Renie scowled at Judith. "Did we know there was a daughter?"

"No," Judith replied. "Hey—it's not my fault."

Sarah laughed. "I suppose she's one of Obsession Shores' dark little secrets. There are quite a few of them around here despite the propensity for gossip. Betsy doesn't socialize much. But for some reason, she comes here once in a while. Vance has talked about her showing up quite often at their place. Don't be surprised if she calls on you. She won't remember the Webers are gone."

"I saw her this morning," Judith said. "I asked how she was and she wanted to know *who* I was. Then she ran off."

Mel nodded. "That sounds like Betsy. She's harmless."

"She never stays long," Sarah said. "She can't, being unable to focus. Extreme ADD, among other problems."

"How old is she?" Renie asked. "Her face is curiously unlined."

Mel looked up at the beamed ceiling. "Oh . . . Betsy's got to be at least sixty. Our theory is that she's never spent a lot of time outside, so she's avoided the sun and whatever else causes wrinkles. We've also wondered if she's been institutionalized along the way."

"When," Judith inquired, "did her mother die?"

The Friedmans exchanged looks. Sarah spoke first. "It was a few years before we moved here permanently. We never really knew her. I doubt I spoke to Blanche more than a dozen times. She didn't go out much. Bad knees, someone told me."

"I wonder," Judith said, "why she didn't get her knees replaced. The Quimbys must have plenty of money. I wasn't keen on getting a new hip, but I realized I had to do it to remain mobile."

"Maybe her general health wasn't all that good," Sarah suggested. "She was older then than we are now."

Renie raised her hand. "Guess what? I can talk. I had my shoulder virtually replaced. Sometimes it squeaks. I think the surgeon used tin."

"Ignore her," Judith said. "She got full mobility back. I'm not so lucky. But I'm not complaining," she added hastily.

"Yes, you are," Renie asserted. "You like the attention."

Judith was indignant. "I do not!"

"You do so," Renie snapped.

The Friedmans laughed. "You're just like sisters," Sarah said. "I wonder if Vance and Ellen have killed each other yet. Every time Ellen and Win come up here to visit, Vance insists her kid sister tries to reorganize their lives. It makes her so mad."

"Aunt Ellen does that with everybody," Judith said. "The family loves to see them coming, but I think they're relieved to see them going. Aunt Ellen really is an amazing woman. She accomplishes more in a single day than most people do in a week."

"Sibling rivalry," Mel mused. "I've got two sisters, and they still live back east. But I've seen those rivalries in other siblings, even up here."

Judith's expression was curious. "I didn't know any brothers or sisters lived at Obsession Shores."

"They don't, except for Quincy and Betsy Quimby," Mel replied. "It was Hank and Tank Hilderschmidt. Tank's company worked on some projects here the summer before last, including a renovation of the boathouse. Much of the original wood had rotted out. The brothers got into it and a fistfight ensued. Frank Leonetti and Zach Bendarek had to pull them apart before they killed each other."

"Gosh," Renie said, "Hank was standing up for Tank at the meeting. They must've made up after that."

Mel shrugged. "I've heard it's more like an armed truce. Hank bought small properties and cut deals with Tank to help develop them with his subcontracting business. I gather they've always greased each other's palms."

"Say," Judith said, "who else has seen that mystery boat?"

"Kent Logan," Sarah replied. "He's seen it twice, but the Logans usually go to bed earlier than we do." She looked at her husband. "You mentioned at least two other people who told you they'd spotted it."

"Right." Mel paused for a moment. "Quimby's son, Quincy. He said it reminded him of the rumrunners his father used to talk about coming from Canada during Prohibition. Ernie Glover mentioned seeing the boat a couple of weeks ago, not long after New Year's." He shook his head. "Poor Ernie. I wish they'd find his killer. All these feeble old folks in the development must be frightened out of their wits."

"The Johnsons didn't act scared this afternoon," Renie said. "Coz shouted to them on the beach just before we came up here."

Sarah smiled. "Charles was a high school principal and May taught at a different high school. Nothing scares them after forty-five years with teenagers."

"How about a refill?" Mel asked, standing up.

"No, thanks," Judith replied. "We're having dinner with the Sedgewicks. We want to be mostly sober when we arrive. But this wine is very good. It has sort of a sweet taste."

Mel nodded. "Sarah and I don't do much of the hard stuff. It gets to be a habit with people who have time on their hands. That's why I moonlight doing dental work for the retirees. I only charge a small fee or an occasional bottle of this stuff." He tapped his empty glass.

"Last Thanksgiving," Sarah said, "the Crowleys gave us a turkey. One of their kids chipped a front tooth falling down the stairs to the beach. We happened to be there at the time, so Mel volunteered."

The cousins had also stood up. "That's good," Judith said. "It's nice to know there really is a sense of community here."

"Sometimes," Sarah murmured as she also got to her feet.

"It's not all bad," Mel conceded—and winced. "At least until some poor guy like Ernie Glover gets killed."

Judith didn't much like that exit line, but she'd heard ones like it before. She didn't pause to tote up the dead people she'd encountered in the past sixteen years. There was nothing sweet about that number. Murder left a sour taste in her mouth. The only cure for that, she realized, was to find the killer.

Chapter 12

The north wind had died down, but it brought heavy rain from Canada. Judith and Renie pulled up their hoods as they walked to the Weber house. The clothes they had worn to the beach were headed for the laundry room. Dinner at Obsession Shores might be informal, but the cousins didn't want to show up looking like beach bums.

"It's a good thing neither of us sat on that white divan," Renie said as she came out of the spare bedroom after changing into brown slacks and an orange mock-turtleneck sweater. "How do they keep all that white furniture clean?"

"The Friedmans," Judith replied, shifting her torso around in her roomy red-and-navy floral wool tunic, "may be tidier than *some* of us."

"I don't know what you mean," Renie said, strolling out of the hall. "I'll check the Sunday Mass times. St. Walburga's, right?"

"Yes." Judith joined Renie at the kitchen counter. "Find it?"

Renie nodded. "Ten o'clock. They have one at seven tonight, but we'll be too hammered to make it."

"We may not have eaten by then," Judith said, sitting at the kitchen table. "I wish I'd asked Jacobson about that boat. There's something strange about it. But it's after four, so he must be off duty."

"So," Renie began, leaning on the back of a kitchen chair, "you seek a motive for murder involving the boat?"

Judith looked up at her cousin. "It's an unusual occurrence. Why would anyone take a boat out so late at night this time of year?"

"Insomnia. Fleeing a nagging spouse. Seeking peace and quiet on the water. People do unusual things for not so unusual reasons." She shrugged. "That's the best I can come up with."

"Maybe somebody's running drugs out of here," Judith said. "That's the only contraband idea I have."

"When do they come back? They can't have a fleet of boats in the boathouse."

"While it's still dark. The sun doesn't come up until around seven thirty in January."

Renie looked skeptical. "I'll bet a lot of these people go to bed early and get up early. They'd see the boat returning in the dark before dawn."

"Then it must be a very short run. Let's check the boathouse tomorrow. I don't know why Uncle Vince never kept his boat in there. I don't see any other boats on the beach."

"He kept it on the beach," Renie said, finally sitting down, "because it wasn't much of a boat. I remember when I was up here years ago, Auntie Vance was giving him hell for not putting it inside. I can still hear him: 'But, Little Girl, getting it up the ramp bothers my bad back. You didn't spend over forty years carrying a dozen gallons of milk in each hand.' Auntie Vance just snorted and told him he should have been a cow."

Judith smiled. "That sounds like our aunt. She probably also called him a few of her favorite unprintable names."

"Oh, sure." Renie sighed. "What do you expect to find in the boathouse? Another body?"

"No!" Judith cried. "I assume we'd find boats. And maybe the names of people who keep them there. The building isn't all that big, so there can't be that many. If anyone has a cruiser or a bigger craft, they probably dock it at the Scratchit Head marina."

"So we'll be watching tonight to make sure the boat comes out from here and not over there?"

"Well . . . I guess we will. One of us, anyway."

"I can't see it from the spare room. I'll have to stay up."

"You can watch for it with me from the master bedroom or we can sit in the living room. In fact, we probably should go out on the deck. Or even down the road for a close-up view."

Renie made a face. "And have the phantom ship's captain kidnap us and turn us into galley slaves? No thanks."

"We're not talking pirates," Judith declared.

"Hey—if your suspicions are right, whoever is using that boat is up to something. I vote for staying safe. Just for once, okay? Besides, it might be raining hard later tonight."

Judith decided Renie was right. "But we'd better get a good look. The boat could be coming from the marina. You can't see it from here."

"Oh, swell." Renie groaned, a hand to her head. "So if we can't tell where it's coming from tonight, we'll have to do a stakeout tomorrow on the other side of the boathouse?"

"That's not a bad idea," Judith said. "Depending on the weather, of course. We could ask—" A rap on the door interrupted her. "Now what?"

Renie got up. "If it's Betsy Nutsy, I'll keep going to the Sedgewicks'. You can fend for yourself." She put her hand on the doorknob. "Are you armed and dangerous?" she shouted.

"Fraklenutty," the male voice called back. Or at least that's what it sounded like to Judith, who remained at the table.

Renie opened the door. "Frank?" she said, letting in a short man with curly silver hair. "As in Leonetti?"

"Right." He came inside, shaking water off his yellow slicker. "Are you the nieces? I got some flyers."

"You got birds?" Renie asked, trying to avoid the excess rain Frank was shedding. "What are you, a magician? Let's see you pull a ptarmigan out of your sleeve."

Frank apparently thought the remark was hilarious. He laughed so much that he had to stagger over to the table and sit down. "That's a good one," he gasped, wiping at his eyes. "Everybody else is so damned grim around here."

"Yeah," Renie muttered, "we're the entertainment committee. And no, we aren't offering you a drink. Food and beverages aren't included."

Frank laughed some more. "I . . . can see . . . you're . . . related . . . to Vance," he finally managed to say. "You're a kick, just like her."

Judith decided to become the voice of reason. "Did you mention flyers? Is there another meeting coming up?"

"No," he replied, growing serious and reaching into his slicker. "I made up some flyers to help find Ernie Glover's killer. Here, have a look." He handed over a sheet of white paper with red lettering on it.

"Calligraphy," Renie remarked, sitting down. "Did you do this?"

"You bet I did," Frank replied. "I learned how to do that for my papa. He owned his own business."

"It's beautiful," Judith asserted before reading aloud.

Attention Obsession Shores Residents: Anyone with information regarding the murder of our good friend and neighbor Ernest Glover should come forward and inform the sheriff. Anything you saw or heard the day of the murder could help find the killer.

"Well?" Frank said. "What do you think?"

Judith set the flyer aside. "It's a good idea. Do you sense people are holding back? We heard everyone has been questioned by the deputies."

Frank leaned back in the chair. "People don't always know

what's important and what isn't. Then there's some folks who don't want to get involved. You know how that goes."

"True," Judith conceded, "but why us? We're strangers."

Frank shook his head. "If Vance was around, I'd have asked her. She's sharp, and I don't just mean that tongue of hers. She's blistered me a few times, but I respect her. Being her nieces, I figured you might have some of your own ideas."

Judith held out her hands in a helpless gesture. "The problem is that we don't really know most of the people who live here. Oh, we've met a few since arriving yesterday, but that doesn't give us the kind of insider's knowledge our aunt would have."

"That's okay," Frank said. "Just keep at it. I've only distributed half of these so far. A couple of the locals I talked to acted like I was crazy."

Judith nodded. "That's natural. Did they act afraid?"

"Some of them did," Frank replied. "I can't blame them, really. Face it, there are a lot of lunatics on the loose these days. My papa had what you'd now call an urban farm. He sold his vegetables and seasonal foods at a stall in the public market downtown. I helped him out there for years. You ever shop at the market?"

The cousins exchanged discomfited looks. "I hate to say it," Judith confessed, "but I can't remember the last time I went to the public market. I own a B&B and I tell my guests to include it on their sightseeing trips because it's so interesting."

Renie uttered a short laugh. "I think I've only stopped in twice in my life. My husband likes to go there, though. He's originally from Wisconsin. I always think of the market as a tourist attraction, not a shopping place."

Frank grinned at her. "You don't want to see the salmon vendors throw the fish back and forth at each other?"

"I do not," Renie replied with a mock-serious expression. "I find that abusive to the fish."

"You're true natives," Frank declared, standing up. "I've got a couple dozen more flyers to deliver and I don't want to be late to supper. Gina's making her special dish tonight—veal Parmigiano-Reggiano."

Judith rose to show Frank out. "I think you're doing something worthwhile with the flyers. If even one person comes up with something that's important to the homicide investigation, it'll be worth the time and trouble. Does the sheriff's office know you're doing this?"

Frank shook his head. "I don't want them to think I'm meddling. Cops don't like amateurs."

"Ah . . . right," Judith agreed. "I'm sure they know what they're doing. Thanks for stopping by."

"Why," Renie asked, "don't we just sit and wait for everybody to come to us? It'd save on our general wear and tear, not to mention walking a lot."

Judith remained by the door. "I think Auntie Vance keeps busy with all these people dropping in on her. She must be the source of common sense as well as a sounding board for Obsession Shores."

Renie looked ingenuous. "So why not just stay put?"

"For one thing, we have to leave for dinner," Judith said, shrugging into her car coat. "It's going on five. Cocktails await us."

"Of course," Renie said wearily. "Let's hurry so we can get liquored up. I'm starting to go through Pepsi caffeine withdrawal. I may get all calm and you won't recognize me."

"Like that'll ever happen," Judith murmured.

The rain was coming down so hard on their faces that they had to squint to see where they were going. "Tell me when we start having fun," Renie muttered, her boots squelching in the muddy road.

Judith didn't answer, saving her breath to climb the stairs to the Sedgewick house. Dick apparently had seen them coming. He opened the door before Judith could sound the brass knocker.

"Come in, come in," he urged them. "Kind of nasty outside, eh?"

"It's wet," Judith agreed.

"I'll bet you two would like a drink," Dick said, leading the way. "Come on into the living room. Jane's making the hot toddy mix in a vat."

The furnishings were an eclectic mix of old and new: some probably brought from their former home in the city; a few pieces of well-worn antiques perhaps found at a garage sale; a mundane brown tweed sofa purchased from a January clearance. But, Judith discovered, it felt very comfortable when she sat down on it.

"We saw you out and about today," Dick said, settling into a big green-and-beige-striped recliner with so many controls that it looked as if it could launch him into outer space. "In fact, Jane saw you leaving the Friedmans' a while ago. Maybe we should've asked them to dinner, too."

Jane entered the room. "I'm glad you didn't. The pot roast shrank." She placed a tray with four steaming mugs on the coffee table in front of the sofa. "Go for it, girls," she said to Judith and Renie, waiting for them to pick up the mugs before handing one to Dick. She sat in an armchair that matched the sofa. Jane hoisted her mug. "Cheers. Got any good gossip? That's our other hobby."

Judith hesitated about mentioning the scene at the tavern. "Well . . . we've met some of the other—"

"Hold it," Renie broke in. "Tell them about the brawl at the bar and the Bennetts' divorce news."

"You," Judith declared, glaring at her cousin, "are so damned lippy. I might've gotten to that in a more tactful way."

"Tactful?" Jane echoed. "Vance left tact in her baby crib. What's wrong with you? You're her niece. Where did the blunt gene go?"

After heaving a big sigh, Judith unloaded. When she'd finished the account of what had gone on between Brose, Fou-fou, and Kent Logan, Dick and Jane looked at each other.

"Didn't I tell you they were in trouble?" Jane asked her husband. "Suzie Logan already hinted as much. I figured Fou-fou would try to finagle some free legal advice out of Kent. Their split-up is all about money, which Fou-fou thinks Brose should share."

"Right," Dick murmured. "The poor wife's always the victim."

"Did I say," Jane shot back, "that I was on Fou-fou's side? She's an idiot. If she wasn't she'd have never married Brose in the first place."

Dick shrugged. "No argument there. They're both idiots. Except when it comes to making money; Brose had a knack for that. He sold his bun company at the right time before the economy started to go south."

"That was luck," Jane declared. She turned back to Judith and Renie. "Now I suppose Brose has got a scam going with finding priceless coins along the beach. It's always something with him."

Before anyone else could speak, they heard the knocker bang on the door. "I'll get it," Dick said, heaving himself out of the chair.

"What else is new?" Jane asked.

"We met Betsy," Judith replied. "She stopped at the Friedmans'. I'd already seen her earlier, but I don't recall Auntie Vance mentioning her."

"Ohhh . . ." Jane shook her head. "Vance has such a soft heart along with that mouth. I suspect she didn't like thinking about the poor creature. Not that Betsy would care or know. I guess she's always been like that. Very sad." Jane looked up as Dick came back into the living room. "What was that all about?" she asked.

"Frank Leonetti," Dick replied, sitting down again. "He's put together some flyers asking people to come forward with any information about Ernie's murder. Not the worst idea I've ever heard."

"He stopped earlier to give us the flyers," Judith said. "I gather he feels that some people are holding back. Do you think that's true?"

"Probably," Jane replied. "They don't want to get involved with anything that's as sordid as murder. It makes Obsession Shores look bad. Most of the people who live here don't like that. They prefer their Eden to remain without sin."

Judith decided to change the subject. "Has Mel or Sarah mentioned the boat they've seen go out from here after midnight?"

Dick nodded. "Mel did say something a week or so ago. We've never seen it. We're usually asleep by then."

"What," Renie asked, "do you think it could be? It's a bit odd."

He shrugged. "Some night owl testing his boat, maybe over at Scratchit Head. Or making sure the running lights work." He chuckled. "You think it's the killer and he was planning his escape route?"

Judith was mildly surprised. "I never thought of that."

"Just kidding," Dick said, before standing up. "How about a warm-up on the drinks?"

Neither Judith nor Renie had finished more than half of their hot toddies. "Well . . ." Judith began. "Okay."

Dick went off to the kitchen.

"The pot roast should be done in about fifteen minutes," Jane said. "I've got carrots with it along with the potatoes. Oh—I made some biscuits, too." She leaned forward, calling out to Dick. "Hey, lover boy, put those biscuits in the oven. I already turned it on."

"I'm the bad-weather cook," Jane informed the cousins after Dick made a brief, muffled response. "During the good weather, he barbecues a lot. So do about half the people up here. The whole place reeks of barbecue when the sun's out. Some people even barbecue in the rain."

The conversation drifted onto other topics. After eating chocolate sundaes for dessert and sipping small snifters of Galliano, the cousins took their leave around seven thirty. It was still raining, though not as hard as earlier. The lights of Scratchit Head glowed below the big bluff. There was little wind and the only sound besides the patter of rain was an unseen owl hooting in the nearby forest.

"Who'll drop in next?" Renie asked when they got inside the house.

Judith stood by the window, watching the lights of a large ship hove into view. "I wonder if this would be a good time to visit the Quimbys. Maybe Mr. Q. goes to bed early."

"Maybe you're insane," Renie declared. "That's one of your worst ideas yet. They probably wouldn't let us in."

"We can't just sit here. Do you really think more people are going to call on us?"

She'd barely gotten the words out when someone knocked.

"Yes, I do," Renie said, going to the door. For once, she opened it without asking their caller's identity. "Hi, come in, sit down, let me fix you a drink." She turned to Judith. "How's that for being neighborly?"

Katie Glover Blomquist's green eyes looked startled. "I don't want to be a bother, really. I wanted to let you—that is, the Webers—know when and where my father's funeral will be."

Judith decided to intervene to keep Renie from making any more mouthy comments. "Sit," she said, pulling out a kitchen chair. "The Webers probably will still be out of town for the next few days."

Katie waited to respond until she and Judith were both seated. Renie was by the sink, devouring chocolate-coated honeycomb chunks.

"Maybe your relatives will get back in time," Katie said. "Mom decided to hold the funeral at their former church in the city, but the pastor is out of town until next weekend."

"Auntie Vance and Uncle Vince might be home by then," Judith responded. "Renie and I will probably head home Monday morning. We both have to earn our livings."

"What," Katie inquired, glancing at Renie, who was chewing lustily on her candy, "does she do?"

"Besides eat?" Judith retorted. "She's a graphic designer. She uses food instead of paints for her artwork. You'd love her crinkly-french-fry design for the state potato growers association."

"Shuddub!" Renie burbled to her cousin.

Judith ignored her. "How is your mother?" she asked Katie.

"Okay. But I worry about her. She's not used to being alone." Katie fretted at the gold-and-diamond wedding band on her left hand. "I'm taking the boys home tomorrow night because I have to teach at the preschool Monday. My brother, Dave, is stuck in Denver. They're snowed in."

Judith offered an encouraging smile. "Your mother seems strong. Besides, I'm sure the neighbors will come calling on her."

Katie flinched. "I don't know. Mom has never been one to have a lot of company. She likes a quiet life."

"They won't expect her to entertain them. They'll only want to show they care. I imagine some of them have already stopped by."

"Not yet," Katie murmured.

Judith hid her surprise. "Maybe they feel awkward. And they probably know you're there with the boys."

Katie got to her feet. "True. It's that Mom . . . is sort of stand-offish."

Judith also rose. "She was welcoming to Renie and me."

"That's because you found Dad," Katie said, moving to the door. "She wanted to hear what you had to say."

"I see," Judith murmured.

Except that she didn't.

How could you still be hungry?" Judith demanded of Renie after Katie left. "You just had dinner."

"So?" Renie flopped onto the sofa. "I always have room for dark chocolate. What do you make of the antisocial Edna? Do her neighbors know about her plethora of pills and stay away?"

Judith took her place in the overstuffed chair. "That's possible. But it also puts a different light on Ernie, doesn't it?"

Kicking off her shoes, Renie turned thoughtful. "That his social life was dull and thus he had to seek companionship elsewhere?"

"That's one possibility," Judith agreed, "but then there's all the drugs Edna was allegedly taking. Yes, she has some arthritis, but so did Grandma Grover, who sewed, made quilts, and did needlepoint."

"Edna may be a bit of a hypochondriac. That doesn't make her antisocial. Maybe it's just her nature."

"Also possible." Judith fingered her chin. "There's got to be a motive for Ernie's murder. Unlike most of the locals, I doubt it was a random nut." She stood up. "Let's call on the Bendareks. We need to get more background. I'll figure out where they live."

"Check for the house with the busted front door," Renie said, putting on her shoes. "Didn't Zach say he broke it?"

"Yes, but he might've exaggerated. Where's the map of the development? I saw it around here somewhere."

"Look under the island phone book," Renie advised.

Judith found the map and realized she'd noticed it after putting the phone away the previous evening. "The streets don't have signs, but we can figure them out easily enough. The Bendareks are on Salmon Road, one down from here—which, as you know, is Mussel Road. They live three doors south on . . ." She paused, recalling the Webers' address. "This house number is even, so the Bendareks' must be odd."

"He *is* kind of odd," Renie remarked. "Maybe she is, too."

"We'll find out," Judith said, getting her jacket. "Let's go."

The rain had dwindled to a drizzle, though the road was muddy, which made for slow walking, especially for Judith. It took them five minutes to reach their destination.

"The door's fine," Renie noted. "Only a dent or two. Maybe Zach tried opening it with his head and forgot he wasn't wearing a helmet."

Judith pressed the bell. The cousins smiled when they heard a chime playing the University's fight song. After almost a minute, the door was opened by a tall, lanky teenage boy.

"What's up?" he asked with a vaguely curious expression. Or maybe, Judith thought, he was vague by nature. She introduced herself and Renie before asking if the boy's parents were home. "Parents?" he repeated. "You mean Pop and Mop?"

"I . . . guess I do," Judith said.

The teenager loped out of sight.

"Mop?" Renie murmured. "Mrs. Bendarek is a cleaning device?"

"Aren't we all?" Judith responded under her breath.

A beautiful, petite woman with a startling mass of auburn curls came to the door. Maybe, Judith thought, the hair was the reason the boy called her Mop. "Hello," she said in a musical voice. "I'm Becca. Chad told me you're related to some of the neighbors. Come in."

The cousins followed her into a darkened room where Zach and Chad sat on a big sofa watching a pro football game on a big-screen TV.

"Mute it," Becca ordered. "We've got company."

The sound was turned off. Father and son kept their eyes glued to the game. "Have a seat," their hostess offered.

"Where?" Renie asked, obviously unable to see anything except some of the wall behind the television set.

Becca looked flummoxed. "Oh, come into the kitchen. We don't want to interrupt the replay of a *pro football game*." She darted a sharp glance at Zach and Chad, but they didn't notice. Their eyes were still glued to the screen despite the fact that it was a commercial break for a digestive aid. Or maybe, Judith wondered, because they needed it. The kitchen reeked of garlic and onion.

After sitting at a table covered with a purple-and-gold paisley linen cloth, Becca asked if they'd care for some wine. The cousins declined.

"Zach called on us," Judith said. "It's interesting to meet people our relatives have talked about. Have you lived here very long?"

"Three years," Becca replied. "We bought this place ten years ago, but waited to move until our daughter was starting high school. Cece's a freshman at the University now, and Chad's a sophomore at Whoopee High." She leaned forward and lowered her voice. "Did you really find Ernie Glover's corpse? Wasn't that exciting?"

Judith was mildly nonplussed. "Not exactly. I'd describe it as . . . memorable." Given her experience with corpses, it was the best word she could come up with. "Did you know Ernie well?"

"Ernie Well?" Becca looked puzzled. "Oh! You mean did I . . . sort of. He used to come by when his wife was entertaining her boyfriend. He didn't like getting in their way."

"Gee," Renie said, "couldn't he have gone into another room?"

"I suppose," Becca replied, "but he wasn't used to having company. Edna doesn't like people. Except for her lover, of course."

"Dare I ask," Judith inquired, "who the lover was? I mean, *is*."

"Of course you dare," Becca asserted. "The problem is that I don't know his name. Ernie never told us. I didn't feel like prying. It didn't really matter as long as it wasn't Zach." She glanced in the direction of the living room. "At least I don't think it could be Zach. Maybe I should ask him after the game is over."

Judith felt as if her head was spinning, but she tried to refocus. "Did Ernie ever mention anyone he'd quarreled with?"

Becca propped her chin on her hands and looked thoughtful. "Yes," she said after a long pause. "Frank Leonetti, for one. They got into it over Gina."

Judith was surprised. "Frank's wife? Why?"

Becca looked at Judith as if her guest must be simpleminded. "Because Ernie was rumored to be having an affair with Gina. He couldn't keep dropping in on us and the other neighbors all the time. He had to find other interests. Besides, Frank still keeps his hand in."

"In what?" Renie asked.

Becca scowled. "In his food. That is, his business with food. He still owns Leonetti and Sons, so he has to go into the city three or four times a month. Frank's the only son left. The two older brothers died in a house fire a few years ago." She grimaced. "I wouldn't want to have found *their* bodies after they were all crispy. It's a good thing I missed that. I'll bet I'd have thrown up."

"Speaking of that," Renie said, sniffing the air, "what did you make for dinner?"

Becca shrugged. "One of those goulashy things Zach likes. His parents came from the old country." She frowned. "Why are they called that? Aren't all those countries in Europe old?"

"Pretty much," Renie murmured, twitching a bit in the chair.

Judith smiled at Becca. "It's because they've been established so much longer than our country," she explained—and saw her hostess shrug. It was time to take their leave before Renie said or did something she might not regret, but Judith would. "We'll be on our way now," she said, standing up. "Thanks for inviting us in. We enjoy meeting the Webers' neighbors."

Becca remained seated. "The Webers? Oh—you mean Vance and the guy who always falls asleep? Yes, she's very funny. You'd think he'd stay awake just to listen to her. Vance always makes me laugh." Her lovely face turned glum. "I don't get to do that around here very much."

"No kidding," Renie said, already almost out of the kitchen.

"I'm not kidding," Becca replied seriously. "Do come again."

When the cousins were back outside, they saw the fog rolling in, its dampness making the air feel even colder than before they'd stopped at the Bendarek house.

"Can we please go home?" Renie begged as they went up the road.

"Maybe we should," Judith responded. "We might get lost if the fog really settles in. I felt kind of sorry for Becca. So far, it

appears there aren't a lot of women in her peer group. She probably gets bored."

"I gather she doesn't like football," Renie remarked, waving
a hand in front of her as if she could push the fog out of the way.
"She could have an affair like everybody else up here seems to do."

"*Seems* to do is the key," Judith asserted. "It almost sounds like
a hobby, if you believe half of what we hear. I suspect the real
hobby is gossiping about affairs that don't exist. Are we here yet?
I can only see about two feet in front of me."

"Becca would ask you who the two feet belong to," Renie said.
"But I'm me, so I say we're five yards away from getting into the
end zone."

"You should have stayed with Zach and Chad to watch the
repeat of last week's AFC play-off game."

"I know who won," Renie replied. "I saw it the first time. The
Panthers beat the Bears. We're here."

Judith turned to glare at Renie—and bumped into something
that moved. She couldn't help herself. She screamed. A hand
reached out to grab her. Judith screamed again.

Chapter 13

Hey," Kent Logan said, steadying Judith, "I didn't mean to frighten you. Really. You were sitting by Suzie and me at the meeting. Are the Webers back yet? Nobody seems to be home."

Judith tried to ignore Renie, who was laughing as she led the way up the steps. "Auntie Vance and Uncle Vince probably won't be back from Nebraska for several days," Judith explained as she cautiously started up the stairs to the deck. "Her sister in Beatrice had shoulder surgery. We came up here mainly to cast their proxy vote at the meeting, but we're staying through the weekend."

"Oh." Kent didn't speak again until the lock was opened and the trio went inside. "I wanted Vance to notarize something for me. She's done it before."

"I didn't know that," Judith admitted, shrugging out of her car coat. "That is, it makes sense, since she retired as a legal secretary."

"Right," Kent said. "I don't suppose either of you is a notary?"

"Not even close," Renie declared, before sinking onto the sofa. "We're retired hookers. Or maybe just tired, being kind of old to—"

"Stop!" Judith yelled. She looked at Kent. "Pay no attention to her. Renie has a bad habit of saying really stupid things that are *not* true."

"And you don't?" Renie shot back, taking off her shoes.

Kent, however, was chuckling. "I can see that you're both related to Vance. She's got quite a mouth on her, too. Hey, I'm sorry to have bothered you." He started to turn around, then stopped. "I just remembered—weren't you at the pub this afternoon?"

"We were," Judith replied, noticing that Kent's left cheek looked faintly bruised. "That was quite a row. Do you need witnesses? We didn't see all of it, to be honest."

"For a change," Renie called from the sofa. "Come on, coz, offer Kent a drink like other people around here do. We *are* trying to fit in."

"Okay," Judith said. "Would you—"

But Kent put up a hand. "No, thanks, but I'll sit for a minute. It's kind of cozy in here."

Judith gestured at the recliner. She shoved Renie a bit to make room on the sofa and posed a question for Kent. "Do you have Auntie Vance do other legal secretarial work for you?"

"Once in a while, when I don't have time to go into the city to my former law firm," Kent replied. "My longtime secretary still works there, so I usually ask for her help. But Vance is very efficient. She likes to keep busy, too. Your aunt isn't the type to just sit and vegetate."

"True," Judith agreed. "That's what bothers me about some of the other people we've met so far. Or at least have heard about. They seem to be merely passing the time. Many of them aren't that old—at least from my point of view. Even the Johnsons have their hobbies."

Kent smiled. "You mean like their collections?"

"You mean of coins?" Judith asked.

"Coins, stamps, books, clocks," Kent replied. "Their house is stuffed with various items. You'd think that at their age, they'd want to unload some of it. I suppose they figure that after they're gone, their daughter and her husband can do it."

Judith nodded. "They probably enjoy the things they've collected. Do their children live nearby?"

Kent looked faintly puzzled. "I forgot you don't know most of these people. Their only daughter is Hilda, Hank Hilderschmidt's wife."

Renie finally found her voice and looked at Judith. "Didn't the Sedgewicks tell us she collected stuff off the beach?"

Judith tried to remember the conversation. "Maybe—or they alluded to it when they talked about her going on long walks."

"Genetics, maybe," Kent remarked. "Hilda does spend a lot of time on the beach. She isn't much for socializing."

"Neither is Edna Glover," Renie said. "What's with the women up here? They don't like people?"

Kent made a face. "I don't want to tell tales, but this is fact. The Hilderschmidts' son was killed in the line of duty a few years ago. I understand Hilda hasn't been the same since."

"How sad," Judith murmured. "Was he in the service or law enforcement?"

Kent frowned, apparently trying to think. "He wasn't in the military, so I assume he was with the city's police department. I don't remember seeing his death in the news, but it might've happened when Suzie and I were abroad. We try to get away every year for at least a month. Last fall we were in China."

"My husband's retired from the police force," Judith said. "I wonder if he knew their son. The name doesn't ring a bell. Of course he could've been with the county sheriff's department."

"That could be," Kent allowed. "I don't really know." He stood up and glanced outside. "I'd better go home. The fog's getting thicker. I don't want to end up in the woods instead of at my house." He paused as Judith rose to walk him to the door. "You two should come to dinner if you stay on past the weekend."

"Thanks," Judith said, "but we'll probably head home Monday morning. We both have jobs."

"Right," Renie called from the sofa. "Got to get back to working those streets with all the sleazy motels. Now you know why I always take off my shoes when I sit down."

Kent grinned. "She's as bad as Vance. Not as profane, though."

"Give her time," Judith muttered. "She's not as old either."

Kent exited chuckling.

"I like him," Renie said, after Judith sat down in the over-stuffed chair. "I hope he didn't kill Ernie."

"I hope so, too," Judith agreed. "Unfortunately, we've met some likable killers along the way."

"Hey—I know a good game—'Categorize the Killers.' Let's start with Crazy as a Bedbug and work our way up to Jolly as Old Saint Nick."

"Stop, you're kill . . . never mind. So the Johnsons are related to the Hilderschmidts. I wonder how many other Obsession Shores people are intertwined."

"Literally?"

"No, but that's another angle. So to speak." Judith leaned back to rest her head against the chair's cushioned back. "Motive—I can't find one that works very well. Even a love triangle involving jealousy doesn't seem to fit up here. Is that because I think older people need something more serious than infidelity in order to commit murder? If so, what could it be?"

"Anger?" Renie suggested.

Judith shook her head. "That is, not a spontaneous outburst. The murder must be premeditated if the weapon was as long as Jacobson indicated. Who'd carry a knife that big onto the beach this time of year?"

"A fisherman? I think they can go for blackmouth and chum here during the winter."

Judith scowled. "Why didn't our husbands do that instead of going all the way to New Zealand? We could've saved a ton of money."

"Because they didn't want to find a corpse on the beach?" Renie retorted. "Get over it. They deserve an adventure of their own. I didn't dare tell Mom where Bill was going. She'd have passed out. You never told me how Aunt Gert reacted."

Judith groaned. "I was so mad about the whole thing that I blurted out the truth. She didn't believe me and insisted that even Needle Noggin—as she referred to Joe on that occasion—wasn't that stupid."

Renie laughed. "So where does your mother think he is?"

"I don't know," Judith replied. "She probably hopes he's in the hospital with terminal spots. Or in prison for impersonating a retired police detective. I've never figured out if she believed Joe was a cop in the first place. She insisted he was another unemployed bum like Dan." Her dark eyes strayed to the phone on the kitchen counter. "I wonder if I should call Mother to see how she's getting along."

"She always gets along with Arlene and Carl," Renie declared. "I'm not calling Mom. In fact, I told her that Auntie Vance and Uncle Vince had their phone disconnected for the time they'd be gone."

Judith shook her head in disapproval. "You're awful. Doesn't Aunt Deb know you have a cell phone?"

"She sure doesn't," Renie said. "When I use it, I always tell her I'm calling from a pay phone and I can only talk for three minutes. You know how much my mother likes to yak on the phone."

Judith nodded. "I understand. But your mother doesn't live in your backyard."

"So? Your mother doesn't talk nonstop to you even in person."

"Aunt Deb doesn't tell you you're an imbecile," Judith countered.

"You know Aunt Gert doesn't mean it."

"I still don't enjoy hearing it."

"It's better than having my mother insist I wear an undershirt under my designer cocktail clothes during the cooler months— like June."

Judith couldn't resist. "Have you ever tried to find a designer undershirt?"

Renie laughed. "Damn, I should. And then flaunt the price tag to make Mom pretend she's going to faint." She suddenly tensed. "What was that noise?"

"What noise? I can't hear anything with you blabbing."

Renie put a finger to her lips. Judith sat up in the chair. At first, she couldn't hear anything. Then, as she was about to speak, a soft, muffled, almost catlike sound could be heard somewhere outside.

"A kitten?" she said softly.

Renie shook her head.

The sound continued. Judith thought it came from near the window behind her. All she could see was fog. Getting up, she started for the door. Renie hopped off the sofa to join her. Both cousins stood in motionless silence, but couldn't hear anything except each other's anxious breathing.

"Dare we open the door?" Judith whispered.

"Let me grab a weapon and stand behind it," Renie whispered back. She went around to the other side of the counter and got out Auntie Vance's rolling pin. "Classic female defense," she murmured. "I feel like a cliché."

Judith cautiously unlocked the door and opened it an inch at a time. The fog obscured her view beyond a couple of feet. Taking tentative steps toward the stairs, she could see only the first two steps—and more fog. She turned around, noticing that Renie now stood in the doorway, rolling pin at the ready. Judith kept moving slowly in the direction of the picture window. She gave a start as she heard the mewing sound nearby. Motioning to Renie and moving one step at a time, she saw what looked like a bundle of clothes on the deck just below the picture window's sill. The bundle moved slightly—and mewed again.

Judith got close enough to recognize strands of fair hair and the strap of a canvas bag. "It's Betsy Quimby!" Judith gasped. "Help me get her inside. She must be sick."

"Take it easy," Renie said, looking over her cousin's shoulder. "She may have broken something. I'll call Dick. Maybe he knows first aid or somebody who does."

Judith nodded. "I'll grab a blanket to put over her. It's chilly."

The cousins hurried back inside. Renie got out her cell while Judith went into the master bedroom to fetch an afghan that was draped over Grandpa and Grandma Grover's old rocking chair. By the time she got back to the deck, the catlike sound had changed to a whimper.

"Betsy," Judith said gently, "are you hurt?"

The bundle moved enough so that Judith could see two wide blue eyes looking out from under a rumpled beige head scarf. The only answer was a moan. Or at least that was what it sounded like. But Betsy repeated it more loudly. "Va . . ."

"Vance?" Judith said.

Betsy gave what Judith took for a nod of assent and closed her eyes. For the first time since coming back to the deck, Judith realized Renie was at her side. "Dick's on the way. He wanted to call 911, but I told him to wait. Was that wrong of me?"

Judith grimaced. "I don't know." She turned at the sound of footsteps. Two sets, in fact. When Dick appeared at the top of the steps, his wife was right behind him.

"Betsy!" Jane cried, rushing past her husband and hurrying to the stricken woman. "Is it one of your bad dreams?"

Betsy opened her eyes, but stared wordlessly at Jane.

"Is it a *dream*?" Jane asked again, emphasizing the last word.

Suddenly Betsy's huddled form went limp. Jane turned to the cousins. "I think she's okay. This often happens. We found her once on the beach last summer when the tide was coming in. Scary." She moved out of the way. "Can you carry her inside, Dick? I'll grab the afghan."

"Hell, I've carried her from the beach twice now. Remember when I found her in Vince's old boat?" Dick said. "I think she's passed out. She usually does after these spells. Better get the brandy, girls," he added, leaning down to pick up Betsy. "Oof! Move it! And don't even think about whacking me with that rolling pin, Renie."

The cousins and Jane plastered themselves against the deck's railing as Dick carried Betsy into the house. "He's the brawn," his wife muttered, "but I'm the brains. Hey, lover boy," she called after they were back inside, "how's your hernia?"

"You're damned lucky I don't have one by now," Dick shot back while Judith arranged the afghan around Betsy, who seemed to be sleeping peacefully. "Are you forgetting I had to carry you up to our house after you trashed yourself at last year's St. Paddy's Day picnic? Hell, we aren't even Irish."

Judith spoke up before the Sedgewicks could continue their good-natured banter. "Are you certain we shouldn't call 911? How do we know she didn't fall and do some serious damage before she went into her dreamlike state?"

Dick shrugged. "She never has before. If she'd broken something, how did she get up the stairs without yelling for help?"

"Good point," Judith conceded. "I'm always worried if a B&B guest has some sort of accident."

"Like getting murdered," Renie said, twirling the rolling pin. "Hey, coz, none of your previous corpses has been done in by one of these."

Jane and Dick exchanged puzzled glances. "What," Jane asked, "do you mean by plural 'corpses'? Vance has mentioned you've had some weird adventures, but I assumed she was joking—as usual."

"She was," Judith said sharply with a warning look at Renie. "Having married a police detective, I've heard about a lot of his cases."

For once, Renie kept her mouth shut and returned the rolling pin to the kitchen drawer. The Sedgewicks sat down at the kitchen table. Even if Betsy didn't need a drink, they apparently did. Judith headed for the liquor cabinet.

"Just a short one," Jane called to her. "Dick wants to see the end of the Texas-Oklahoma basketball game."

"Hell, it's probably over by now," Dick said, then turned to his wife. "But haven't you got one of your *Real Housewives* on tonight?"

Jane shook her head. "That's tomorrow. It's all glitz and unrealistic. Half-assed, as Vance would say. They should do one on 'The Real Housewives of Obsession Shores.' Maybe we could figure out if one of them did in poor Ernie."

Judith handed two medium-size snifters of brandy to her guests. "You think it was a woman?" she asked.

Jane shrugged. "Why not? This is an equal-opportunity country."

"Damn!" Dick exclaimed. "I didn't know that. Now I don't dare turn my back on you, hot lips. You might do me in."

Jane shot him an arch look. Judith retrieved the other two brandy snifters and sat down. Renie, however, had remained in the living room. Before anyone could speak again, she called out to the others.

"Hey, guess what's in Betsy's bag?"

"The knife?" Judith asked, trying to stifle her excitement.

"No," Renie replied, sitting down before removing several pill bottles from the canvas bag. "Check out the labels."

Everyone kept quiet while Judith examined each of the almost two dozen containers. "Xanax for Edna Glover? Percoset for Mel Friedman? Diphenhydramine for Suzie Logan? Methocarbamol for Gina Leonetti? Vicodin for Hilda Hilderschmidt?" She stopped reading off the prescription labels. "How did Betsy get hold of all these meds?"

Jane sighed. "I suppose she sneaked into houses and stole them. I can see through some of those bottles and they look like there are still plenty of pills inside. How recent are the dates?"

Renie had picked up a couple of the meds. "This Plavix for Fou-fou Bennett is dated January nineteenth," she said. "The other one's from January tenth, Coumadin for Hank Hilderschmidt."

"Here's one for Brose Bennett," Judith noted. "Naproxen, January sixteenth. These are all recent, none going back beyond the first week of this month. Have you two missed any of your medications?"

The Sedgewicks exchanged glances. "Not lately," Dick finally replied. "I thought I'd mislaid my ibuprofen after Christmas, but figured I'd never picked it up the last time it was reordered. I don't need it very often. My gorgeous bitter half hasn't given me a migraine lately."

Jane sneered at her husband. "I only got crabby because I'd run out of my Premarin and wasn't sleeping well." Her eyes widened. "No wonder my doctor's nurse was reluctant to renew it when I called. She told me I should have another month's supply, but I couldn't find the bottle. I assumed I'd tossed it."

"Why," Dick murmured, glancing in the direction of the sofa, "would Betsy steal meds? She's apparently not taking them. The bottles all look fairly full."

"Maybe," Judith suggested, "she only takes one or two when the whim strikes her. Betsy must've pinched this stuff quite recently. Do you know if she's on medication?"

"I'd guess she may be," Jane replied. "But I've no idea what it is."

Renie had checked out the rest of the bottles. "It seems she never took more than one prescription from each person. Are there any medical professionals living in Obsession Shores?"

"Virgil Payne," Dick said. "He and Greta spend their winters in Mexico. The retired pharmacist Will Lindquist and his wife, Amy, are in Palm Springs and have been since just after Christmas."

Judith had checked the names of the prescribing doctors. Only three of the bottles had been ordered by the same physician. "Is Dr. Emil Klontz on the island?"

"Yes, he's in Langton," Jane replied. "That's who we see since we moved up here permanently. Your aunt and uncle kept their doctor . . ." She stopped, as all eyes turned to the sofa where Betsy was calling Vance's name. "Let me take care of this," Jane murmured, getting up and going into the living room.

Dick downed the last of his brandy. "Jane and I'd better take Betsy home. If she'll let us." He rose and joined his wife by the sofa.

"No!" Betsy cried. "I want Vance!" Jane started to explain that Vance was on a trip, but Betsy shook her fists and yelled, "No, no, no!"

The cousins got up to join the Sedgewicks. For some reason, Betsy stopped yelling. "Betsy," Judith said calmly, "would you like to talk to Vance on the phone tomorrow?"

Betsy frowned. "Why can't I see her?"

"She and Vince are taking care of Vance's sister, Ellen, who hurt her shoulder. You know how Vance likes to take care of people, right?"

Betsy nodded. "I like Vance. I like Vince, too, but he sleeps a lot. Vance makes soup for me." She looked around the sofa and the floor. "Where's my kit?"

"Your bag?" Jane said.

Betsy nodded. "It's gone." Her face crumpled. "They hid it, didn't they? They hate it when I collect things."

Renie hurried to fetch the canvas bag from the table. "Here. You left this on the deck."

Betsy snatched the bag out of Renie's hand and looked inside. "Oh, good," she said. "You got rid of the nasty stuff for me. Thank you."

She struggled trying to stand up, but Dick helped her. "It's getting late," he said. "Jane and I'll walk you home. That fog's pretty bad."

"I like the fog," Betsy asserted. "I can find my way."

Jane started to speak, but Betsy shook her head. "Hush. No talking in the fog. Voices carry. So do ghosts. Don't move. Your shadows can't follow me in the fog."

Judith felt mesmerized, but found her voice just as Betsy reached the door. "Let me help with the lock," she said. "It's tricky."

Betsy wagged a thin finger. "No tricks. I can walk through walls." To prove it—or not—she took another step and bumped against the door. "Sometimes I can," she murmured. "Tell whoever's outside to stop leaning against it or I won't be able to go home. I'm tired now, you see."

"I'll have to open the door to do that," Judith said. "Okay?"

Betsy nodded. As soon as the door opened less than halfway, their frail, wraithlike guest scooted outside. Jane and Dick had put on their jackets. "We'll see she gets home okay," he said. "Thanks for the brandy." The Sedgewicks made their exit.

"Gosh," Renie said as Judith locked the door behind them, "we've got our choice of party pills. How about a Vicodin high?"

"I feel high already," Judith replied, going over to the table where Renie was standing. "Or at least on another planet. I suppose we should return all this stuff to their owners tomorrow."

"Another open season on grilling," Renie remarked. "I'll put these pills in my tote bag. How do we explain where we found them?"

"I'll think of something," Judith muttered. "Now I'm trying to figure out what Betsy meant when she said we got rid of the nasty stuff for *her*. Did she mean we saved her the trouble of disposing it or of returning it? Or was she implying that the prescriptions were *for* her?"

"How would I know?" Renie retrieved the tote bag she'd stored under the kitchen counter. "Betsy may not know what she means. I noticed she referred to the canvas bag as a kit—as in doctor's kit, I presume. How about those ghosts? Who does she think she sees? Her mother, maybe?"

"I've no idea. If she's taking medication, she could be seeing Elvis." Judith paused, watching Renie stash the bottles in her tote. "I think I'll call the Sedgewicks in a few minutes to see what happened when they took Betsy home. The Quimby house isn't far from here, if I remember its location from the Obsession Shores map." She walked over to the window. "It's still socked in out there. I assume you'll want to have breakfast in Langton after Mass tomorrow."

"Damned straight," Renie shot back. "If I have to get up at nine, I want a reward of buttermilk pancakes, hamburger steak and eggs, served by an aging waitress with a bad perm and rubber-soled shoes."

"You are such a brat," Judith said, though without malice.

"Hey," Renie responded, folding up the afghan before she collapsed onto the sofa, "it's not my fault you have to get up early every morning to feed your paying guests. I'm usually still working while you're sound asleep. I'm more creative after it gets dark."

Judith merely shrugged. "I'm going to call to see what happened with Jane and Dick." She picked up the phone and dialed, already having memorized their number. Jane answered on the third ring.

"I hate to be a pest," Judith said, "but did you have any problems taking Betsy home?"

"Are you kidding?" Jane retorted. "We never found her after we left the deck. She disappeared as if she was invisible. Or a ghost."

Chapter 14

Renie was unmoved by the news of Betsy's disappearance. "Betsy can't get lost. Even if she did, she seems capable of sneaking into other people's houses to steal their meds."

"You have a point," Judith said, putting the brandy snifters in the dishwasher. "She's cunning. I wish Auntie Vance had told us about her. It's obvious that she bonded with Betsy."

"Ha!" Renie shifted around on the sofa. "Now that I think it through, you know our aunt has a perverted sense of humor. I'll bet she purposely didn't tell us because she thought it'd be funny to let us find out for ourselves—and deal with it."

Judith sat down in the overstuffed chair. "True. I've decided not to call her tomorrow."

"Revenge for not warning us about Betsy?"

"No." Judith made a face. "Auntie Vance is tough, but she's softhearted. She'd worry about putting us in danger. Even if I didn't tell her about Ernie getting killed, she'd sense something was up. Worse yet, she'd tell Aunt Ellen, who'd want to get involved despite being in postsurgery mode. You know what a take-charge kind of person she is."

Renie nodded. "Even from over a thousand miles away in Beatrice. But she's sharp. You have to admit that. And she's goodhearted, too."

Judith laughed. "That could be said about most of the women in our family." She turned to look out the window. "The fog's still thick. I guess there's no point in watching for the mystery boat tonight."

"Good," Renie said. "If I'm getting up early, I'm going to bed early."

"Now?" Judith asked.

Renie checked her watch. "No, but maybe around eleven. And no to playing cribbage. Let's watch an old movie on TV."

Judith found the *TV Guide* in the end table by her chair. "*Saving Private Ryan* started at nine."

"And he'll be saved without me watching—again. Bill has shown the DVD eight times. Skip World War Two movies. I'm really sick of Hitler. I've gotten so I don't even like certain parts of Asia and the South Pacific anymore. I don't want to see anybody in military uniform. Got it?"

"Guess I won't mention that *Stars and Stripes Forever* comes on at ten," Judith murmured.

"Good. I've nothing against John Philip Sousa, but I'm not in the mood to . . ." Renie frowned. "Didn't we see that one together at the old Poseidon Theater? We had to leave before it ended because some pervert grabbed your leg."

"Yes, but we went up to the balcony and watched the rest of it from there. I think you discouraged him by shoving your empty popcorn box down over his head."

"Oh—right, I forgot that part."

"You always were protective of me," Judith said with a fond smile.

"You've always needed protecting," Renie countered. "You're too kindhearted for your own good. Not to mention that your search for truth and justice has almost gotten us killed a few times."

"People get killed in vehicular accidents every day," Judith responded matter-of-factly, still scanning the TV listings. "The other movies are *Gladiator, The Patriot,* and *Heavy Metal.*"

"*Patriot* has uniforms, so does *Gladiator*—sort of. It certainly has weaponry, and I'm too old for heavy-metal bands."

"It's not about music," Judith asserted. "It's sci-fi."

Renie buried her head in a sofa cushion. "I loathe sci-fi! I'd rather play cribbage!"

Judith sighed. "Let's see if there's anything on PBS. I didn't look at their schedule because it's often science." She studied the listings. "How do you feel about coal?"

"Find the crib board," Renie said, her voice muffled by the cushion.

Judith got out of the chair. "Auntie Vance keeps her playing cards and games in the china closet. Remember playing Scrabble with her and how she always beat the stuffing out of us?"

Renie sat up. "I sure do. She ruled over all those triple-letter and triple-word squares. I got so frustrated once that I almost swallowed the Q tile just so she couldn't get it."

Judith had found the games in the drawer. "Here's Scrabble. Want to try it without the unfair advantage of playing against our aunt?"

"Why not?" Renie responded, sitting up. "We'll have to put it on . . ." She stopped as a knock sounded on the door. "Now what?" Getting off the sofa, she hurried to ask the identity of their latest visitor.

"Jacobson," the deputy said. "Open up."

Judith set the game on the end table before joining Renie. Jacobson entered, wearing civilian clothes. He shut the door, but remained standing.

"When," he asked somberly, "did you last see Betsy Quimby?"

"Nine-ish," Judith replied. "Why? Has something happened to her?"

"She's missing," the officer replied in a tense voice. "It's after ten. According to her sister-in-law, she never stays out past nine, despite not owning a watch. Apparently, she's afraid a ghost will get her."

Judith was puzzled. "How did you know she was here?" Before Jacobson could answer, she asked if he'd like to sit down.

"Well . . ." He grimaced. "Nan Quimby thought she called on your aunt and uncle quite often. A patrol officer should be showing up in a few minutes. Saturday nights are always busy for us, especially with this fog. I'm off duty, of course."

They sat down at the kitchen table. "If," Renie said, "you're not official, do you want a drink? We understand that's the first question anybody asks around here."

The deputy's expression was wry. "I'd like to accept, but I won't. Thanks anyway." He turned to Judith. "I did some checking earlier tonight. I knew there was something unusual about you. You're FASTO."

Judith groaned and slumped in her chair. "Damn! I do not advertise that nor do I endorse the stupid website."

"Obviously not," Jacobson said with a slight smile. "But I wish I'd known that before. Ordinarily, so-called amateur sleuths are highly unreliable, but your résumé is impressive. It explains why you knew what kind of questions to ask about the corpse. Even a cop's wife might not do that. I noted that your last investigation was a cold case."

"I got it wrong," Judith declared.

"Your fans believe you were so close as to be right," he pointed out. "I gather it was some kind of coconspiracy."

"Skip the history," Judith said. "Let's stick to current events."

Jacobson seemed to relax a bit. "In the past month, Betsy has visited your aunt and uncle frequently."

Renie was frowning. "Why so often lately? We figure Betsy's been hanging out here for some time."

The officer shook his head. "Betsy has spent several long periods in various institutions. I was informed that she's only been back at the family home since early November. I get the impression—brief as it was—that the other Quimbys consider her an embarrassment."

"Ha!" Renie exclaimed. "And Quentin Quimby *isn't* an embarrassment? We've seen him in public. He's gruesome."

"And rich," Jacobson noted drily. "The wealthy prefer 'eccentric.' If Quimby didn't have so much clout, I wouldn't be here when I'm officially off duty." He shrugged. "So how was Betsy when she left an hour ago?"

"She had one of her spells," Judith replied, then explained what had happened before Betsy disappeared into the fog. "That's it. She hasn't been back, unless you saw her crawling around on the deck."

The lieutenant shook his head. "I didn't. It's almost impossible to find anybody with the weather so socked in."

"What," Judith inquired, "did you mean about a ghost getting her?"

"Betsy has talked to her family about a ghost she's seen on the beach late at night. That's why she always comes back home by nine. She told them the ghost doesn't walk until much later." He shrugged again. "That's not a great deal of help in trying to find her."

"But," Judith said, "it does mean she sees someone in the late evening. Not that it couldn't be just another person."

Jacobson stood up. "It's hard enough to get straight answers out of sane people, let alone the mentally unbalanced. I'd better see if the patrol is here. We have to search for Betsy."

Judith followed him to the door. "If we hear or see anything, we'll let you know. Is there another number where we can reach you directly?"

"Yes." He waited for Judith to grab a pen and a notepad off the counter before giving her his cell phone information. "I'll be in touch," he said as he went out the door.

Judith clenched her fists. "Darn! Now Jacobson knows about my annoying habit of finding dead bodies!"

"But you finally stopped biting your nails," Renie said.

"True." Judith retrieved the Scrabble game and put it on the kitchen table. "Let's compete with mere words. I need to clear my brain. If you get the Q, you can't spell out 'Quimby.' It's not in the dictionary."

"Fair enough. I've got a total of thirteen points on my tiles. Unlucky, I'm sure. How many have you got?"

"Fourteen," Judith replied. "I go first."

Shortly before eleven, Renie had won by eighteen points. Judith asked if her cousin really was going to bed early.

"I need to settle down for a bit," Renie replied. "Have you managed to rid your brain of murder for the rest of the night?"

"I might have if you hadn't used the words 'corpses' and 'knifed.'"

"You put in 'coins,' 'surf,' and 'tides,'" Renie countered.

Judith sighed. "Tomorrow we're going to call on the Quimbys if only to find out if Betsy has been found. I'd worry if I didn't think that somewhere in her scrambled brain she has a survival instinct."

"Maybe she's watching football with the Bendarek males," Renie suggested. "Do you know which house belongs to the Quimbys?"

"I can find it on the development map. It can't be anything lavish. Everything here is fairly modest, at least by city standards. I assume that's due to Quimby's restrictions on lot sizes and view obstructions. I won't criticize him about any of that."

"I *have* noticed a few ultramodern places sprinkled around," Renie said, putting the game pieces in the box. I wonder if there are any undeveloped lots left. It's hard to tell from the beach because of the surrounding trees. Quimby may own some of the forest land."

Judith stood up. "I noticed what could be an empty lot right above the beach off to the right. Maybe that's one of the lots where potential buyers discovered the ground didn't perc. I'm going in the bathroom to get ready for bed. I hate to turn off the heat. It feels kind of cold and drafty in here. Have you noticed that in the last half hour?"

"No," Renie replied, "but you've been sitting by the hall door. That might make a difference."

"True," Judith agreed as she headed out of the kitchen area.

Fifteen minutes later, she returned to the living room, where Renie was reading a copy of *National Geographic*. She grinned when she saw Judith. "This issue has a space exploration article in it," Renie said. "Uncle Vince must love it. You know how keen he's always been on 'little green men from outer space.'"

Judith laughed. "Oh, yes. He's convinced they exist. I'll let you turn the heat down. It still felt drafty in the hall. I'll wake you at nine. I'm aware that you're clueless when it comes to setting an alarm clock."

"You're right about that," Renie conceded. "Sleep well."

Judith bade her cousin good night and headed into the master bedroom. As soon as she turned on the light, she gasped—and raced back into the living room.

"Coz!" she gasped, trying to keep her voice down. "Betsy's asleep on Auntie Vance and Uncle Vince's bed!"

Renie's jaw dropped. "You're kidding! No," she went on quickly, "of course you're not. Are you sure she's asleep and not . . . ah . . ."

"She's breathing," Judith said. "I turned on the lamp just inside the door so I could see movement. Come look. I wonder how she got in."

The cousins tiptoed to the bedroom door. Renie paused before quietly walking past the bed. Judith watched as her cousin approached the curtained window by the dressing table. Renie pushed the curtains aside—and closed the window before rejoining Judith.

"No wonder you felt a draft," Renie whispered. "Better check your meds to see if she pinched any of them. Now what do we do?"

"Call Jacobson. We'll let him tell the Quimbys. Unless we—"

"No!" Renie interrupted without raising her voice. "We're not going out in this fog. Let the law handle it. It does, alas, give you a perfect opening to visit the Quimbys tomorrow."

The cousins returned to the kitchen, where Judith had left the deputy's cell number. "I suppose," she said, dialing the phone, "he may be home by now. I wouldn't blame . . . Lieutenant? This is Judith Flynn. Betsy's sleeping in the Webers' bed. Where are you?"

A heavy sigh was heard at the other end. "Halfway home, but I'll turn around. It'll only take ten minutes." He rang off.

Judith passed the message on to Renie. "Maybe we should keep an eye on Betsy. She obviously can move quietly, like a—"

"Ghost?" Renie broke in. "You take watch duty. Maybe you can change into your bedclothes without waking her up. I'll go into the bathroom, but keep the door open, okay?"

Judith returned to the hall, but hesitated before entering the bedroom. Betsy was still sound asleep. Approaching quietly, Judith noted she had a faint smile on her thin lips and she was clutching the canvas bag to her breast. It appeared to be empty. Judith checked the three bottles of meds on the little side table. They seemed untouched. Turning around, she saw Renie in the doorway, attired in her tiger-striped nighttime ensemble.

"Good grief," Judith whispered after going back into the hall, "did you have to put on your . . . animalwear?"

Renie looked affronted. "You prefer me to show up in my underwear?"

"Of course not," Judith retorted, "but couldn't you have waited?"

"For what? Tigers don't change their stripes and Renies don't bring spare sets of nightclothes on a weekend trip."

"You're lucky if Jacobson doesn't call the World Wildlife Federation," Judith said, returning to the kitchen.

A knock sounded at the door. Renie rushed over to do the unlocking honors. The deputy's usually impassive face looked startled.

"What's wrong?" Renie asked with a scowl. "You got something against cats?"

"Only the ones who walk on two feet," he replied stoically. "Which way is the bedroom?"

To avoid a flippant remark from Renie, Judith answered the question. The deputy kept going. Judith followed Jacobson at a discreet distance. He walked to the bed, stood for a moment with fists on hips, then leaned down to softly call Betsy's name. She shifted slightly under the comforter, but didn't react. The deputy returned to the hall.

"She's really out of it," he said. "I've only seen her once before, two or three years ago, when she climbed a utility pole and wouldn't come down. Betsy may not remember me, but I don't want to scare her."

"You're not in uniform," Judith pointed out. "If she's like most people—even normal people—she may not recognize you in regular clothes."

"Hey, Lieutenant," Renie said from the kitchen doorway, "want to put on my peignoir?"

"No thanks," he replied quietly, barely glancing at her before heading out of the hall via the door to the living room. "Here's the thing," he went on in his normal voice. "If she's on medication, she probably should be allowed to sleep until she wakes up on her own. Disturbing her now could have some ugly results."

Renie had also entered the living room. "Uglier than coz having to sleep on the sofa?"

Judith made a face at her cousin. "The spare room has a double bed. I can sleep with you. Can you try *not* to chew gum?"

"I doubt it," Renie replied. "That's what puts me to sleep. Maybe Uncle Vince has some earplugs. He could use them when Auntie Vance gets mad." She looked at Jacobson. "Do the Quimbys know she's here? What happens if she wakes up and leaves?"

The officer nodded. "Quincy—the son—advised against startling Betsy. In fact, he thinks she can be dangerous."

"Oh, great!" Renie twirled around in a flurry of stripes. "You're going to leave us alone with a violent crazy person?"

"No," he said in a weary voice. "I'll sleep on the sofa."

Judith looked at Renie. "I don't see that we have much choice, coz." Her gaze shifted to Jacobson. "Do you think I'll wake her up if I grab my own nightgown and robe?"

He shook his head. "She seems to be in a fairly deep sleep."

"Okay," Judith said. "I'll do that now. Help yourself to whatever you need, Lieutenant. One of those pillows on the sofa ought to be okay. I'll grab a couple of blankets from the hall linen closet. Oh—there's the afghan, too." She headed back to the master bedroom.

Renie gave the deputy a bleak glance, mumbled "good night," and went off toward the spare room. Judith joined her a few minutes later.

"At least," she said as Renie burrowed under the covers, "we have police protection tonight."

"You have that every night," Renie responded. "You're married to a cop. Where does Joe keep his weapon at night?"

"Under the mattress," Judith replied. "Just like your father did despite your mother worrying it'd go off and shoot her in the rear end."

"You know how Mom fusses," Renie said, reaching for a package of Big Red chewing gum. "It's a wonder she ever slept at night."

Judith narrowed her eyes at Renie. "You're not really going to chew that gum, are you?"

Renie hesitated. "How about a three-piece limit?"

"None."

"Two?"

"No."

"One?"

Judith pondered the offer. "Okay. Good night." She rolled over and turned off the lamp on the nightstand. To her surprise, Renie kept her word. Judith fell asleep almost immediately.

She wasn't sure what awakened her in the dead of night. Maybe it was a sound, but as her sleepy eyes focused on the illuminated clock, she saw it was 5:10. Judith wondered if Jacobson and Betsy were still on the premises. And suddenly she remembered that she'd forgotten to take her nighttime pills. She slipped out of bed and tiptoed into the hall. Passing the bathroom, she saw a form just outside the master bedroom. *It has to be Betsy,* she thought, backpedaling to reach the bathroom light switch.

The sudden brightness made Judith blink. When she focused her eyes to look straight ahead, she saw Betsy standing four feet away. Her right hand held a very sharp knife.

Chapter 15

Judith sucked in her breath. "Betsy," she said, hoping her voice sounded calmer than she felt, "are you hungry?"

Betsy's fingers tightened around the knife's black handle. She stared at Judith for what seemed like a very long time.

"Yes," she finally said. "I want some soup. Please." Betsy looked at Judith as if she expected something that might have been hope.

"Okay," Judith said. "Let me get my robe. You can sit down at the kitchen table. I'll turn on the light for you."

Betsy put the knife inside her jacket. Judith hurried into the spare bedroom, where Renie apparently was still asleep. She grabbed her robe, put it on, and returned to the kitchen. She could hear Jacobson stirring on the sofa.

"I have a friend sleeping here tonight," Judith said, going to the cupboard to find some soup. "Maybe he's hungry, too."

"Who is it?" Betsy asked in a guileless voice.

"His name is Erik. He's a very kind man." Judith took out a can of beef vegetable soup, found a small kettle, and turned on the stove. "You may know him. He's been here before," she continued as she opened the can and poured its contents into the kettle.

"Erik." Betsy mused on the name. "Kind man. Is he married to . . . Suzie?"

"No," Judith replied, getting out some soda crackers, a bowl, and a soup spoon. "Suzie is married to Kent."

Betsy was silent for a moment. "My brother likes Kent." She frowned. "Maybe Vince lost the knife when he took a nap. But why?"

Judith was puzzled, but before she could question Betsy further, Jacobson strolled into the kitchen. He looked less than his usual alert self and his clothes were somewhat rumpled. "Hi, Betsy. How are you?"

"Hungry," she replied. "Vance is making me soup." She frowned. "No, not Vance. But she's like Vance."

"I see," Jacobson said, sitting down at the table. "Maybe I'll have some soup, too. Would you mind?"

Betsy shook her head. "Vance always has enough to go around. She tells me that every time I come here." She nodded three times.

Judith placed another bowl and soup spoon on the table. "Why don't you show Erik your knife, Betsy?"

She scowled at Judith. "Why should I? Finders, keepers."

"Where did you find it?" Judith asked.

Betsy shut her eyes, apparently in an attempt to remember. "In Vince's boat. The one that Vance laughed about."

"Ah." Judith could hardly conceal her excitement. "Was that after Mr. Glover . . . died?"

Betsy looked vague. "Maybe. It was after the fire engine came. And went. There was no fire, no pretty yellow ribbon by the boat. Did Vance want the firemen to burn it up? She told me it'd make good firewood."

Judith and Jacobson exchanged quick looks. "Vince bought the knife for Vance to cut up vegetables for her soup," Judith explained. "If you give it to me, I can give it back to Vance and Vince."

Betsy took a long time to think about it. The soup boiled. Judith edged toward the stove, her eyes still on her strange guest. Jacobson, meanwhile, seemed intrigued by a pair of Aunt Ellen's fruit decoupages that hung on the wall behind the table.

Finally Betsy reached inside her jacket. "Here," she said, putting the knife down in front of her bowl. "Tell Vance I took good care of it."

"I will," Judith promised, rescuing the soup before it boiled over.

Betsy began to hum to herself. Then, as Judith finished pouring the kettle's contents into the two bowls, Betsy gently slapped herself on the cheek. "No singing at the table!" she growled in a strange, deep voice. "That's what Papa always says. Papa is always right." She made an angry face. "He doesn't like it when I call him Papa. Why is that?" Apparently not expecting an answer, she crushed two crackers between both hands and dumped the crumbs into the bowl.

Silence fell over the table. Judith turned off the stove and put the kettle in the dishwasher. She decided to take advantage of the moment to retrieve her pills and started for the hall.

"No!" Betsy shouted—and choked on something in her soup.

Judith patted her on the back. "Okay, I'll stay here," she reassured Betsy, who immediately recovered.

Jacobson nibbled on a cracker. At last, he spoke to Betsy. "Papa wants you to come home after you've eaten. He's worried about you."

"No, he's not," Betsy declared in an unconcerned tone. "Papa only worries about Papa. And his buried treasure." She put the spoon down and looked at the officer. "What good does it do if it's still buried?"

Judith leaned on the back of an empty chair. "What kind of treasure is it?"

Betsy scowled. "Money. It's deep in the ground, where it's safe." She laughed. "Guess what? I tell Papa *he's* crazy." She lapped up the rest of her soup and rose from the chair. "I'll go now. Thank you for feeding me."

Jacobson got to his feet. "I'll walk you home. It's very late."

"So?" Betsy looked pugnacious. "It's not midnight, is it?"

"No," he said, "but it's still foggy and dark. I'm going in that direction anyway."

"Okay." Betsy looked at Judith. "Please thank Vance for the soup."

"I will," Judith promised while the deputy put on his jacket. He let Betsy go first before mouthing the words, "Wait for me."

Judith nodded and hurried to get her pills. She took them into the kitchen and had just swallowed the two tablets when Renie staggered out of the hallway. "Are they gone?" she asked, shoving strands of chestnut hair out of her eyes.

"Yes," Judith replied, "but Jacobson's coming back. Did you hear any of that?"

"All of it," Renie said in disgust. "I'm going back to bed. You can entertain your new best friend. If I have to get up at nine, I need to go back to sleep. Alone." She disappeared from view.

Judith cleaned off the table. A glance at the kitchen clock told her it was a quarter to six. She wondered if there was any point in going back to bed, but hoped Jacobson wouldn't stay long. He'd put in a harder day than she had.

The deputy knocked on the door at exactly six. He went straight to the table where Judith had left the knife.

"Is that the weapon?" she asked.

He shrugged. "Have you got a plastic bag I can put this in?"

"Somewhere," she said, but had to pull out three drawers before she found the stash of paper, plastic, and aluminum products. "Can your lab get anything useful off that thing?" she inquired.

"Dubious." Jacobson put the knife in the recyclable bag. "By the way, nice work getting Betsy to believe this belonged to the Webers."

"It was a long shot," Judith admitted. "My only hope was that Betsy thought enough of Auntie Vance and Uncle Vince to please them by leaving the knife where it supposedly belonged. What happened when you took Betsy home?"

Jacobson looked beleaguered. "The door was locked. I had to

get somebody to hear me over the barking of guard dogs inside, but they roused Quimby's son. He didn't seem surprised by Betsy's return this time of night. Or morning."

"Where *is* the Quimby house?" Judith asked. "I keep forgetting to check it out on the development map."

Jacobson gestured up and to his left. "It's the fairly big gray house at the top of the hill. It must have three stories and a basement. I noticed earlier that it looked like the oldest structure in Obsession Shores."

"That makes sense," Judith said. "Quimby inherited the property from his family, but selling it off lot by lot was his wife's idea."

"Oh?" The deputy looked intrigued. "I don't know much about the development's history. That's interesting. I feel remiss, having grown up here, but it's a huge island."

"It's also a long and rather narrow chunk of land." Judith suddenly remembered the mystery boat. "I hate to bring this up, but . . ." She succinctly related the sightings. "Has anyone mentioned this to you?"

"As a matter of fact," Jacobson replied, "someone did, but it was a Scratchit Head resident, one of the people who reported a break-in. Of course we've no idea why the boat goes out so late in January. With this fog socked in, it's probably moored somewhere tonight."

"Did it seem to be coming from here or Scratchit Head?"

"The person couldn't tell," the deputy responded, and moved to the door. "He saw it just off the point. In fact, he thought it was stopped. I'd better go before I fall asleep at the wheel. Thanks for the soup. Maybe I can sleep in and skip breakfast."

Judith wished him well before turning off the lights and heading to the master bedroom. She soon fell into a dreamless sleep. When she finally awoke, it was bright daylight and the fog was gone.

A glance at the digital clock told her it was 9:50. Stunned, she struggled out of bed in search of Renie. She found her cousin still asleep. The alarm clock was on the floor. Shaking her head, Judith went into the bathroom. It was too late to go to Mass. By the time they got dressed and drove into Langton, the liturgy would almost be over. Feeling a twinge of guilt, she showered and prepared to face the day. Maybe God would forgive them for their sin of omission. Most people's excuses for sleeping in on Sundays didn't include someone else's sin of commission.

Renie showed up in the kitchen right after the coffee had begun to perk. "We're going to hell," she muttered. "I think I knocked over the alarm clock when I reached for more gum."

"Are you sure you didn't throw it on the floor?" Judith asked.

"The gum? I always throw it on the floor after I finish chewing it. Are we still going out for breakfast?"

"No. We'll eat here. I'll start cooking while you put yourself together. Those tiger stripes are making me dizzy."

Renie wandered into the bathroom. She returned to the kitchen fifteen minutes later just as Judith was removing bacon from a skillet. "What," she asked "is your revised plan for the day?"

"Tackling the Quimbys," Judith said. "Then joining the folks who are already on the beach. Some of them are clam digging. The tide's already fairly far out. We should give clamming a shot, too."

Renie put a slice of bread in the toaster. "Go ahead. It's Sunday, a day of rest. I thought you wanted to explore the boathouse."

"I do, but if you'd bother looking through the window, you'd see a half-dozen boats out there already. I'd rather check the boathouse when it isn't in use. Do you want a fried egg?"

"I'll do it myself," Renie said, opening the refrigerator. "I have my own method. I use only butter for frying and I like to arrange my egg in a visually pleasing manner."

Judith ignored the comment. She finished preparing her own breakfast and sat down at the table. Renie joined her a few minutes later after doing whatever it was she did at a stove that seemed to require some serious cussing. Neither cousin spoke until Judith finished eating and Renie devoured several mouthfuls of food.

"Did you catch Betsy-and-the-knife bit?" Judith asked.

Renie shook her head and kept chewing toast while Judith explained how Betsy apparently had found a knife in Vince's old boat. "Judging from the time frame," Judith continued, "Betsy must've come to the beach while we were being taken back here by the firefighters. You recall that neither of us gave Uncle Vince's boat a cursory look."

" 'Nothing to see here, nothing to see here," Renie murmured. "Except there was, and we missed it."

"A huge mistake on our part," Judith declared. "Of course we thought Ernie died of natural causes."

Renie's smile was ironic. "With your history, we should've known better. Still, if that knife is the weapon, wasn't it stupid for the killer to leave it so close to the scene of the crime?"

"That's what bothers me," Judith said. "Did the killer panic? Was someone else nearby? But no witnesses have come forward nor has anybody admitted being on the beach. Betsy had to move quickly before the other emergency personnel showed up. She does skitter around very fast, especially for someone her age."

"Her whole persona is childlike," Renie pointed out. "It's as if she's still three years old. A safe age for hiding."

"Good point," Judith noted. "I'm not sure I blame her."

It was going on eleven by the time the cousins headed up the hill to the Quimby house. Judith remarked it could use a new paint job. "Even gray fades," she said as they approached a peeling white picket fence. "The roof could use some work, too."

"You're right," Renie agreed, opening the gate, which creaked on rusty hinges. "If this place was an older architectural style, it could stand in for the house in *Psycho*."

"Well," Judith murmured, "Betsy does live here."

The grass was overlong around the slate stepping-stones that led to the small porch. "Quimby must be too stingy to pay for upkeep," Renie asserted. "Check the broken windows on the second floor and what seems to be a third floor or big attic."

Judith grimaced. "I didn't notice how shabby all this looks from down below. It's a nice house, but it sure hasn't been maintained."

"No wonder Betsy wanders around outside," Renie said, after ringing the doorbell. "It's depressing."

The cousins waited. And waited. Renie punched the bell again. "I can't hear the damned thing ring. Maybe they can't either."

"They heard Jacobson earlier this morning," Judith noted. "He could hear barking dogs inside before anyone showed up."

"Let's hope nobody has released those hounds outside," Renie said, looking as if she was ready to kick in the door. Before she could do any damage, the knob turned in her hand.

"Yes?" the woman reputedly called Nan said warily. "Are you lost? Or . . ." Her voice trailed away as if it had run off down the darkened corridor behind her.

"We're the Webers' nieces," Judith said quickly, before Renie could say something less polite. "We were the ones who . . . hosted Betsy last night. How is she?"

Nan shrugged. "Betsy's fine. She always is. My sister-in-law tends to wander. Thanks for asking." The door began to close.

Judith stopped it with her foot. "We wanted to thank her for returning the knife," she said.

Nan looked shaken. "The . . . knife? What knife?"

"The one that belonged to our aunt and uncle," Judith replied. "It was kind of Betsy to bring it to us. We wondered what had happened to it. I hate staying at somebody's house and mislaying their belongings." She took advantage of Nan's still-startled expression to step just inside the door. "Could I speak to her for a moment?"

"Ah . . ." Nan turned to look behind her as a sound came out of the darkness. "Later, maybe," she mumbled, trying in vain to close the door. "I must—"

"What's going on?" a rasping voice shouted. Quentin Quimby rolled into view. "Who dares show up at my house?"

"Mr. Quimby!" Judith cried excitedly. "What a thrill! You're quite famous around here. Could I get your autograph?"

The old man's wrinkled face scowled up at Judith. "What the hell do you mean by that?"

"Ginger at the Sun Store told us so much about you," Judith gushed. "Of course, Auntie Vance and Uncle Vince never stop singing your praises."

Quimby pounded a gnarled fist on the wheelchair's arm. "Bah! That Vance woman's got a big yap and her old man's always unconscious. Get out of here before I . . ." He stopped and glared at Nan. "Throw them out, girl. They're trouble. Now."

The "girl" appeared to be at least sixty. Having only glimpsed Nan amid the clubhouse hubbub, Judith noticed that Quimby's daughter-in-law looked almost as thin as Betsy and far more wrinkled. Nan's watery blue eyes were pleading. "Please go," she said to the cousins in a tremulous voice.

Renie shrugged. "Sure. We could always get a ladder and crawl in through a broken window. See ya." She stomped off the porch.

Judith didn't have much choice but to follow her. "That was a bust," she muttered after the door had been firmly shut behind them. "Still . . ." She stopped talking and turned around to stare back at the grim, gray house. "This isn't a home, it's a prison. The only one free to come and go seems to be Betsy. I wonder . . ."

"What?" Renie asked when her cousin didn't continue.

Judith shook her head. "Never mind. Let me brood awhile."

Renie knew better than to prod. Before reaching the gate, they heard dogs barking. A moment later, Quincy Quimby came into view, leading two Rottweilers on leashes.

"Hi," Judith called out to the spare, slightly stooped man. "You have a couple of handsome pooches."

He paused at the gate, the dogs reduced to snarling. "Hansel and Gretel," he said, straining to open the gate and keep the dogs under control. "Are you from the county? If so, you'll have to talk to my father."

"We already did," Judith replied. She and Renie stepped aside to let Quincy and the Rottweilers go by. "We're house-sitting for the Webers."

Judith thought a relieved expression passed over Quincy's deeply lined face. "Oh." He frowned. "The Webers are gone?"

"Just for a few days," Judith said. "I'm sorry to say that your father apparently doesn't like visitors."

"No." Quincy kept moving. "He's elderly. My father finds it difficult to entertain." He paused by the porch. "Say, didn't I see you somewhere before? Maybe at the clubhouse?"

"Yes," Judith responded. "We had the Webers' proxy vote."

Renie spoke up. "We also were sitting by you at the café in the Sun Store. Your old man's a real pain in the butt, frankly. I came very close to dumping his lunch over his head."

Quincy looked shocked. "That's a very unkind thing to say. I told you—he's elderly. Please go away. You probably hurt his feelings." He yanked on the leashes with one hand while unlocking the door with the other. Before either Judith or Renie could respond, Quincy and the dogs disappeared inside.

"You really didn't have to say all that," Judith chided as they exited through the gate.

"Yes, I did," Renie countered. "I don't care what the Quimbys think because I don't have to. Somebody needs to tell them they're a bunch of weirdos. Maybe I'm lacking in Christian charity because I missed Mass this morning, but truth is also a virtue. Bullying is wrong. I tried to tell you that when you were married to Dan, but you ignored me. If he hadn't eaten and drunk himself to death, you'd still be stuck out in the Thurlow District and we wouldn't have had all these homicide adventures during the last sixteen years."

Judith rolled her eyes. "You think I like finding dead people?"

"You seemed to like living with a man who was intent on killing himself." Renie laughed. "Just think how many unsolved murder cases there'd be if Dan hadn't died at forty-nine."

"You're terrible," Judith murmured, though she couldn't help smiling. Renie sometimes had a way of putting things in perspective.

By the time they reached the beach steps, a woman in a mauve hooded coat was coming up the stairs carrying a plastic grocery bag.

"Hi," Judith said in greeting. "Lovely change in weather today."

The newcomer wore an inquiring expression on her plain face. "I ignore the weather," she remarked. "You can't change it. Have we met?"

Judith repeated the Weber connection. "And you're . . . ?"

"Hilda Hilderschmidt," she replied. "Are you going to the beach?"

"Yes," Judith said, judging Hank's wife to be barely fifty. "It looks as if several people are there already. We might dig clams later on."

Hilda wrinkled her nose. "I don't like clams. They're icky. I'm from South Dakota. I moved out here with my parents when I was fifteen. I never saw a clam when I was growing up."

"Really?" Renie said in feigned surprise. "I thought those Black Hills were full of them."

"Hardly," Hilda responded. "You should get out more often." Her emerald eyes veered away from the cousins. "Oh, damn! Here comes Tank. What's he up to now? Excuse me." She hurried off up the hill.

Judith spotted a dark green van turning onto the road halfway down from the Weber house. "Maybe Tank's here to get the skinny on the sewer vote—or lack thereof. Eventually, they'll have to resolve the issue."

"After all this nightmare, the sewer proponents may give up,"

Renie said as they headed down the steps. "Did we ever figure out where the Hilderschmidts live?"

"I don't think so," Judith said. "Hilda must have been very young when she married Hank if they had a son old enough to be a cop." Looking out to the bay, she noticed that most of the half-dozen boats were heading into shore. "I'll bet if those are fishermen, the orcas showed up. That means they ate all the fish."

Renie nodded. "I remember that happened last year on the Christmas cruise when I went with you and Kristin and your grandsons. The ship went off course so we could watch the orcas play."

Judith laughed. "We adults were more agog than the boys were." She lowered her voice. "I see people we haven't met. Let's get acquainted."

Renie groaned, but trudged along beside Judith in the direction away from the boathouse. "Two men and a woman," she murmured. "Another triangle?"

"Digging clams together?" Judith responded. "That's fairly tame."

The plump, pretty dark-haired woman and the two middle-aged men looked up when the cousins approached. The shorter of the two men doffed his snap-brimmed cap. "Hi there," he said. "Don't mind me or my brother. We belong to Gina. She'll vouch for us. We're visiting her and Frank for the day. Sis won't let us stay very long because one time my bro ate three pizzas including the boxes they came in."

Gina's brown eyes were wary, but she offered her hand to Judith. "I'm Frank Leonetti's wife. And you are . . . ?"

Judith kept her smile in place as she shook Gina's hand. "We're related to Vance and Vince Weber. They're out of town for a few days, so we're staying at their place."

Gina nodded. "Frank did mention they had house-sitters. These two are my brothers, Pauly and Pete."

"We're freeloading," the taller man said, his long face beaming. "I'm Pete, so you can probably figure out this other rascal is Pauly."

Gina shot Pete a disparaging glance. "Cut the clowning. We're not far from where Ernie Glover was murdered. I'm in no mood for jokes."

"Hey, sis," Pauly said in a deep voice that belied his short if bulky stature, "lighten up. I thought you didn't like that Glover guy."

Gina's olive skin turned pale. "That's not true. It's his bitchy wife I can't stand." She tossed aside the shovel she'd been holding and hurried toward the steps.

The brothers exchanged puzzled glances. "What's up with Gina now?" Pete muttered.

"Hell, bro," Pauly said, "you know Gina's touchy. Let sis go. She's Frank's problem, not ours. He's had enough lousy stuff happen to him the last year or so. Cut both of them some slack."

"Yeah, right, fine," Pete muttered. "Seems like a lot of people up here are carrying heavy loads." He gave Judith and Renie a sheepish look. "Ignore us, even when we talk smack about our sister. Gina's a fine woman, but she feels marooned up here on what they call The Rock."

"I gather you all grew up in the city," Judith said.

Pete nodded. "Seven of us. Gina's the only one who moved away. Pauly and I keep the family business going. You ever buy Melba's Toast?"

Renie blinked a couple of times. "You mean the baked goods line? Yes, I do. So does my husband."

"Good for you," Pauly said in his deep voice. "We've never sold out our operation to a big faceless company like some people have." His dark eyes moved up to the houses on the hill. "Greedy, and that's that."

Judith forced herself to look innocent. "Surely you don't mean anyone around here?"

Pauly started to speak, but Pete put a hand on his shoulder.

"Let's not cause trouble. There's enough of that here already. We'd better finish filling these buckets so we have something to take home to Mama."

"Right," Pauly said, doffing his cap again. "Pleased to meet you."

The cousins wandered down closer to the water. Renie spoke first when they were out of earshot. "Competition from Ben's Buns, huh?"

"I guess so," Judith agreed. "But then the victim should be Brose Bennett or a member of Gina Leonetti's family. Does anybody get murdered over baked goods?"

Renie made a face. "That depends how long I have to wait for my number to be called at Donner & Blitzen's bakery department downtown. Some of those old bats take forever to make up their minds. Five minutes to choose between raised or cake doughnuts? Really?"

"Ah . . . right," Judith murmured. "Maybe we can cross off Gina's brothers as suspects. They can probably prove they weren't here Friday. As for any rumors about Gina's alleged amorous adventures, she *is* good-looking."

"Suitable for being Ernie's paramour? It crossed my mind," Renie said, kicking at an empty clamshell. "*If* he had one."

Judith shrugged. "Too much gossip. It's Gina's reaction to the mention of Ernie's death that caught my attention."

Renie looked bemused. "You're thinking it isn't that she dislikes Edna as much as she liked Ernie?"

"Exactly." Judith stopped a few feet away from the outgoing tide. "I'm wondering about a lot of things. I was so tired last night while I was dealing with Betsy and Jacobson that I almost forgot about the treasure comment. Did you catch that?"

Renie grimaced. "No. That went right by me. Who said it?"

"Betsy. She was talking about her father's treasure and mentioned that it was safely buried. Where? I wonder."

"Why does Betsy say most of what she babbles about?"

"Is it babbling?" Judith gave a shake of her head. "I'm trying to figure out if there's a method to Betsy's madness, but I can't."

"If you can't, I sure can't," Renie said. "You're better at reading people than I am. I assume you're not implying Betsy isn't really nuts."

"I'm not. It's more like *how* nuts she is," Judith replied. "It's possible that some of her eccentric behavior is a shield against reality."

Renie shuddered. "That house and old Quimby are enough to make *me* a bit peculiar. Both Quincy and Nan look like wrecks. Ginger's right—no amount of money is worth putting up with a virtual dictator."

Judith's expression grew wistful. "It can happen. It's what you're used to. 'Normal' to one person isn't 'normal' to somebody else." She turned away from Renie to look out over the bay, but her dark eyes didn't see the sparkling Sound or the Peninsula's mountains. Instead, she saw herself working two jobs to make ends meet and coming home to a lazy, drunken, verbally abusive husband. It wasn't money that had kept her a prisoner for nineteen years. It was fear.

"Why," she said out loud, "didn't somebody kill him?"

"I guess," Renie said, "everybody figures he's eventually bound to die of old age."

Judith turned sharply to stare at Renie. "I didn't mean Quimby," she blurted. And understood how a so-called normal person could be tempted to snuff out someone else's life.

Chapter 16

Judith silently blessed Renie for her innate understanding. Her cousin had merely shrugged—and kicked at another empty clamshell. They continued walking away from the steps. Some of the clam diggers had moved farther out as the tide continued to expose more wet beach. A couple with two young children had just given up for the day and were coming toward the cousins. Judith recognized Katie Glover Blomquist and the two boys, but wondered if the man was her brother or her husband. Brad suddenly stopped in his tracks and started to cry.

"Mine!" he screamed. "Mine money! Josh took it!"

"Please don't be so loud," Katie admonished. "He'll give it back when we get to Grandmom's house. You have to learn to share. Josh already promised to give you some of the shells he found." She suddenly focused on Judith and Renie, who were some ten feet away. "Oh! Hi, Mrs. Flynn . . . and Mrs. Jones," she added warily.

Renie held up her hands. "I confess! I didn't give your kids Valium." She paused. "It was Xanax."

Judith shot her cousin a dirty look. "Mrs. Jones didn't give them anything. She likes to make inappropriate jokes now and then."

The tall man with the shaved head frowned at Renie as he

picked up the now-whimpering Brad. "Some joke. I was about to pay you a call. I don't take well to anybody messing with my children."

"The Wobble-Dobble made me do it," Renie declared, wide-eyed. "I plead temporary insanity."

A glint of humor showed up in Greg's brown eyes. "You might make that work in court. Or you could sue the toy maker."

Judith felt it was time to change the subject. "Have you been digging for buried treasure?" she asked with a smile.

Katie smiled back. "Oh, yes! Very special." She tapped Josh's head. "Show the nice ladies what you and Brad found in the big hole."

Josh hesitated, but moved closer. "See?" he said, opening a grubby hand. "It's old money from an old ship. From pirates, maybe."

Judith leaned down cautiously to study three grimy coins. "Canadian pennies with Queen Elizabeth. That's fantastic, Josh!"

Katie patted her older son's head. "There's been a lot of talk about coins being found around here lately. Someone mentioned a stash of old French coins. Greg doesn't think that's likely. He teaches American history and knows the subject really well."

Her husband shrugged. "French explorers didn't have a big presence in this part of the country."

"True," Judith agreed, turning to Katie. "Is your brother here yet?"

Kate shook her head. "Denver's still snowed in. Maybe tomorrow. Mom told him not to miss work, so he might wait until the funeral. She doesn't see any point in him making two trips in such a short time."

"We'd better go," Greg said, still holding Brad, who was rubbing his eyes. "It's an early nap after all this fresh air." He nodded at the cousins. "Nice to meet you. Next time, Mrs. Jones, give the boys a shot of Scotch."

The Blomquists continued heading for the staircase.

"At least," Renie remarked, after the family was out of hearing range, "Greg's got a sense of humor. It's good to meet a normal person."

"Greg and Katie don't live here," Judith said. "Have you noticed that except for a mention of the Crowleys—who were gone when the murder occurred—none of the other people we've met have talked about the younger residents except in a vague, general way?"

Renie looked pained. "Does this mean you can't be a suspect if you're under fifty? What about the Bendareks?"

"Borderline," Judith said. "Zach would bash in somebody's head, not resort to weaponry. Becca might use a knife, but I can't think why she'd kill Ernie. In fact, that's the biggest problem. I don't see a motive for anyone. I keep going back to the remark about Quimby being the person who should've been killed. This whole case is backward."

Renie was silent as they continued along the damp sand. "What about Edna Glover? A spouse is always the first suspect."

Judith shook her head. "If she wanted to kill her husband, she could've poisoned him with all the meds she takes. Poison is more of a woman's weapon and it's harder to detect." She frowned. "I didn't ask Jacobson if a full autopsy was being done. Maybe I should call him."

"Would that be automatic in a homicide investigation?"

"I think that depends on the jurisdiction and the immediate survivors," Judith replied. "Let's check out the boathouse. It looks as if all the fishermen have come off the bay. I'll call Jacobson later. I kind of hate to, since he's off duty. That sort of thing always annoyed Joe when he was on the police force."

The tide was out so far that the cousins gave the murder site a wide berth. "They can't store very big boats in that building," Judith remarked, nodding to a couple they didn't recognize who were clamming nearby. "You'd think Obsession Shores would have its own marina."

Renie shrugged. "It's not too far to drive to Scratchit Head."

"That's so," Judith agreed. "I've never noticed if you can get from here to there at low tide."

"You can't," Renie said. "I mean, Bill tried to do it once when we were up here. Just beyond the boathouse, the bluff rises so sharply that there's no way to get around it, even when the tide's out." She waved a hand in the direction of the forested land beyond the development. "You'd have to climb up that hill and it's really steep. As for driving to Scratchit Head, you go back to the main highway and turn due west instead of going south to get here."

Judith nodded as they approached the boathouse's wooden steps. "Come to think of it, I've seen the sign for Scratchit Head. Let's hope this place isn't locked."

Renie went first and turned the knob. "It's not," she said—and gasped as the door opened, almost knocking her into Judith.

"Sorry!" Zach Bendarek cried. "You okay, tiger lady?"

"I guess," Renie replied, catching her breath. "You're dangerous when it comes to doors, big fella."

Zach looked sheepish. "Wish I'd been more dangerous on the field. You got a boat in here?"

"No," Judith said. "We're just visiting, remember?"

"Oh, right." Zach pounded a fist into his palm. "Darn! You already told me. Your uncle's got that old beat-up boat on the beach, right? How come he doesn't use it for firewood? That thing's a wreck."

"Uncle Vince keeps hoping it'll heal itself," Judith murmured.

Zach frowned. "It won't. The only thing it's good for is when Betsy Quimby sits in it and pretends she's a pirate. The poor lady doesn't know it'd sink if she ever put it in the water."

"Betsy's in her own little world," Judith said kindly.

"Good place to be," Zach murmured, edging around the cousins to get down the steps. "I wouldn't want to live anywhere near . . ." He stopped speaking as soon as reached the sand. "Never mind. See you around. If you're still here."

"You know what?" Renie said as they went inside. "I'd like to listen to Zach and Betsy hold a debating contest."

"You're mean," Judith declared, closing the door behind her. "As we thought—they're pretty basic and lightweight with room for no more than six people. Most seem to be made of aluminum and have some kind of canopy, unlike Uncle Vince's. I wonder what he did with the motor."

"He had a motor?" Renie asked. "I could've sworn he used oars when I was out in it."

"Maybe he did," Judith said. "He always had trouble starting it. The boats in here are probably used mainly for fishing and crabbing. I wouldn't want to go out farther than the bay in any of them."

"Right," Renie drawled. She gazed at the thirty or more craft lining the walls. "It might get choppy out in the Sound. I see a couple of kayaks, too. They all look seaworthy to me, though. I can't see any visible holes."

"I hope not. You're the one who had a seagoing father." Judith studied a printed list near the door. "This shows who stores boats in here along with the time they go out and come back. I don't recognize most of the names except for Bennett, Hilderschmidt, Leonetti, and Logan."

"What about Bendarek?" Renie asked.

Judith scanned the list a second time. "No. He's not listed." She was puzzled. "So why was Zach here?"

"Because he forgot he doesn't own a boat?"

Judith didn't answer right away. "I wonder if he was in a boat with somebody else and lingered after they came in. It took us a couple of minutes to walk over here. I didn't see anybody go inside, only a couple of people coming out. The ramp's not wide enough to accommodate anything but small craft. It goes off at an angle, maybe the better to catch the tide."

"You think Zach was looking for another body?"

Judith sighed. "No. It just seems odd. But Zach *is* a little odd.

Heck, maybe he's thinking of buying a boat and was checking the ones here. Let's go. We haven't learned a blasted thing. Do you really want to dig clams?"

Renie didn't answer until they were outside again. "Well, why not? The tide's still going out. You stay here. I'll get a bucket and a couple of shovels. Or do the Webers have a clam gun?"

"I don't think they've ever bothered to get one," Judith replied. "Auntie Vance likes the exercise. I've never seen Uncle Vince dig clams. He might doze off and end up facedown in the sand." She winced. "That reminds me of Ernie. I think I'll stay away from that log."

Renie gave her cousin a thumbs-up sign and trotted off to the staircase. Judith strolled on, noting there were only four clam diggers still on the beach. Closer to the bank, several teenagers were clambering over driftwood on the far side of the staircase. One of them looked like Chad Bendarek. To her surprise, he jumped off a weather-beaten stump, gestured to a young girl, and hurried to join Judith.

"Hi," he called out, coming closer. "Mop told me you found Mr. Glover's body. Is that for real?"

"I'm afraid so," Judith admitted. "My cousin was with me."

"Awesome," Chad murmured, putting a hand on the girl's arm. "This is Em. She thinks she knows who whacked Mr. G."

Em gave Chad a disgusted look. "I never said that. I only thought they looked like they were arguing when I saw Mr. Glover talking to Mr. Hilderschmidt that afternoon." She turned to Judith. "I had to stay home from school that day because I had a bad cold. I don't want to get Mr. Hilderschmidt in trouble, even if he is a total doof."

Judith kept her tone neutral. "No blows exchanged?"

"No," Em replied. "Mr. Hilderschmidt waved his arms, though."

Judith glanced up the hill. "Do you live close to the beach?"

Em nodded, her frizzy golden curls highlighted by the noonday sun. "Halfway up on the right—from here, I mean. I was using binoculars so I could bird-watch. We're doing a science project on sea life."

Judith nodded. "How did Mr. Glover look?"

"He was sort of turned away," Em responded. "But he looked . . . like maybe he was sort of like . . . trying to back off?"

"An argument, perhaps?" Judith suggested.

Em shrugged. "I stopped watching. I thought I saw a crane, but it turned out to be a weird-looking seagull."

"What time was that?"

Em's round face scrunched up. "Um . . . just before two? I was watching a soap. While I studied, I mean. It was the last commercial break before the Friday cliffhanger. I hate those. I zonked out after that. The decongestant I take makes me sleepy. I didn't get to see the excitement after you found Mr. Glover."

"It wasn't exactly exciting," Judith said. "In fact, my cousin and I left almost as soon as the emergency people arrived." She saw Renie coming down the steps with a bucket and two shovels. "Here's Mrs. Jones now. Did the police talk to you?"

Em's plain face looked blank. "No. Somebody came to our house, but he only asked Mom a couple of questions." She looked at Chad. "Hey, let's go. I don't want to talk to some guy in a uniform. That is so not cool." She didn't wait for Chad, but headed back to join the other teens.

"Sorry 'bout that," he murmured, and sauntered off after Em.

Renie kept walking right past Judith. "Come on," she called over her shoulder. "We'll have better luck closer to the water. Nobody's dug there yet. Skip the horse clams and geoducks. They taste like tires."

"Right," Judith shouted, following her cousin.

Renie stopped some ten feet from the outgoing tide. "So now you're interrogating the younger set?"

"Chad volunteered Em," Judith replied. "I don't know her last name, but she saw Ernie and Hank having what appeared to be an argument not long before the murder occurred."

Renie was looking around for clam holes. "Over here," she said, motioning for Judith to join her. "Do you believe the kid or do you think she likes attention?"

"I don't know. After she unloaded on me, I found out that whichever deputy went to their house spoke to her mother, but not to her." Judith paused to take a shovel from Renie. "Em stayed home from school because she had a cold. She was using binoculars, so she couldn't have misidentified the two men."

"Drama queen?" Renie asked, starting to dig by some tiny holes in the sand that indicated clams were spitting in the vicinity.

"No." Judith plunged her shovel into the wet sand a few feet away from Renie. "Very ordinary sort of fourteen-, fifteen-year-old girl. It's plausible, though it's not exactly evidence."

Renie laughed. "Since when has a lack of that quantity stopped you? You tend to go by your gut, coz."

"That's what I'm doing," Judith said, finding the digging fairly easy. "What would Ernie and Hank be arguing about? A woman? Ernie playing around with Hilda doesn't sound right. Edna's a beauty queen by comparison. Not that looks count for everything. It'd work better the other way around with Hank and Edna getting it on."

"Gack," Renie muttered. "Hank's about as appealing as a geoduck. If I . . . whoa!" She got down on her haunches, one hand gripping the shovel for support, the other reaching into the hole she'd dug. "I think I've found some buried treasure," she said, standing up and coming to show Judith what was in her hand. "See for yourself."

"I can't see much," Judith retorted, "except that it's a black coin with markings."

"Look closer," Renie urged. "Can you make out what looks like a flower—a rose, to be precise—on the right of the inner circle?"

Judith squinted at the blackened coin. "It could be a flower of some kind, but why not a camellia or a gardenia or a—"

"Hold it." Renie scraped the coin with her long thumbnail. "This doesn't help much, but see if it's a little better defined."

Judith refocused. "Okay, if you say it's a rose, I'll go with that. Do I see a profile? Whoever it is seems to be wearing a houseplant on his or her head."

Renie let out an exasperated sigh. "Okay, okay. It's a Tudor rose and that's Queen Elizabeth the First. She's wearing a crown, not a ficus. I can see the word 'regina' and part of her name in the outer circle."

"Your eyes are better than mine," Judith said, "though now I can tell it's a profile. But is it authentic?"

Renie picked up the coin and stared at it again before responding. "Heck, I don't know. It has to be from the latter half of the sixteenth century. Elizabeth didn't become queen until 1556. No English ships ever came this way back then. Mr. Moffitt's the local numismatic expert."

"As I recall, he's closed Sundays, at least in winter. Do you think there could be more of those . . . can you tell the denomination?"

Renie put the coin in her parka's pocket. "No. I can't make out the rest of the letters after *E-L-I-Z*. I'll dig farther down to see if there are any more. I might even find a clam."

Judith found one before Renie did. Two, in fact. "Littlenecks," she exulted. "Yum!"

"Don't gloat," Renie warned her. "This hole's a dud. Except for the coin. I'm moving farther down toward the tide."

The cousins dug in silence for the next quarter hour. Renie had uncovered enough clams that she had to carry them on the shovel, treading cautiously to make sure she didn't lose any along the way.

"We've got enough for more chowder," Judith said. "Or should we steam them tonight?"

Renie considered the half-full bucket. "I say we dig for more. I can eat piles of steamed clams."

"So you can," Judith said drily, scanning the beach. "I see some other people have come onto the beach. Is that the Logans just below the clubhouse?"

Renie shielded her eyes with her hand. The sun was starting to move to the west. "I think so. They're coming this way. Haven't you already grilled them?"

Judith shook her head. "Only Kent. I haven't met Suzie."

"Here's your big chance," Renie said, moving off to seek fresh sand.

Judith kept digging, but didn't lose sight of the Logans, who were definitely headed toward her. From some thirty yards away, Kent waved. Judith waved back, leaning on the shovel.

"We're seeking our supper," she said as the couple came closer. "Are you the rare locals who don't like clams?"

Kent laughed. "We do, but only once a week. This is my wife, Suzie. I told her about you and your cousin."

Judith grimaced. "I won't shake hands. I'm kind of grimy."

Suzie smiled, showing perfect white teeth. Indeed, everything about Mrs. Logan seemed flawless, from her glowing rosy skin to her sleek silver ponytail. "I saw you at the meeting Friday. What a farce! We didn't get a chance to introduce ourselves before the stampede started."

Renie had wandered over with another dozen or more clams. "Hi," she said. "I'm the other niece."

Suzie nodded. "It's nice to have normal people around here like your aunt and uncle. Sometimes I wonder if we made a mistake retiring here. There are some odd ducks at Obsession Shores."

Kent looked apologetic. "The problem is that it's a very small community. Scratchit Head's probably the same way. People's eccentricities tend to be more glaring."

Suzie shrugged. "Maybe someday I'll buy that argument." Her attractive features turned gloomy. "I can't imagine how horrible it was to find Ernie's body. That must've happened not long after you arrived."

"True," Judith replied, hoping to look suitably distressed. "We thought we'd take a walk before the rain started."

Kent put an arm around his wife's shoulders. "We'd planned to do that but I got held up on a long call to a client. By the time I got off the line, the weather had turned bad."

Suzie nodded. "I'd been practicing on the piano. I didn't know the firefighters had come and gone. In fact, I had no idea anything had happened until I saw the ambulance. We only found out Ernie had been killed when a deputy showed up to ask if we'd seen or heard anything."

Kent nodded once. "We hadn't, of course. That's the problem with staying focused on what you're doing. You block out everything else."

"I understand," Judith said, hoping she didn't sound glib. "Witnesses seem scarce." She glanced at the pile of driftwood, noting that the teenagers were gone. "Luckily, some of the younger folks were paying attention that afternoon."

Kent looked startled; Suzie turned pale. "Who?" she asked, her hazel eyes wide. "What did they see?"

Judith laughed. "We don't live here. Renie and I refuse to get involved in local gossip."

"Right," Renie agreed. "We're those big-city types who never get involved. God help us to get mixed up in anything as sordid as murder." To Judith's surprise, her cousin sounded almost sincere.

"But," Kent protested, "surely if someone told you . . . something helpful to the investigation, you'd share it with the police. Or inform the rest of us for our own protection. There's a killer on the loose."

"From what little we've heard," Judith said, "most people think it was random. A head case, probably."

Suzie moved even closer to Kent. "What if they're wrong? The sheriff's deputies haven't told us anything. At least we'd like to know if they have some leads."

Judith shrugged. "Early days, as they say in law enforcement. The sheriff's personnel have to be very cautious."

Kent frowned. "I forgot. Your husband's a retired policeman, right? Have you discussed the case with him?"

Judith shook her head. "He's fishing in New Zealand."

Kent looked at Suzie. "Maybe we should call a meeting. I mean, a real meeting to figure out how we can learn about progress with the investigation. Frank Leonetti handing out flyers doesn't seem to be doing much to find the killer. We need some answers."

"Good thinking," Renie asserted. "You should chair the meeting, Kent. Hank Hilderschmidt doesn't know a motion from a potion."

"She's right," Suzie said, smiling at her husband. "You're a pro."

Kent hugged Suzie. "Okay, let's get organized. Maybe we can set it for tonight." He looked at the cousins. "Would you two come?"

"Dubious," Renie replied. "We're outsiders. People get murdered all the time in the city. The meeting might bore us. Don't you folks have a neighborhood watch?"

Suzie seemed to take umbrage. "We haven't needed one. Until now," she added, lowering her gaze.

Kent had kept his arm around his wife. "Let's go, Suze. We've got work to do."

After the Logans hurried off, Judith gave her cousin a dirty look. "You went too far on that one. I thought you liked Kent."

"I do," Renie said, "but did they have to try out their alibis on us?"

"Yes," Judith responded. "Practice makes perfect. The question is why do I think they need alibis in the first place?"

Chapter 17

Judith leaned on her shovel. "People give themselves away by overdoing their lies," she said. "When I'm forced to tell a fib, I keep it simple. Kent and Suzie Logan not only told us too much, but they know too much to be telling the truth about their lack of awareness."

Renie laughed. "I've known you to stitch some fancy embroidery of your own. But you're right. For one thing, how did they know we hadn't been here very long before we found Ernie's corpse?"

"Exactly." The wind had risen off the bay and Judith paused to tuck a strand of hair behind her ear. "The Logans have a reason for not wanting anyone to know what they were doing at the time of the murder. Kent's alibi isn't worthy of him because it could easily be broken. The call itself could be checked or the person at the other end would have to lie for him."

"But why make up such a bunch of twaddle?" Renie asked.

Judith raised an eyebrow. "Because they were on the beach?"

Renie made a face. "Kent wouldn't resort to violence. He'd take an enemy to court. And I can't see Suzie stabbing anyone. It's messy. She's a very tidy person, not a hair out of place despite the wind. A knife means blood. Wouldn't the killer have got some on him or her?"

"Good question." Judith stared out across the bay to the snow-covered mountains on the Peninsula. "I wonder if Jacobson has found out anything about the knife Betsy found. I wish he was on duty today. I hate to bother him on a Sunday."

"He *is* the lead detective on this case, isn't he?"

"He's the lead at the scene," Judith replied. "Someone at the county seat in Cooptown is probably in charge, maybe the sheriff. With fifty thousand people living on the island, they must have a fairly large police force because most of the towns aren't incorporated."

Renie's expression was quizzical. "How do you know that?"

Judith grinned. "I read it in the island phone directory while I was trying to get hold of Jacobson. Frankly, I was surprised by the number of people who live up here now. I'll bet it's doubled since Auntie Vance and Uncle Vince bought their lot."

"Too much growth everywhere in this part of the country," Renie said glumly. "We should charge visitors just for coming here."

"That's mean," Judith chided. "I'd go out of business."

"Oh. I forgot about that." Renie grabbed her shovel and moved farther down the beach.

The wind picked up after another fifteen minutes had passed. Judith found at least another three dozen clams, but her back began to ache. She checked her watch, which told her it was a quarter to two, and called out to her cousin, who was some thirty yards away.

"Let's quit," she shouted.

Renie looked up from her digging and yelled something Judith couldn't make out. Apparently her cousin had found more clams. Leaving the bucket where it sat, she walked toward the staircase. She was halfway there when she saw Brose Bennett coming down to the beach.

"A niece," he called out, coming to meet her. "You seen Fou-fou?"

"No," Judith replied as he joined her a few yards from the steps. "Was she coming to the beach?"

Brose's long face grew even longer. "No. I can't find her any-place. I guess she's gone."

"Gone . . . where?" Judith inquired.

"Left," he replied, tugging at his left earlobe. "Left me, that is. Oh, hell, it's no surprise. She's threatened to do it for years. Fou-fou better not try to get her gloms on my money. I earned it with my buns."

"Ah . . . yes," Judith said. "I'm sure you did. I gather your wife didn't take part in running your baking business."

"Hell no." Brose pulled up the hood on his rain jacket. "She likes to spend what I made, though." He looked beyond Judith. "Here comes the other niece with a bucket. Looks like you've both been digging clams. Find anything else interesting?"

Judith turned enough to see her cousin trudging across the sand. "As a matter of fact, we did." She waited for Renie to join them. "Hey, coz, show Brose what you found."

Renie's eyes grew wide. "You mean the astonishing discovery of the Elizabethan coin? Hang on while I disencumber myself."

Brose frowned at Judith. "What's she mean by that? It sounds like I should look the other way."

Judith didn't bother enlightening him, since it took Renie only a couple of seconds to set down the bucket and the shovel. She removed the coin from her pocket and held it out in her palm.

"What do you make of that, bun boy?" she asked, making a clicking noise with her tongue.

"Wow!" Brose exclaimed. "That's incredible! Where'd you find it?"

Renie turned around, scanning the beach. "I don't remember. It's hard to tell now that the tide's almost out."

"Well . . ." Brose stroked his long chin. "That's a funny thing. I found an old coin on the beach a couple of weeks ago. It made the local paper."

"Slow news day, huh?" Renie murmured.

"Right, right," Brose agreed. "I got to admit, I created quite a stir." He glanced at Judith before speaking again to Renie. "Your cousin knows all about it. I'm surprised she didn't spread the word. Now other folks are hunting for more rare pieces. Got to be money in it somewhere. I mean, besides that they're coins."

Judith decided to speak up before Renie got them in any deeper than she already had. "We noticed a rare coin shop in Langton yesterday. Have you had the one you found appraised?"

"No," Brose replied. "It's not about the value, it's about the thrill. Of finding stuff like that, I mean. If other people want to cash in, that's fine with me. Besides, old Moffitt is gaga." He glanced at the boathouse. "I wonder if Fou-fou's in there. Maybe I should have a look-see. Let me know if you find any more treasure." He ambled off along the beach, his rain jacket flapping in the wind.

"How," Renie asked, "is Brose working this scam? Or is he really stupid enough to believe what he's saying?"

Judith crossed her arms, feeling a bit chilly. "I'm not sure. He ran a successful business, so he isn't a complete dope. Betsy talked about her father and hidden treasure. Maybe there are some legends around here, but I never heard the Webers mention them. I suspect you're right. Brose has himself a little sideline. Middleman, maybe for brokering deals if somebody actually comes up with a valuable item. He strikes me as the type who'd enjoy a good con."

Renie turned to look out at the bay. "Over the years some ships with valuable cargoes have sunk in the Sound, but none were this far south. Of course that doesn't mean it's impossible. It could be rumrunners from Canada during Prohibition, though if they came by sea, they usually crossed to the mainland north of Whoopee Island or over on the Peninsula. Just enough real history to make Brose's claims credible."

Judith grew thoughtful, trying to conjure up full-masted sailing ships with gun portals on each side, and three times smaller than the ferry the cousins had taken to Whoopee Island. "Your dad taught me everything I know about ships," she said. "Which, frankly, isn't a lot."

Renie smiled. "As a seagoing man, he knew his stuff. You didn't have to learn how to identify every type of vessel from every different era. I actually liked doing that."

"Speaking of boats," Judith said, "I want another look at Uncle Vince's. Do you mind carrying the clams? I'm wearing down a bit."

Renie scowled. "I'm smaller and I have to do the heavy lifting?" But she didn't hesitate, picking up the almost full bucket and walking with Judith over to their uncle's derelict little craft.

"The crime-scene tape is almost gone," Judith noted. "A stranger probably wouldn't realize someone had been murdered on this beach." She looked back at the spot where they'd found Ernie. "Why here?"

"What do you mean?" Renie asked.

"Daylight, out in the open, where anybody could see. It makes no sense." Judith looked up at the overhanging bank above the big log and their uncle's small boat. "Let's try an experiment. It's about the same time of day that Ernie was killed. You go up to the first row of houses and I'll stand where the deed was done."

"Okay," Renie said. "I'll take the clams and the shovels. I don't want to have to call 911 because you dislocated your spare part."

Judith smiled wanly. "Thanks, coz." She waved her cousin off.

As soon as Renie started up the staircase, Judith studied Uncle Vince's beat-up boat. One of the two seats was broken. There was a cushion under the other plank. She pulled it out, noticing that it was an embroidered pillow, soiled and tattered. There were rust-colored blotches on the faded satin cover. In one corner, she could make out Edna Glover's signature. She was still turning the pillow in her hands when Renie yelled at her.

"Hold on!" Judith called back, moving to where Ernie's corpse had been found. She couldn't see her cousin. Thus Renie probably couldn't see her. They met at the top of the stairs. "That," Judith stated, "helps explain why nobody above the beach saw the murder." She thrust the pillow at her cousin. "Tell me what this is all about."

Renie's examination was thorough. "Did you see it Friday?" she asked, handing the pillow back to Judith.

"Of course not. I didn't look inside the boat."

"Neither did I. You might be tampering with evidence. Could that brown stuff be dried blood?"

"Maybe." The cousins started up the hill. "The pillow must not have been there Friday," Judith finally said. "Jacobson would've bagged and tagged it. I'm wondering if Betsy put it in the boat. The blood may have been on the knife. Maybe she swipes more than meds from the locals. I'm guessing she swiped the pillow from the Glover house."

"You figure Betsy often takes a nap in Uncle Vince's old boat?"

Judith sighed. "Who knows what Betsy does? It's hard enough to understand allegedly normal people, but this time we've got a ringer. Dick mentioned her sleeping in the boat. I suspect Betsy is on some kind of pills. Maybe they make her sleepy." She paused halfway up the hill and turned around. "Darn. I was thinking that from this angle you could see more of the upper beach because we're higher on the hill. But we can't."

Renie was looking off to the road on her right. "Why is Hank Hilderschmidt hugging Edna Glover?"

Judith remained fixated on the beach. "At some point, Ernie—and his killer—had to be seen by somebody other than the sick teenage . . ." She stopped to stare at Renie. "What did you say about hugging?"

"Hank hugged Edna," Renie said, adjusting her parka's hood. "She's getting into that pale green car. I guess they're going for a spin."

Judith saw Hank open the door on the driver's side. "Keep

walking," she said to Renie. "We don't want them to think we're spying."

"Why not?" Renie retorted, though she kept moving. "They're not doing anything illegal. Hank will probably honk when they go by."

But the green car passed them without so much as a nod. "Edna didn't even look at us," Judith said. "Is that a Cadillac?"

"I think so," Renie responded. "Cars all look alike these days."

Judith made a face, but kept walking. "Edna doesn't entertain, but rides around with Hank? Was Zach right about Edna having a lover?"

"Eeeew," Renie said, wincing. "Hank is not an attractive man."

"To you," Judith said. "Maybe he is to Edna. That could explain the argument that the ailing Em watched from her window."

"You're suggesting a motive for murder?" Renie asked.

"It's always a good one," Judith replied, "but I'm not jumping to conclusions." She grew silent as they turned off to the Weber house. "Let's hose down the clams and leave them outside. We need to do research."

Renie set the bucket by the garden hose faucet just off the steps. "On what? I know how to take care of clams."

"We haven't done the basics to find the killer," Judith replied. "Yes, we've met several people since we arrived, but what do we really know about them? Just random bits and pieces. All we have are rumors. We need facts. Deep background, as they say."

"Good thing I brought my laptop," Renie murmured, covering the clams in water. "Ooof! This thing's heavy. I should've waited to fill the bucket after I got it up the steps." She used her free hand to steady herself on the rail. "If you fall down, you're out of luck."

Five minutes later, they were both on the sofa with a box of Ritz Crackers and a jar of soft cheddar. Judith had a glass of ice water and Renie had her usual Pepsi.

"Let's start with a known quantity," Judith suggested, spreading cheese on a cracker. "Brose Bennett; real first name, Ambrose. Put his name in the *Times* search engine."

Renie kicked off her shoes. "Why didn't our aunt and uncle put a fireplace in here? That would be really cozy."

"It probably would've cost too much," Judith said. "Find anything?"

"Quite a bit," Renie said, eyes on the screen. "All old news and mostly about the sale of the company. See for yourself. I need chocolate." She got up to fetch her white bag from the fridge.

Judith was disappointed. "You're right. Nothing recent. I might as well stay with the *B*s and put in Zach Bendarek. Careful, you'll get chocolate all over the keyboard."

"Idwoodabeedafurztym," Renie said with her mouth full.

"I can see that from whatever residue you've left on previous occasions," Judith declared. "It's a wonder the keys don't stick."

"Sometimes they do," Renie said, after swallowing.

"Shoot," Judith murmured after sipping her ice water. "One hit, two years ago, about a California high school recruit Zach found for the University football team. Here's another one, but it's the same as from the previous year, except there's a quote. 'The kid's got legs. He can run.' That sounds like Zach."

"Master of the obvious," Renie remarked.

"Maybe this was a dumb idea," Judith said. "I'll try Hilderschmidt. Here's a Helmut Hilderschmidt. Could that be Hank's real name? No—this is about H&H Construction. It must be Tank."

"Is it of interest?"

Judith shook her head. "It's in the business wrap-up about a new building in South Lake Onion. I guess Tank keeps busy. Ah! Here's Henry, three years ago this month. He's a junior. Oh, no!" She put a hand to her breast. "It's the son, a firefighter." She read the story aloud: " 'Three people were killed and two were injured when the roof of a burning house caved in early Tuesday morning . . .' " She stopped, scanning until she found young Henry's name. "'A three-year veteran of the city's fire department, Hilderschmidt was killed when a beam fell on him while he was trying to rescue an elderly couple trapped on the second floor.'" She paused. "The rest is speculation about what caused the fire. He wasn't a cop, as Kent assumed, but he was killed in the line of duty."

"There must be an obit," Renie said.

"There is. Hank was only twenty-six. Private services, memorials to Medic One and the firefighters retirement fund. No wife or kids."

"No wonder Hilda's a bit odd," Renie murmured. "Who's next?"

"Frank Leonetti," Judith replied, typing in the name. "Nothing. Maybe it's Francesco?"

Renie shrugged. "If not, try Franco."

Her cousin's suggestion paid off. "There are several references, all related to the family produce business. After the elder Leonetti died in 1982, his three sons turned it into a wholesale company. They later expanded the line of grocery products. Two brothers, Antonio and Claudio, were running the business along with Franco as of 2000." Judith kept scrolling—and gasped. "In October 2003, the brothers drowned while fishing in the Santa Lucia Islands." Judith skimmed the article. "A storm came up, overturning their inflatable boat."

Renie chomped on another piece of honeycomb. "Infwadubel bo in Akdobah?" She swallowed. "That's not very smart. We were lucky with the weather when I went with you to B&B-sit your old pal's inn, but that was in September. To quote Uncle Vince, it really can get choppy up there later in the fall."

"I suppose," Judith murmured. "I'll check their obits. Several people at Obsession Shores have had their tragedies."

"A lot of them are old," Renie said. "Nobody who lives to retirement age gets a pass on the bad stuff."

Judith clicked *Obituaries* again, then entered *Leonetti*. "It's a single article about the brothers—and it's long."

Renie dug a chocolate-covered raisin out of the bag. "Condense it."

Judith scanned the two columns that ran a good six inches. "Background on the family business. Antonio was sixty-eight, Claudio was sixty-six." Judith skipped down to the survivors. "Brothers never married. Survivors are Frank and two nieces, Angela Leonetti Burke and Maria Leonetti Jordan. They must be Frank's daughters."

"Even I could figure out that much," Renie said. "That's it?"

"More about the business's earlier expansion. The usual affiliations, activities and hobbies along with the funeral and burial info. Memorials to their parish school's scholarship fund. This explains the comments Gina's brothers made about Frank's bad luck. You want to read it?"

"No. Just asking. Did they collect coins by any chance?"

Judith ate another cheese-covered cracker before answering. "Both brothers fished, hunted, and liked music, especially Italian folk songs. They made a pilgrimage to their father's hometown of Terracina, Italy, in 1990. I wonder if Frank went with them."

"Why?" Renie inquired. "You figure Frank wanted the business for himself and tried to push Tony and Claud off the Amalfi Drive? When that didn't work, he put a hole in their inflatable boat? Get real."

"No," Judith said with a scowl. "Though especially as business partners, brothers can have a falling-out."

Renie's expression was impish. "The brothers did fall out of their boat. Check Hank Senior. Maybe he's been arrested for window peeping."

"Hank's name drew a blank," Judith said, after finding no references. "He bought up all those old corner grocery stores, remember? I suspect that Tank probably took over from there with demolition and replacement. I'm guessing he built houses."

Renie had a quibble. "Tank's a subcontractor. Somebody else probably built the places. Still, the Hilderschmidt brothers made money off of Hank's real estate savvy."

"No doubt." Judith drank more water. "Let's see what I can find on Kent Logan."

There were at least a dozen references going back for the past three years. All of them pertained to personnel moves within his law firm except for one that caught Judith's attention.

"Listen to this, coz," she said, noting that Renie's eyes looked rather glazed. "Kent was involved in a lawsuit last March where he represented Quincy Quimby suing Helmut—that's Tank—Hilderschmidt for building-code violations in connection with work done on the boathouse. They settled out of court."

Renie looked mildly interested. "So Quincy stabs Ernie Glover because he remarked that he didn't think Tank did such a bad job?"

"Of course not," Judith replied, mildly exasperated. "But it shows contention between the Quimbys and the Hilderschmidts, with Kent on Quincy's side. Of course that makes sense because as far as we know, Kent's the only lawyer here at Obsession Shores." She waited for Renie's response, but her cousin merely popped more chocolate into her mouth. "Okay," Judith muttered. "I'm checking Ernie next."

Renie got off the sofa and walked over to the window. "It's clouding up. I'm going to rescue the clams. We might as well get them cleaned."

"Fine," Judith said, scowling. She was about to enter Ernest Glover's name when she heard Renie talking to someone outside. A minute or so later, her cousin staggered inside with the bucket of clams.

"I would've dumped the water out," Renie gasped, "but some bozo was down below the deck. He wanted to know if the Webers were home." She set the bucket down and rummaged in the cupboard.

"What did you tell him?" Judith asked, fingers poised on the keyboard.

"That they were killed in a tragic hot-air balloon accident," Renie replied. "He was probably trying to sell them something. He looked like a salesman. Who else would wear a trench coat up here?"

"A private detective?"

"I exaggerated. It was a regular raincoat." Renie hauled a big metal kettle out of the cupboard and began filling it with water. "Come to think of it, maybe the Quimbys hired someone to follow up on the old man's suspect as the killer. But why call on the Webers?"

"Maybe the guy's checking all the residents," Judith suggested.

"I doubt it. His Nissan was parked by the mailbox. He took off."

Judith set the laptop aside and got up from the sofa to join her cousin in the kitchen area. "What did he look like?"

"Oh . . ." Renie paused to put the kettle on the stove and turn on the heat. "About forty, fairly tall, sort of blond hair, average in every way. Help me toss clams into the kettle. I refuse to lift the bucket again."

Judith complied. "I wonder . . ." she murmured, more to herself than to her cousin.

"What?" Renie inquired, using a metal bowl to scoop clams out of the bucket.

"When we were in Langton, do you remember me telling you I saw the reporter who stayed at the B&B?"

"Vaguely. Eeek!" Renie made a face and rubbed her right eye. "One of those clams just spit at me."

Judith laughed. "They don't want to be boiled." She quickly grew serious. "Now you've piqued my curiosity. Why is Jack Larrabee hanging out around here? Granted, he said he was heading north, but I thought he meant straight up the freeway to Canada. He's doing a series on vacation spots in the Pacific Northwest."

Renie shrugged. "Whoopee Island is a vacation spot."

"So it is," Judith agreed. "But it's off the beaten track for anybody who isn't a local."

"I suppose that's why he's here," Renie said, dumping the last of the clams into the kettle. "He's avoiding all the usual tourist stops."

"You're probably right, but that doesn't explain why he'd want to talk to Auntie Vance and Uncle Vince." Judith wiped her hands off on a towel. "Now I wish you'd let him come in. There's something odd about his coming here. I have his cell number, but it's at home. I wonder if Arlene and Carl are at the B&B. They could look it up for me."

"Oh, coz!" Renie exclaimed. "Don't tell me you've got the hots for this guy. He's really kind of average-looking."

Judith gave Renie a disgusted look. "I'm only curious. It's my nature. The only reason I can think of is that Auntie Vance seems to be the go-to person for reliable information around here."

Renie looked miffed. "She sure kept a lot of that information to herself when it comes to what really goes on at Obsession Shores. I'll admit she didn't know there'd be a murder, but still . . ." Her voice trailed off as the cousins heard a pounding noise from somewhere outside.

"The back door?" Judith said.

"I'll go see," Renie offered, heading for the hall. "Betsy, maybe."

Judith turned down the water under the boiling kettle. A glance out to the deck showed a few raindrops splattering the picture window. She gave a start as she heard Renie talking to someone. A moment later, her cousin came out of the hall with a teary-eyed Nan Quimby.

"Mrs. Quimby is seeking sanctuary," Renie announced in a bemused voice. "She's afraid of being killed. Do we have enough steamed clams for three?"

Chapter 18

A tremulous Nan Quimby followed Renie into the kitchen area. Her thin hands clutched at the drawstrings of her brown cloak. "I'm sorry to intrude," she said, dark eyes zigzagging every which way as if she expected an unseen attacker. "The only person I trust is your aunt."

"She *is* trustworthy," Judith declared. "What's wrong?"

Nan grimaced, the hood slipping off her graying brown hair. "I only found out she was gone when that nice man brought Betsy home. I couldn't say anything to you when you came to the house. I'm sorry." She grabbed the back of a kitchen chair before sitting down. "You won't make me leave, will you?"

"Of course not," Judith said quickly, though she caught Renie giving her a warning look. "Would you like something to drink?"

Nan shook her head. "No, thank you." She rubbed her hands together. "Something strange is happening. I wish I knew what it was."

Judith sat down at the table. "Is it about Betsy?"

"No. She's always been as she is now. I don't blame her. She can escape into her own little world. I can't."

Renie, who had retrieved her candy bag, remained standing. "Can't your husband help you?"

Nan rubbed at her left eye. "He doesn't want *Père* to disinherit him," Nan replied.

"*Père?*" Judith echoed.

Nan nodded. "Quincy's mother—Blanche—was French. His parents were always called *Maman* and *Père*."

"Does your father-in-law speak French?" Judith asked.

"Not really," Nan replied. "Blanche spoke excellent English. She'd gone to school in England before the war. Her parents were what she called *la crème de la crème*. She and her family fled to England before the Germans invaded. They were all killed in the Blitz—except Blanche."

"That's so sad," Judith said. "How old was she?"

Nan had to think for a moment. "Twenty, twenty-one, I think. She joined the Red Cross. That's how she met *Père*."

Renie, who had eaten all of her chocolate, tossed the empty bag into the garbage and sat down. "How," she asked, "did you meet Quincy?"

"We went to high school together here on the island," Nan replied, her eyes in shadow. "We didn't date until later. After a year he proposed. I hadn't yet met his parents." She looked down at her hands, which were in her lap. "*Père* was opposed to the match, but Blanche overrode him. We had a simple ceremony at the county courthouse in Cooptown. Blanche, you see, was Catholic. *Père* isn't. He and Blanche were married in a London registry office. She'd hoped to have the marriage blessed by the Church eventually, but that was the one war she couldn't win. It made her very bitter." Nan finally looked at the cousins. "In the thirty-odd years I've lived in that house, it's never been a happy place."

"But you stayed," Judith said, trying to keep the incredulity out of her voice. "That's remarkable."

"You must think I'm insane to have done that," Nan said.

"Of course not," Judith assured her.

"Nothing else would explain it," Renie declared.

"Coz!" Judith glared at Renie. "That's unkind." She turned her gaze back to Nan. "My cousin doesn't always think before she speaks. What she means is . . . unf!" She winced as Renie kicked her under the table. "Leg cramp. Sorry. But I assume you had your reasons for remaining with your father-in-law. Do you and Quincy have children?"

Nan grimaced. "We wanted to, but I had several miscarriages. I felt I was cursed. Then I realized it wasn't me—it was the house."

"Was the house new when you moved in?" Judith asked.

"No," Nan replied, "but it was the only house here back then. The original family home was razed by *Père*'s father after the war to build on the same site. His family had homesteaded here over a century ago. They had a small farm and raised cows, chickens, and goats."

Renie finally sat down. "Were things any better when Blanche was alive?"

Nan sighed. "No. It was just a different kind of unhappiness. After she died, we wondered if *Père* could live long without her. He's had several serious illnesses over the years, but he always rallies. Quincy talked of moving away, but *Père* would threaten to leave all his wealth to the county to build a memorial to him and Blanche. I hate saying it, but Quincy has never really worked except to handle this swath of land. It's as if he's chained to Obsession Shores—and his father."

"But," Judith pointed out, "you're finally rebelling. Why now?"

"Because of the murder," Nan said without hesitation. "A decent man like Ernie Glover is killed. That shows how evil this place really is. I don't care who killed him—I mean, I *care,* but it's like a symptom of the disease that comes out of the very ground. I hate this place. I hate *Père* and sometimes I almost hate Quincy, who refuses to understand why I loathe living here. All he can think of is his stupid inheritance. Why can't he think about *me?*" Nan burst into tears.

Judith paused before speaking. "Quincy is at the mercy of his father, who is obviously a control freak. Your husband can't fight that this late in life. How old is . . . *Père*?"

"Ninety-six, come February twenty-ninth." Nan grimaced. "He only has a birthday every four years, so *Père* insists he's only twenty-four."

Renie's face expressed irritation. "Your complaints are justified and all that, but I don't see how we or Auntie Vance or anyone else can help. Face it, you're stuck. So why the sudden urge to unload?"

Nan's dark eyes revealed a spark of defiance. "Because I feel threatened. So does Quincy, if he'd admit it. Even *Père* is a bit put off by what's been happening around here lately."

"You mean," Judith said kindly, "Ernie's murder?"

Nan shook her head. "Not just that. I can't explain it. People are behaving oddly. It's like . . . you know that sudden eerie calm before an earthquake?" She saw the cousins nod. "That's how it feels."

"It's hard for us to understand," Judith admitted. "Renie and I have never stayed here for more than a day at a time until now. But I admit there's something strange about the atmosphere. Could it have a connection to the rumors about buried treasure?"

Nan looked alarmed. "You've heard about that?"

"Yes," Judith replied. "Of course Brose Bennett found some old coins, but we understand their authenticity is questionable."

Nan frowned. "Why?"

"By chance," Judith responded, "we stopped in at Mr. Moffitt's coin shop yesterday."

Nan sniffed. "He would say that since he's never forgiven *Père* for buying up their property when the Moffitts defaulted during the Depression. It was sold off long ago after the end of World War Two. I'll say this much for *Père*—he's very canny about money, as was his father before him."

"Since when," Renie inquired, "is parsimony a virtue?"

"It's called thrift," Nan declared—and lowered her head. "At least that's what *Père* calls it." She suddenly scrambled out of the chair. "I must go. Quincy will wonder where I am. I never stay more than twenty minutes when I visit Vanessa. *Père* considers your aunt a troublemaker." A sly smile touched her thin lips. "I think he's secretly afraid of her. She does tend to speak her mind."

Not waiting to be shown out, Nan rushed to the door and left.

Judith had stood up, but Renie remained seated at the table, resting her chin on her hand. "Nan's not as crazy as Betsy, but she's not exactly all there either."

"She's a victim," Judith said.

"Victims often have no one to blame but themselves," Renie declared. "Nan must have had her eyes shut tight when she married Quincy. Or else she figured she'd end up rich."

Judith resumed her place at the table. "I don't see it quite that way. Nan and Quincy were married over thirty years ago when old Quimby was in his sixties. The house probably seemed like a logical stopping place until he died from one of his medical problems. Nan couldn't know the ornery codger had an iron constitution. I'll bet she has no idea of how these properties were handled. Quimby didn't start selling the lots until around the time his son got married."

Renie looked thoughtful. "Dick Sedgewick told us the idea was Blanche's. Obviously, Quimby went along with it."

Judith's dark eyes danced. "Blanche has been a shadowy figure so far. I think we need to do more digging, and I'm not talking about clams."

Five minutes later, Renie was eating clams out of the shell. "These aren't enough for dinner," she announced. "One bucket of clams does not a dinner make. Let's go to that French restaurant in Langton."

"Cabaret?" Judith said. "We should get a reservation."

"They don't take reservations. They don't have a menu either. You love a mystery. Why not try it?"

"Oh . . . sure. But it's only a little after four. And what do we do about the clams?"

"Eat them. Then we won't have to order appetizers." Renie tossed two clams into her mouth at once.

"Well, we didn't have lunch. Bring the bucket over to the sofa so we can get back to our research." Judith stood up.

"We need some melted butter," Renie declared. "I'll do that while you take the bucket."

Judith complied, pausing to check the weather. "It's starting to rain," she said before sitting back down on the sofa.

"So? That's not news."

"If it gets socked in, it'll hamper our watch tonight for the mystery boat. Maybe we should scout a location while it's still daylight."

Renie almost dropped the microwave dish holding the butter. "You're serious about doing that over by Scratchit Head?"

"Of course I am," Judith replied, making herself comfortable. "Bring the Obsession Shores map along with the bucket. I want to see if there's any way we can avoid driving around to Scratchit Head and still see where the phantom ship comes from."

"Jeez!" Renie shut up as the microwave timer went off. She gathered up everything and joined her cousin. "I'm older, you know."

Judith looked sheepish. "Sorry, coz. All that digging got to me."

Renie grinned. "I know. It's fine. Have some butter. What or who are you going to check into now?"

"I forget where we left off," Judith said, studying the development map. "This is odd. There *is* one parcel of land that's vacant. Take a look. It's next to the Quimby house on the edge of the forest."

"Hunh," Renie said. "How come we didn't notice that when we called on the Quimbys? Did we figure it was part of their garden?"

Judith tried to remember what the area north of the Quimby house looked like. "There wasn't much of a garden," she finally said. "In fact, the only things that were growing besides some kind of straggly grass were native plants. The house took up most of the lot. That's odd. If I remember correctly the vacant spot was covered with more wild stuff, as if it had been cleared for sale, but left untended."

"That sounds right," Renie murmured. "That's weird."

Judith set the map aside and stood up. "Let's take another look while it's still light outside."

Renie frowned. "You sure you want to walk up there?"

"It's not very far," Judith asserted. "I've been sitting around for a couple of hours."

"Your call," Renie said, eating the last clam as she got to her feet. "At least it's not pouring. I'll dump the shells with the rest of the garbage on the way out."

The rain had actually dwindled, blowing southward. They could see over to the Peninsula, though the mountains were obscured by clouds. Judith noticed that a few lights had been turned on in some of the surrounding houses. But not at the Quimby residence, a fact she mentioned to Renie.

"They're in the dark in more ways than one," her cousin remarked.

"I'm afraid they live in a very dark world," Judith said ruefully as they turned past the Sedgewick house. "I wonder if Betsy stays inside when it rains."

Renie looked up at the derelict home from which the old man ruled over Obsession Shores. "I wonder if she notices the rain that much. We don't, unless it's a downpour. We're natives." She involuntarily shivered as they approached the vacant lot next door. "I think I'm spooking myself."

"Take it easy," Renie cautioned. "I doubt they'll release the hounds."

They stopped just beyond the Quimby property, gazing at the

overgrown lot that remained unsold. Vine maples, wild black-berry bushes, salal, Oregon grape, and several varieties of ferns had sprung up in nature's attempt to reclaim the vacant lot.

"Why?" Judith said under her breath.

"Why what?" Renie asked.

Judith shook her head. "I don't understand why this lot was never sold. Didn't it perc? If not, why didn't the Quimbys plant vegetables or something? They went to the trouble to clear it. If a sewer system is put in, it's probably worth close to a hundred grand. Like all the other lots, whoever builds here has an amazing view."

Renie smirked. "And live next door to the Quimbys? No thanks."

"The buyers wouldn't know that," Judith said. She walked carefully off the road and onto the property. A glance to her left surprised her with a narrow view looking over to Scratchit Head. "Hey, coz," she called to Renie, "I forgot about the adjacent community of Dandy Look. How do you get there from here?"

Renie joined Judith, craning her neck to glimpse the narrow spit with a single road between the homes on each side. "You don't. You take the road just before the turnoff to Obsession Shores. Hey, that means if you really want to carry out your phantom-ship sighting tonight, all we have to do is drive back out to the highway and turn into Dandy Look."

"You're right," Judith agreed. "It's a smaller community, but they have their own marina. Maybe that's where the mystery boat is kept."

"Of course." Renie grinned. "That solves that. We don't have to go out tonight after all."

"Yes, we do," Judith declared. "I want to be certain. It could come from Scratchit Head or . . . some other place," she murmured.

"How about Uranus?"

"What?"

Renie sighed. "Never mind. Are we done here?"

"I guess so," Judith said, but walked carefully up the slight slope, trying not to let the wet underbrush dampen her slacks. "I'll bet the deer come here quite often. Lots of greenery for them to munch on. Too bad they prefer Auntie Vance's rose . . . oops!" She staggered slightly as her right foot struck something solid. "Damn! I hit my toe."

Renie hurried to her cousin's side. "Did you do any damage?"

"To myself, or whatever I hit?" Judith didn't wait for an answer. "I'm fine. It was my good hip's side."

Renie looked relieved. "What was it? A root?"

"No." Judith moved her foot around, trying to make sure she wouldn't stumble again. "Here. You bend over. It feels like a rock."

"It's cement," Renie replied after yanking away the tall grasses and a couple of ferns. "Good grief," she gasped. "It's a tombstone."

Judith moved closer. "I can't lean down. Can you see the name?"

"Yes," Renie replied. "It's not that old. Let me brush off more dirt and leaves." She worked quickly, clearing the simple marker to reveal a name and dates. " 'Blanche Marie Moreau Quimby, born April 3, 1921, died August 31, 1998.' "

"Quimby's wife," Judith murmured, crossing herself. "She was several years younger than he was. *Is,* I mean, still being alive. But why bury her here? And not keep up the grave site?"

"Good question," Renie agreed. "He wanted her close by, but . . ." She shrugged. "It's futile trying to make sense of Quentin Quimby's mind-set."

Judith sighed. "It certainly is. I suppose this burial site is why the lot's never been sold. Let's get out of here. I don't like this place. If I believed in ghosts, I'd swear it was haunted."

The cousins trudged back to the Weber house in silence. The rain had stopped and the pale sun was setting over the Peninsula. Judith finally spoke when they reached the deck.

"I wonder if the Sedgewicks know about Blanche's grave. I think I'll call them when we get inside."

Renie undid the lock and opened the door. "Go ahead."

As soon as Judith took off her car coat, she went to the phone on the kitchen counter. Jane answered on the second ring.

"Good timing," she said. "We're about to have a cocktail. Want to join us?"

"No, thanks," Judith said with an appropriate amount of regret. "Renie and I are going into Langton to have dinner at Cabaret."

Jane laughed. "We haven't been there in ages. Dick swears he never knows what he's eating. It's always good, though."

"That's encouraging," Judith said. "We just got back from a little walk. What do you know about the vacant lot next to the Quimby place?"

"Oh . . ." Jane paused. "Not much, really, except that Mrs. Quimby's grave is there. I guess the old coot didn't want to spend the money on a cemetery plot."

"He could've made more money selling the lot," Judith pointed out.

"Probably. But he's an odd one. Got to go. The cocktail lamp is lit." Jane rang off.

"That's strange," Judith said as she put the phone in its cradle. "I could swear Jane's fobbing me off about that empty lot."

"Why would she do that?" Renie asked from where she'd parked herself on the sofa. "Did she know about the tombstone?"

"Yes." Judith sat down next to her cousin. "What I'd really like to know is why that lot gave me the creeps. Did it affect you that way?"

Renie shook her head. "Seen one empty lot, seen 'em all."

The response didn't help Judith shake off her eerie sense of doom.

Chapter 19

There was only a brief wait at Cabaret. The small dining room was full after Judith and Renie were seated at six thirty. Their table wasn't by a window, but darkness had descended, so they didn't complain.

"How do we know what we'll be eating without a menu?" Judith asked.

"We won't," Renie replied. "For all I know, they only prepare one item each night. Let's hope it's something we like. If not, dinner's over, as Grandma Grover used to say when anybody griped about what she'd cooked."

Happily, the bespectacled, middle-aged server identified herself as Wanda and informed them that the entrée du jour was prawns with truffles. Renie licked her lips.

"We get greens and bread, too," she exulted. "And all for under thirty bucks."

"You call that a bargain?" Judith shot back. "There better be at least a dozen prawns."

"Hey, I'm the one who's supposed to be a pig," Renie chided. "You're irked because you haven't spotted anyone to interrogate."

Judith's gaze roamed to the entrance. "I have now. Here come the Bendareks and the Blomquists."

"Great," Renie muttered, craning around to glimpse the newcomers. "Just when I wanted to take a sleuthing break."

Judith squinted in the candlelit interior. "Relax. They haven't spotted us."

Wanda arrived with the wine that she'd suggested as an accompaniment.

"The Chardonnay is from Sonoma," she whispered with a hint of apology. "The French wines are a bit pricey for our clientele."

"No problem," Renie said. "They all taste like mouthwash to me."

Wanda smiled weakly. "How . . . clever." She practically galloped away, almost colliding with the foursome of women who were getting out of their chairs at the adjacent table.

"Oh, drat," Renie said with a sigh. "Now the Bendareks and the Blomquists will be grilled along with the prawns."

"Stop griping and start drinking like everybody else." Judith lifted her wineglass. "To finding a killer."

Renie looked disgusted, but lifted her own glass to touch Judith's. "Before he or she finds us. Gosh, I feel better already, you twit."

Judith was unmoved by the sarcasm. "Motive. We still don't have one. Don't forget this seems to be a premeditated homicide. Well timed, if there really were no witnesses."

"Imminent storm scared everybody off the beach," Renie noted. "Except Ernie, of course." Her eyes strayed beyond Judith. "End of discussion. Obsession Shores crew about to be seated at the adjacent table for four."

If the newcomers noticed the cousins, they didn't react. The quartet seemed caught up in their own company, especially Becca and Katie. Judith was glad to see that Becca looked happy, no doubt because she was in the company of a woman who wasn't eligible for Social Security.

Judith made a face. "I am not trying to eavesdrop," she declared.

"And the world ends tomorrow. Which," Renie continued,

"reminds me to ask if we are, in fact, leaving here in the morning."

Judith couldn't help looking put off. "Well . . . under the circumstances, I feel it'd be wrong to turn away from what's happened. Wouldn't Auntie Vance say we were chickens?"

Renie looked askance. "She'd be more likely to think you'd had a personality transplant. It's fine with me, but what about the B&B?"

"You're right." Feeling guilty about imposing on her neighbors, Judith grabbed her purse and car coat. "I'll alert the Rankers now before they get Mother settled in for the night." She stood up to go outside.

Judith didn't have to worry about noisy traffic on Langton's main street. Only one car and a small van passed by as she placed the call to Hillside Manor. To her surprise, Gertrude answered.

"You're still alive?" the old lady inquired, sounding faintly disappointed. "You picked up any sailors yet?"

"No, Mother," Judith replied. "Is Arlene there?"

"Who's Arlene?" Gertrude shot back. "What's the matter with you? Are you asking for bail money or have you and that squirrel-bait niece of mine kept out of trouble?"

"We're fine," Judith assured her mother. "But we're going to stay over another night. Are you okay?"

"Other than waiting for the Grim Reaper? Carl and I are playing cribbage. Arlene makes dinner at a sensible time—on the table by five fifteen. We had chicken and dumplings tonight. No feathers on the chicken either. Unlike yours."

"That's . . . good," Judith said. "Could I talk to Arlene?"

"I suppose you could," Gertrude grumbled, "but what for? You think I can't tell her you're not coming back tomorrow?"

"We still might," Judith said, "but it'd be more toward evening. I wanted to make sure that—"

"Judith?" Arlene's voice was at the other end. Obviously, Gertrude had handed off the phone. "Is something wrong?"

Judith was glad her neighbor couldn't see the grim expression on her face. "Not really. Renie and I didn't want to fight Sunday-night traffic, so we may not be back until later tomorrow. Is that okay with you?"

"Of course!" Arlene exclaimed. "It's been quite a while since Carl and I've been able to spend time with your darling mother. She's such a joy, like a burst of sunshine in the middle of August."

"You mean January," Judith said with a weak little laugh.

"No, I don't. Yes, Carl and I will be delighted to spend more time here. Your guests have all been well behaved. Except for the Turk."

"The Turk?" Judith didn't recall any guest reservations with Turkish names. "Dare I ask what happened?"

"He misplaced his fez," Arlene replied. "I found it. Sweetums had dragged it into the kitchen and seemed quite intrigued by the tassel."

"Oh. That's . . . good." Judith recalled that the weekend guests included a man and his wife who were passing through town en route to a meeting in Portland for the Shriners' children's hospital. The last name was Olsen. "I'm glad everything's fine. Any new reservations?"

Arlene laughed. "How would I know? We don't own a computer. Nobody's called, though. You're certain everything's all right with you up on the island?"

Judith had been hoping Arlene wouldn't ask, but perhaps the homicide story had been on TV or in the newspaper. "Yes, really. Renie and I are always cautious in these situations."

"Good," Arlene said. "Those ferry rides can be risky. So often they run into other boats or go aground. Do make sure the captain on your return trip is sober. I must dash. I promised your dear mother an extra serving of blueberry cobbler for dessert. Oh, dear—I think she just won again at cribbage. Poor Carl." Gertrude's triumphant cackle could be heard in the background as Arlene hung up.

Judith clicked off the cell, wondering if the Rankers and her mother had missed seeing the news about the Whoopee Island homicide. Given that it had happened out of town, the big city daily might have relegated the report to a mere paragraph. The local TV stations wouldn't bother sending a crew out of town.

After putting the cell in her purse, Judith noticed a man walking toward the restaurant. As he passed under the streetlight, she recognized him as Jack Larrabee. He stopped a few paces away. "Mrs. Finn?" he said in surprise.

"Flynn," Judith responded. "I saw you here in Langton yesterday."

"Yes." Jack seemed amused. "You were right about the weather. It's been kind of gloomy until late this afternoon."

"Where are you staying?" she asked as a car carrying a bunch of teenagers drove too fast down the main drag.

"At Scratchit Head," he replied. "A former colleague retired here. He and his wife invited me stay with them." He paused. "Are you going inside or do you enjoy hanging out on small-town street corners?"

"I had to call the B&B to see how things are going without me," Judith said, trying not to be annoyed by his comment. "My cousin and I are waiting for our entrées."

"In that case, let's join her." Jack reached around Judith to open the door and allowed her to enter first.

To Judith's chagrin, he followed her to the table, where she saw that the main course had been served. "You'll have to get a chair," she told Jack as Renie stared at her cousin's companion.

"You were out picking up a guy?" she asked after Jack went off to find an empty chair.

Judith sat down. "It's the reporter, Jack Larrabee. He's staying with an old pal at Scratchit Head." She picked up her fork and stared at her plate in disbelief. "Where are my prawns?"

"I ate them," Renie replied. "There were only seven. Another serving's on the way. The dessert is crème brûlée. Yum!"

"You're such a hog," Judith declared, trying to keep her voice down. "Selfish, too. How could you?"

"Easy," Renie replied as Jack arrived with a chair. "Here comes your entrée and your new boyfriend."

"Well," Jack said, sitting down, "you must be the cousin. You have a name?"

"It's Pig," Judith asserted. "She ate all my prawns."

Wanda set a plate in front of Jack. "Oh, dear—did I forget to bring your sides?" she asked in an anxious tone.

"That's okay," Jack said. "Any time will do."

"Wait!" Judith all but shouted. "Prawnie ate my reens! I mean—"

Renie waved her fork. "Bring her another entrée. Some people are never satisfied. Oh—we could use more bread, too. Lots more bread."

Wanda hurried off. Judith noticed that the Bendareks and the Blomquists were staring at them.

"Yo, tiger lady!" Zach shouted. "Anybody take a shot at you yet?"

"No," Renie called back, "but I've seen you take a shot at another lineman and get a fifteen-yard penalty for unnecessary roughness. Didn't you notice he was on *your* team?" She turned to Jack. "I'm Renie, by the way. Nice to meet you."

"Right," he murmured. "Good prawns."

Zach was guffawing so hard that Judith thought his chair would break. She held her head and wished she were back at the B&B, listening to her mother bitch and watching Sweetums mangle Mr. Olsen's fez. Jack gobbled up two prawns at once.

"So," Renie said to their unexpected guest, "are you here to cover a story or just to hang out with all these fun folks on The Rock?"

"Both," he replied between mouthfuls. "Where are you staying?"

Judith decided that since Renie had stuffed the last of the bread into her mouth, she might as well join the conversation. "We're house-sitting for our aunt and uncle at Obsession Shores."

Jack put his fork down. "No kidding. In that case, I may interview you. But not here."

"Why?" Judith asked. "We're not residents. We don't know much more about the island's tourist sights than you could find in a brochure on the ferry."

"So?" Jack ate a bite of *pommes frites* before speaking. "I'm not focusing on the getaway series right now. I'm talking about the murder."

He'd lowered his voice, but Judith noticed that the Bendareks and the Blomquists seemed absorbed in their food. "Why would that be of interest to Midwest readers?" she asked.

"It's not intended for them," Jack replied. "Your local media isn't covering it. That means I get an exclusive and maybe a wire service byline. Assuming there's enough human interest, of course. Is there?"

Judith was momentarily distracted by the arrival of her entrée, another basket of French bread, and an abject apology from the server. "Have you begun interviewing anyone yet?" Judith finally inquired after Wanda rushed away.

Jack shook his head. "I only started this morning with the sheriff's office, but the deputy heading the investigation is off today. I did nose around Obsession Shores before I came to dinner here. I went down to the beach, but I couldn't figure out where the murder occurred."

Renie apparently noted that Judith's mouth was full. "How did you know there was a murder in the first place?"

"Some people were talking about it at that general store down the street," Jack said, perhaps aware that the Bendarek table had grown quiet. "Let's back off. I'd prefer not to be overheard. I'll follow you back to Obsession Shores after dinner. Unless," he added, his gray eyes mocking, "you two plan to make a wild night of it in Langton."

"Fine," Judith said politely. "It's not a suitable dinner topic. In any event, there's nothing we can tell you."

Jack shrugged. "There's always something people can tell me." He finished buttering a chunk of crusty bread. "It's what they *don't* tell me that makes my job so interesting."

I don't trust that guy," Judith declared, pulling away from the curb after dinner.

Renie laughed. "You're just ticked off because you couldn't spend the dinner hour speculating about whodunit."

Judith braked for the arterial. "Maybe I also got annoyed because somebody ate my prawns."

"They looked lonesome," Renie said.

Turning onto the highway, Judith checked to make sure Jack was still behind them. "Okay, I'm over it," she asserted. "But we don't give Jack one word about the murder case. Got it?"

"Yeah, fine, sure," Renie mumbled. "But I don't understand why you mistrust him. He's a journalist and maybe a bit of a hustler. The poor guy is working for the dinosaur-like print media. You can't blame him for trying to make a name for himself so he can put food on the table. Writing blogs that nobody reads isn't very profitable."

Judith frowned. "Have you considered that I don't want to tell him what we've learned about the Obsession Shores residents?"

"Frankly, we haven't learned much," Renie replied, sitting up straight again. "At least nothing that helps finger the killer. I'd like to be there when he comes up against the Quimbys, especially the old duffer."

Judith remained silent until they reached the turnoff that led to Obsession Shores. "Journalists have good sources. On second thought, I might humor Jack. He could do some legwork."

"Why not? As far as I can tell, he has two good hips."

"Maybe," Judith said sheepishly, "what really bugs me is that he slipped by us and was prowling on the beach while I was on the computer and you were stuffing your face with dark chocolate."

"I wouldn't have it any other way," Renie declared. "Be reasonable. You can't keep track of what everybody's doing around here. Have you forgotten that we were innocently sitting in Auntie Vance and Uncle Vince's house while someone whacked Ernie Glover?"

Judith's shoulder's slumped. "No. Damn. It's all in the timing."

"You mean because nobody else saw it happen either?"

Slowing for the turn into Obsession Shores, Judith glanced at Renie. "I think somebody did see it happen."

"Who?" Renie asked, staring at her cousin.

"I want to be sure before I tell even you," Judith said, steering the Subaru into the garage. "Even then, it might not matter."

Renie threw up her hands before getting out of the car.

Five minutes later, the cousins were inside, sitting on the sofa—and still waiting for Jack Larrabee.

"Wasn't he right behind you?" Renie asked.

"He was, the last time I looked," Judith replied. "That was when we turned off to the development road by the sign."

"Have you got a cell number for him?"

"No." Judith made a face. "I do at home, though. I wonder if Arlene's still there."

Renie checked her watch. "It's going on eight."

Judith sighed and reached into her purse. "I'll give it a shot. Check to see if his car has pulled up by the mailbox."

A breathless Arlene answered. "I was about to take your mother back to her cozy little apartment. She's had us in stitches over her adventures as a flapper in the Roaring Twenties. She even tried to show us how to dance the Black Bottom."

"That's . . . adorable," Judith said. "I need a quick favor. Go to the computer and check the heading for last week's guests. I need a phone—"

"Judith," Arlene interrupted, "I've told you, I have no idea how to turn on a computer, let alone use it. Carl might, but he went home to let Tulip out. Our poor doggie has been inside since just after Mass. Oh—your mother wants to wish you good night. Don't you, dear Gertrude?" There was a pause. "Don't you think that would be *nice*?" Arlene's voice was pleading.

Judith heard her mother mutter something, but a moment later the old lady was talking at the other end. "Yeah, I'm still alive. Quit hoping for otherwise. When are you two noodle heads coming home? Your aunt Deb's called me about ten times today."

"I just wanted to say good night," Judith fibbed, seeing Renie come back inside, shaking her head.

"Don't hurry on my account," Gertrude rasped. "I don't know what you're up to there on The Rock, but we're having *fun* here. And I've never figured out what Vance and Vince do up there either. I'm sure glad we never got suckered into buying that empty lot next to the old grump."

"The . . ." Judith almost dropped the cell. "You mean next to the man who owned all the property?"

"Who else? He and his foreign wife gave me a pain in my backside. Had a funny name too, like Quinsy. That's an old-fashioned disease, you know. I guess it went out of style. Nobody gets sick with it anymore. Hang up now so I can watch my favorite TV show at eight o'clock. If I can remember what it is." Gertrude rang off before Judith could say good-bye.

"What now?" Renie asked. "You look as if you've been Gert-smacked."

"I have," Judith said in a weak voice. "Mother told me that the vacant lot was the one they were going to buy. No wonder I felt as if it was haunted."

"Your father wouldn't be haunting it," Renie asserted. "You were the apple of Uncle Donald's eye."

Judith smiled wistfully. "I know. Mother was always the disciplinarian. But that still doesn't explain why the lot wasn't sold to another buyer or why it feels so creepy."

"Only to you," Renie said, though she sounded more puzzled than indifferent. "Maybe it's because the lot represents a dream that your father had, but he died before he could make it come true."

"Perhaps," Judith allowed. "I got the impression just now that Mother wasn't all that keen on buying it in the first place. Back then, they still had the family cabins on the river. I honestly don't remember much about the whole thing. I guess I was too caught up with my own life in those days." She smiled again, still melancholy. "No sign of Jack?"

"Maybe he got a hot news tip on his cell or somehow missed seeing you turn off here," Renie suggested. "If he really wants to interview us, he'll show up eventually."

"True. By the way, Arlene couldn't look up Jack's number. I forgot about her lack of computer knowledge."

"That can't be helped and if anybody's desperate to stay at the B&B, they'll call," Renie said, sitting down on the sofa. "What now? More online background?"

Judith looked glum. "It hasn't gotten us anywhere so far. We could call on Edna Glover again. Katie and Greg may still be at Cabaret." She stood up and marched over to the peg by the kitchen wall. "If you want to sit there like a lump, fine."

"As a matter of fact," Renie responded, sounding unusually bland, "I'll do that. I'm tired of walking. I have flat feet, in case you've forgotten."

"Fine," Judith said, putting on her coat. "Use your fallen arches to get up so you can lock the door behind me."

After waiting to hear a click from inside, Judith walked carefully down the steps. It occurred to her that she could spare her tired hip by driving to the Glover house. Five minutes later, she was parking the Subaru on the verge in front of the modest cedar-shake dwelling. A light glowed behind the living room window.

Judith got out of the car, noting that the wreath was still in place on the front door. She waited only a few seconds before the teenager known to Judith as Em greeted her with a surprised expression.

"I thought you were Mr. and Mrs. Blomquist," she said, speaking louder as gleeful childish voices could be heard from the living room.

"They don't have a key?" Judith asked, stepping inside.

Em looked embarrassed. "I wondered if they lost it. I shouldn't have opened the door. I can't see who's on the porch because the wreath covers the peek hole. I'm trying to get the kids to settle down, but they're in the living room with their sleeping bags. I've already turned off the lights in there twice. Come into the kitchen."

Judith followed Em down the short hall. "Actually, I came to see Mrs. Glover. Edna, I mean. I gather she's not home."

"That's right," Em replied. "She's gone."

"Gone to dinner?" Judith asked.

Em shook her head. "Gone away. I don't know when she plans to come back. Would you like to sit down?"

Struck dumb by Em's words, Judith could only nod. And sit.

Three or four minutes passed while Em was laying down the law to the two Glover grandchildren in the living room. By the time the babysitter returned to the kitchen, Judith had regained her aplomb. She complimented Em on her handling of the little boys. "You must've have had a lot of practice, Em. Do you have younger siblings?"

Em nodded as she sat down. "I've got two brothers, ten and eight. There aren't many kids to babysit around here."

"I suppose that's so," Judith conceded. "Did you mean that Mrs. Glover—the grandmother—wasn't coming back tonight?"

"I guess," Em said. "All I know is her daughter told me her mom was on an important journey."

"Do you know how long the Blomquists are staying here?"

Em shook her head. "I hope it's for a few days, though. They have some plans, so maybe I'll get to babysit again."

"Plans to . . . maybe stay on for Mr. Glover's funeral?"

"I don't know about that. I just heard the kids' dad say something about a plan. Or plans. Brad was crying, so I didn't catch all of it."

Puzzled, Judith surrendered, deciding that she shouldn't badger Em any longer. "I should go. It's quiet in the living room now. You probably want to watch TV."

"There isn't a TV here." Em smiled wryly as she and Judith both stood up. "Kind of weird, huh? But I've got my homework."

"You're very conscientious," Judith said. "Do you live close by?"

"In back of this house," Em replied. "If my parents weren't right there, I'd be kind of scared to stay alone with little kids."

"I don't blame you." Judith paused with her hand on the doorknob. "If anyone else comes to the door, ask who it is before you open it."

Em grimaced. "I will. That was really dumb of me not to do that. But their parents told me they'd be home by eight. It's almost that now."

Judith wished Em good night and left. Sure enough, a car was coming along the road in her direction. She hurried to the Subaru, but once inside, she waited to make sure it was the younger Glovers. Up close she saw that the vehicle was some kind of big SUV. It slowed down next to her and stopped. The driver rolled down the window.

"Hey," Zach Bendarek shouted in a suspicious voice. "What's up?"

Judith pressed the button for the passenger window. "It's me," she called back, glimpsing Katie and Greg behind the Bendareks. "I'm just leaving."

"Oh," Zach said. "Take it easy. I think somebody's trying to break into the Weber house. Have a good one." He rolled the window back up.

Chapter 20

Judith couldn't see any cause for alarm at her aunt and uncle's house. She assumed Zach had seen Jack Larrabee trying to get Renie's attention. But as she turned onto the main road to reach the garage, she saw no sign of Jack's car. Mild panic set in as she hurried up the stairs and pounded on the door. There was no immediate response. Heedless of what anyone within hearing range might think, she yelled Renie's name.

To her relief, she finally heard her cousin's voice. "What's the password?" Renie inquired.

"Pig," Judith yelled. "Open up!"

It took Renie several seconds to unlock the door. "Is someone chasing you?" she asked. "You look awful."

"Never mind. Zach told me someone was trying to break in here."

"Oh. Right." Renie stretched and yawned. "It was Jack. He's in the can. His car broke down right before he saw us turn off. He's been waiting for AAA to rescue him. The Nissan was towed into Langton."

"You mean we've got another overnight guest?" Judith asked, struggling to get out of her car coat.

"Probably," Renie said grudgingly. "We seem to have inherited Auntie Vance's knack for hospitality. Or yours."

"I get paid for it," Judith murmured. "Wait," she said, brightening. "We can drive him over to Scratchit Head and then watch for the phantom ship."

"Oh . . ." Renie twirled around the kitchen floor. "I'd hoped you'd forgotten that nutty idea."

Jack had emerged from the bathroom and was about to sit down in the recliner. "What nutty idea?" he asked.

"You don't want to know," Renie said, opening the wooden bread box on the kitchen counter. "I forgot about Auntie Vance's coffee cake."

"You can't be hungry already," Judith declared.

"Homemade coffee cake?" Jack inquired. "I haven't tasted that since my wife left me for the piano tuner."

"It has to be warmed up," Renie said after cutting off a slice. "Vance must've made it Wednesday or Thursday."

"You got any coffee to go with it?" Jack asked.

"No coffee this late," Renie shot back. "Have some booze like everybody else does up here."

Jack declined the liquor. "Why do you think my wife left me?" he murmured. "She doesn't know how to play the piano." He turned to Judith, who'd sat down on the sofa. "You know anything about Ernie Glover's murder?"

"Not really," Judith replied. "Do you?"

"Just snatches of information I've picked up in Langton and the folks at Scratchit Head," Jack said, staring at his scuffed black leather boots. "Unreliable for a reporter. I need facts. I figured out approximately where the victim was found because my pal Jerry's wife had spotted what looked like emergency people congregating on the beach Friday afternoon." His gaze flicked over the cousins. "I've no idea who discovered the body and called the cops. Evelyn—Jerry's wife—thought she saw a couple of women." The keen gray eyes finally fixed on Judith.

"Okay," she said reluctantly. "So Renie and I found Ernie Glover. That doesn't mean we have any idea who killed him.

We'd just arrived less than an hour before we went down to the beach. And no, we'd never met the victim."

Jack's expression was bland. "Your relatives must've known him. How did they react to his murder?"

"They haven't reacted," Renie asserted. "They're in Nebraska."

The hint of a smile touched Jack's wide mouth. "I think they have phones in Cornhusker country."

As if on cue, a phone rang. Judith started to get up, but stopped when she saw Jack reach into his shirt pocket and take out his cell. "Larrabee," he said, and listened to whoever was at the other end. "Okay, so what time will you be back?"

Renie was still in the kitchen. "Damn. This coffee cake's stale. I'll make popcorn. Those portions at Cabaret weren't very big, not even two of them put together."

Judith sighed, but turned her attention to Jack, who was looking resigned as he listened to the caller. "Then I'll have to walk back to Scratchit Head," he said into the cell. "My hosts are out for the evening. Tell the auto repair shop to call me tomorrow at this number when they get finished." He paused. "How backed up can they be in a little town? . . . Right, I know it's a big island. Is there a car rental nearby?" Another pause. "How I am supposed to get way up to Hoak Arbor? . . . Screw it." He clicked off the cell. "Damned isolated small towns. Only one mechanic at this end of the island and he's busy. Why didn't I stay on the mainland?"

"Quit bitching," Renie called from the stove, where she was heating oil in a kettle. "You think you've got a problem? The Webers don't have any microwave popcorn. I have to do this the old-fashioned way."

Jack shot her a dirty look, but when he spoke it was to Judith. "You're stuck with me because Jerry and Evelyn are out for the evening. They won't get back until after midnight. I should call them now to see if they can pick me up on their way home from Libertyville." He reached again for the cell.

"Wait," Judith said. "We can drive you over to your friends' house, around eleven. Do you have a key?"

"I know where they keep the spare," he replied, "but why wait?"

Judith raised her voice to be heard over the sound of popcorn popping. "Well . . . I'm kind of tired. It's been a long day. We dug clams earlier. And," she went on, kicking herself for admitting it even if the excuse was exaggerated, "I have an artificial hip. I have to rest it."

"Oh. Of course." Jack seemed satisfied with the explanation.

"Hey," Renie called out as she removed the kettle from the stove, "we can play three-handed pinochle. How about it, Larrabee?"

"I'm game," he said.

"Then we're on," Renie declared.

For the next two hours, Judith put murder out of her mind. Instead, she made a killing of her own, collecting a dollar and fifty cents' worth of the quarters they had put into the pot for each game. At ten after eleven, they left the house, driving out into the moonless night. The clouds still hung low, but no rain had fallen. Nor were there many cars on the road. Shortly after eleven thirty they let Jack off at the well-tended rambler owned by Jerry and Evelyn. The cousins waited to make sure he found the key and got inside before they drove away.

But they didn't go far. Judith parked at the end of the Scratchit Head road that stopped where the narrow inlet cut into the island. They could see out not only to the bay, but also to the small, narrow settlement below Obsession Shores and the marina belonging to the spit's homeowners.

Renie peered at her watch. "We've got fifteen minutes to wait for the phantom ship," she informed Judith. "I can't believe we didn't have any visitors while we were playing cards."

"I can't either," Judith admitted. "In fact, it's kind of creepy."

Renie stared at her cousin. "What do you mean?"

Judith shook herself. "I don't know. It's as if . . . it's like the lull before the storm. That's the only way I can describe the feeling."

Renie gazed out through the windshield. "Storms aren't uncommon up here this time of year. But I assume that's not what you mean."

"That's right. I don't."

"Hey," Renie said, straining for a better look at Scratchit Head's main road, "I see a car. That must be Jack's friends."

"Probably," Judith murmured, but kept her eyes fixed on the marina. "Fifty boats, but only thirty-six houses. Interesting."

"It is?" Renie sounded skeptical. "Why?"

"It could mean that people who don't live along the spit can rent marina space to outsiders."

"Or," Renie said drolly, "some of the residents have more than one boat. Are you suggesting that the phantom ship comes from there?"

"That's my best guess," Judith responded. "I keep waiting for somebody to come down to the marina. It'd take some time to start the boat and head out toward the bay."

"Most of the houses are dark," Renie noted. "I wonder if they're permanent residents or summer retreats. I don't recall Auntie Vance ever talking about the people at the spit."

"They're very isolated. Not much of a view, except at the west end by the bay. The bluffs on both sides cut them off. There's not a lot of room for gardens. Maybe the people who live there are privacy fiends. From what little I can see, the houses are rather handsome. It could be a gated community. You certainly can't see anything from the road."

Renie checked her watch again. "It's seven to midnight. Maybe the mystery boat's skipper doesn't go out on Sundays."

"Just our luck if he doesn't." Judith shifted uncomfortably in the driver's seat. "Damn. I've been sitting too long. I've got to get up and stretch. Don't take your eyes off the marina."

"I can't," Renie muttered. "I'm starting to feel as if I'm hypnotized."

"Stay that way," Judith said, opening the door. "I'll walk around the car a couple of times."

"Go for it." Renie kept staring.

The damp air invigorated Judith as she carefully walked around the Subaru once before pausing to look over to Obsession Shores. There was nothing she could see. The bluff by the spit blotted out everything except the forest between the development and the road. Shrugging, she started to take a second turn, but suddenly stopped as something to her left caught her eye. Judith stood transfixed, watching the single running light move from what must have been the boathouse at Obsession Shores. She hurried back to the driver's side of the Subaru, leaning in to alert Renie.

"Mystery ship just came out of the boathouse. Quick, take a look."

Scrambling out of the car, Renie glanced again at her watch. "I'll be damned," she breathed. "It's midnight!"

"Who is it?" Judith muttered, as much to herself as to her cousin. "I was certain the boat must've come from here or even Scratchit Head."

"At least you've narrowed the suspects," Renie remarked. "Too bad we don't know all of the boat owners."

"Whoever it is appears to be turning north and out of sight," Judith said. "Let's go back to Obsession Shores. We can't find out anything from standing here."

The cousins drove back in virtual silence, both lost in thought. And conjecture. But five minutes later, when they reached the Weber house, Judith turned off the headlights, but kept going.

"Oh, no!" Renie cried. "We're not staying up all night waiting for the boat to come back, are we?"

"Cut me some slack," Judith pleaded, driving slowly down the road to the beach steps. "Twenty minutes, that's all. I can't think what any of those rather small boats would be doing every night, especially during the winter. Aren't you curious?"

Renie shot Judith a disparaging glance. "Only about whether or not you've lost your mind."

Judith braked, then put the car into reverse as she backed away from the staircase while keeping the boathouse within view. "Go ahead, time me."

"I'll give you until twelve thirty," Renie replied.

"Fine." Judith sat back and folded her arms.

"I see a ship," Renie announced after a few minutes had passed. "It's a freighter. Do you care?"

"Not unless it rammed the little boat."

"It's a pretty sight, though. I wonder where it came from," Renie mused. "Malaysia, maybe. Or Costa Rica or Madagascar. Cargo might be bananas or coconuts or petroleum. It could bring vast wealth to our hometown. Tuna fish, maybe, or tires. It might even be a slave ship from a country that has its name changed so often that I—"

Judith glared at Renie. "Would you please stop jabbering? You're getting on my nerves."

Renie uttered an exaggerated sigh. "I'm bored." She peered at her watch. "It's twelve eighteen."

"So?" Judith kept her eyes fixed on the area by Scratchit Head. "A rendezvous at sea? No, that's unlikely. Collecting something from a person on shore? Keeping watch on—"

"Stop!" Renie shouted. "Now *you're* driving *me* nuts."

"Okay, okay," Judith said, "but keep your voice down. You'll wake up whoever lives around here."

Renie, who felt no compulsion to keep watching, tried to look up the hill. "Everybody seems to have gone to bed. The closest lights I can see from here are the ones we left on."

"I suspect most people are early to bed, early to rise," Judith said, wishing her own eyes weren't becoming tired. "No wonder whoever takes out that boat doesn't worry about being seen this time of night."

"Check that." Renie rolled down the window. "I see a small light bobbing around about halfway up the hill. Wait—I see another one further up by the Sedgewicks'."

Judith was tempted to take a look, but she suddenly spotted a light coming from around Scratchit Head. "There! That must be the mystery boat. Do you suppose whoever is walking around here is coming to meet it?"

"No," Renie replied. "The lights are moving up the hill. I see a third one now."

"Damn!" Judith cursed under her breath. "Why is so much happening all at once? And this late at night? I don't suppose you'd like to walk up the hill to—"

"Stick it," Renie interrupted. "For all we know, it's the Ku Klux Klan and they're going to lynch somebody."

"Hardly that," Judith murmured. "Maybe a child ran away. Or an elderly person got lost."

"Something's up," Renie said. "I see a fourth light and it looks as if it's coming from the Bendarek house. Or across the street from them."

"The phantom ship's almost up to the boathouse." Judith paused. "Now it's disappeared, so it went inside."

"No kidding. Isn't that where it came from?"

"I wanted to be sure," Judith replied, realizing she sounded defensive. "Now all we have to do is wait to see who was in the boat."

Renie held her head. "If it isn't George Clooney, I don't care. At this point, I'm not sure I'd care if it was Bill."

Judith ignored the comments. "It shouldn't take long for the boat owner to put it back. Then we can check out the people with flashlights."

"Gosh," Renie wailed, "whatever happened to sleeping at night?"

"You're the one who stays up late working. You should be alert and feeling . . . Here he comes. Or she. I can't tell. Whoever it is, isn't using a flashlight."

"They probably ran out of them with so many people wandering around Obsession Shores with flashlights."

"I think it's a man," Judith said. "He's carrying something in each hand. Some kind of contraband, maybe? He's almost to the stairs."

"Want me to get out and yell 'boo'?" Renie asked.

"Just be quiet. We don't want him to notice us." Judith sucked in her breath. A few moments later, a man wearing a baseball cap appeared at the top of the stairs. "Frank Leonetti," she whispered excitedly. "What on earth is he carrying?"

Renie leaned forward. "Crab pots. Gee, that's really thrilling."

Judith scowled, but kept quiet as Frank trudged by the Subaru without so much as a glance. After he'd gone up the hill some twenty yards, Judith turned to Renie. "It may not be thrilling, but this time of year it's illegal. No wonder he goes out so late. But why would he keep doing it? Even you couldn't eat that many crabs."

"Because he's selling them?" Renie responded. "He does own a wholesale grocery business. You were right about contraband."

Judith gnawed on her index finger. "I wonder if Ernie knew what Frank was up to." She stared at her cousin. "That could be the motive."

Renie made a face. "Isn't that a bit much? Even if Frank got caught poaching, he'd get off with a big fine, but no jail time."

After making sure Frank was out of sight, Judith started the car, but still didn't turn on the headlights. "I'll bet Frank's the ghost Betsy saw when she stayed out later at night. Do you know where the flashlights ended up?"

"The leaders headed past Auntie Vance and Uncle Vince's house," Renie replied. "That indicates they weren't going to break in and kill us."

Judith frowned. "How many?"

"I couldn't tell. It's so dark, and the flashlights—or maybe they're lanterns—were pointed in front of whoever was carrying them. Are you sure it's a good idea to track them down?"

"Someone talked about holding a meeting tonight," Judith said. "The Logans, remember? They wanted to get everybody together to pressure the sheriff about the murder investigation."

"Oh." Renie sounded indifferent. "That's a useless effort."

"They don't know that." Judith slowed down as they passed their aunt and uncle's house. "Are you sure the people you saw were going up farther than this?"

"I'm not even sure they were people," Renie replied. "They could be poltergeists who can't see so well in the dark. But whatever or whoever, they went past the Sedgewicks'. I couldn't see anything beyond that."

Judith almost came to a stop by the octagonal-shaped home above the Weber property. "Who lives there?"

"Summer people," Renie said. "I forget their name. There's only one other house behind the Webers' on this side of the road. It's a vacation retreat, too. I suppose that's why Auntie Vance never talks much about either of the owners. They don't stick around long enough to annoy her."

Judith turned the Subaru to the left, creeping along past the darkened Quimby residence. "That place looks better in the dark," she murmured. "Do you see a sign of anybody around there?"

"No." Renie frowned. "Where could they go? There's nothing else up this far except that vacant lot—and the remains of the late Mrs. Quimby."

"Did you have to say that?" Judith asked. "I told you, I don't like that piece of turf."

"That's stupid," Renie declared. "Your father liked it well enough to want to buy it. Where's your usual rock-solid logic?"

"Okay, so for once I let my imagination get the better of me,"

Judith shot back. "Your flashlight friends must've gone into some-body else's house. I'm turning around."

"Good," Renie said, leaning back in the passenger seat. "I'm beat."

Judith couldn't find a place to turn the car around. She decided to go to the road's end and hope for more maneuvering room. But as she reached the vacant lot, she saw several bobbing lights—and people. "What on earth . . . ?" She hit the brake.

Renie sat up. "They're not poltergeists! I'll be darned."

Apparently, no one in the small gathering had heard the car's approach. "They're digging," Judith whispered. "Why?"

Her cousin didn't answer right away. "I don't mean to creep you out," she finally whispered back, "but it looks as if they're disinterring Mrs. Quimby. Here comes the casket."

Chapter 21

Gruesome!" Judith said under her breath, leaning to look out through the passenger window. "Why?"

"How do I know?" Renie muttered. "I'm rolling down the window to see if we can hear anything."

Before she could get the window more than halfway down, a voice called out to her. "Hey—who's there?"

The cousins exchanged quick looks. "Hank Hilderschmidt?" Judith whispered.

Renie nodded. Hank and Hilda were hurrying toward the Subaru. Judith and Renie froze in place.

Hank leaned down to look into the car. "The nieces? What are you doing up here?"

"That's our question," Renie shot back. "You go first."

Hank looked conflicted. Hilda sighed heavily. "We're righting a wrong, that's what. If you want to call the cops, go ahead."

Judith found her voice. "We won't do that. It's none of our business. But we sure are curious. Is it okay if we get out of the car?"

Renie was aghast. "Coz, are you nuts? Aren't you going too far to look at a dead body?"

Judith shook her head. "Check out what they dug up. It's a

casket all right, but not big enough for Blanche Quimby." She leaned to her left to look at Hank. "Am I right about that?"

Hank chuckled. "Yeah, yeah, but forget you ever saw it. We're done here. How about a ride for me and Hilda, at least as far as the Weber place? My back's killing me."

"Get in," Judith said. "I can drive you home, but I don't know where you live."

Hilda didn't answer until she was settled in the backseat. "Two houses this side of the clubhouse on the street below your aunt and uncle's place. Come on, Hank, untangle those long legs of yours."

"Right, sure . . . ahhh!" Hank finally arranged himself. "That was something."

Judith struggled trying to turn the car around without running into the other people who were coming away from the vacant lot. She recognized the Bendareks, the Logans, the Bennetts, and Edna Glover, who was carrying the little casket that up closer looked like a big jewelry box.

"What was that?" Renie inquired, taking up the slack for Judith.

"Hey," Hank said, sounding weary, "it's a long story. We're worn out. We had to wait to do all this until we were sure the Quimbys—especially cuckoo Betsy—weren't outside."

Judith finally switched on the headlights and got the Subaru turned around, but still had to be careful not to run over the more than two dozen people who were walking along the road. "Is Blanche Quimby really buried in that vacant lot?"

"Blanche!" Hilda exclaimed. "What a greedy woman. I think she drove Quentin insane. It was her idea to sell off all this property. She ruled that family with an iron fist."

Hank snorted. "A golden fist is more like it," he grumbled. "That's what she was all about—money. Meanest woman I ever met."

Turning onto the main road, Judith couldn't stifle her natural empathy. "Having a daughter with mental problems may have affected her adversely. A tragedy like that can change a person's outlook on life."

"Dubious," Hilda murmured. "The son, Quincy, let it slip some time ago that he thought his mother had coerced his father into marrying her after the war and bringing her to this country. Once the Germans were out of France, the authorities might've been on her trail."

"Why?" Judith asked. "Had Blanche collaborated with the Nazis?"

"Hell no," Hank asserted. "She was still real young, but she'd worked at one of those big Paris museums. Blanche made off with a bunch of rare coins. Something to do with Napoleon."

Renie turned to look at the Hilderschmidts. "Is that what was buried in the case you guys dug up?"

"No," Hank said. "It's . . ." He paused. "Should I shut up, Hilda?"

"Yes," his wife replied. "Wait until Kent Logan and Edna open the case. Kent's a lawyer, so he can advise us on what to do. We won't know what's in that box until they see it."

Judith took a left onto the Hilderschmidts' street. "Would I be right in guessing that you think those Napoleon coins are inside?"

"That was our idea," Hilda responded. "It doesn't rattle like it's coins, though. But what else would the Quimbys bury in it? It sure isn't Blanche's ashes. She wasn't cremated. I wouldn't be surprised if they dumped her body out in the bay."

"Is that legal?" Renie asked.

"Burial at sea?" Hank chuckled. "Only if you don't get caught. Or if you get permission. Hell, I remember a couple of ferryboat skippers who were asked to do it over the years. Hey, we're on the right-hand side of the road just up ahead. See the big stone chimney? That's us."

Judith could barely make it out, but slowed down. "Good luck," she said, pulling up by the cement walk.

Hilda waited for Hank to extricate his gangling frame from the car. When he finally got out, she looked Judith in the eye. "We don't care about luck. We want justice. Thanks for the ride."

"Could I be more confused?" Renie said while Judith reversed the car. "What's the point of digging up a bunch of coins that belong to a dead woman? She may've stolen them from a French museum, but it's too late to bring her to justice if she's at the bottom of the bay."

"It sounds more like a grudge," Judith said, slowing to a stop before they reached the main road. "Now we wait."

"For what?" Renie yipped. "Are you insane?"

Judith gestured to her left. "See that green house? It's where the Logans live. They ought to be arriving any minute."

Renie slumped in her seat. "Damn, why didn't I stay at the Webers'?"

"Go ahead, take off," Judith said. "I *can* do this alone."

"You know I won't leave you," Renie retorted, sitting up again. "For all I know, Kent and Suzie are a couple of crazed killers."

"I'm not sure about that," Judith murmured. "What's taking them so long? Unless . . ." She paused. "Of course. They walked Edna home. They wouldn't let her go by herself."

"Because she's a crazed killer?"

"Coz," Judith said earnestly, "I don't know who the crazed killer is. That's what really bugs me. I still can't figure out the motive for Ernie's murder. Maybe I *am* losing my knack."

"So we sit here while you hunt for your self-esteem," Renie muttered. "Fine. Why not let Jacobson solve this? He might get promoted. All you'll get is an urge to find another corpse."

Judith started to defend herself, but decided not to argue. Five minutes passed in silence except for the first few drops of rain sprinkling the windshield. In between the Logans' contemporary home and a shake-covered cottage, she saw a large ship gliding north to open water. As she was about to check her watch, Kent and Suzie came around the corner. He was carrying the mysterious rectangular case.

Judith got out of the car. "Hi," she called in her friendliest fashion. "You can't blame me for wondering what's in that thing. Do you mind if I come in?"

The Logans exchanged puzzled glances. "It's rather late," Kent finally said. "Why are you so interested?"

Judith shrugged. "You know Auntie Vance. If we don't give her a full report of what's happened while she and Uncle Vince have been away, she'll kill us. Excuse the expression, of course."

Suzie poked her husband's arm. "Why not? It turns out to be much ado about nothing. Edna's so disgusted."

"You're right, Suze," Kent agreed. "When everybody finds out about the contents, it'll be a big letdown."

Judith started to follow the Logans into the house, but paused as Renie called to her. "Wait. I'm not sitting out here in the dark. You want *me* to get bumped off?"

Suzie flipped on the hall light. "Come into the kitchen," she said. "I wouldn't mind a nightcap. How about you two?"

"I never wear them," Renie replied. "They ruin my coiffure." For emphasis, she ran a hand through her unruly chestnut hair.

"Ignore her," Judith said with a stern glance at her cousin. "Thank you for the offer, but no. It's a bit late for us."

Kent pulled out a chair for Judith. "Have a seat. This whole endeavor has been disappointing. But we couldn't refuse Edna's request. She was certain that whatever was buried in the vacant lot was connected to Ernie's murder. As you'll see, that's very unlikely."

The cousins and Kent sat down. Suzie busied herself with getting out snifters and a bottle of brandy. Judith realized that the buried item actually was a jewelry box. The lock had been pried open, probably by Kent, since the faint scratches looked recent.

The leather case, however, was mottled, moldy, and rotting around the edges.

"There," Kent said, flipping open the lid. "Polaroid photos and unopened letters returned to Blanche Quimby. Probably a case of unrequited love. Sad, but neither interesting nor valuable."

Judith picked up one of the Polaroids, gasped, and turned pale. With trembling fingers, she handed the picture to Renie.

"What the . . . ?" Renie gaped at her cousin. She reached in the case to remove more photos. "Good Lord! These are all of your father!"

Instead of saying anything to Renie, Judith turned to Kent. "Maybe," she said in a trembling voice, "I should have some of that brandy after all."

All four of them seemed to be talking at once. Kent shut up and raised his hands to silence the women. "What about your father?" he inquired. "Is he this Donald Grover that the letters are addressed to?"

Judith nodded, but didn't speak until Suzie handed her a snifter of brandy. "Yes. That's my mother's handwriting on the envelopes. She and my father considered buying property up here when the Webers did. But he died suddenly of a heart attack. I noticed that all these photos were taken from a distance. At first, I wasn't sure it was him, but I recognized his duffel coat. My mother had given it to him the previous Christmas."

Renie smiled. "I remember the duffel coat, too. He's wearing that snazzy tweed cap Uncle Al gave him to go with the coat. Your father always dressed so conservatively. The rest of the family wondered if he was having a midlife crisis. Or Aunt Gert was."

Judith nodded vaguely, still trying to marshal her thoughts. "Does this mean Blanche was infatuated with my father? Or . . ." She picked up one of the half-dozen letters sent to Hillside Manor's address long before it became a B&B. "This one was mailed after my father passed away."

"Maybe they all were," Kent said, handing the other letters to Judith. "How soon did he die after they considered buying in here?"

Judith frowned, trying to remember. "Not very long."

Kent smiled faintly. "Blanche must've fallen for him at first sight. Maybe she'd never been in love before. He must've been a charmer."

Judith laughed. "Dad was a schoolteacher, quite prim and proper. But he had a wonderful sense of humor and he was very smart. Mother certainly fell for him and she's a bit of a hardcase."

"Speaking of a case," Suzie said, "maybe you should have that one. Or at least the contents. It doesn't mean much to the rest of us."

Judith hesitated. "Well . . . I am curious as to what Blanche wrote. I wouldn't mind keeping the Polaroids, though. But the case belongs to the Quimbys. Renie and I should go. It's very late."

Suzie found a big manila envelope for the letters and photos before seeing the cousins to the door. Once they were in the car, Renie couldn't help but needle Judith. "Wait until I tell Auntie Vance that her brother was a real heartthrob. Are you going to reveal all this to Aunt Gert?"

Judith grimaced. "I don't know. She might have a stroke."

"No, she won't," Renie asserted. "She may've guessed Blanche was infatuated with your father. Women are often more percep-tive than men. It'd also explain why she didn't want to buy the property."

"True," Judith allowed, turning into the Webers' garage. "Weird."

"Why?" Renie asked before opening the passenger door. "Uncle Donald wasn't exactly homely."

"I don't mean that," Judith said. "In fact, I'm not referring to Blanche's alleged infatuation. But I know who killed Ernie Glover."

She bit her lip, got out of the Subaru, and headed for the house.

You," Renie shrieked, practically on Judith's heels as they went inside, "aren't getting away with your I-can't-tell-you-until-I'm-one-hundred-percent-sure stunt this time. Unload or I pitch a five-star fit."

Shoulders slumping, Judith looked at her cousin with a wan expression. "What if I told you I think I must be nuts?"

Renie simmered down. "Well . . . I suppose if you said you think Blanche is the killer, I'd agree."

"Okay," Judith said, looking chagrined, "that's what I think."

"Oh, no." Renie staggered over to the sofa and collapsed. "I'm not sure I want to ask any more questions."

Judith rested a hand on the sofa arm. "Don't take off your jacket. We've got to get inside the Quimbys' house. Now, before everybody finds out Blanche isn't buried in the vacant lot."

"Not a chance." Renie shook her head so hard that she made herself wince. "The only way I go into that place is with police protection. I want weaponry nearby."

"You mean a gun?"

"I don't mean a slingshot and a handful of rocks."

Judith knew from Renie's mulish expression that drastic action was required. "Give me five minutes," she said, starting for the hall.

"If you intend to call the cops," Renie shouted, "you're going the wrong way."

Judith paid no attention. She had to focus on thinking back to what Auntie Vance had once said to Uncle Vince when two deer had invaded her precious rosebushes in back of the house. "Wake up, Weber!" she remembered her aunt yelling. "I've had it with these damned deer. Get your damned gun out of the damned . . ."

Judith stopped in the middle of the bedroom. What had Auntie Vance gone on to say after she got through cussing? *Close your eyes,* she ordered herself, *reach down, and bring back those words. . .*

The Lost Sock Box in the closet. Auntie Vance kept every unpaired sock she'd ever found from the dryer in a shoe box along with the .38 revolver Uncle Vince had brought back from World War II. Judith hurried to the closet, scouring the shelves above the clothes rack for a shoe box. She didn't see it. Using her left foot to move aside several pairs of the Webers' footgear, she spotted the box in a corner.

"Coz!" she yelled. "Help me out here."

Renie wearily trudged into the bedroom. "Now what?" she asked.

"Can you pick up that shoe box? I don't dare bend over."

"Why," Renie inquired in a beleaguered tone, "do I feel I should refuse? Oh, I give up. You've got some crazy idea and you won't let it go." She retrieved the box and handed it over to Judith. "What do you think is in here? Blanche's remains?"

"Hardly," Judith replied, setting the box on the dresser.

"Socks?" Renie remarked after Judith lifted the lid. "You *are* nuts."

"You may be right." Judith removed the gun, making sure to keep it pointed out of harm's way. "I wonder if it's loaded. It's like one of Joe's guns. Maybe I can figure out how to—"

"No!" Renie was backing away. "You can't be serious."

"But I am." Judith noticed that Renie had taken off her jacket. "I'll see you later. I'm going up to the Quimby house."

Renie looked dumbfounded. "Good grief," she finally said, following Judith out of the bedroom and into the hall. "I'm calling the sheriff. I don't care who I have to wake up."

Judith opened her mouth to argue, but realized Renie was right. Somebody must be on patrol at the south end of the island. "Okay, but tell whoever it is to meet me at the Quimbys' house."

"Meet *us*," Renie muttered, dialing the emergency number with one hand while grabbing her jacket with the other.

Judith had gone down the steps by the time Renie emerged onto the deck, still trying to get her arms into the right sleeves. "Why should I bother locking up? We're going to face a killer. What could be worse?"

"Lock the lock anyway," Judith hissed. "We don't want someone stealing Auntie Vance's precious unmatched socks she's been saving since 1982. And keep your voice down. People are sleeping."

Renie joined Judith. "You're right. I can hardly see any lights around here. Oh, it's raining. Good thing we've both got hoods. Hey, why don't we drive up there?"

"Because cars make noise," Judith whispered. "It's less than thirty yards to the Quimby place. Think of it as well within field-goal range."

"About now I wish we had Zach Bendarek with us," Renie murmured. "He may be dumb, but he sure is . . . dumb."

"I wonder. In fact, I wonder if anything up here is as it seems. Tonight at the vacant lot, I felt as if we were watching a play."

Renie thought for a moment. "To what point?"

"Distraction," Judith replied, passing the Sedgewick house. "To throw the Quimbys off guard. Act One was the goofy club-house meeting."

"What's the point? The old guy's ornery, the son's a pathetic stooge, the daughter-in-law's a mess, and Betsy's mental."

"But they still have all the power," Judith asserted, adjusting her hood. "That's what matters at the fiefdom called Obsession Shores. The peasants are revolting."

"Well . . . some of them are annoying, but . . ."

"You know what I mean," Judith said as they walked off the road and paused to gaze through the drizzle at the shabby old house. "What did you hear about a sheriff's deputy being close by?"

"You know how that goes," Renie said. " 'We'll inform a patrol officer who will assist you as soon as possible.' At least that's what they say when you're out here in the wilds."

Judith opened the gate. "I almost expected it to be locked at night," she whispered. "It has a lock, but part of it is broken."

"How do we get in?" Renie asked. "I assume that's your intention."

"The basement, maybe. Let's see if we can find a window. There isn't one in the front." They walked to the side of the house facing the road. "We can see the deputy arriving from here," Judith said softly.

"We can't see much else," Renie noted. "They've let everything grow up so that the foundation or basement or whatever is covered in shrubs and bushes. I can only glimpse what might be concrete." She jumped as a nearby noise startled her. "What was that?"

"A chipmunk? A squirrel?" Judith gazed at her surroundings. "It's a rat. He's burrowing under the shrubs. Maybe he's trying to get into the basement."

Renie grabbed her cousin's arm. "Shoot him! I hate rats!"

"I don't even know if the gun's loaded," Judith admitted. "I was afraid to check. It might've gone off. The rat isn't bothering you."

"I loathe them. You lived with a pack of rats in those dumps you and Dan rented. The rest of the family figured they were your pets. You couldn't afford a dog."

"Never mind," Judith said with a touch of indignation. "That was then, this is now. Let's check out the back of the house."

"I can hardly see anything," Renie griped. "Why didn't we bring Uncle Vince's big flashlight?"

Judith grimaced. "Because we were too stupid to think about it. Wait—look beyond that old trellis that's leaning against the bushes that are leaning against the house."

"I can't see all that leaning stuff," Renie retorted. "What is it?"

"A door, like to a root cellar," Judith replied, grabbing Renie's sleeve. "Come on, have a look."

Reluctantly, Renie joined her cousin. "That's what it is, all right. If you think I'm going in there, think again. The rats are rooting around inside. They're the only creatures who stir around here this late."

"The door looks kind of flimsy," Judith remarked. "I'll bet we could pry it open. Did you say you had your nail scissors?"

"Yes. No. I lost them."

"All I want to do is see where this goes," Judith asserted. "Okay?"

Renie sighed as she dug in her purse. "Why don't you have your own nail scissors? Is that because you really do still bite your nails?"

"Not very often," Judith replied. "Only when I get really nervous."

"I'm nervous now," Renie said, but she found the scissors. "Let me do the prying so you don't have to bend. Then you can do the snooping."

It took what seemed like a long time and several mumbled cusswords that would have done Auntie Vance proud, but Renie finally loosened the door enough to open it. "You're on your own," she said, stepping back. "All I see is more dark."

"Hey," Judith said under her breath, "don't you have that little light on your key chain? Let me use it."

"It doesn't shine very far," Renie warned, delving again into her purse. "Here. I took the key chain with the light off my big key ring, just in case you don't come out of the basement. Good luck."

Judith clicked on the light, which covered about a three-inch swath. She moved it to see how many stairs led to the basement. Only five were in view, but they were steep. There was a wooden handrail, which Judith grasped before leaving solid ground. Maybe it was a root cellar or a storage area as opposed to a full basement. Testing the wooden surface of the top step, she felt slick, damp moss underfoot and decided to take the steps one at a time.

Renie hovered above the opening. "For God's sake," she whispered fervently, "don't fall!"

"I'm hanging on," Judith assured her, counting the steps. *Five, six, seven . . . solid ground,* she thought—and realized she'd been holding her breath. Still moving cautiously because of the little light's restricted glow, she was able to see some discarded chairs piled on her left. The air smelled damp, even fetid. As she moved forward and her eyes seemed to grow accustomed to what little light that might have come in through the open door, Judith noticed the wall on her right was filled with cupboards. One of the doors hung open, its hinges broken. She glimpsed jars of what looked like cobweb-covered canned goods. Peering straight ahead, she saw a big wooden box. As she got closer, the big box's contents seemed to be protected by heavy plastic or maybe glass. Judith stifled a sneeze. From above, she heard a skittering sound, probably from the rats. Undaunted, she approached the box. The little light glinted on what Judith recognized was thick glass. She made out some kind of floral fabric, rotting with age. Moving the light over the glass, she saw what looked liked a pair of old kidskin gloves. She gave a start when she saw a face—and realized it was her own reflection. Judith laughed at herself for being so skittish and moved the light to the end of the box.

She took one look and almost dropped the key chain. Nausea overcame her. Covering her mouth with her free hand for fear of throwing up, she staggered to the staircase. Shaking all over and unsure of her footing, Judith croaked out the words, "Help me!"

Renie scrambled as fast as she dared down the steps and reached out to her cousin. "What is it?" she asked in a low, anxious voice.

Judith grabbed Renie's hand. "Wait," she said in a barely audible voice, taking deep breaths.

"Take it easy," Renie urged. "I'm hanging on to you. If you fall, you'll land on me. As usual."

Her cousin's normal tone helped Judith regain her composure. Wordlessly, they climbed the slick stairs and stepped onto the ground. Renie waited patiently, using the time to put the door back into place and retrieve the key-chain light from Judith's trembling hand.

"Well?" Renie finally asked, ignoring the rain that was dripping off her hood. "What happened?"

"I was wrong," Judith confessed, sounding almost normal. "Blanche didn't kill Ernie. Blanche isn't buried anywhere. Blanche is a . . . mummy."

Chapter 22

I could make a really bad joke here," Renie murmured, "but I'll refrain. In fact, you look as if you need a really stiff drink."

Judith pressed her hands together as if she was about to pray, which, she realized, wasn't a bad idea. Neither was a stiff drink. "I flunked again," she said between clenched teeth. "Damn!"

"Let's go back to the house," Renie said, taking her cousin's arm.

"Fine. Where's the deputy?"

"Not here," Renie replied. "I kept an eye on the road. Nothing."

"It doesn't matter now," Judith muttered in a dejected tone. "The sheriff can't arrest a corpse. And just when I thought I'd solved this case in a way that nobody else would ever consider."

"I'll give you points for creativity and originality," Renie said.

"But where did I go wrong?" Judith asked as they started down the road. "It all fit. Blanche, faking that she died, but staying in the shadows and keeping control because nobody else had the mental or physical capability to murder Ernie Glover."

"Ah . . ." Renie made a face. "I'm missing motive here."

"Does it matter now?"

"Of course it does. I want to know how you arrived at such a weird conclusion."

"Wait until we get inside," Judith said as they turned toward the stairs that led to the deck. "Frankly, it seemed obvious, if wrong."

Once they were safely back in the friendly confines of the kitchen, Renie poured two short but stiff drinks. "Let's hear it," she urged, joining Judith at the table. "You do realize it's two A.M.?"

"We can sleep in," Judith said—and yawned. "It was Ernie's looks. We'd both noted a resemblance to my father. Of course we never saw Ernie up close when he was still alive, and we certainly couldn't see what he looked like when we found his body. He was facedown."

"I do remember the incident," Renie drawled. "It seems like it was only last Friday."

Judith ignored the sarcasm. "I assumed that Blanche had lost her marbles and become a recluse. Maybe Quentin or even Quincy didn't want anyone to know. It was bad enough that Betsy suffered from mental illness. They decided to tell everyone she'd died and had a marker made to prove it." Judith paused to sip her drink.

"What did they do with her?" Renie asked. "Lock her in the basement until she finally croaked?"

"I doubt that," Judith replied. "I've no idea how long she's been dead. A coroner can figure that out. But old Quentin was now in control of the money. Yes, he probably had handled the actual sales, along with Quincy's help. But while Blanche was still of sound mind, she ruled. Everybody seems to agree on that, according to the Hilderschmidts. When her remains weren't found in the vacant lot, I was convinced she was still alive. When I saw the Polaroids and the returned letters, I suspected she was the killer. In her muddled mind, even their last names were alike—Glover and Grover. She thought Ernie was my father. It even made sense that she could have come up with the idea of pretending she was dead and had buried the souvenirs of her unrequited love under her grave marker. That might've been part of the madness that afflicted her."

Renie leaned back in her chair. "That's all so twisted I could almost believe it. Of course, the Quimbys are a very bizarre family. Nan must've known, but when she was here, she talked about Blanche's death some years ago. Didn't that blow your theory?"

Judith shook her head. "Nan was following the party line. I figured that Quimby had indoctrinated her—and no doubt Quincy—to keep the ruse alive, even if Blanche wasn't."

"I guess I can follow your logic," Renie said, "which is usually spot-on. Anything to do with the Quimbys could derail Einstein. But what do you think has become of the French coins Blanche brought with her from the Paris museum?"

"I honestly don't know," Judith said, shaking her head. "They may be tucked away in her box. I mean, it's more of a coffin, though . . ."

A knock at the door made both cousins jump.

"What now?" Renie said under her breath. "I'll get it." She crossed the room and asked for the visitor's ID.

"Jacobson," he called back.

Renie undid the lock. "You're on duty tonight?"

"Do I look like it?" he asked, indicating his civilian attire.

"In that case," Renie said, "how about a drink?"

The deputy sat down at the table. "I can't . . . hell, why not?"

Renie opened the cupboard where the liquor was kept. "Bourbon, Scotch, vodka, gin?"

"Bourbon, rocks, and water," he replied. "It's a good thing I stayed home today and schlepped around the house. At least I'm not exhausted."

"So," Judith asked, "why did you answer the call?"

"We got a big wreck between Langton and Cooptown," Jacobson replied. "Five cars involved, possible fatalities. Teenagers out too late racing on the wet roads and probably doing booze and drugs. All the on-duty deputies are tied up at the scene. Your call was sent on to me, since I'm the one handling the homicide case."

He paused to take his drink from Renie. "So what's happening here now?"

Judith was embarrassed. "I jumped the gun—so to speak. I thought I'd fingered the killer. I was wrong." She bit her lip. "I'm so sorry. I've made you come out in the middle of the night for nothing."

Renie held up a hand. "Whoa. That's not true. What about the dead body in the Quimby basement?"

"Oh," Judith said. "That. It's not exactly an emergency."

Jacobson's eyebrows shot up as he took a deep swallow of bourbon. "Let me be the judge of that. What are you talking about?"

Judith winced. "We sneaked into the Quimbys' basement. Old Mrs. Quimby is . . . moldering down there. Is that against the law?"

"Is 'moldering' against the law?" Jacobson shook himself. "You mean . . . she's dead?"

"Very," Judith replied. "Don't make me explain. It'd take too long."

The deputy frowned. "I knew she'd died, but . . ." He took another swig of bourbon. "There's nothing I can do tonight about the corpse. You're sure it's Mrs. Quimby?"

Judith realized she wouldn't know Blanche Quimby from blanc mange. In fact, given the state of decomposition, the face had looked kind of like a very unsavory pudding. "Who else could it be?" she asked.

"The Quimbys will have to answer that question," Jacobson said. "I don't suppose you'd care to tell me why you broke into their house in the first place?"

Judith her head. "I really wouldn't. Do you mind?"

The deputy grimaced. "All things considered, no." He polished off his drink. "I'd better go now while I'm still sober."

Renie walked him to the door. "Be careful out there," she called out before closing the door and locking up. "You're lucky he knows you're FASTO. Otherwise, he would've busted us."

"Don't mention that stupid nickname," Judith snapped. "I feel more like SLUGGO."

"Wasn't he in the comics when we were kids?"

"Yes," Judith replied testily. "He hung out with Nancy, who was a little fat girl with black hair. You told me I looked just like her."

"You did. She always had all the answers."

Judith gave Renie a bleak look. "And I don't. That's why I feel like Sluggo. I'm going to bed."

"Good idea," Renie said. "Tomorrow *is* another day."

"Don't be so optimistic," Judith retorted. "That's not like you."

Renie shrugged. "For once, I thought I'd act like *my* mother instead of yours."

Judith didn't comment. But for some reason, her cousin's words followed her to bed. She didn't realize that they were the answer to who had killed Ernie Glover.

By morning, fog had once again settled in over Obsession Shores. To Judith's surprise, she'd slept until almost ten. Not to her surprise, Renie was still asleep. Judith showered, dressed, and went out to the kitchen to make breakfast. She noticed that she couldn't see much beyond the deck.

The phone rang while she was frying bacon. "Jacobson here," the deputy said. "In case you were wondering, we're going to have to get a warrant to get inside the Quimby house. I figured you might be puzzled about why I hadn't shown up yet this morning."

"I couldn't see far enough in this fog to tell if you were here or not," Judith responded. "I'm wondering if Renie and I should head for home."

"I can't tell you what to do," Jacobson said, "but I'd advise staying put for now. The fog's all over the south end of the island. It's not a good idea to be out on the roads until it lifts. Besides, the ferryboats to the mainland are having some problems. Of course they're overloaded with the Monday-morning commuters."

"I have to wait anyway," Judith told him. "Renie's still asleep."

The deputy told her that was just as well and rang off. Judith finished preparing her breakfast of bacon, boiled eggs, and toast. She was almost done eating when she heard Renie stirring in the spare bedroom. A few minutes later, as Judith was putting her dirty dishes and silverware into the dishwasher, Renie leaned into the kitchen.

"Don't say it," she muttered, staggering to the bathroom. "Nothing good about mornings except for committing suicide, as my grouchy dad used to say to my cheerful mom. Gack."

Judith couldn't resist. "Good morning," she said in a chipper voice. Renie slammed the door behind her. Pouring a mug of coffee, she picked up the manila envelope from the counter and sat back down at the table.

Looking at the ten photos of her father evoked mixed emotions. He looked much younger than she remembered him. Maybe that was because there were no close-ups, the pictures having been taken from quite a distance. Two of the Polaroids included Gertrude, looking unusually benign. Her mother had always had a sharp tongue, but the toughness came later, after Donald Grover died too soon.

The half-dozen letters hadn't all been postmarked prior to her father's death, though the two that weren't had been sent only the week before the first heart attack. He'd lingered for several days in the hospital before succumbing to the ravages of the rheumatic fever that he'd suffered from as a child. Judith guessed that Gertrude hadn't bothered to check the mail. She'd spent most of the time at the hospital with her husband.

"Well?" Renie said, seeing Judith holding one of the letters but obviously reluctant to open it. "Are you scared to find out what erotic messages Blanche sent to Uncle Donald?"

"You've shed your tiger stripes," Judith noted. "It didn't take you long to get ready for the day."

"I took a bath last night," Renie replied, pouring coffee into a mug inscribed with the words KEEP CLAM. "You know I prefer doing that. I'm afraid if I wait until morning, I might drown, not being fully conscious."

"Smart," Judith murmured. "I'm about to read the first of Blanche's letters."

"Read it out loud. I'm going to get some cereal."

Judith winced. "If they're too gushy, I might get nauseous." But she unsealed the first of the ecru envelopes. "Drat! It's all in French."

"Did your father speak French?" Renie asked, bringing a bowl of cornflakes to the table.

"French and Spanish," Judith replied. "I only took a year of Spanish. I wasn't good at languages. You know French. I remember that from when we were in Europe."

"I studied Spanish a lot more than French," Renie said. "I'm really rusty at both languages, though I can usually read some of it better than I speak it. Let me take a look." In between spoonfuls of cereal, she frowned at the elegant yet not entirely legible handwriting. "Rough— *really* rough—translation is that she finds your father handsome, debonair, intelligent, gallant, and proposes a tryst."

"Are you sure about that?"

"The word she uses is *rendezvous*. Even you can figure that out."

Judith handed over the second letter. "I'm not sure I want to hear more of her drivel."

Renie opened another envelope. "More gack-making stuff. Written the next day, grand passion, *mon seul et unique amour*. Her only love. Blah blah. Cut to the chase and give me the last letter. That might be more revealing about Blanche's state of mind."

A full minute passed before a scowling Renie finally spoke

again. "Her heart or her flask is broken. I can't tell if the word is *coeur* or *cruet*. She's dying of unreturned love. I suppose she got that way from getting the returned letters."

"It's kind of pathetic," Judith said. "I can't help feeling pity for her."

"You would. I don't," Renie declared. "She's middle-aged before she actually falls in love? I wonder what she looked like."

"Not very good when I saw her," Judith said, making a face. "I must confess," she went on with a smile, "you're back to being you."

"Right. Renie rhymes with Meanie. At least we resemble our mothers in looks. I guess that's not the worst thing that could happen."

Judith didn't comment. Her mind had wandered off on a tangent. "I'm thinking about heading home after the fog lifts, but I'd like to find out what happens when Jacobson confronts the Quimby clan. Maybe we should walk up that way. It's almost eleven. The fog should start to lift."

"You're sure you want to leave?" Renie inquired after polishing off her cornflakes. "Auntie Vance might be disappointed."

Judith had gone to the window, where she didn't notice much change in the weather. "She can ask the Sedgewicks or the Friedmans."

Renie took her bowl and spoon over to the dishwasher. "Did you see any of them at the vacant lot last night?"

"No," Judith said. "It was so dark. When I was trying to avoid hitting the people along the road, I was focused on my driving."

The phone rang. Thinking it might be Jacobson, Judith hurried to pick up the receiver. "Vance?" a vaguely familiar voice said at the other end. "We're going to do it."

"Do what?" Judith blurted, too curious to bother mentioning she wasn't her aunt.

"Confront . . . is this Vance?"

Judith recognized Becca Bendarek. "No, it's Judith, her niece. The Webers are still gone."

"Oh. I thought they might be back today. Sorry." She hung up.

"Now, what's that all about?" Judith murmured.

Renie was pouring more coffee. "Who was it?"

Judith repeated the brief conversation with Becca. Her cousin looked stumped. "Something about not digging up Blanche or valuable French coins?"

"I don't know." Judith picked up her car coat. "Let's visit the Sedgewicks. We can brave the heavy fog."

Renie scowled at her cousin. "I'm still in a fog. I need more coffee. What do you think happened to those coins?"

"I bet they're still in the Quimby house, maybe with Blanche and her box. I'd love to see Mr. Moffitt get hold of those. Payback for losing his family home to the Quimbys. Maybe after we get home I'll call the old dear and put a flea in his ear."

"Good idea," Renie said. "I wonder if Mr. Moffitt would find me comely in my tiger stripes?"

"How about terrifying?" Judith shrugged into her car coat. "To quote your husband, 'Let's boppin'!'"

Renie growled. But five minutes later, the cousins were calling on the Sedgewicks. To Judith's bewilderment, the couple's welcome lacked its usual warmth.

"We're about to take off for the grocery store," Jane said. "The fog's starting to lift."

Dick's usually jovial expression seemed forced. "This area's always the last to clear up. The fog gets trapped in the bay. We should expect sunshine once we get out on the main roads."

"Are the Bendareks going with you?" Judith asked.

Jane's hazel eyes were wary. "What do you mean?"

"Something's up," Judith asserted. "Becca let it slip. Does it have to do with Ernie's murder?"

Judith thought both Sedgewicks looked relieved. "No," Dick stated in a firm voice. "That's up to the sheriff's department." He looked at his wife. "What the hell, Jane. Vance will end up telling them."

Jane hesitated, then shrugged. "Come into the kitchen. It's after eleven thirty. Almost time for a prelunch cocktail. What'll it be?"

"Got any of that hot toddy mix left?" Renie asked.

Jane laughed. "Maybe enough for you two. That's about it. Dick and I will settle for a shot of Scotch. You do the honors, lover boy."

Dick busied himself with the drinks. The three women sat at the kitchen table. "The whole thing started with Vance," Jane said. "A while ago, Quincy Quimby engaged Kent Logan to represent the family in a lawsuit against Tank Hilderschmidt, Hank's brother."

"The boathouse remodel?" Judith asked.

"Right," Jane said. "Did Vance tell you about it?"

Judith shook her head. "We did some research. Tank was liable and it was settled out of court."

"Yes. But," Jane went on, "Kent had looked deeper into some of the Quimbys' property sales and how they'd been conducted. Vance helped him because she was savvy about real estate, since both she and Ellen worked for that big law firm after the war. In fact, one of the senior partners was elected governor, as I recall."

"True," Renie said. "He and his wife came to Aunt Ellen and Uncle Win's wedding. Uncle Corky took home movies of the future governor imbibing strong punch at the reception. Aunt Gert wanted to give the film to the local newspapers because the guy was running as a Republican and had publicly announced he was a teetotaler."

Jane shook her head. "Your family. They're a caution. Naturally, Vance was able to point out some of the irregularities in the real estate contracts, especially the freehold section. She also consulted Ernie Glover, who had been an auditor for the state.

He agreed that there were irregularities in the agreements that didn't conform to Revised Code of Washington requirements. Kent wasn't as knowledgeable as your aunt when it came to that kind of expertise. His practice was confined to other fields."

Judith was puzzled. "Why hadn't Auntie Vance figured that out when they bought in here?"

"She had," Jane said with a wry smile. "That's why the Webers—and us—are the only ones in the development to *not* sign such a contract."

Renie rocked in her chair. "Only she could pull that off."

Dick set the hot toddy mugs in front of the cousins and sat down. "Sheer brass on her part. But with that mouth of hers— not to mention her brain—she can get away with it. The only thing bigger than her bazooms is the heart that beats under them."

"So what happens now?" Judith asked, still in awe of her aunt.

Jane frowned. "Kent called a special meeting a week ago Friday night at the grade school outside of Cliffton. They didn't dare hold it here. Vance and Vince were there. In fact, Vince stayed awake for almost the whole thing. At first, some of the younger people like the Crowleys thought it was all a distraction to avoid discussing the sewer issue. But they caved, especially since they were leaving town this weekend."

"You mean," Judith said, "the Friday meeting was a setup?"

"Right." Dick chuckled. "Originally, it was to be the real deal because Quimby and his family knew the sewer question had to come to a vote. That's why Vance wanted you two on hand to cast your ballots for them. But that afternoon Ernie got killed." Dick's voice dragged a bit and he took a sip of Scotch. "We all lost heart. Frankly, we were scared."

Jane put her hand on his arm. "We still are. But Kent has put everything together for the confrontation with old Quimby and his offspring. We're waiting for the rest of the information Kent has ordered from the county courthouse. Then we'll sound the alarm."

"Literally?" Renie asked.

"Of course," Jane replied. "It's the one we ring during the summer to announce the cocktail hour."

Judith thought the bell sounded like it should have been a death knell.

Chapter 23

I feel like a dupe," Judith declared after she and Renie had taken their leave.

"A dupe or a dope?" Renie asked.

"Both, maybe. No wonder I felt we were watching a play."

"What about the hidden treasure and the French coins and the phony ones Brose collected? Fact or fiction?"

"French coins, probably real," Judith replied, stopping at the road's edge. "The other coins seem like a scam Brose dreamed up. Maybe it's a ploy to get Fou-fou back."

Renie looked skeptical. "Why? She's a real twit."

"So's he. They make a good pair. Hey, if it gives these folks something to do, why not?" Judith sniffed at the damp, foggy air. "The fog's lifted enough so that I can see almost to the Quimby house, but I can't tell if Jacobson's arrived. Let's find out."

Renie groaned. "Why do I think more sleuthing is a bad idea? You were talking earlier about leaving. Worse yet, we had pre-lunch cocktails, but no lunch. Those cornflakes weren't very filling. I'm hungry."

"You had breakfast less than an hour ago," Judith reminded her. "Come on, let's go."

"You really are annoying sometimes," Renie grumbled.

"And you really like to complain," Judith retorted as the outline of the grim old house loomed up ahead of them. "No cruiser in sight. Maybe he's come and gone."

"We could be gone if we turned around," Renie muttered.

Judith stopped near the Quimbys' fence. "I wonder if . . ." She grew silent, seeing Betsy step out from behind the house.

"Hello," Betsy chirped in greeting as she approached the cousins. "How are you? I am fine."

"That's good," Judith said with a smile. "Are you going for a walk?"

Betsy grimaced. "I'm not sure. I have to take some pills."

"Well," Judith responded, "you could take the pills now and then go for a walk."

"No, no, no!" Betsy looked annoyed and stamped her foot. "I have to *take* them first. Then *you* can take them. Like before."

"You mean when I took the other pills for you?" Judith asked.

Betsy brightened and nodded. "Yes. Please. I hate pills. People shouldn't have to swallow them. They aren't at all tasty. Sometimes they make my tummy hurt and I get *so* sleepy." She whirled around, pointing toward the house. "*Maman* is leaving. I'm glad."

Judith frowned. "*Mam—*"

Renie interrupted. "Your mother is going away?"

Betsy nodded. "I'm glad." She wrinkled her snub nose. "Do you want to say good-bye to her? I mean, adieu."

"No," Judith said in what she hoped was a kindly tone. "We don't want to intrude. We've never been farther than your front door." *A bit of a stretch,* she thought, *but does the basement really count?*

"I see," Betsy said, tapping a finger against her cheek. "I'll let you in the back door. Then I'll start taking the pills. Come through the gate." She scampered away, heading for the opposite side of the house.

"We," Renie announced, "are not following her."

"I am," Judith declared. "Betsy's harmless. This is our big chance." She moved quickly to the gate.

"Coz . . ." Renie shut up, knowing that arguing was futile. She followed her cousin into the yard and around to the side of the house, where Betsy was standing by two sagging wooden steps that led to an entrance behind a battered screen door.

"The back door's not in back," Betsy said. She laughed merrily, then paused after opening the screen door. "Where did Hansel and Gretel go? I thought Quincy let them out. Oh, well." She tugged at the doorknob. "Stupid thing." Betsy launched a big kick. The door creaked open. "Come in, come in," she called to the cousins. "Let's play hide-the-pills."

Judith went up the two steps. Betsy ran off down the gloomy hall, calling to the Rottweilers before disappearing out of view.

"Are you coming?" Judith asked Renie.

"Do I have a choice?" Renie muttered, joining her cousin just inside the doorway. "Where did Looney Tunes go?"

"Down the hall," Judith replied. "Maybe we should leave the door open. I think Betsy's going to let out the dogs." She peered into a room off to her left. "That's the pantry. It probably leads into the kitchen. What's on the other side of the hall?"

"A wall," Renie said. "Not uncommon in most houses. Why are we here instead of just about anywhere else I can think of?"

"Stop bitching." Judith started down the hall. "Where did Betsy go? The pantry's the only room . . . There's a door on the right. Let's check it out." She turned the knob. "It's locked." She started to move on, but saw that Renie was leaning against the door. "What are you doing?"

"I'm sleuthing," Renie said. "I hear running water, so I deduce this is a bathroom. No wonder the door's locked."

They moved on, pausing at double doors that revealed storage for linen and china. Turning the corner, they saw two more doors, one straight ahead and the other on their left. The latter was ajar. Judith pushed it open, revealing a cluttered, windowless room where a single lightbulb dangled on a frayed cord from the ceiling. What had probably been used as a study was jammed with piles of books, newspapers, magazines, photo albums, and file folders.

"Firetrap," Renie observed. "Nan must not like housecleaning."

"I hope the rest of the place doesn't look like this," Judith said. "No wonder they don't encourage visitors. You're right. This wasn't one of my brighter ideas. It smells musty in here. I wonder why the light's on. Let's go before I start sneezing from all the dust."

A rustling sound made the cousins jump before they could get to the door.

"You're not going anywhere," a raspy old voice said.

Quentin Quimby rolled his wheelchair out from behind a stack of books and albums. He had a cigarette lighter in his hand. "Blanche isn't going anywhere either. At least not without me." He made as if to flick the lighter. "We're all going to hell, where the flames will burn forever."

"Don't," Judith said sharply. "There's something you should know."

The agatelike eyes stared at her as his hand faltered slightly. "There's nothing I *don't* know," he growled. "I saw you from my window when you arrived Friday at the Weber house. That's when I knew your husband had to die. Now you know too much, snooping all over my property. You and your smarty-pants husband! I fixed him. Stupid schoolteacher man. Who's to say the lot wouldn't perc? I say it does. Pshaw!" He spat on the floor.

Judith opened her mouth to speak, but clamped it shut. She felt Renie's arm brush against her elbow. The empathy they'd shared since childhood often allowed them to read each other's mind. Judith knew Renie also understood Quimby's delusion.

"He died a long time ago," Renie said. "He had a heart attack."

The old man's sagging jowls seemed to droop even more. "No! That's a lie!"

"Why do you say that?" Judith asked, hoping Quimby didn't notice the quaver in her voice.

"I know because I watched him die," he said with a twitch of a smile. "I told you, I know everything. I own everything. I *am* Obsession Shores." He flicked the lighter.

Judith sucked in her breath; Renie let out a little gasp.

Nothing happened.

Quimby clicked and clicked, using every cussword in the English language and a few more in French. His wrinkled face was turning purple. Judith was certain that he was apoplectic. But instead of collapsing, he dropped the lighter, heaved himself out of the wheelchair, and staggered toward the cousins.

"Hansel! Gretel!" he howled, clenching his fists. "Kill!"

Judith involuntarily looked around. She saw no sign of the dogs. But the door opened behind her. The Rottweilers charged into the room.

And stopped. Betsy was behind them, holding their leashes. "You called, *Père?*" she asked. "I brought the dogs back in. They had to pee-pee." She frowned at her father. "You look all funny. Are you sick, *mon cher père?*"

Quimby's eyes grew wide and he opened his mouth to speak. Nothing came out. He pitched forward, collapsing at the cousins' feet. The dogs sniffed at his prone body before settling in beside him.

Betsy frowned. "Is he dead?"

"I don't know," Judith said.

Renie knelt down, lifting the hand that had held the lighter. "I can't feel a pulse. Let me try his neck." She touched the crepelike skin by his right ear, waited a few moments, and shook her head. Renie crossed herself and stood up. Judith bowed her head, offering a silent prayer.

"Oh, my," Betsy said, "if he's dead, I'll have to tell the man to go away. Or should I have him see Quincy?"

"You'd better tell your brother about your father first," Judith advised, trying to discern any sign of distress on Betsy's curiously unlined face. "In fact, maybe we should go with you."

"No, no, no," Betsy replied. "*Père* shouldn't be left alone. You go. I'll stay here with the dogs. And *Père.*"

Judith realized she had no idea how to get to the main part of the house. "Where does the door at the end of the hall go?" she asked.

Betsy didn't answer right away. She was studying the old man's body in a detached sort of way. "To all the other rooms," she finally said. "If you see my brother, tell him *Père* is dead. Quincy will be so happy. Now he's rich."

Once outside of the cluttered room, Judith leaned against the wall. "I need to find my nerves. I know they must be somewhere."

Renie rubbed her eyes, then blinked several times. "I thought I'd die—literally. That's the first time we've had a killer croak on us." She frowned. "The old coot is . . . I mean, *was* the killer, right?"

Judith nodded. "I never suspected him until those letters showed up and we discovered Blanche really was dead. All along it bothered me that there was no apparent motive. Nobody commits murder over a proposed sewer. But several people mentioned that the victim should have been Quimby. Why didn't I realize that if you flipped that around, the answer was that *he* was the killer?"

Renie grimaced. "Because that's not the way your usual sound logic works?"

Judith shook her head. "Maybe not. It doesn't matter now. Let's find Quincy and Nan. Oh, let's not forget the visitor Betsy mentioned."

"I'll bet it's Jacobson," Renie said as she opened the door at the end of the hall that led to a more narrow, dimly lighted corridor.

"Maybe not, since Betsy knows Jacobson as Erik, so she'd . . ." Judith stopped, seeing Quincy, Nan, and Jack Larrabee come out of a room up ahead on their left. "What the . . . ?"

Quincy and Nan both looked startled. Jack seemed bemused.

"Fancy meeting you here," he remarked as the cousins approached.

Quincy stared at Jack. "You know these women?"

Jack grinned. "I've spent the night with Mrs. Flynn. She makes an excellent breakfast."

The flippant remark helped ease the tension that was still making Judith feel a bit wobbly. "Could we all find somewhere to sit down?" she said to Quincy.

He looked discomfited. "I suppose. But why? What's going on?"

Nan tugged at his arm. "Please, Quin. I told you I had a premonition, even before Mr. Larrabee arrived. *Père* seemed very odd."

Quincy led them into what he termed the parlor, a room with closed drapes, shabby furnishings, and a Persian carpet that was threadbare in places. Judith and Renie sat down on a faded blue settee. The others seated themselves in worn side chairs flanking a fireplace sealed off with a piece of plywood.

Judith didn't mince words. "Mr. Quimby is dead, apparently from a stroke or heart attack. Betsy is with him. I'm sorry for your loss."

Quincy's jaw dropped. Nan simply stared at Judith. Jack looked mildly curious. In the silence that followed, a mantel clock chimed the half hour on a weak, quivering note.

Then Nan shot out of her chair and flung herself at Quincy. "We're rich! We're free! I love you, Quin! Let's have a cocktail!"

After being told where the body could be found, the two Quimbys rushed out of the parlor. Judith stood up, with Renie following suit.

"We're leaving," Judith said to Jack. "Are you sticking around?"

"No," he said, also getting to his feet. "I was on my way out when you two showed up. I don't suppose you want to tell me why you're here."

"Betsy invited us," Judith replied, noting that Jack looked puzzled. "Quincy's sister. How do we get out of here? We came in the side door."

"Follow me," Jack said, going out the way they'd come into the parlor, but turning to his right. "There's the front door. May I?"

He opened it and followed the cousins outside. The fog had lifted, so that they could see the beach, if not the bay. "I don't suppose," he mused, "you've heard anything new about the homicide case?"

Judith paused at the bottom of the steps. "Check later with the sheriff's office," she replied. "Did you come here to question the Quimbys about the murder?"

Jack looked pained. "I lied."

Judith was taken aback. "About what?"

"I'm not a reporter," he said, looking sheepish. "I'm not from the Midwest. I'm a private investigator from Portland. Becca Bendarek is my sister. She was designated a week ago to find a PI to look into the senior Quimby's shenanigans with the property sales here. She found a Joe Flynn, but he turned down the case . . ." Jack chuckled. "You know why."

Judith didn't know whether to laugh or get mad. "Is that the reason you came to the B&B?"

Jack shrugged. "I had to stay somewhere overnight to do background in the city. I worked with Joe a couple of times when he was still on the force. When I realized you were his wife, I thought I could get information about the island from him, but he'd already left town. I decided I didn't want to blow my cover. You never know who's connected to who, even in a city as large as your hometown. My hunch was right. You did have ties to Whoopee Island. I almost turned tail and took off when I recognized you outside the café."

Renie couldn't contain herself. "You used my cousin? That's a cheap shot. It serves you right that she doesn't know zip about the case."

"Hey," Jack said, holding up his hands, "it's my job."

"Then you'd better do it," Renie snapped. "So long, Jack."

Judith followed Renie down the walk. "That was sort of mean of you," she said, but sounded more amused than upset.

"I knew you wanted to call Jacobson," Renie said. "In fact, here he comes now. Do you want to talk to him?"

Judith paused at the road's edge. "I'm worn out. Let's go back to the house. I'll call him from there. Right now *I* need a cocktail."

The deputy came to see the cousins an hour later. Judith explained everything in detail. He listened stoically, asking only a few questions. When Judith had finished, he sadly shook his head.

"Mistaken identity from over thirty years ago," he murmured. "Incredible. Of course Quimby's death saves the county the cost of a trial, though I doubt it would've come to that. He sounds deranged."

Judith nodded. "Yet cunning. And ruthless. He would've preferred killing all of us and himself rather than being exposed as a criminal."

"Nonagenarian jealousy," Renie said, "and without a real reason. Judith's father never knew Blanche had fallen for him."

"Jealousy," Jacobson asserted, still faintly incredulous, "is always a strong motive—along with revenge. That vacant lot was a symbol to both Quimbys of someone who had thwarted them in different ways. But I marvel that the old guy had the strength to commit the crime."

"He was stronger than he pretended," Judith said. "We'd heard he could walk, but preferred being pushed around by his son and daughter-in-law. Of course adrenaline gives people extra strength."

"That's true," the deputy agreed. "I still don't understand what set him off after all this time."

Judith made a face. "I'm not sure either. Maybe everything had been festering for so long that it suddenly erupted."

Renie burst out laughing. "Coz! What's wrong with your mighty brain? Quimby saw you arrive Friday. That triggered the memory of Blanche's infatuation with your dad. Blanche may've taunted her husband about finding a new man. Quimby was obviously jealous. He went back thirty years when your parents came here to look at the property. Didn't I always say you look like your mother?"

Judith wondered if she should have another drink.

The cousins packed up later that afternoon and headed for the ferry. They stopped first at the Sedgewicks' house to say goodbye, but Jane and Dick weren't home, probably having gone to grocery-shop.

They reached Cliffton in time to catch the three-thirty ferry. The line of vehicles took up only a lane and a half, but Judith noticed there were two security guards with sniffer dogs on duty.

"I hope the ferry schedule isn't still disrupted," Judith said.

Renie shrugged. "It looks as if the incoming ferry's arriving on time. I think I'll go up for popcorn again."

"I'll stay here," Judith said. "I may take a quick nap. This wasn't a very restful weekend."

"No kidding." Renie grinned at her cousin. "You must be worn out. Usually you want even the loosest of loose ends tied up. I gather you don't care about Frank's illegal crab pots or the French coins or Edna's icy demeanor or any of the other strange doings on The Rock."

"I'll leave all that to Auntie Vance," Judith said. "It's clear that everyone seems to like and respect her. I'm an outsider on her turf. Yes, I finally fingered the killer. Our aunt and uncle like living at Obsession Shores. It's a flawed community, but human beings are flawed. When they had to act, they banded together in a common cause against Quentin Quimby's injustices. That speaks well for them."

Renie nodded. "Now that Quimby's dead, maybe they can work through the property issues. But I suppose they'll go back to quarreling among themselves, having affairs, arguing over sewers, and shooing pesky deer into each other's gardens."

"Human beings are . . . human," Judith said, noticing the ferry was almost in the slip. "I'd like to think that removing Quimby from the equation would ease tensions in the community."

"Let's hope so," Renie remarked, leaning forward in her seat. "Just be thankful we aren't smuggling illegal Dungeness crab across the Sound. A security guy is making the driver in front of us open his trunk."

"We don't even have clams," Judith said. "We ate them. Looks as if the driver doesn't have anything of interest either. Just routine."

"The ferry's in the dock," Renie noted. "There still aren't many cars waiting. Our turn to be possible terrorists."

The fair-haired security guard stopped on the passenger side and asked Renie to open the door. "May I look inside your purse?" he asked.

"Sure," Renie replied. "Don't swipe my gum. I can't get to sleep without it."

The guard didn't crack a smile. "Fine. Thank you." He came around to the other side of the car and made the same request of Judith.

"I don't have any gum," she said with a smile.

He didn't smile back as he opened her purse. "You don't have any gum," he said sternly, "but you have a gun. May I see your carry permit?"

Judith gaped at the guard. "I . . . forgot . . . it's not mine . . . I don't even know if it's loaded!"

The guard remained stoic. "This weapon isn't registered to you?"

"No, of course not," Judith said. "It belongs to . . . let me explain . . ."

He cut her off with a wave of one hand. "Would you please step out of the car and put your hands on the top of your head. You're under arrest for unlawful possession of a handgun. I'll read you your rights before turning you over to the on-duty officer for this part of the island."

Judith looked at Renie. "I guess we'll have to catch a later ferry."

"Darn," Renie said. "They better not be out of popcorn by then. Now I'm really hungry."

AUNTIE VANCE'S BEEF NOODLE BAKE
(as she would tell you how to make it)

Before you start messing with this, boil a lot of GOOD egg noodles. Don't go cheap. Life's too short.

1 lb. hamburger—skip the lean stuff; get the grade with the most
fat or you might as well eat a cardboard box
½ cup chopped onion
½ cup cut-up celery
½ cup green, red, yellow or orange sliced pepper—green isn't as
good for you as the other three—so what if they cost more?
1 can tomato soup
½ cup water
Dash of Tabasco—BIG dash, don't skimp—nobody lives forever
Dash of Worcestershire sauce—see above. You got eyes, right?
1 tbsp. or 2 of soy sauce
Salt & pepper—plenty of it—you got something against flavor?

Heat a skillet, a frying pan, whatever you call the damned thing, and melt 1 tbsp. of butter. REAL butter. Forget you have arteries. Add hamburger and brown—briefly. Add onion, celery, and pepper. Add everything else and cook until heated. Grease* a baking dish big enough to hold this stuff. Add the noodles (don't forget to drain them . . .) and all of the above. Bake in a 350° F oven—you can tell when it's done. If you're too dumb to figure it out, you shouldn't be reading this. Meanwhile, make a green salad. You need those greens, right? Some crusty French bread goes good with all this. When it's ready, wake up your husband/partner/whoever and serve. It tastes better than it looks.

---

* Use Watkins Cooking Spray. It's a Canadian product, but so what? You want to start a border war?

About the Author

MARY RICHARDSON DAHEIM is a Seattle native with a communications degree from the University of Washington. Realizing at an early age that getting published in books with real covers might elude her for years, she worked on daily newspapers and in public relations to help avoid her creditors. She lives in her hometown in a century-old house not unlike Hillside Manor, except for the body count. Daheim is also the author of the Alpine mystery series, the mother of three daughters, and has three grandchildren.